Soul Transfer

Carol Treacy

First published in 2022 by Carol Treacy

ISBN (print book): 978-0-9964474-3-0
ISBN (eBook): 978-0-9964474-4-7

Printed in the United States of America

What the world needs now is love.

Love for all beings.

Love for the planet.

1

Emma wanted to dance with it. She wanted to fling it in the air and catch it with her teeth. She knew exactly how Charlie Bucket felt when he unwrapped the Willy Wonka chocolate candy bar and found the golden ticket. Sheer glee. She had an urge to tell anyone within shouting distance that this boarding pass in her hand was going to take her to Turin, Italy. *Italy*! As the crow flies, it's 6,248 miles from San Francisco, but it has lived inside Emma from a very young age. She has a vivid memory of toddling up to the television screen and slapping her sticky hands on the Piazza Castello, the ancient central square in Turin. Despite her parent's and sister's pleas to sit back down, she stood there mesmerized until a loud, intrusive Ford truck commercial replaced the hypnotic city. Posters of Turin, known as the city of magic, were taped up on Emma's adolescent bedroom walls alongside a psychedelic Led Zeppelin poster and a poster of Bobby Sherman. At the same time tomorrow, Emma would be strolling down via Lagrange, breathing in the ancient city's history, along with the rich aroma of pasta pomodoro and espresso. It took nearly sixty years to plan the trip, but here she was, sporting a silly grin as she checked the gate number one more time.

Emma's cellphone rang, interrupting her reverie. She looked at the number and groaned. "I'll be damned if he's going to ruin my moment," she said to no one, putting the phone on mute and sticking it in her purse. A few minutes later, her phone vibrated. Him again. Against her better judgment, she reluctantly answered. "What is it?"

"Hello to you, too."

"Not in the mood, Vin. What do you want?"

Vin was Emma's third ex-husband. When she first met the tall, slightly overweight investment banker, she loved his name. It sounded exotic, like it was short for Vincento or Vinaldi. And his accent. She couldn't quite place it, though it sounded like a cross between French royalty and a feisty German Chancellor. After two years of being married to the pathological liar from Kentucky, she was convinced his name was short for Vinny the Vathead. One of the reasons for Emma vacationing in Italy was to cleanse her psyche of the accumulation of paperwork and legal wrangling the divorce had had her entangled. It lasted almost two years, due to Vin's convoluted financial statements, many of which were falsified. She chastised herself for getting involved with a man who thought scruples was a board game. She should have known better, but Emma was coming off her second marriage and vulnerability must have been oozing from every pore. She was ripe for the picking and Vin had smelled her susceptibility from a mile away. At least a barstool away. In the darkened chambers of the Judgement Inn, a bar across the street from San Francisco City Hall, Vin turned on the charm so high, she thought he might pass out from the effort. Her intuition was silently yelling, imploring her to turn away from his advances, engage in conversation with the elderly, suited gentleman to her left, or simply sit somewhere else and enjoy her chocolate martini in peace. Instead, Emma's bruised ego soaked up every compliment Vin served her on a faux gilded platter.

Vin did his best to sound sincere. "I wanted to make sure you were okay. My lawyer can be quite an asshole."

"You think? I don't even like sitting close to the guy. I'm afraid he'll take a chunk out of me. I swear he's part werewolf."

Vin was going to miss Emma's sense of humor. "He gets the job done."

"And then some. That's why you called?"

"In part. I also…"

A large group of travelers plopped down on the empty chairs across from Emma. They all appeared to be in hyper drive, no less excited for their impending journey.

Vin continued. "Are you at a party?"

"Airport."

"Airport party?"

Emma got up, grabbed her purse and carry-on bag, and walked over to the window. She would have liked to have been staring at the Air Italia plane, the one that would be taking her away from her job and her home and the stench of her divorce. But their flight was delayed by a few hours, so she looked out at the empty runway, still wet from a passing storm.

"Just the airport. You know, where people get into big flying machines and go to places far away?"

"Where are you going, Emmy?"

"None of your business and don't call me Emmy. For the third time, what do you want?"

Vin cleared his throat and Emma instinctively closed her eyes. When he made that sound, she knew something was coming and it wasn't going to be pleasant. "You know the armoire that I gave you for our anniversary? Well, I'd like it back. It has special meaning for me."

Emma laughed a little too loud, drawing the attention of a young couple standing next to her. "I bet it does. Isn't that where Cindy was hiding when I came home unexpectedly and caught you with your pants down, way down?"

"She wasn't in there." Vin cleared his throat again. "She was in the closet. The point is, the armoire has been in the family for generations, and I was hoping that I could have it, you know, for old time's sake."

Emma was trying very hard to keep her cool. She vowed that she wouldn't lose it when talking to Vathead, but lost it she did. "The armoire stays with me and don't try to tell me that growing up in Bumfuck, Kentucky, your family had anything of value, except the still where your daddy made whiskey. You bought that piece of furniture at an antique store. Did you forget that I saw it years before and fell in love with it? I'm getting off the phone and I'm going to do my best to forget that we had this conversation. If I really try hard enough, maybe I'll also forget that we were married. The papers have been signed. You and I are officially divorced or as you say in your native language, unhitched. Goodbye, Vathead."

Inner sanctuary cracked. Composure fractured; Emma walked hurriedly to the bar. Normally she would meditate, but the airport was hardly the locale to regain her tranquility. She swung her purse over her shoulder a little too hard, accidentally hitting a man walking in the opposite direction. When she turned to apologize, she was taken aback. He looked like he had recently been released from prison. Shaved head, rock hard pecs underneath a thin tank top, tattooed arms, and a scowl on his face, a look that would have been followed by a litany of cursing if they weren't in a public place. His friend sported a similar look with a tattoo that was hard to miss: a black boot stomping on a bright red heart. Emma didn't have a chance to offer her apology. The two sidestepped her and continued to walk away quickly. She involuntarily shuddered as she watched them disappear into the bookstore.

Emma grabbed the last seat at the bar. She swung her legs around, knocking her knee into the purse hook attached to the bar's underbelly, and let out a quiet groan. The bartender, a young woman in her 20s, came over and wiped away the remnants of a spilled drink. She smiled at Emma and said, "What can I get you?"

Still rubbing her knee, Emma answered, "How about a weapon capable of wiping out the entire male population."

The bartender turned and did a quick check of the bottles displayed on the shelves. "Sorry, we're out of that. Second choice?"

Emma ordered a scotch on the rocks with a twist. Rattled by her conversation with Vin and the brief but intense encounter with the two skinheads, she quickly downed the scotch and ordered a second. After all, she wasn't piloting the plane. All she had to do was hand her boarding pass to the attendant, take her seat, buckle up and prepare to be in the air for almost eight hours. How hard could it be?

As she sipped scotch number two, Emma read over her itinerary. She'd be staying at a B&B on the outskirts of Turin. The small cottage came highly recommended by her neighbor's brother, Forest, who had recently returned from a solo trip. Normally, Emma wouldn't trust the advice of a twenty-three-year-old, but Forest and his sister, Petal, were the coolest people Emma knew. Children of self-proclaimed hippies, the siblings were more cosmopolitan than earthy. A slight dusting of their parents' radical views along with their love of nature appeared to stick to their ideals. Forest had been showing his sister pictures of his trip on his laptop. Emma had always wanted to go to Turin, so it was no coincidence that she dropped by Petal's to return a hand mixer the day Forest visited. He told her about his tour of the city's magical highlights. A Turin expert, Emma loved hearing firsthand about the city's location, said by some to be a kind of vortex between good and evil, where black magic and white magic can be found throughout the city. Fascinated by magic, this was one tour she didn't want to miss. Emma was also delighted by Forest's photos of the Forte di Bard, a barrage fortress built in the early nineteenth century. The multi-leveled structure carved into the mountain exemplified the mystical quality of the city.

"I told you we didn't have to get here so early. We breezed through baggage check-in and security. We now have two hours to kill. Get me a martini with 3 olives."

With a silent nod, her husband Bob walked over to the bar. Norma Ekhart looked up as Emma turned to see who had interrupted her solace. They must have been at least five feet from each other, but before she was struck by Norma's commanding presence, she was transfixed by the woman's eyes. They were turquoise, the shade of the ocean off the coast of Oahu. It was a color Emma would never forget. She had grown up next to the Pacific Ocean. It was a deep, dark blue. It wasn't until she honeymooned in Hawaii with her first husband that she was in awe of the translucent quality of water and its color: an enticing turquoise. Same ocean. Different shore.

Norma was the first to turn away, concentrating instead on a small stack of papers. She studied them in earnest, waiting for her martini with three olives. Her long, slender fingers turned the pages of the report. She frowned, pulled a Mont Blanc gold pen out of her purse, and circled a paragraph.

Emma suddenly felt frumpy. She looked down at her T-shirt and jeans. They were clean, but she'd had the tee for years, so the "Eat Your Ethics" logo was faded, the letters crinkled and cracked, but still legible. It was slightly worn as were the jeans. She glanced at her left arm, partially covering her itinerary. The skin was wrinkled and dry. She grimaced and repositioned it, eliminating the crepey skin, if only momentarily.

Bob placed the martini in front of his wife, put his rum and coke on a napkin, and sat down opposite her. He leaned forward to read the papers. "What are you reading?"

"What do you think?" Norma replied without looking up. She played with her earring, the teardrop shaped ruby hung close to her jaw, turning it gently between her thumb and forefinger.

After a moment, he said, "Rick's synopsis from the meeting?"

Norma clapped her hands. "That wasn't too tough now, was it?" She took a sip of the martini and made a face. "What kind of vodka did they use? This is putrid. Grey Goose. Please." As she looked back at the papers, her shoulder-length ash blonde hair fell into her eyes. She swept it back behind her ear, her 10-carat diamond ring getting caught in the strands. Norma deftly removed the hair and once again perused the report.

After deliberately taking a long sip of his drink, Bob picked up the offensive martini and brought it back to the bar. Before he could speak, the bartender said, "One Grey Goose martini coming up. Sorry about that."

"No problem." He looked over at his wife and internally sighed. At fifty-six, Norma was a royal pain in the ass, yet he still found her attractive. And she continued to turn heads. She looked every bit high society, from her perfectly coiffed hair to her manicured nails, custom-tailored suit, and Christian Louboutin heels. Coming from old San Francisco money, she was born demanding attention.

This time when her cell rang, Emma ignored it. She was enjoying her scotch high and didn't want to ruin it with a conversation. She was debating whether she should have a third drink when she noticed that the man waiting for his wife's martini was staring at her map of Turin.

"Have you been there?" Emma said.

"Italy, yes. Not to Turin. I hear the mayor is turning her city vegetarian friendly. Can you imagine that?"

"Yes, I can," said Emma. "It's most likely one of the healthiest cities in Italy, if not the world. Of course, vegan would be ideal. Don't you think?" Emma loved messing with omnivores, which she knew he was by his comment.

Bob shook his head. "Have a nice trip." He grabbed the new and improved martini and brought it to his wife for approval. She took a sip and smiled.

"Now that's a martini." Norma circled a paragraph on the synopsis and handed it to Bob. After reading it, he put the paper down.

"Does Rick really think that building the racetrack will cost that much? I doubt it."

Norma said, "I doubt it, too. I'd like to get an estimate from Dolcini and Sons. My parents were good friends of the family. I'm sure they could give us a better quote. When we get back from the wedding, I'll call John."

Norma checked her watch, then downed the rest of her drink. "We should get to the gate in case they board early. Drink up."

Bob did as he was told, grimacing as he downed nearly half of his rum and coke. Emma watched them leave, then turned to the bartender and said, "That woman gives a whole new meaning to the term pussy whipped. She uses a cat o'nine tails."

The bartender laughed as she poured a jigger of rum into the shaker. "I'm betting she's got the money. Otherwise, why would he put up with that shit?"

"Beats me."

"Gigi? Gigi Cantella?"

Emma turned and watched as an elderly woman approached, then hesitated.

"I'm sorry," the woman said. "I thought you were someone else."

Emma stood and smiled sadly. "Gigi was my sister."

"Was?"

"She died two years ago last June. Car accident."

The woman put her hand to her mouth. "I had no idea. I'm so sorry. We had taken a class together at the junior college. She was such a sweetheart and what a sense of humor."

"Thank you. She was a wonderful sister. I'm Emma." She extended her hand and the woman shook it. "Where are you off to? Vacation, I hope."

"Yes, a much-needed vacation. I'm meeting friends in Cancun. You?"

"Italy."

"How lovely." The woman looked for an empty seat at the busy bar. All were occupied.

Emma said, "I was just leaving. Take my seat." She grabbed her purse and let the woman slip past her to the stool. "Have a wonderful time in Cancun."

"I will. Enjoy Italy. Again, I'm so sorry to hear about Gigi."

Emma nodded and left the bar. Not quite ready to sit at the gate, she went into the Global Duty-Free Shop, wandering mindlessly up and down the aisles, perusing the jewelry, objet d'art, books, and bottles of high-priced alcohol. A day didn't go by when Gigi wasn't lurking around the corner of her sister's mind. They were friends the moment Emma was born. At two years old, Gigi would marvel at her sister's teeny toes and fingers. She loved to make her laugh by tickling the baby's mini feet. When she got mad at her, she would call her by her full name: Esmerelda Conklin Banks. Emma was able to return the favor as soon as she could pronounce her big sister's name. With her slight adolescent lisp, she would shake her finger and say, "Griselda Locke Banks, what have you done?"

The sisters shared friends, clothes, and dates. Actually, only one date. And even then, it wasn't intentional. When Emma got the news of Gigi's death — her car rear-ended, pushed off the freeway overpass and into the traffic below — her knees buckled. She had sat on the floor of Quinley Books for what seemed like a lifetime. Memories ran through her brain like a relay race. Once one finished, another would take its place, from the time the family adopted Puddles McGee, the terrier hound mix from the shelter, to when Emma broke her leg skiing and Gigi bought her the entire Sex and the City DVD collection. And watched it with her in a marathon screening.

Emma was grateful her parents hadn't lived to experience their oldest daughter's death. It would have exacerbated their already fragile physical conditions. The family she did have circled around her and gave her the support she needed to get through the tragedy. She also leaned heavily on Gigi's husband, Grant. Married for over thirty years, the loss for him was immeasurable. The two had a marriage that Emma unsuccessfully tried to duplicate three times. After her split from Vin, she was convinced that, due to her lousy choices in men, she wasn't meant to be married. It was the universe signaling the end of matrimony for Emma Banks. Third time wasn't a charm.

When her focus landed on the merchandise, Emma was standing in front of a crystal necklace, her hand grazed the multi-faceted heart with a smaller red heart carved in the middle. Emma turned the price tag over: $45. She brought it to the counter and the saleswoman rang it up. As she handed the sales slip to Emma, she said, "That's my favorite necklace in the store."

"My sister loved hearts. She must have had a dozen in every size and color in earrings, necklaces, and rings." Emma put it on. "I'm wearing this for her."

The saleswoman held up a hand mirror and positioned it for Emma's view. She said, "It looks lovely on you. Wear it in good health."

"Thank you." Emma's eyes filled with tears. She left before the saleswoman noticed.

A quick stop at the Starbuck's kiosk to pick up bottled water and

Emma headed to gate 39. It was still early, but she figured she could read her book while waiting. Her hand involuntarily went to the necklace, gently tracing the heart with her finger. She was still thinking about Gigi when a family of three whizzed by, clearly rushing to get to their destination. They were a good ten feet ahead of Emma when the child's doll fell out of her backpack. It rolled a few times on the well-traveled floor and landed face up.

Emma ran over and picked up the doll. She held it over her head and yelled to the family who were now at least forty feet away. "You dropped your doll!"

The little girl turned and felt her backpack. Panicked, she looked at her mother and said something that Emma couldn't make out. The mother nodded and started walking swiftly toward Emma.

"Throw it to me," she yelled as the space closed between them.

As Emma watched the doll fly through the air, a deafening blast erupted in the utility room, three feet away. Massive chunks of concrete, tile and piping broke free from the wall, flying through the space where seconds before the hum of travelers returning from and leaving to their destinations seemed soundless in comparison. The floor rose and fell and rose again under their feet, causing people to scramble to safety. In their panic, they ran in all directions, unaware of where the explosion originated. Others fell on the uneven floor. A child tripped, getting stuck between a jagged gap in the concrete. She screamed as she tried to free her leg. A broken pipe coughed up water. Clouds of debris and dust danced wildly through the acrid, toxic air.

2

The entrance to San Francisco General Hospital was swarming with reporters. Television satellite vans occupied most of the parking lot while perfectly groomed reporters aggressively vied for those unlucky enough to enter the hospital, hoping to catch a particularly moving, newsworthy story.

The foyer and waiting room were overflowing with a cross section of the city's elected officials, grieving friends, and family members. Seated in the corner, a man in his early twenties, wearing an expensive suit, punched his legs oblivious to the pain, repeating, 'Goddamn terrorists, goddamn terrorists, goddamn terrorists.' The woman next to him barely heard his inflamed mantra. She was too busy calling relatives on her cell, crying as she told one after the other that her sister was in surgery, the doctors hopeful that they could save her legs. Outside, with cameras rolling, well-groomed talking heads recapped the events at San Francisco International Airport. Microphones were unsympathetically thrust into people's faces, the obvious questions asked: "Do you know anyone who was a victim of the attack?" "How did you feel when you found out your loved one was injured?" "Were you at the airport when the explosion occurred?"

Some people turned away, repulsed by the intrusion. Others were only too eager to talk, wanting to express their sorrow, frustration, anger, and helplessness.

In the pediatric wing, on the third floor, Paige Anderson was asleep in a hospital bed, her father by her side. He held her small, bandaged hand against his chest and pushed a strand of hair away from the purple and blue marbled bruise on her cheek. When they first arrived, the emergency nurse had gently cleaned the wounds on her arms and face. Most were superficial. He was grateful that she was sleeping. He didn't want her to see him crying. He closed his eyes and relived the life-changing event. Alec must have squeezed her hand a little too tight because Paige opened her eyes and looked at her father. She tried to sit up, but her head began to throb.

"Where's Mommy?"

Alec leaned over and kissed Paige's forehead hoping she wouldn't see the tears in his eyes. "How are you feeling, sweetie?"

A light knock on the door saved Alec from answering his daughter's question. Nurse Murphy smiled as she went to Paige's bedside. "I see you're up."

"I have a headache. It really hurts." Again, the six-year-old tried to pick her head off the pillow, but it only made the pounding in her head worse. "Ow!"

"I have just the thing to make that headache go away, but first I need to take your blood pressure." Nurse Murphy partially removed the covers, exposing her patient's arm and the doll Paige embraced. She tried to take the doll out of Paige's arms, but the little girl yanked her back and screamed, "Leave Marilyn alone! Don't touch her!"

Emma Banks opened her eyes. She was surrounded by darkness. She tried to turn but couldn't. Her arms. Numb. Her legs. Numb. No feeling at all. She felt like she was encased in a small box, the size of her body from head to toe, from left arm to right arm. A type of panic overtook her that she had never experienced. One of total helplessness. She tried to scream, but nothing came out. The only sounds she heard were the muffled voices of others, like they were talking through gauze. Then she heard a woman's voice with crystal clarity.

"Emma."

Emma tried to say, "I'm here!" Again, no sound.

"Emma. Come toward my voice."

The voice sounded so familiar, and she would have liked to follow it, but without being able to communicate or feel a thing, Emma's ferocious anxiety only intensified making it nearly impossible to know from where the voice was coming. Again, she tried to scream, but was enveloped in inky silence. Once again, she heard the voice. This time it was right next to her.

"Follow the sound of my voice." Gigi began singing one of Emma's favorite songs, Garth Brook's The Dance. It felt eerily appropriate as she continued singing, slowly moving away from Paige's doll.

Without thinking, Emma did as she was told. Total darkness became light as she floated upward. Then she saw her sister.

"Gigi! Oh my God!"

Emma went to embrace the woman she hadn't seen in over two years. Their 'bodies' merged. Startled, Emma retreated. She felt surges of energy coursing through her, like waves undulating from her core. She looked at her arm and gasped. She could see right through it. It was then Emma realized that she was floating above the room. She looked at the scene below and was confused. She didn't recognize the people, but the doll looked very familiar. A brief, intense flashback hit her hard. She gasped.

"That doll. At the airport. Now I'm...what am I? What's happened to me? Am I...dead?"

Gigi sighed. "Let's go somewhere else. Hospitals give me the creeps."

As she lightly touched her sister's fingers, Gigi transported them both to the edge of an enormous planter at the Palace of Fine Arts, one of the last remaining structures of the San Francisco World's Fair of 1915. On either side of the sisters were the weeping female statues gracing the corners of the planter boxes above the colonnade designed to hold flowers and vines "watered by their tears." Gigi thought it was an appropriate location to discuss her sister's demise. When they both lived in the Marina District, they would come to the Palace with its walking trails meandering through the lush landscape. Emma would look up at the planter boxes and wonder what the women were looking at. Using the planters for flora had been abandoned decades ago, so they appeared to be looking at something else.

"As much as I love seeing you again, I really need you to tell me what the hell is going on. One minute I was at the airport on my way to Italy and then..." Emma once again looked at and through her body, no longer corporeal. Even though she was confused, she also felt a sense of calm, like the time she took a Zoloft after learning of Vin's deceptions.

Gigi nodded. Again, she put her hand near Emma's. Her smile was soft and sympathetic. "You probably don't remember this, but when you threw the doll to that woman, a bomb exploded about three feet from you. You didn't survive."

Emma sat very still. The words, 'you didn't survive,' sliced through her. She was immobile. Frozen. Finally, she spoke. "So that's how it happens, huh? You wake up in complete darkness and can't move? It's a horrible way to find out you're no longer alive."

"It's definitely horrible, but it's also not normal. What I'm going to tell you is going to sound crazy."

"Any crazier than this? I'm sitting…"

Gigi raised her hand to silence her sister. "You threw the girl's doll in the air at the same time of the explosion. Its impact thrust your spirit out of your body and into the doll. You know how Dad always called you his living doll? Well, now you are."

"You're making a joke out of my predicament?"

Gigi laughed. "Sorry, Esmerelda, but I have to add some levity to this unbelievable situation, otherwise I'd be interminably depressed and when you're a spirit, that's a very long time."

Emma was trying to process the latest revelation. She had never been convinced that there was life after death. Reincarnation, though a fascinating subject, was dismissed as too esoteric. She looked at her sister, then down into the urn. It all felt fake, like she was dreaming and would wake up on the plane. The flight attendant would be announcing their arrival into the Turin Caselle Airport, so she needed to put her seat in the upright position and fasten her seatbelt. She blinked a couple of times, hoping that would bring her back into the world she knew. The world she wasn't ready to leave. Nothing changed. She could hear people below, walking around the columns, posing in front of the lagoon, snapping photos, and laughing. She longed to join them.

"I wasn't ready to leave."

"Most people aren't."

Emma sighed. "Remember in the movie, Superman, when Lois Lane dies? Superman reversed the direction of the Earth's rotation to the time before the accident that took her life. Can't you do that?"

Gigi shook her head. "Now you're just being silly."

"No. I'm just being…dead and I don't want to be dead. You're my big sister. Undo the accident. Send me on my way to Italy. I promise I'll visit your grave once a week and bring you your favorite flowers. Purple freesias, right?"

"If I could, I would send you back to the living in an instant."

Emma absently nodded. She sat very still and listened to the sounds below: a child running after her older brother, her feet crushing pebbles lining the walkway, laughing as she grabbed the back of his jacket. A helicopter circled above, Emma embraced the whirring of the blades, a sound she always took for granted. Now, it was the sound of the living, life on Earth which she was no longer an inhabitant.

Gigi broke Emma out of her reverie. "Here's the thing. When your spirit flew into the doll, it sort of got…stuck."

"What do you mean? I'm out of it right now. I'm here with you. I don't have to go back."

"Yeah, you do."

"No, I don't, Griselda."

"Sweetie, I know this all must be very difficult to understand."

Emma's spirit darkened as she hovered above her sister. "You have no idea how difficult this is to understand. I can't…I don't know what's happening. I'm flesh and blood one minute and the next…" She looked through her body and shuddered. "It's all so horrific. I want to go back to being Emma. I want to continue to work at Quinley's and drink coffee at Café Le Dance every morning. I want to jog to Fort Point with Petal. I want to go to Italy. Please, Gigi, just let me go back."

Her older sister knew firsthand how difficult it was to come to terms with mortality. Gigi's life ended abruptly, too. She was killed instantly in the car crash, her spirit mercilessly ripped from her body, not allowing her any time to assess the situation. Like Emma, she was alive and vibrant and in a split second, her life was taken from her.

Gigi patted the spot next to her and Emma sat down, the anger dissipating, replaced with sadness. "I know this is all very upsetting. Believe it or not, there is a bright spot. Since you're in Paige's doll – her name is Marilyn – you're still earthbound. Because the doll is inanimate, you can travel out of it a lot easier than when you were human, but there's a catch: you need to find another human body to inhabit. Basically, finding a soul that's weak enough so you can essentially push it out. Sounds weird, huh? It's super strange. This phenomenon happens more than you think. Most spirits make an easy escape from the body at the time of death, but when there's an explosion where objects are destroyed, spirits can get trapped in the debris and, in your case, a doll."

Gigi waited for a response, but Emma said nothing, just nodded, so she continued. "When a spirit inhabits an inorganic entity, exteriorization is easy at first. The longer it's housed, the more difficult it becomes to leave because the spirit's comfort level and attachment to the object becomes stronger. See what I'm getting at?"

"Not a clue."

"What I'm trying to say is that you don't have a lot of time to find another human body. Eventually, the doll will be your new body and since there's no 'down time,' like sleeping, you won't have a chance to leave like humans do when their bodies dream. You'll only be released when the doll is destroyed."

Emma shook her cosmic head. The flood of information on spiritual protocol and survival in an inorganic object was overwhelming. "How do you know all this? Are you really God disguised as my sister?"

Gigi laughed. "This is information we all know. It's easier to access when you're free of the trappings of the human form. You're still in shock from the accident. Once you become acclimated, you'll be able to tap into the Universal Mind, or as I like to call it, UM."

"You're just a barrel of laughs, aren't you?"

"Sorry, Emma. Turns out laughter is the best medicine." Gigi slapped her hands together and sparks of light flew, charging the air around them. "You've got your work cut out for you and I would be happy to help you find your new body. Shall we get started?"

Emma was about to answer when she heard a woman yelling. A young man, hiding in the tall reeds near the lagoon, had leapt out and snatched a tourist's cellphone as she was taking a photo of her husband and young daughter. The thief darted down the pathway with the family in pursuit. Emma and Gigi flew down to get a better look.

Panicked, Emma said, "Can't we do anything to stop him?"

"You mean like Patrick Swayze did in Ghost, when he chased down the guy who set him up to be robbed?"

"Exactly."

"Welcome to the real world of spirits. We're as effective as mist. Good movie, though." The sisters watched as the woman grabbed the thief by the back of his shirt and threw him to the ground. She snatched her phone from his hand and called 911 as her husband, a good foot taller than the thief and twice as wide, apprehended him.

Emma said, "How difficult is this body snatching going to be?"

"That, I don't know. Human's spirits are all different. Someone who might look like an easy target, may have a strong spirit and the person's potential hasn't yet been fully developed. On the other end of the spectrum are humans who appear strong and commanding, yet their spirits are young and weak."

"What you're trying to say is that it's a crap shoot and I'll be playing the spiritual version of dodgeball. You know when you throw the ball at someone hoping you'll knock them down and..."

"I remember how to play. I was good at it, too."

"You were the best."

Emma watched her spiritual legs swing back and forth. Processing her new life was like being plucked from a job and thrown into a new one without training and in a different language. "Any words of wisdom from the spiritual realm?"

"The Beatles said it best. All you need is love."

"You're kidding, right?"

Gigi laughed. "Sound too simple? You wanted something more earth shattering?"

"Yeah."

"If every person felt love for everyone and everything, earth would be a paradise. No war, no poverty, no murder. I would call that pretty damn earth shattering. When you're back in a body, think about it. Try to love without exception. Try to love and forgive the men who planted the explosives at the airport, then tell me how simple it is."

3

Norma Ekhart was putting the finishing touches on her nearly completed ensemble. Rick and Marlo Standish were coming to dinner, and she wanted to look more beautiful than her guest. Marlo was Rick's latest trophy wife, the third, the youngest, and possibly the most stunning. Realistically, Norma knew that she couldn't compete with a woman twenty-five years her junior, but she was going to give it her best shot. At fifty-six, Norma's face and neck were toned, nary a wrinkle could be detected, all without the aid of Botox, fillers, or surgery. From an early age, she treated her skin like a one-of-a-kind work of art. Growing up in San Francisco and spending every summer at the beach, her friends would make fun of their fair-skinned friend for wearing sunscreen and wide-brimmed hats while they slathered on Hawaiian Tropic Dark Tanning Oil, smelling like ripe coconuts, papayas, and mangoes. They laid on the beach for hours while Norma read the latest novel by Leon Uris beneath a six-foot umbrella. The hat was surrendered only when she body surfed or played volleyball. Years later, her beach friends would pay large sums of money to eradicate wrinkles, age spots, and mottled skin. Not one to pass up an 'I told you so,' Norma enjoyed visiting her friends while they recuperated from a face lift or cheek implants, reminding them that she had yet to require the services of a plastic surgeon. "You look so uncomfortable, Pamela. Remember you used to say that to me when I was sitting under the umbrella at Ocean Beach? Ironic, isn't it?" Then Norma would take out her mirror and study her flawless skin, her reflection admired for its beauty. She'd point to a spot on her face and in mock horror say, "Is that a line? Ah, no, my mistake. It's just an eyelash."

She applied mascara last, sweeping the brush on her lashes above her turquoise eyes. Finished, she turned to the side and studied her profile in the 3-way mirror. A flash of anger disrupted her viewing as she was reminded that her daughter's small, upturned nose was identical to her own.

"I don't know where I went wrong with that girl." Norma turned from the mirror and put on the evening dress laid out on the bed. Five years ago, she would have wriggled into a dress and admired the way it hugged her perfect figure. She hadn't gained extra weight. Age and menopause simply redistributed the curves, fat settling on her abdomen and giving a once shapely rear in need of a lift.

Norma turned to the side and frowned. She put her hand on her stomach and pushed it in, granting her the vision she desired. She vowed to suck it in whenever Marlo had viewing access to her belly.

The doorbell rang at exactly 7:00. Betsy, the Ekhart's maid, brought Marlo and Rick into the living room where they were greeted by their hosts. Bob and Norma internally gasped at the same time. Marlo looked splendid in a mini dress. The lime green toga-style tog lovingly hugged and caressed Marlo's tight body. Rick couldn't hide his satisfaction. His wife served her purpose. Norma was the first to break the silence. She hugged Rick first, her arms embracing his portly frame, letting her body linger. She could have sworn he was wearing Spanx.

"So nice to see you again. You look as handsome as ever." She gave Marlo a cursory hug. "And look at you."

Once Norma stepped away from Marlo, Bob took his turn. His hug was anything but cursory. He said, "You look lovely, my dear."

"Thank you, Bob."

Darby arrived with cocktails at the appointed time. Norma picked up her martini, acknowledging the family chef with a near imperceptible nod.

Rick took a sip from the perfect vodka martini, then turned his attention to the hostess. "Bob told me that you were at the airport during the bombing. It must have been horrific."

Norma said, "It was dreadful. We were boarding our plane when we heard the explosion. It wasn't too far from our gate." Her hands gently flew up in the air, making it look more refined than chaotic. "Maybe now they'll stop those damn Muslims from entering our country."

Marlo said, "Didn't you hear? The bomb was planted by a white supremacist group. I think they call themselves the Guiding White Light or it might have been the Guiding Knights. Two men were arrested in the airport parking lot. They found more explosives in their car."

"Obviously I didn't hear. Thank you for the clarification, Marlo." She intentionally turned to Rick. "Why would they kill Americans?"

Rick shrugged. Marlo answered. "Maybe they thought they could kill more foreigners by targeting the airport." She inhaled deeply. "Instead, they ended up murdering five white Americans, three of them women. The cowards."

Norma said, "It's a matter of time before we have another terrorist attack. We can't stop white extremists from invading America, but they can stop the Muslims from living amongst us." She sat down and patted the seat next to her. "Right here, Rick." She carefully stirred her martini. "Is the sale going through next week as planned? I'd like to break ground on Francisco Downs Racetrack as soon as possible."

"It's coming together." Rick sat back and took a long sip of his drink. The martini was perfectly chilled. The vodka slid down his throat like a cool, slippery waterfall. He pulled the olive off the 14-carat gold martini toothpick and offered it to his wife. Her lips parted as Rick gently placed the olive in her mouth. "Cliff at Barclay's said if there aren't any entanglements, we should be signing the papers two weeks from Thursday."

Norma sat up straighter and instinctively pulled in her stomach. "Entanglements? What kind of entanglements?"

Rick smiled. "Nothing to be alarmed about, Norma. You know that the property abuts Sternwood Creek. Even though the plans clearly show that we have the proper clearance between our structures and the creek bed, Citizens for Environmental Protection is contesting the track."

Norma's voice was tight. "I thought Jim Harper took care of that. He said he spoke to the director of CEP and they agreed to drop the complaint."

"Apparently, they changed their mind. I wouldn't let it concern you. Harper is working on it." Rick popped the remaining olive in his mouth.

"Do you want me to call Lonnie?" Norma said.

"No," Rick replied.

"Are you sure?"

"I'm sure, Norma."

Marlo said, "Who's Lonnie?" Her husband replied, "A mutual friend in the financial sector."

Sensing tension in the air, Marlo went over to a statue sitting on the mantle. The winged god Mercury looked as though he was taking flight, the chandelier reflecting light off his bronze body. "Is this new? I don't recall seeing it last time we were here."

Bob followed her lead. He walked over to where she was standing and was about to answer, when Norma said, "It's been in the family for years and I'm going to say it's been in that exact location for at least ten years. I'm sure this conversation is boring for you, Marlo. Bobby, why don't you show her the other family heirlooms in the den while Rick and I discuss business?"

"No need," said Rick. "I don't want to talk business right now. Honey, tell the Ekharts about your plans for the backyard. You're going to love this, Bob."

Marlo sat back down and put her hand on her husband's leg. She swept her long hair to one side. "You know how there's kind of an empty space next to the pool where the old cabana used to be? Well, I thought it would be so cool to extend the pool and create an underwater grotto, like the one at the Playboy mansion. We could have a hot tub in there, too."

Rick added, "And I'd love to build a bar. Did you know Marlo was at the mansion? She even met Hef." He gave Marlo a kiss. Norma couldn't help but look over at Bob. She could have sworn he was getting a hard-on.

"Imagine the honor of meeting Hef." Norma's sarcasm wasn't lost on anyone in the room, including Darby who had just walked in.

The petite Irish woman announced, "Dinner is ready."

As Darby circled the table, filling the diners' bowls with roasted garlic and parsnip soup with sage lemon butter, Sandy Ekhart sat shivering in the north corner of Colbert Park, not more than three miles from the Ekhart mansion. Her arms were wrapped tightly around her body. Despite a sweater and wool coat, the wind found its way through her many layers and chilled her to the bone. She was trying hard to concentrate on the two figures huddled next to an unruly grove of sycamore trees, but a nasty headache was making it difficult. A few minutes passed, then one of the men hurriedly disappeared into the night and the other walked toward Sandy. He waved a small baggie in the air, his dirty fingers clutching the bag like a lifeline, while he stuffed a larger bag into his coat pocket.

"I told you I'd get it," the man said, flashing a nearly toothless smile. He was pushing forty, but he looked like he was in his sixties.

Sandy weakly smiled back, extending her hand to grab the bag, but the man pulled it away.

"There's a price to pay. I told you that."

"I don't have any money, but you can have this." She dug into her pants pocket and held up a small sapphire ring. Its worth was much greater than the contents in the baggie.

The man's doughy smile was anything but charming. "I ain't asking for money or jewelry." She knew his intention and so badly wanted to get high, taste the milky smoke in her mouth, feel it expanding in her lungs and, ultimately, removing her consciousness from reality. But the cost wasn't worth it. Her insides ached when she thought of that man putting his filthy hands on her body. She didn't even know his name and didn't care. It was irrelevant. Sandy shoved the ring inside her jeans and started to walk away. "That's okay. I don't need it that bad."

The man walked after her. "Fine. You win. I'll let you have a small toke. That okay with you?" She nodded. He pulled the baggie out of his pocket, along with rolling papers and cocked his head in the direction of the wooded area in the park. Sandy followed.

A few minutes later, they came to a clearing. It was obvious that others had used this spot. A crude fire pit had been constructed with various sized rocks from the surrounding area. Branches and twigs, some charred, were piled in the middle of the pit. The man motioned for Sandy to sit down while he took off his backpack and pulled out a rolled-up newspaper. While he used it to get a fire started, he began singing. His voice was as crude as his looks. Off-key and guttural, it wasn't until the end of the song that she realized he was singing Justin Timberlake's, *Can't Stop the Feeling.*

Sandy began to thaw, her skin tingling with the heat from the fire. "My name's Ellis. Yours?" he said as he handed her the joint.

"Sandy." She took a big drag and kept it in as long as she could. She wanted a high as tall as the trees. She wanted to block out the park and her companion. Nothingness was best.

Ellis took the joint from Sandy's hands, letting his fingers linger. She quickly dropped her hands into her lap, interlacing her fingers until they hurt. As she exhaled, she could feel her mind leaving her head, piggybacking on the smoke. She looked up and watched it float away. She felt blissfully numb. She could no longer smell Ellis' rank body odor. The chirping of the crickets and occasional breaking of twigs was muted. It was the first time since she was forced to live on the streets that the humiliation she felt dissipated.

Her artificial bliss was short-lived. Sandy was about to ask Ellis for the joint when he pounced on her. Her petite frame was no match for his two hundred forty-pound body. He wasn't strong, just big and determined. He clamped one hand over her mouth while the other unzipped her pants and roughly pulled them down. Sandy tried to fight back, but his body had all but covered her. Pinned, she was unable to move her arms. They ached under his weight. The same high that brought her happiness came crashing down like a felled tree, sending splinters of terror through every part of her body.

Sandy's anguish was replaced with excruciating pain. She screamed into Ellis' dirty, calloused hand. It seemed to excite him more. A few more minutes and it was over. The rapist rolled off her, patting her exposed belly like he had done this many times before. He was breathing heavily and the rancid odor once more permeated her nostrils.

"You're one tight little bitch, you know that?" Ellis picked up the joint lying on the ground and lit it. He inhaled too quickly and began coughing, spittle hitting Sandy's face and neck.

Very slowly, Sandy sat up. She wiped her face, the dirt from her hands mixing with fresh tears. She gently touched her crotch. Her fingers came back bloody. The pain she felt was piercing, like Ellis had ripped her in two. Sandy wanted to curl up into a tiny ball and disappear. Instead, she stood and pulled up her pants. She tried to run but gasped as the pain shot up from her groin. Her legs buckled. She held her breath and rose, then slowly, very slowly walked away. Ellis shook his head. "You don't get nuthin' for free. Remember that little girl, 'specially if you're gonna be livin' in the great outdoors."

Stoned and in pain, Sandy walked in the direction of the homeless camp. At least she hoped she was. Her sense of direction was poor and worse when she was high. Eventually, she saw faint lights in the distance and what looked like outlines of tents. When the pain became too intense, she stopped. Looking up at the starless sky, Sandy screamed, "You did this to me, Norma! I hate you, you bitch! Do you hear me, I hate you!"

When Sandy reached the homeless encampment where she had left her few belongings, most of the residents were asleep. She was grateful that her backpack, sleeping bag, and shopping bag full of clothes were still there. She still wasn't sure how she would get through another cold night. It chilled her beyond her bones, seeping into her organs, especially her heart. Growing up in the city, she was used to the weather, the foggy nights, frigid winds, but she had always been well fortified, wrapped in Versace jackets, Gucci scarves, Prada boots.

Sandy unfurled her sleeping bag and pulled it around her body, hugging it as if it could heal her.

"What's the matter?"

Sandy's head jerked up. Standing before her was a diminutive Asian woman. A knitted cap was pulled down below her ears and she must have had on four layers of clothing. With her small head sticking up out of the scarf wrapped around her neck, she looked like a tick full of blood ready to burst. If Sandy wasn't so miserable, she might have laughed. The woman made a second attempt at communication.

"Are you deaf? If so, you're shit out of luck because I don't know sign language."

"I'm fine," Sandy lied.

"Then why are you crying?" She pointed to Sandy's tears with a hand encased in a dirty mitten.

Sandy put her hands up to her face and felt her cheeks. They were wet with tears.

"It's nothing."

"The hell it isn't. There's blood on your hands. Follow me." She noticed Sandy looking down at her worldly possessions. She grabbed the backpack and looked at the sleeping bag and shopping bag. "Pick up your stuff."

Reluctantly, Sandy followed the woman through the maze of lean-to's, oversized cardboard boxes, tents and outstretched, sleeping bodies until they came to the corner of the encampment. She stopped at a two-person tent. It wasn't the mansion that Sandy grew up in on Broadway in Pacific Heights. It was tattered and ripped at the stake points. The sun had bleached its original hunter green exterior a few shades lighter, and a paisley sheet had been draped over what appeared to be a nasty tear, held down by duct tape. As if reading her mind, the woman said, "It's not an estate, but it'll keep you out of this nasty wind." She unzipped the doorway and crawled inside, then held the flap open and beckoned Sandy inside.

"I'm going to make you some hot tea. Go ahead and sit. My name is Kaitlin."

"I'm Sandy." She tried to sit cross-legged, but the raw pain made her involuntarily cry out. Kaitlin dropped the tarnished tea kettle and reached out to Sandy. "What the hell's wrong?"

Without a thread of dignity left, Sandy broke down and told Kaitlin about meeting Ellis. When she finished, she looked down at the makeshift floor, a polyester rug, the pattern of large and small circles in orange, red, green, and yellow. "It was my first time."

"Being raped? I hope so."

Sandy shook her head.

"My lord. That bastard took your virginity? I don't know who this Ellis character is, but he's not getting away with it."

"No!" Sandy cried. "I don't want him to hurt me again. Please, don't tell anyone. Please."

Kaitlin promised she wouldn't breathe a word to anyone, but it was only to placate her guest. "I'm taking you to the clinic tomorrow to make sure you're okay down there. Right now, go lay down and I'll make us some tea." She crawled over to the corner of the tent and uncovered a small single-burner camp stove. "I don't know what I'd do without this baby." She turned the knob and after a few clicks, the fire came to life. Kaitlin filled her kettle with water from a very used plastic bottle and placed it on the burner. She then grabbed two mugs from a duffle bag and put a teabag in one of them. She glanced over at Sandy and shook her head. It reminded her of when she was thrown out on the streets not too long ago. At least Kaitlin was in her thirties and had more street smarts than Sandy. It wasn't easy, but she could defend herself against a rapist. At least she hoped she could. She put her hand inside her pants pocket, touching the switchblade, a present to herself when she realized that living under a roof and the comforts of a home wasn't possible.

4

Alec Andersen felt like someone had filled him with sandbags. Normally, he was one of those rare individuals who bounded out of bed, optimistic about the new day, ready to take on whatever was presented. Not this morning. His head was throbbing, and he could barely lift his arm, the one draped across Paige. The six-year-old was still asleep, lightly snoring. He would have liked to remain in bed, but Alec felt it was time to get up and fulfill his duties as a single parent. He and Janet discouraged Paige from sleeping in their bed, but her first night home, after she was released from the hospital, his daughter woke up at two in the morning, screaming for her mother. He calmed her down, then carried her to his bedroom, not before she refused to leave without Marilyn. The American Girl doll was still wearing her gray beret, though it was singed and dirty from the accident. One of her flower buttons was partially melted and, no matter how hard Alec scrubbed at her with a damp cloth, she smelled of concrete dust and smoke. He promised Paige that he would order another pair of shiny black shoes. Both were lost in the rubble.

Three glasses of orange juice sat on the kitchen table. At first, he was confused. Did he pour the juice and forgot? Was he sleepwalking? Then his mother-in-law walked into the kitchen. She was dressed in running gear. Her skin glistened from a rigorous jog.

"Good morning," Rebecca said.

"I must be losing my mind. I totally forgot you were here." Alec rubbed his eyes and sat down at the table. Rebecca went over to him and put her arm around his shoulder. As soon as he felt her touch, he broke down. He tried to muffle his sobs so he wouldn't wake Paige. "I miss her so much."

"I know Alec. I miss her, too." Rebecca began to cry. The room filled with their grief, pain and disbelief that Janet Andersen wouldn't be walking into the room, joining them for breakfast, and helping Paige get ready for school.

Rebecca took a handkerchief out of her jacket and blew her nose. She got a tissue from the kitchen counter and handed it to Alec. He thanked her and went over to the refrigerator, grabbed the loaf of sourdough bread and almond butter, and placed them next to the toaster. "Would you like some toast?"

She shook her head and pointed to the Vitamix. "I drink my breakfast. Thanks, anyway."

"That's why we have half the produce department in our fridge." 2 stalks of celery, a bag of apples, 3 cucumbers, a bunch of red and yellow beets, and 4 lemons. "Would you mind making enough so I can try it? It may be a great way to regain my mental strength."

"I'd be delighted. I'll make enough for Paige, too. All that organic juice will definitely boost your immune system and give you both some much needed energy."

Alec was putting two pieces of bread in the toaster when Paige appeared in the doorway, arms tight around Marilyn. She saw her grandmother and her eyes lit up. "Grammy!"

Rebecca scooped up Paige and hugged her tight. "How's my little munchkin? Did you sleep well?"

"Kind of. Mommy was in my dreams. I think I had five of them. The first one…"

Alec had to smile. His little girl had the ability to vividly recall what seemed like every dream she had had the night before, up until she awakened. Smells, colors, events. She remembered everything with perfect clarity. Normally, he had trouble concentrating on her seemingly endless recitation, but this morning his interest was purely selfish. He wanted to hear about Janet.

"…and then the dog jumped on the bed and turned into Mommy. She took my hands and started jumping up and down and I was laughing and then Marilyn turned into a lady, but she didn't look like Marilyn. Her skin was my color, not cocoa color. She wasn't wearing her hat either. In my next dream, Grammy and I were at the park."

Rebecca cut in. "You must be psychic. I thought I'd take you down to the park after breakfast. How does that sound?"

"What's psychic?"

Rebecca laughed. She forgot she was talking to a six-year-old. "It's when a person knows what someone else is going to do or say before the person does it."

Paige said, "Maybe I am psychic." She went over to her dad. "I think I knew you were going to make toast."

"I make toast every morning. That's not being psychic. That's having a good memory. Go sit down sweetie and drink your orange juice."

Paige did as she was told. She sat Marilyn next to her, but when she pulled the doll's chair closer to the table, Marilyn slid off and fell on her head. Emma woke up with a start. Immediate disorientation set in. So did panic. She still wasn't used to her new body, especially since inside the doll she couldn't see, feel, or touch. Sound was her only sensory perception and even then, it was muffled. Emma didn't have any trouble leaving Marilyn for hours, but eventually she was forced to return, the luminous silver cord that had connected her to her corporeal body now was attached to the doll.

Emma was curious about her new family. She willed herself out of Marilyn and gently floated above the doll. She watched as Paige picked her up from the floor and lovingly brushed off a few hairs that caught in her beret.

"I can clean her up for you, if you'd like," Rebecca said. "We could wash her clothes and…"

"I like her this way," Paige replied. She straightened out Marilyn's dress, her hand resting on a burn mark in the hem. "She's perfect."

Rebecca looked at Alec and shrugged. He gave her a weak smile. "Yes, she's perfect," he said and set a plate of toast in front of her. "Eat up so you and Grammy can go to the park."

Paige took a bite of bread, slathered with almond butter and bananas. "Are you coming with us?"

"I have to go to work, but I'll be home early. Maybe we can take a walk. The three of us."

Don't you mean the four of us? Emma thought to herself. She liked these people. If she had to be temporarily stuck in a doll, she couldn't have chosen a better family. Their energy felt solid, loving. It also was tainted with intense pain over the loss of Janet Andersen, a raw pain that Emma mirrored. Free from the doll's confines, she moved from room to room, observing the décor, most of it eclectic. An antique oak and walnut dining room table and chairs rested on a mosaic-patterned rug in shades of blue and green. She drifted over to the living room; its walls washed in a light peach. One of the walls was covered with photos, mostly of the family. Emma felt a tightness, a rip in her soul as she glanced at one of the photos. Janet is holding Paige who looked to be about two years old. The little girl's arms were wrapped around her mother's neck. They smiled at each other, pure sweet love between them. Emma could feel it, sense it. She had never considered having children, but regret washed over her. Maybe I'll be a mother in my next incarnation, she thought.

Back in the kitchen, Emma observed Rebecca. She looked to be about the same age as Emma before the accident. Her salt and pepper shoulder length hair was pulled pack in a ponytail, revealing a strong jawline. Her almond shaped eyes were hazel. Light age spots were visible on her olive skin. Even through the loose-fitting sage green long-sleeved shirt and black sweatpants, Emma could tell that the woman was in great shape for being in her fifties. I really should have exercised more, she thought, then she wondered where Rebecca's husband was or if she had one, where she lived and how long she'd be staying with her son-in-law and granddaughter. She made a note to herself to find out.

Rebecca was glad she had brought a sweater for Paige. It was late morning and, even with the sun shining, it felt like it was in the mid-sixties. Perhaps she was being more cautious, more doting than usual. She wasn't the typical grandmother who hovered over her granddaughter. She wanted Paige to make decisions for herself, provided they wouldn't put her in danger. With her mother gone, Rebecca's instinct to protect Paige was heightened.

They rounded the corner and as soon as Paige spotted the swings, she ran toward them. Rebecca took a seat on the bench and laid the sweater next to her, along with her cellphone and book. She watched as Paige buckled Marilyn into the swing, then did the same for herself. She worked slowly into a forward and back movement until she could use her legs to propel herself higher. Satisfied that she was at a sufficient height, she grabbed the chain on Marilyn's swing and the two of them flew through the air, swinging back and forth like good friends, their bond even tighter than before. Occasionally, Paige would look up at the sky and say something. Her grandmother was too far away to hear, but Emma was above her and the little girl's plea to her mother broke her heart. "Can you see me, Mommy? I miss you. Marilyn does, too."

Moments later, Emma noticed a bright beam of light hovering above the swings. She glanced over at Rebecca and then at the other people in the park, wondering what their reaction would be seeing this phenomenon. No one noticed, even those looking up at a plane flying overhead. Emma came in closer to get a better look. As soon as she did, the light disappeared as quickly as it had appeared. Emma wondered if it was Janet. Gigi had told her that spirits whose bodies had undergone a traumatic death were disoriented and it took them longer to acclimate to the afterlife. She thought of following the light, then decided against it. She was more concerned with learning about the Andersen family and looking for another body to inhabit, not chasing after spirits.

Sandy walked slowly, almost shuffled, on the periphery of the playground. She glanced over at the children playing, jealous of every one of them. They were taken care of and loved, especially the little girl on the swing set with her doll. Sandy watched an elderly woman blow a kiss to the child and the child responded by blowing one back.

She didn't want to be out during the day, amongst the 'normal' people, but her body ached; it felt worse than the night before and she promised Kaitlin that she would go to the free clinic. Her new friend had given her specific directions and she was doing her best to remember them. Even sober, she had to concentrate so she wouldn't get lost. This wasn't a part of the city that Sandy was familiar with. Up until a few days ago, she had never been here, even though it was only a few miles from where she grew up in Pacific Heights, one of the more prestigious addresses in San Francisco. Across the street from the park, the Victorian-style homes nearly touched each other. The small rectangular lawns were well-groomed. Flower boxes were filled with begonias, peonies, primrose, and other colorful, showy flowers. Sandy barely noticed. She tried to keep her head down so she wouldn't have to acknowledge pedestrians walking in the opposite direction. A grey cat sauntered down the stairs of a hunter green house with gold gingerbread trim and begged to be petted. A soft spot for animals, Sandy stopped and bent down to pet the cat. As she did, it felt like her skin was being ripped apart. She gasped and held her breath, hoping that would ease the pain. Slowly she stood, leaning on a mailbox for support. What did I do to deserve this, she thought, admonishing herself for being so trusting?

An hour later, Sandy braced herself as she walked through the doors of the San Francisco Free Clinic. She expected to find a poorly lit room filled with desperate-looking transients sitting on metal folding chairs. Instead, she walked into a room painted light pink, the linoleum floor a brighter pink. The waiting room was filled, but as Sandy scanned the room, looking for an available seat, she appeared to be one of the most unkempt people there. Most weren't going to win awards for their fashion sense, but the majority were clean, their hair combed, presentable. She walked up to the receptionist window and gave the woman on the other side of the opening a pained smile. The young woman smiled back.

"Can I help you?"

"I'd like to see a doctor, please."

"Have you been here before?"

Sandy shook her head. The woman handed her a clipboard and a pen. "Fill out this form on both sides and bring it back to me."

At the other end of the room, an elderly man was leaning back in the chair, stroking a small dog on his lap. As soon as he saw Sandy, he stood and offered his seat to her. He could tell that she was in pain by her knotted brow and tight smile. She willingly took the chair and thanked him.

Twenty minutes later, Sandy returned the form, completed to the best of her ability. Without an appointment, it would be another two hours before her name was called. During the first hour, Sandy read a few of the magazines designated for the patients. By the second hour, she became antsy. As hard as it was to leave her coveted seat, she went to the restroom, pulled out a small bottle of Jamieson's Scotch and finished off half of it. It helped dull the pain both physically and emotionally. When she returned to the waiting room, her seat had been taken by a pregnant teenager. Her vision altered, Sandy made her way to the other side of the waiting room and sat down on the floor between a side table and an office door. Legs sticking out in front of her, she leaned back against the wall and closed her eyes. She woke up when the nurse touched her on the shoulder and requested that she follow her to the examination room.

"The doctor will be right with you." She handed Sandy a paper exam gown. "Please put this on so the open part is in front. You can leave your socks on."

Before the nurse left, Sandy said, "I requested a female doctor on my application form."

The nurse gave Sandy a sympathetic smile. "We're just a tad short-staffed here, so you'll be seen by the first doctor available, unless you want to wait longer and, honestly, I'm not sure when Dr. Drexler will be free. Do you want to take that chance?" Sandy shook her head. Under normal circumstances, like a routine exam, she wouldn't have cared. This was not a normal exam. She had always had a female gynecologist and the thought of a male physician checking her out and asking her personal questions made her very uncomfortable.

There was a soft knock on the exam room door. Sandy was sitting on the exam table, her legs crossed and her arms over her chest, holding the flimsy gown together. "Come in."

The doctor walked over to Sandy and held out his hand. "I'm Dr. Remini and you must be Sandy Ekhart."

"There's no one else here, so that must be me."

Sandy couldn't help but notice how the doctor reminded her of her first crush in high school. Teddy Logan wasn't the most popular boy in school. Most of the girls probably didn't even notice him, but Sandy thought he was adorable. He was average height and wiry with shoulder length wavy blonde hair and a warm smile. Behind his horn-rimmed glasses were sage green colored eyes. Dr. Remini had the stature, the glasses, and even the same eye color, but his hair was short. The smile was the same, big and friendly. Sandy must have been looking at him funny, because he said, "Are you okay?"

"If I was okay, I wouldn't be here, would I?" She laughed but it came out as a snort.

"Good point. It was just you were looking at me as if you knew me."

"Are you Teddy Logan?"

Will Remini was used to his patients being somewhat…different. He had joined the clinic staff a few months ago. In that time, he had treated the homeless, drug addicts, and illegal immigrants. The conditions ranged from stab wounds to chlamydia to gangrene. Sandy would be his third rape victim. Dr. Remini knew from her chart that she was homeless, but there was no indication that she suffered from a mental disorder, so her question took him by surprise.

"No. My name is William Remini. Who's Teddy Logan?"

"Never mind. I'm not here to talk about a guy I went to high school with." Sandy shifted on the exam table and grimaced. "I'm in a lot of pain. I need meds or something. Can I get some?"

"I'm going to do my best to alleviate that pain, Ms. Ekhart, but first I need to do an examination. Can you tell me what happened?"

As Sandy told the doctor about last night, she kept her gaze on her hands which began to shake as she told him about the attack. When she was done, she wiped her eyes and looked up.

Dr. Remini looked sincerely upset. "I'm very sorry. It must have been traumatic. Have you told the police?"

"No and I don't want to. What if he's not arrested? He'll be pissed and then he could do it again or even kill me. I don't want to take that chance."

There was a short knock followed by the entrance of Nurse Halliday. She went over to the cabinet and took out the necessary medical tools for the procedure.

"Ms. Ekhart…"

"Sandy, please. My mother is Mrs. Ekhart and the last thing I want is to be associated with or reminded of her. The bitch."

Nurse Halliday glanced over at the doctor and gave him a disapproving look. Sandy caught it. "If you knew my mother, you'd understand. She takes the word bitch to another level. Another galaxy, actually." Sandy laughed, then grimaced as the pain from her groin was ignited. She shifted uncomfortably and rearranged her examination smock.

Dr Remini said, "Sandy, we're obligated to report your rape to the police. If your statement is true, this Ellis character will be jailed. It sounds like he's attacked women before. Can you remember where he took you in the park?"

Sandy closed her eyes and tried to imagine the spot, but she found it hard to concentrate. Dealing with the police and retelling her attack was making her agitated. She opened her bloodshot eyes. "I don't know. It was dark and I'd only been at the park for a couple of days. It's all muddled in my head. Can we get this exam over with?"

The doctor nodded and instructed his patient to put her feet in the stirrups. Sandy gingerly slid into position. When Dr. Remini saw the dried blood and inflammation, he discarded the speculum and requested a cotton swab with a numbing agent. It wouldn't alleviate the pain, but it would definitely decrease the intensity.

After Sandy dressed, Dr. Remini returned. He handed her three pieces of paper. "I've prescribed an antibiotic and the morning after pill. The antibiotic is a precaution in case you have an infection from the unsanitary nature of the perpetrator and the morning after pill will protect you in case you were impregnated. There's also a prescription for Tylenol."

"Can't I just get that at a store? I'm in pain. What the hell is that going to do? Oh, I get it. You're afraid of giving me real pain drugs, like Percocet, aren't you? Afraid I'm a druggie? Well, I'm not."

"Sandy, the Tylenol being prescribed has Hydrocodone and is by prescription only. It's strong enough to alleviate your pain, which I have no doubt you're feeling. We don't even carry Percocet because, unlike you, we have many patients who are addicted to drugs. I will ask you, however, that when you come in for your follow-up appointment, you're sober."

Sandy looked at the third piece of paper. "325 Hill Road, five to seven p.m. What's this?"

Dr. Remini smiled. "That is the address for the soup kitchen, and I invite you to come over tonight and have a nice hot meal. I'll be serving my vegetarian chili. I've been told it's excellent."

"You a veg head?"

"Vegan, actually."

"Well, what a shocker. How come you're not wearing Birkenstocks with white socks?" She sniffed the air. "And is that patchouli oil I smell?"

He laughed. "I give you permission to shoot me if I'm ever wearing that combination or any variation thereof. I'm surprised that a San Francisco native is stereotyping a vegan. We come in all flavors and sizes. It's the healthiest diet and the most compassionate. If you ever want more information, let me know."

Sandy stood up and went for the door. "Before I make my shopping list and head over to Whole Foods, I'll be sure to give you a call. You can tell me all about the nuts and seeds and tofu I need to buy. And why would you assume that I grew up in San Francisco? This city is a melting pot for all 50 states."

"The name Ekhart is a giveaway. Your family is synonymous with San Francisco history."

Sandy winked and clucked her tongue. "Got me there, Doc. You're smarter than you look."

Dr. Remini was taken aback. "I beg your pardon?"

"Remember when I asked you if you were Teddy Logan? Well, he wasn't the brightest bulb on the tree, just the cutest." And with that, Sandy walked out of the exam room and asked the first nurse she saw where she could get her prescriptions filled.

Dr. Will Remini had just enough time to check his messages in his office before his next patient. He had an email from his sister, Gloria. She invited him to dinner next Friday. He had another email from her son, Makelo. He requested that his uncle please come to dinner next Friday. Before he went to the bathroom, he wrote a note on the pad next to the computer to look up the Ekhart family. His curiosity surrounding Sandra was acute. How did a young woman from one of the richest San Francisco families end up in the free clinic, inebriated and homeless?

By the time Sandy returned to the park, it was dusk. She couldn't wait to get back to her belongings and get high. Her nerves felt thin and exposed. Touching her skin hurt. The interview at the police station took hours. They must have asked her more questions about herself and details of last night than she could have imagined. At one point, she felt like she was the guilty party. As she suspected, the cops also wanted her to take them to the place where she was accosted by Ellis. As she had told the doctor, it was dark and she wasn't familiar with the park, only the area where the homeless encampment was and even then, Sandy's sense of direction couldn't be trusted. When she asked one of the officers for protection, they suggested she go to the shelter, where she would be safer. He even offered to drive her there, though it was less than a mile from the police station. She declined. Sandy knew they would have a list of rules that she would be forced to abide by. The last thing she wanted was to live by others' rules. She was done with that for good.

She recognized the children's area. Without a watch or cellphone, she assumed it was around six o'clock, because the swings were empty as was the slide and carousel. A father was scooping up his young daughter from the sandbox, holding her pail and shovel in his free hand. Wanting nothing more than to rest, Sandy picked up her pace as she got closer to the homeless tents. Kaitlin insisted that she stash her worldly possessions just outside of her tent. She was hoping she'd remember where her friend's tent was located. Dr. Remini was right about the Tylenol. Her physical pain was almost gone. It was her emotional anguish that she was going to work on eliminating, even if temporarily.

She could smell the homeless camp a hundred feet before she walked through the weather-beaten entrance. For people who didn't have a lot of belongings, Sandy was amazed at how much crap they accumulated. And how much it reeked. Socks worn for weeks on end, clothing too, through rain and heat. The stench of body odor and unclean skin wafted through the air and settled on everything it touched. Rotted food was the second worst odor. Moldy fruit and vegetables smelled offensive, but old meat and expired milk and cheese won the foul-smelling contest by a landslide. Maybe Dr. Remini was onto something with his vegan diet. As she walked past her neighbors, Sandy wondered if she would be one of those ladies who pushed a shopping cart full of errant papers, clothes, food collected from the back of restaurants, and miscellaneous junk found on the city streets.

"Over here!" Kaitlin waved her arms over her head until she caught Sandy's attention. As her new friend walked toward the tent, Kaitlin noticed her gait was quicker and her face softer, not pinched. "You must have gone to the clinic, because you look a lot better than you did this morning." Kaitlin sat down in one of two folding chairs. She liked to call it her veranda. She motioned for Sandy to join her.

Sandy made a beeline for her backpack, then took the seat next to Kaitlin. She grabbed a bottle of Dark Eyes vodka and unscrewed the cap, then offered it to Kaitlin who just as eagerly put the bottle up to her welcome lips and took a healthy swig. She noticed the surprised look on Sandy's face and laughed. "Did I drink too much?" she asked as she handed the bottle back, one quarter of its contents gone.

"It's all good," Sandy said as she tilted her head back and took a big gulp, now only half the liquid remaining. "Damn, that's fine. Spending hours with the police can make you want to empty the liquor cabinet."

Sandy told Kaitlin about her day, starting with the good doctor. By the time her recounting was over, the women had finished the bottle. They were buzzed and enjoying every moment of their altered state.

"I think you have a crush on Dr. Remini," Kaitlin said, her words slightly slurred.

"I had a crush on Teddy Logan. He was so sexy with those black-rimmed glasses. I always was a sucker for a bespectacled man. Remini's kind of cute. I don't know. He's one of them."

"What does that mean?"

"Establishment. I want nothing to do with their world. Not anymore." Sandy made a cursory scan of the area. "Got anything to drink? It seems I'm still thirsty."

Kaitlin rose. Her leg caught on the chair. She stumbled but righted herself before falling into the tent. "That could have been bad."

"But it wasn't."

"Nope." Kaitlin disappeared into the tent, giggling. Sandy could hear things being moved and thrown. Moments later, she emerged with a handle of Jack Daniels. "Woo hoo! Mama scored big time. We're going to party like it's 1999. I mean 2999 and that's some big ass partying. Am I right?"

"You're never wrong."

Will looked up at the clock. It was 6:30 in the evening and the soup kitchen was filled to capacity. He kept one eye on the door while he spooned out the vegetarian chili to the grateful recipients.

"Don't ever change this recipe Doc or there will be hell to pay." Annie was a regular. She lived in the homeless shelter and was proud to claim the title of oldest resident. At eighty-three, the petite, white-haired woman had been homeless for years. It was Will Remini who convinced her to take up room and board at the shelter. She had come into the clinic with a nasty case of bronchitis and if she had continued to live in the harsh conditions the city streets threw at her, she wouldn't have lasted much longer. That was almost two years ago. Her health wasn't optimal, but she was clothed and sheltered and fed and for Annie Soleski that was as good as living in paradise.

"Don't I know it? I'll make you a deal. I won't change my chili if you come in for a check-up next week. It's been a while since I last saw you at the clinic."

Annie smiled, revealing a mouth full of crooked and concrete grey teeth. "It's nice to know that someone's looking out for me."

"Is it a deal?"

"Deal. Now give me some chow."

He did as he was told and filled Annie's empty bowl with a generous helping of chili. The volunteer next to him placed a square of cornbread next to the bowl.

Will once again glanced at the front door. He was hoping that Sandy Ekhart would take him up on his offer and come in for a much-needed warm meal. An hour remained before they closed, and she hadn't yet shown up.

After his last appointment, Dr. Remini googled the Ekhart family of San Francisco. Rudolph Ekhart, Sandy's great grandfather, had come over from Germany with his wife, Enta, and his brothers, Heinrich and Hans. Together, they started a small electrical company. The brothers made a decent living, working with construction companies on various projects. After the earthquake and subsequent fire leveled the city in 1906, Ekhart Electric was in high demand. Their reputation for excellent work kept them busy, so busy that they had to hire more workers. By the 1930s, Ekhart Electric was one of the largest electrical contractors in the Bay Area. Rudy had moved his family into a custom-built mansion in Pacific Heights. His children Robert, Gretchen, and Samuel enjoyed the luxury of growing up in the upper crust of society. When Robert met Estelle Davenport, he knew that her family's wealth and influence would only bolster his own reputation and that of his family's.

The family's wealth continued to increase along with their reputation for charity work. They were regulars in the society pages of the San Francisco Examiner. Robert and Estelle's two sons, Robert Jr. and Jeffrey, were perfect specimens of the rich and famous, at least famous in the San Francisco Bay area.

Robert, Jr., better known as Bob, married the daughter of another Pacific Heights family. Norma Trainor Nathaniel, the stunning woman with turquoise eyes, captured Bob's heart, despite her reputation for being strong headed, demanding, and intensely narcissistic. All Bob saw was a woman who would look great on his arm and would produce beautiful offspring. Despite Bob's desire to have at least three children, Norma had a different plan. She didn't want to be a mother. Her compromise was having one child. Sandra Eloise Ekhart was born on October 17, 1992. From what Will could tell, she had the privileged life that all the Ekharts enjoyed. Obviously, something went very wrong. Sandy was now homeless, living not too far from the neighborhood where she grew up.

It was past eight when Will opened the door to his two-bedroom apartment on the third floor of a 1920s Victorian. Even though it was renovated in the eighties, the hardwood floors creaked, doors stuck, and hairline cracks were visible on nearly every wall. Will made sure that he took off his shoes and walked softly to his bedroom. Soundproofing had only reduced the noise level by a small percentage. His downstairs neighbors went to bed early and he didn't want to disturb them. After changing into sweats and a T-shirt, Will made a mug of roasted green tea and plopped down on the living room couch. He resisted the compulsion to turn on his laptop and read more about the Ekharts. He never thought of himself as having an addictive personality. This determination to read up on his client's family was verging on cyberstalking. He had to remind himself that this was the first time he had more than a medical interest in a client. It was hard for Will to understand how a young woman born and raised into extreme wealth could end up destitute. Could her family life have been so corrosive that she chose homelessness over asking for help? His thoughts were interrupted by a familiar scratching noise above his balcony. He set his mug down and opened the sliding door. In a wooden box, between the eaves and the top of the balcony roof, Minky moved around his precious pile of leaves, trying to make himself comfortable. As soon as the urban rat saw Will, he stopped mid-scratch, and struck a paralytic pose for nearly fifteen seconds.

"Hey Minky, how was your day?"

Sensing friend, not foe, the medium-sized rodent wiggled his nose and went back to fluffing up his nest. When Will first encountered the rat, it was burrowing into the eaves of the house. With his shiny, dark brown coat, Will thought he resembled a mink, thus the name. He knew that one rat could lead to an infestation and take over the attic, but he also didn't want to kill him, so he bought a humane trap, placed peanut butter on the tripping device and after the second night of avoiding it, Minky walked into the trap to dine on the sticky delicacy.

The metal door shut, trapping the rat. It happened at two in the morning, so he was forced to live in the cage until Will could take him to a vet.

When Minky came home, neutered and slightly groggy, he was placed in a wooden box that resembled a log cabin, his pile of leaves nicely arranged. Will found the cabin at a local pet shop. It had a feeding tray inside and two holes, the smaller one a window and the larger a door. Will loved the irony of a rural log cabin affixed to a Victorian in the heart of the city.

Will went into the kitchen and returned with a bag full of shelled, unsalted mixed nuts. He put half a handful into Minky's tray, then watched as the rat's tiny hands grabbed a peanut and began turning it while his nose sniffed the exquisite meal. As if he desired privacy, Minky turned his back to Will while he ate the nut.

"I can take a hint. Enjoy your dinner, my friend."

Back on the couch, Will turned on the television and punched in the Comedy Central channel. The Daily Show had just begun. It was exactly what he needed to unwind and forget about the day. He took a long, deep breath in and exhaled slowly, pushing out the negative comments, patient rantings, everything that didn't belong in his inner sanctum, as well as his outer sanctum.

By 9:30, the doctor to the poor and homeless was fast asleep, oblivious to the banter between Trevor Noah and his guest. Less than a few miles away, another San Franciscan's evening was just beginning.

5

Paige slept soundly; her arms wrapped tightly around Marilyn. The doll was her refuge, her security blanket. As Emma's body, it was finally at rest, so she was free to leave her plastic hull easily.

As soon as she drifted through the roof of the Andersen home, Gigi was hovering close by and caught up with her.

"Here's your hat, what's your hurry? Oh wait, could it be that you're encased in a prefabricated plastic body?"

Emma stretched out her spiritual form, feeling like she was just released from solitary confinement. "Who died and made you a comedian?"

"I did. Follow me."

Two beams of light shot up into the night sky. They were magnificent. They were glorious. Sisters, spirits temporarily separated, now together as perfect beings. Speeding through the air without the weight of flesh and bone filled Emma with euphoria. When she was alive, she remembered having this feeling a few times. She always thought it was a dream, flying through the air. Now, she realized that it was her spirit being released from her sleeping body, free to wander and roam until she awakened, once again trapping her ethereal form in its human tomb.

As quickly as they took off, they stopped. Emma looked around. She could feel activity around her but couldn't see forms or shapes. The energy pulsed and she felt more alive than ever. In the distance, she saw two bright lights racing toward her and Gigi. When they approached, Emma watched the lights take on human attributes. She began to cry.

"Mom! Dad!" Emma forgot what she had become and went to

hug her parents. Their spirits co-mingled. Her 'arms' hugged nothing but air. It didn't matter. She was with her family. Emma looked over at Gigi. Her sister was surrounded by a golden aura, filling the darkness. Her mother spoke first.

"Emma, my beautiful daughter. I knew we would see you again, but not under these circumstances." Her father looked like he was in his 40s. Her mother, too. Appearing at whatever age you desired was one of the perks of being a spirit. Because Emma would be re-animated, hopefully soon, she preferred to look the age she was when she died. As a result, she looked like the parent and her parents, the children.

Her mother said, "We felt the explosion. It was as if we died again."

"I don't understand. If you're dead and way up here, how could you have possibly felt it?"

"We'll always be connected. In life and death, we have a thread that ties us together. You, me, Gigi, your father, my parents, his parents, and so on. The connections are never broken and they grow exponentially. When my father died, you weren't born yet. You were only a couple of hours old and I remember looking into your eyes and seeing my father. Life went on and the memory faded, but there were things you did and said that I swear my dad used to do and say. You know how you used to say 'lickety split' as a kid? That was my dad's expression, too. I never used it, so I thought it was odd that you adopted a colloquialism that was popular fifty years before your time. After I passed on, I discovered that you – your spirit – and my father's were one and the same."

After Emma's dad saw his daughter trying to absorb the revelation, he gave his wife a look of disapproval. "Come on, Helen, you know that kind of information is too much for a newly minted spirit to absorb." His hand lighted on his daughter's. "Sorry, Emma. We're just so happy to see you that we want to share the splendor of spiritual life with you."

"It's true. Sorry, sweetie. Gigi told us that you're a 'tweener.' Getting blown into tiny pieces sucks, but at least you can go back to earth in another being."

Emma laughed. "Don't sugar-coat it, Mom."

Her mother replied. "You know I call them as I see them. You told me that was one of my best and worst attributes."

"True." Emma noticed her sister was quiet. The telepathic conversation didn't include her. It was unusual for Gigi not to participate. She looked over at Gigi and was awestruck. The initial golden glow around her sister at the beginning of the family reunion had increased ten-fold in intensity. It was magnificent.

Helen said, "Gigi is absorbing our family's love. It sounds corny, but…"

"Not at all. It's beautiful." Emma drifted over to her sister and extended her spiritual arms, touching the intensely bright gold light. Immediately, she was filled with a love so strong and complete, Emma never wanted it to end. Her parents joined in and for what seemed like eternity, the family was bathed in pure, unconditional love.

When Emma awoke, she could hear Paige asking her grandmother for toast with peanut butter and jam, so she assumed Marilyn was still in the bedroom. Free to travel, the restless spirit lifted out of the doll and said a silent good-bye to her temporary family.

While Emma scanned pedestrians on Market Street for a possible 'takeover,' she was suddenly yanked back inside Marilyn. Exteriorizing when Paige was awake had its pitfalls. This was one of them.

Fifteen minutes later, Emma cautiously lifted herself out of the doll. She was back at Colbert Park, Marilyn sitting on the bench beside Rebecca, who was reading the newspaper. There must have been twenty children playing on the jungle gym, digging in the sandbox, and randomly running around. Paige wasn't among them. Panic set in as Emma scanned the park for the little girl, finally spotting her walking in the direction of a crop of trees.

Leaning up against a large sycamore on the periphery of the children's area, arms around her body, Sandy shivered as the wind whipped around her. A thin blanket she borrowed from Kaitlin provided nominal warmth, even though she was wearing a jacket and sweater. Eyes closed and teeth chattering, she willed the sun to come out.

"You can have my jacket." Paige held out her hot pink Patagonia thermal jacket to Sandy. "It's very warm."

Startled by her voice, Sandy's eyes shot open. They were bloodshot and the rims were red from squeezing them tightly shut. She was shocked to find a little girl smiling at her. Too tired to feel self-conscious, she returned a weak smile.

"Where do you live?" Paige asked a very hungover Sandy.

"You're looking at it, kid."

Paige raised her eyes to the hundred-plus-year-old sycamore. "Up there?"

Despite a very nasty headache, Sandy laughed. "Nope. Right here." She pointed to the ground.

Paige stared at the ground. "Is that why you smell a little funny, because you don't have a shower?"

"You don't mince words, do you kid?"

"What does mince mean?"

"Doesn't matter. What's your name?"

"Paige. What's yours?"

"Sandy."

Paige looked at the ground around Sandy. Small tufts of weeds and grass were surrounded by dirt, leaves and pine needles from the nearby trees. An empty Pepsi can and crumpled fast food bag wasn't too far from an overflowing trash can. "Why don't you live in a home?"

"That's a very good question."

Emma could tell by the conversation that this homeless woman was most likely harmless, but she was still uncomfortable with the situation, especially since Paige's grandmother was unaware of the child's whereabouts. She came in for a closer look at the woman. She was young, probably around twenty-five. Despite her eyes being red and bloodshot, they were a beautiful light turquoise. She'd seen that color before but couldn't remember where. They were deeper and darker than this young woman's. She's pretty, Emma thought. She definitely had the homeless vibe, but she didn't look hardened enough from living on the street, fighting the elements. Emma lived in the city her whole life. She'd witnessed everything from teens begging for money so they could buy the latest PlayStation game to the unbridled crazy Vietnam vets, their brains so scrambled by the horrors of war, reality was a memory.

"I think she would be perfect." Gigi hovered next to her sister.

"What do you mean?" It took a second for Emma to get it. "Seriously? You think taking over a druggie's body would be perfect? You've been dead too long, Griselda. These people are hopeless."

Gigi said, "Au contraire, mon amie. This girl is ripe for the picking. I suggest you do some research. Find out about her history, her family, stuff like that."

"What good will that do me? I find out that she's from an abusive household, her folks are alcoholics, deadbeats. She's a loser. I don't want to be in a body that's been neglected and exudes self-hate."

"Hold your horses there, missy. What makes you think, no assume, that she's burdened with all these social handicaps? Maybe she's from a wealthy family and couldn't take the pressure from a crazy father or abusive mother. Maybe she's in graduate school, going for her masters in psychology and this is part of her thesis, studying the life of the homeless as a street person. Whatever the scenario, your spirit will inhabit her body, so if she is messed up, you can rectify her life. You could be doing that body a huge favor."

The sister's conversation was interrupted by the commotion below. Rebecca was running over to Paige, calling her name with a sense of urgency and panic. Once she reached her granddaughter, she knelt beside her. "Don't ever run off like that again. I was worried sick." Rebecca hugged Paige, then turned to Sandy. "I hope she wasn't bothering you."

Sandy sat up a little straighter despite her discomfort. "Not at all. She's very sweet."

"And probably cold. Put your jacket back on, honey."

Paige held it out to Sandy again. "I wanted her to have it, Grammy, because she's cold and this is a very warm jacket."

Rebecca was touched by Paige's generosity. "That's very kind of you, honey, but it's too small for the lady." She took off her own jacket. "Please, take this. Hopefully, it will help keep you warmer."

Reluctantly, Sandy accepted the jacket. She thanked Rebecca as she took off her blanket and put the bright blue jacket on. The effect was immediate. She inhaled deeply, the scent of sandalwood and lemongrass that hung to the fabric replaced the acrid smell of Sandy's blanket, even if for a moment. She stuck her hands in the pockets and felt something in the right pocket. She pulled out a twenty-dollar bill. Before she could say anything, Rebecca said, "Keep it."

"Thank you."

"You're very welcome." Rebecca turned to Paige. "Let's go back to the playground."

Paige took her grandmother's hand. "See you later, Sandy."

Not if your grandma can help it, Sandy thought as she waved goodbye. Gigi and Emma followed Sandy as she slowly rose. Wearing the jacket, her blanket tucked under arm, she looked more like a visitor to the park than a resident. Walking back to the encampment, Sandy reminisced about being with her grandmother. Even though she died when Sandy was only ten years old, the time she had with her was memorable. Her father's mother, Beatrice, or Grandbee as Sandy liked to call her, was sweet and loving and smelled like gardenias. She always had time for her granddaughter and would take her places that Sandy's parents did not. One of her fondest memories was when Grandbee took her to the Warrior's basketball game. The woman was crazy for the team. Sandy had never been to a game before. When they were taken to the courtside seats, she was in awe of how close they were to the players. Stuffing her mouth with popcorn, she loved the sound of the players' tennis shoes squeaking on the shiny hardwood court, their movements fast and deliberate. And Grandbee was shouting and cheering on her team just like everyone else. At halftime, she asked her grandma if she could live with her. It was more like pleading. The request was denied and Sandy was told that she was a lucky little girl to be living in one of the most beautiful mansions in the city. Little did she know the misery Sandy endured at the hands of her mother and her father's indifference to the abuse. Even if she asked Grandbee not to tell anyone, she knew she wouldn't have been able to withhold the information from her own son. As a consequence, Sandy would pay a higher price than she currently suffered.

By the time she made it back to her sleeping bag, Sandy's mood had darkened. She went from grateful for meeting two generous people and owning a warm jacket to resentful for having to live with the bare minimum. It wasn't her fault that she didn't have a home. It was her mother's, and she despised the woman for making her life miserable. Buried under a pile of shirts and pants, she pulled out a small bottle of vodka. She couldn't unscrew the top fast enough. It didn't go down smoothly. It never did, but it numbed her and for that, she was grateful. For the second time today. She leaned back on her overstuffed backpack and closed her eyes.

From above, Emma and Gigi watched. Emma shook her head. "Really? You want me to take over that very damaged woman's body? Who knows what her liver looks like. All that drinking has to be doing harm."

Gigi ignored her sister. She flew down and sat next to Sandy, careful not to touch her. The comingling of her with Sandy's spirit could cause confusion and, in the woman's present state, Gigi didn't want to further upset her. After a few minutes, she reunited with her sister and said, "Follow me."

Seconds later, the sisters looked down on an opulent entryway. Hovering at the foot of the winding stairway, they were dazzled by marbled floors and original paintings by Picasso and Renoir. Those were the two they recognized out of the many that hung on the walls. Gold railings, enormous crystal chandeliers, exquisite furniture that screamed expensive.

"I'm impressed," Emma said. "Now tell me where the hell we are. I'm thinking museum?"

Without answering, Gigi ascended to the second floor and went through the wall to the master bedroom, Emma in tow. Wearing an aqua chiffon shirt and black leggings, Norma Ekhart sat in front of her vanity. She was deliberate and precise, applying the eyeliner flawlessly.

Emma got closer. As soon as she saw Norma's eyes, she said, "I know her! She was at the airport with her husband. We were at the same bar. Those eyes. They're incredible. Wait a minute. Is this...Sandy's mother?"

Gigi nodded.

"How did you know?"

"As a spiritual entity, we have the ability to view any person's history. It's called the Akashic records and it's like the universe's supercomputer system. It acts as the central storehouse of all information for every individual who has ever lived upon the earth. When I sat next to Sandy, I tapped into her past and it brought me here. You're supposed to ask permission from the person before you scan their records, but I had to make an exception for obvious reasons. Can you believe Sandy Ekhart grew up in this place and now she's passed out drunk in a homeless camp?"

"This does change the circumstances, you know. If Sandy's

upbringing includes a good education and the best medical and dental care rich folks can afford, then she may be a perfect specimen. How long has she been homeless?"

"Only a week or so."

Completely unaware that she was not alone, Norma finished applying her make-up. She opened the door to her closet and walked inside. Emma was dumbstruck. "This is bigger than my house. Damn! You got to wonder why Sandy gave this up for a life under the stars."

While Emma followed Norma into the boutique-sized room in awe of the seemingly endless wardrobe, Gigi hovered just outside the entrance, never one for having extravagant taste in clothes or even having a lot of clothes. "If you witness Sandy's Akashic records, you'll know exactly why she'd prefer to live on the streets than inhabit the same living space with this woman you are so whorishly following."

"Why don't you give me the abridged version?" Emma said. She seemed hypnotized by all the colors and fabrics. Norma's closet reminded her of Nordstrom's Studio 121 department, the section of the store where high end designer clothes are displayed for the wealthy, mature women. It was the section Emma had only dreamed of shopping in. Unless there was a big sale.

And the shoes. "Will you look at this? There must be over 200 pairs! The woman has more shoes than Imelda Marcos."

"Imelda Marcos? She's dead you know."

Dripping with sarcasm, Emma said, "Aren't we all?"

"I forgot what a nut you were."

"No you didn't."

Gigi laughed. "No, I didn't." Her ethereal body sat at the foot of Norma and Bob's California King-sized bed, covered with a white brocaded bedspread, nearly half of it swallowed up in decorative pillows. "Get out here and I'll tell you the sad tale of Sandra Eloise Ekhart." After one more tour of the closet, Emma reappeared and sat next to her sister.

"I feel drunk on couture. You should see her collection of Ralph Lauren jackets. Amazing." Emma could tell that her sister was getting bored. "Okay, I'm ready for the lecture on randy Sandy. Tell me about my next body."

"From her earliest memories, Sandy was verbally abused by her mother. The kid couldn't do anything right and when she did, she wasn't acknowledged for it. Dear old dad kept his mouth shut and continues to do so, never admonishing or complimenting his daughter. He let Norma handle the discipline, which she did with glee. Sandy's self-esteem is practically non-existent, eroded away by an unrelenting mother and a silent father. No wonder the woman is on the streets. I don't think she feels that she deserves any better. She moved out of this place six months ago and in with her best and only friend, Sandra Henstrom. Without a job and no desire to find one, Sandra kicked Sandy out. As you can surmise, they're no longer pals."

Emma digested the information. "Doesn't our Sandy have a trust fund or something? With such wealth, I'm surprised she's not a rich bum, drinking and partying in her own manse."

"Good question, but I wasn't in her records long enough to glean that info. I could go back and check it out while you spiritually drool over Evil Norma's wardrobe in yonder closet."

"Good plan. I definitely got the better assignment." Emma went back to the closet and found Norma still deciding what jewelry to wear. She was holding up blue topaz halo drop earrings against her ears. Emma watched as she slowly turned the earrings, letting the recessed light catch the facets in the reflection. "You may be a mean, twisted mother, but you have amazing taste."

Gigi called from the other room, "I have some juicy financial data that you'll be interested in learning."

Emma reappeared next to her sister. "When I went into Sandy's records, I couldn't find anything related to her finances. Basically, as far as she's concerned, whatever she has in that smelly backpack is everything she owns. When she moved out of her parent's place, Norma refused to let her take her furniture, even most of her clothes. She told her daughter to get a job and start from scratch. I went into Norma's records and, boy oh boy, what we have here is a case verging on deception.

"Grandbee, Bob's mother, was Sandy's favorite relative. The woman spoiled her and was the only one who treated her with love and respect. She died when Sandy was ten. In her will, she left her granddaughter $15 million in a trust fund. Most trustees are entitled to the money when they reach twenty-one, but Norma talked Grandbee into creating the trust in such a way that Sandy could access it only with Norma's signature. Conversely, Norma can't access it without Sandy's signature. The woman has no idea she has the trust fund. Norma never told her."

Emma was dumbstruck. "Where was Bob-o all this time, under a rock? Is the man that much of a milquetoast?"

"Here's the kicker: Bob doesn't know about the trust fund. When his mother died, he was heartbroken, so Norma told him that she would handle everything. Believe it or not, he didn't care about his inheritance. Between the two of them, they have millions."

"I'm assuming his father passed away."

Gigi nodded. "He died five years before Grandbee."

"I feel like I'm going to be joining a reality show family. Dysfunction doesn't begin to describe their relationships."

"To top it off, Norma and Bob have no idea that their daughter is homeless. They think she's still living with Sandra."

The conversation was abruptly halted when Norma began talking on her cellphone. "Rick Standish, please...It's Norma...thank you." While she waited, she played with her earring, twirling it between her fingers. After a few moments, Rick came on the line. "I thought that secretary of yours forgot about me."

Rick leaned back in his leather chair. "Now who could possibly forget about you?"

"True. Any word from Barclay's?"

"Not yet. I'll be sure to let you know when it's time to sign the papers. At dinner the other night, Bob intimated that it could take a little longer to secure your share of the funds. Is that accurate?"

Norma twirled her earring a little faster. "Not at all. The money has been allocated for months. You misinterpreted Bob's bland demeanor for problems. Not the case."

"If you say so, Norma."

"I do. Not everyone can have the charming, gorgeous spouse that you are so lucky to have landed. Some of us are stuck with duds."

Rick knew that was coming. Every time they spoke privately, Norma would toss him an exaggerated compliment and bury her own husband under a finely tuned insult. Her jealousy toward Marlo was transparent. Who could blame her? Norma was very attractive, but Marlo was stunning and thirty years her junior. It was not even close to a competition in Rick's view. "I have another call. As soon as I hear from Cliff, I'll let you know."

"Fine." Norma hung up and tossed her cellphone on the bed. "Son of a bitch," she whispered under her breath as she hurried downstairs and into Bob's office. Bob looked up from his computer as Norma glared at him from the other side of the monitor.

"Can I help you?" Bob said in his calmest voice so as not to upset his wife's hair-trigger temper.

Norma's turquoise eyes darkened to a deep, dark blue. "Do we have the $40 million earmarked for Francisco Downs in the Wells Fargo account?"

As if he sprung a leak, Bob began to perspire. First under the arms, then his upper lip and forehead seeped tiny beads of sweat. "I believe so."

Norma planted her hands on Bob's desk. The way the light played against his wife's hair, he swore he saw horns popping out of the perfectly coiffed blonde locks. "You believe so? What's going on?"

Before Bob could answer, Norma slammed her hands against the desk. "Goddamn it, Bob, talk to me!"

Gigi and Emma cosmically jumped. It reminded Emma of the airport explosion. It simply scared the shit out of Gigi. She turned to her sister. "This ought to be good."

As soon as he hesitated when talking to Rick about the funds, he knew he was in trouble. He saw the look in Rick's eyes and prayed he wouldn't mention it to Norma. Now he was at the mercy of Stormin' Norman, a nickname she wasn't privy to. Sweat trickled under his collar, sliding down his back. I might as well get this over with, he thought, as he came around the desk to face his wife.

"A few months ago, I had an opportunity to invest in a once-in-a-lifetime deal. Dennis guaranteed that he could double our money in less than sixty days. I talked to him last week and he said there was a slight delay, but the investment will pay out in the next month."

Norma was doing her best to keep her temper in check, a skill she had yet to master. "How much did you invest without consulting me first?"

"Twenty million."

"Twenty...million...dollars...earmarked for the racetrack." Norma took off one of her $1,710 Louis Vuitton Snakeskin Eyeline pumps and threw it at her husband. It made a thunk as it bounced off his forehead, the heel leaving an indentation in the shape of a gumdrop.

Bob put his hands up to his face. "Son of a bitch! What did you do that for?"

"In case you hadn't noticed, BOB, we need $40 million for the investment, not twenty. We can't wait another month and I don't have $20 million at my disposal. How could you be so careless?"

Bob gently touched the mark on his head and cringed. It was quickly turning dark purple, the pain radiating like a mini beacon. Norma picked up her shoe, examined it for any damage, and put it back on her size eight foot. She gave her husband a menacing look, then turned and faced the fireplace. She closed her eyes and tried to take deep breaths so she could think clearly. It wasn't working. She was still agitated. When she opened her eyes, she glanced above the mantle. Despite her insistence that they give it to Goodwill, Bob kept the portrait they commissioned of Sandy when she was twenty-one. Her smile was disingenuous, and the young woman's sadness bled through the canvas and acrylic. As Norma stared at the painting, normal breathing started to return. Without another word, she strode out of Bob's office and upstairs to her bedroom. Once his wife was out of sight, he raced to the bathroom to examine his injury. He flinched as he touched the deep purple and black bruise. "She will be the death of me."

Norma opened the vanity drawer and took out her address book. She turned to the E's and scanned down the page until she found the phone number for her daughter.

6

Will couldn't believe his good luck. Instead of parking blocks away, he found a spot one block from his destination. Bernal Heights, like every other San Francisco neighborhood, was low on available parking spots, especially when residents were allowed to park on the street for longer periods of time than visitors.

He picked up his pace as he glanced at his watch. Late again. This time it wasn't his fault. His last patient at the clinic went into cardiac arrest and he had to facilitate getting them to Mercy Hospital's emergency room. Luckily, the patient survived.

He turned right onto Powhattan Avenue and took the steps two at a time up to the bright red door. Before he could knock, Gloria opened the door. The tall, thin woman with hair the color of paprika and light green eyes stared suspiciously at Will. "What's your excuse this time?"

Before he could answer, she broke into a grin and gave him a big hug. "Just funnin' with you. You're a tad sweaty. Did you run here?"

"I walked at a fast clip. Being late keeps me in shape."

"Uncle Willy!" Five-year-old Danya took a running leap into Will's arms.

"My little sweet pea." Will swung his niece around by her waist, her ponytail horizontal with her body. "How was school?" He put Danya on the couch and sat next to her.

"It's not school, it's kindergarten."

"Excuse me. I stand corrected. So, how was kindergarten? Did you make anything?"

"Yes!" Danya leapt off the couch and ran up the stairs to her room. Seconds later, she returned with a lump of clay. Except for 4 skinny tendrils on the top and bottom, it reminded Will of a breast. It was bulbous and slightly misshapen with a smaller ball of clay stuck on top. Danya proudly held it out in front of her like it was an original Rodin. "Do you know what it is?"

"I'm going to pass on guessing. You tell me what this amazing sculpture is."

She looked at the clay and then glanced up at Gloria. "It's mommy."

"Ah. I was going to say that, but I think your mother's head is a little smaller. Excellent job, Danya."

"Very funny," Gloria said and playfully punched her brother in the arm.

"Dinner's ready. Everyone please sit." Monica emerged from the kitchen holding a platter full of roasted vegetables. Corn, eggplant, potatoes, sliced onions, and yellow peppers all donned grill marks and glistened with marinade. Following her, Makelo placed a large bowl of brown rice on the table.

"Hey, Uncle Will." He went over and gave Will a hug. "Can I come to the soup kitchen with you tomorrow? I told Old Joe that I would bring him a bar of raw chocolate because he didn't believe there was such a thing."

Will was convinced that Makelo was an old soul. A wise old Buddha soul. Gloria and Monica adopted the half Syrian, half Turkish boy when he was three years old. His home was the Bayti orphanage in Reyhanli, Turkey, close to the Syrian border. At a young age, the boy's sensibilities and compassion were honed. His identification with human and non-human animals was intense. After every meal, no matter how small his portions, Makelo would scoop half of the food into a napkin, toddle outside and feed the stray cats that hung around the back of the kitchen. He wouldn't leave until all five cats ate their share. The fair-skinned boy with large brown, almond-shaped eyes and an infectious smile stole the women's hearts. Their intention was to adopt one child, but Makelo refused to leave without Sisi. She was the scrawniest and ugliest of the stray cats. Makelo knew in his heart that the black and white cat with open sores and scars on her backside wouldn't survive without him feeding her and giving her the attention and love she had grown used to from the 3-year-old. Reluctantly, they agreed to adopt Sisi, too. With veterinary care, proper feeding, and a lot more love, the fellow Turk thrived and Makelo became her companion and hero. Sisi knew that this little boy saved her life. Gloria swore that when Sisi looked at Makelo, she could see the love emanating from the cat's eyes.

When Makelo was six, he found out that his uncle volunteered at the soup kitchen. Whether he felt a kinship for those without families or he was drawn to others less fortunate, Makelo begged his mothers to let him go and help serve the food. Understandably wary of the environment, they hesitated, but Will assured them that he would watch his nephew and make sure he was safe.

Will spooned the brown rice on his plate and stabbed a couple of grilled veggies. "Of course you can come with me. Old Joe was asking about you the other night. He thought you forgot about him."

Makelo said, "I just saw him three days ago. I guess that's why he's called Old Joe." He took the serving spoon from Will. "He needs that chocolate more than ever. You know it's good for memory and the heart. I learned that on Google."

Monica laughed. "When I was your age, I had to go to the library to find out about the benefits of chocolate. I also could have looked it up in our encyclopedias, but I hated those things. All my friends had World Book encyclopedias. Not our family. My dad said the Encyclopedia Britannica was more comprehensive. They were and they were also a bitch to understand, and the text was teeny and there were no color pictures. And it was also a lot less expensive." She took a bite of the potato. "But I'm not bitter."

Gloria patted her wife on the back. "That's my girl."

Will held up a piece of eggplant. "This is delicious. Good job, Mon." He took a bite. "You went to Pacific Heights High, didn't you?"

"Sure did."

"Did you know Sandy Ekhart?"

"Of Sandy and Sandra fame? Of course." She saw the funny look on Gloria's face. "Sandy Ekhart and Sandra Deloise were best friends. They were also both socially awkward. Aside from each other, they didn't hang out with anyone else. I would say hi to them, but most of the students ignored them."

Gloria said, "Why are you asking about Sandy?"

Will knew he couldn't disclose how he knew Sandy. Client confidentiality was sacred. "I found out she's living on the street."

Monica dropped her fork. "The poor little rich girl? Her family is worth millions. I'm surprised she's not a trust fund baby."

Will said, "I looked up the Ekhart family. They made their fortune after the 1906 quake. They've been traveling in high society ever since. Seeing Sandy was quite a shock."

Gloria got up from the table. "Does anyone else want a glass of water?"

Two hands shot up. From the kitchen, Gloria said, "Makelo, tell Uncle Will about your school project."

Makelo was in the middle of chewing. He held up his hand for emphasis. When he was done, he said, "Our English teacher, Mrs. Kornfeld, wants us to interview a person completely different from us. Someone we've met, but have nothing in common with, so I'm going to pick a person from the soup kitchen. It's not due for another couple of weeks, so I'll have a chance to really study someone there. That's okay, right?"

Will beamed. "Makelo, you make me very proud. Trying to understand a person that most people look right through, is admirable. So many of the soup kitchen participants have mental illness. Others are shell-shocked from trauma in their lives. And still others are veterans, living with war inside their heads."

Danya, who hadn't spoken a word since they sat down for dinner, let out a big sigh. "Can we talk about my Sparkle Pony? She's feeling very left out."

Will mouthed, 'later' to Makelo, who gave him a knowing nod. Gloria placed a glass of water in front of her daughter and handed the other glass to Will.

"I'm sure Uncle Willy wants to hear all about Sparkle Pony, don't you, Uncle Willy?"

"Definitely."

"Good," said Danya, "because Sparkle Pony broke her leg walking over the rainbow bridge and I told her that you would fix it because you're a doctor."

"I normally work with humans, but I think I can take on an animal with no problem at all. As a matter of fact, broken legs on horses are my specialty."

When the dinner table was cleared and Will's offer to help with the dishes was declined, he went up to Danya's room to check out his patient. In their wildest dreams, Gloria and Monica never could have imagined that they would be affixing glow-in-the-dark pixies and fairies to the ceiling of their ultra-feminine daughter's room. Plastic toadstools as big as cushions sprouted up from the hardwood floor and a smattering of fairy dust in the form of glitter clung to the walls. Princess dolls, magical horses and any other creature that looked like it was born in the enchanted forest, or immortalized by Disney, shared space with Danya. Will loved telling his friends about his sister and her wife with the exclusively pink and lace daughter.

Laying in a crib, covered in a pink blanket with rhinestones, Sparkle Pony looked more at peace than in pain. When Danya picked her up, Will could see a Band-Aid covering the pony's back right leg. She handed the injured animal to her uncle. He cradled it in his hands.

"May I take the bandage off so I can see the injury?"

Danya solemnly nodded. "She was jumping over the rainbow and fell."

Will peeled the multi-colored Band-Aid off. "Yes, this is a break, but I have just the remedy." He fished a lip balm out of his pocket and waved it across the pony's leg. When he was done, he handed Sparkle Pony back to his niece. "She's all better. Next time she wants to jump over the rainbow, tell her to go around."

Danya hugged her uncle hard. "Thank you, Uncle Willy." She ran over to her closet. "Close your eyes. I have a surprise for you." Will did as he was told. A few seconds later, he felt something lightly falling on his head. When he opened his eyes, he touched the top of his head. He wasn't sure what he grabbed, but when he looked in his hand, he saw glitter. Lots of it. He started to shake his head. Danya protested.

"Don't do that! You need the fairy dust to protect you."

Will stopped shaking his head. "Thank you, sweetie. I definitely feel protected."

Before Will left the house, he made plans to pick Makelo up after work. As soon as he got outside, he furiously ran his fingers through his hair in an attempt to rid most of the fairy dust. He thought it wise to keep a little for luck…and safety.

Emma and Gigi sat atop the Eiffel Tower. The lights sparkled all over the 984-foot structure. Emma was delighted. Gigi, not so much.

"Couldn't you have picked a less famous spot for our rendezvous? This is so pedestrian."

"The Eiffel Tower, pedestrian? Au contraire, mon amie. There's nothing else like it in the world. It's inspirational."

"To whom? It looks like an erector set project on steroids. I don't see the beauty."

Gigi looked down at the tower's lights, which were admittedly quite stunning. She settled into the steel beam, becoming one with the structure. "Having second thoughts about body snatching Sandy? You'll be walking into a scene from *Mommy Dearest*. Norma is cuckoo crazy."

Emma sighed. "There's a nasty strain of entitlement and a twisted sense of righteousness in that family. Bob is a total wimp. No wonder Sandy is such a mess. Strangely, I feel more compelled than ever to take over her body. I can help her and, honestly, I wouldn't feel any obligation to keep up ties with Norma and Bob. On the other hand, it wouldn't hurt to have a substantial chunk of money from them. So, what's the next step?"

Gigi said, "I need to show you how to read Sandy's Akashic Records, then Norma's and Bob's, so you have a history of the family. When do you…"

Emma vanished. "Paige must have had a nightmare," Gigi said to the Parisian sky, then looked down at the city, a jumble of lights blinking, flickering. Her focus was on the Opera District. Dottie's Café was sandwiched between La Florist Elegante and Opera Boulangerie. It was five years ago that Gigi and her husband sat across from each other at the café on a balmy evening, savoring their cappuccinos and glazed donuts. After returning home, coffee never tasted as rich, the aroma never as intoxicating. "I wish I could get a cappuccino one more time. Sometimes it sucks being dead."

The jolt took Emma by complete surprise, leaving her momentarily disoriented. She heard crying and realized she was back at the Anderson home, Alec was rocking Paige in his arms and stroking her hair, damp from perspiration.

"It was a bad dream, that's all. You're okay now, sweetie."

Through her tears, Paige cried, "The loud noises and people

screaming. I saw Mommy and that lady. They turned bright red." Paige looked down at her covers, turning right then left, panic in her voice. "Where's Marilyn?"

Alec leaned over the side of the bed and found the doll on the floor, face down. He picked her up and gave her to Paige. "Are you okay, Marilyn? Are you hurt?" The doll's eyes slowly closed as she was laid back down on the bed, her head resting on the pillow. Emma could only imagine the nightmare Paige had and most likely would be having more of for a long time. She also hoped Alec could get his daughter back to sleep as soon as possible so she could continue her conversation with Gigi. She was getting used to the sensory deprivation. Sometimes, when Paige was at school, Emma was left alone with her thoughts. Instead of leaving the doll, she would relive memories. The details were vivid. The re-creations realistic.

Five minutes later Emma could still hear Alec speaking to his daughter, slightly above a whisper, comforting her. She sensed that Paige was falling back asleep. Her small, fragile emotional state calming back down. To normal? Perhaps never again. For now, the images that tore her family apart dissipated as sleep took over. Emma was beginning to feel fatigued as well. She decided to stay in for the night and resume her study of Sandy tomorrow.

7

Kaitlin gently shook Sandy awake. "Did you hear? They arrested the jerk that attacked you." Still feeling the effects of the vodka she drank last night, Sandy heard every other word. "I'm under arrest?"

"No. That asshole who raped you got arrested. They picked him up on the other side of the park this morning. He was grabbing some woman and she started screaming. A couple of guys held him down until the police showed up."

Slightly more lucid, Sandy sat up and rubbed her eyes. Her breath tasted like polluted water, and she had crust stuck to her lashes. She yawned. "They got him, huh? That's good."

"It's great. He won't be assaulting women anymore. You know they're going to want you to identify him, right?" She broke off a chunk of bread she was eating and handed a piece to Sandy. At the sight of food, she became nauseous and put her hand up.

"I'm not hungry."

"I bet you're not." Kaitlin laughed. "You and Lila were really gettin' it on. Drinking wise. I'm surprised I could wake you. Maybe you should take it easy."

Sandy lashed out. "You didn't complain the other night when we were drowning in booze. Why are you suddenly Mother Teresa?"

Kaitlin was about to answer when the roar of motorcycles filled the air, sounding more like a giant horde of mosquitoes. She gave Sandy a dirty look and walked off in the direction of Center Street. Others from the encampment joined her.

Curious, Sandy left her sleeping bag, straightened up the clothes she slept in the best she could, ran her fingers through her hair, and followed the crowd.

Seven motorcyclists pulled up to the curb, their Harleys stopping in front of the homeless crowd that had gathered, expectantly. Dressed identically, all the riders wore black helmets with an illustration of a viper on the front, its red eyes glowing against lime green and yellow scales, the scales outlined in blue. Their black jackets displayed the viper hugging a large red 'V'. When they took off their helmets, Sandy discovered they were all women. Some were in their 20s, others in their 60s. Thin, full-figured, gray haired and blonde, the eclectic-looking group dismounted their bikes and greeted the crowd, many holding empty bags, anticipating the bikers' bounty. Sandy tapped a man next to her on the shoulder. "Who are they?"

"The Vegan Vipers. They come by every so often and bring us food and clothes and whatever else we need."

Veronica Schatzki grabbed her messenger bag off the sissy bar. Normally, the large black Harley bag was made of leather, but Veronica convinced a local artisan to recreate the bag with synthetic materials. Once the leathersmith was sold on using an alternative, he began seeking out sturdy, eco-friendly materials. A few months later, he presented Veronica with the prototype. It so closely resembled leather that she was blown away when he told her it was made from pineapple leaves. After showing the other vipers, Veronica ordered seven of the thick, sturdy bags.

"Got a viper in the bag, Ronnie?" Taylor's laugh was rusty and hollow, the result of years of smoking whatever he could find and being homeless for over ten years.

Someone in the crowd shouted, "Can't you come up with something better than that, Taylor? You say it every time."

Taylor wiped a bit of spittle from his mouth with his dirty coat sleeve. "Maybe I want to see a viper every time. Got a problem with that?"

Veronica, also known as Ronnie, pulled a toy viper out of the bag. "Ask no more, Taylor. Here's your very own rubber viper. Do with it what you will." She threw it to Taylor. Despite the declaration that it was fake, a couple of people screamed. Taylor caught it with both hands and hugged it close to his chest. "I still get food, don't I?"

"Of course." Ronnie walked through the crowd, along with the other Vegan Vipers, dispersing leftover food from her restaurant, The Big V, Lydia handed out last night's fare from her restaurant, The

Olive Branch, and Cecily gave the crowd last night's entrees from her diner, Sprouted Plate. Along with the food, the Vipers provided the homeless with toiletries. On other visits, they passed out clothing and blankets.

With her short black hair, high cheekbones, almond-shaped blue eyes, and tall stature, the lanky restaurateur was a hit with the crowd, especially the men. They thought she looked like a young, feisty Joan Jett.

Sandy watched as the Vipers chatted it up with her neighbors and handed them sandwiches, fruit, slices of apple pie, and whatever else was being served at the three vegan restaurants over the past day or two. She loved their look, all clad in black pants, red T-shirts, and black jackets. A wave of shame washed over Sandy. Some of these women were close to her age. They had jobs. They had homes. They had a purpose. Sandy had a second-hand sleeping bag and a backpack filled with nearly everything she owned. She wanted to run and hide. Instead, she held out her hands when Ronnie came by and asked her what she'd like.

"I have a couple of slices of sourdough and brioche left. Oh, here's a lentil loaf sandwich on rye."

"They all sound good." Sandy studied Ronnie as she pulled the food out of her bag. She eyed her jacket and pants. "I thought vegans didn't wear leather."

"We don't." Ronnie stroked the arm of her jacket. "This is called eco-leather. Feel it."

Tentatively at first, Sandy touched Ronnie's sleeve. The thick material had a nubby texture, eerily similar to leather. "Are you sure they didn't lie to you? I think this is cow hide."

Ronnie said, "I'm positive. Pretty amazing, huh?" She handed the food to Sandy. "I'm Ronnie, by the way."

"Sandy."

"Nice to meet you, Sandy. Enjoy the food."

"Thanks." The longer Sandy watched Ronnie move with grace and confidence, the more she felt small and insignificant. She wanted to climb into a crack in the sidewalk and disappear. Instead, she walked back to her spot next to Kaitlin's tent and pulled out her bottle of Smirnoff. It was empty. She threw it against a makeshift campfire which was essentially a pile of small rocks and concrete chunks from a neighboring demolition site. The flask-sized bottle shattered, sending shards flying in every direction. One hit Sandy in the arm. It punctured her skin enough to make her bleed, but not enough to cause alarm. She put her hand over the wound and applied pressure. "Just my luck." She looked up to the sky and yelled, "Are you happy, Norma? I bet you are."

Actually, Norma wasn't happy. She was furious. She had just gotten off the phone with Sandra only to discover that her daughter moved out a few weeks ago and she had no idea where Sandy was living. The ex-best friend offered little help. "For all I know, she's living on the street. She had very little money, you know."

Flustered, Norma said, "I don't understand. Sandy told me she was working as a paralegal for a law firm in the financial district."

"Yeah, right. The only job Sandy had when she lived with me was taking out the trash every Wednesday and she didn't even do that with regularity."

The next number Norma dialed was Lonnie's. He answered after only one ring. "How's it hanging, Norma?"

Norma rolled her eyes. Her lack of fondness for Lonnie King wasn't lost on the private investigator. He wasn't as brash and uncouth as some of the others in his line of work, but he couldn't compare financially, culturally, or even scholastically with many of his clients, Norma Ekhart being one. It didn't bother the 6-foot 2 native from Oakland, the city across the Bay Bridge from San Francisco. With his unkempt sandy blonde hair, ruddy complexion, and soul patch, he looked more like a surfer than a P.I. It worked well in his favor and that's why Norma liked dealing with him. He would never grace her party invitee list and Norma would deny knowing him if asked.

Norma grabbed for her left ear and played with the dangling earring, the solitary pearl rotated between her thumb and forefinger. "It's hanging just fine, Mr. King. A few weeks ago, my daughter Sandy moved out of an apartment she was living in with a friend. No one knows where she went. She may not even be living in the city anymore. I need you to find her as soon as possible."

Lonnie loved time-sensitive jobs. He was able to charge more and get the investigation off his plate to make room for other work. He took a sip from his can of Pepsi and licked his lips. He asked Norma to replay the conversation she had with Sandra, then requested that she email him a recent photo of her daughter, her last known address, vital statistics, likes, dislikes, places Sandy frequented, and a list of her friends and relatives. "How much time are you giving me?"

"The sooner the better, Mr. King, and I'd rather give you the requested information in person. I don't like computers."

"Call me Lonnie, Norma, and meeting is fine with me."

"I'm working against a two-week deadline on a substantial project, Lonnie, and Sandy is a big part of the final planning process."

Lonnie finished the Pepsi and tossed the can into the garbage, despite the recycle bin sitting to its right, then he pulled out a moustache comb and raked it through his soul patch.

"I'll do the best I can." He hesitated, then added, "Was there anything else you wanted?"

"After you find my daughter, we can discuss the next step."

"Sounds like a plan. As soon as I receive the info, I'll get on it. Sandy's as good as found."

Norma reapplied her lipstick and smiled at her reflection in the vanity mirror. "I certainly hope so."

8

As soon as Paige left for school, Emma knew that Marilyn's caretaker would be gone for hours. "Time to get my spiritual ass to Turin."

Determined to fulfill her dream of visiting the ancient Italian city, Emma mentally imagined being at the Fréjus Rail Tunnel monument. It was the first destination she had planned on visiting before the explosion. It wasn't a beautiful memorial. Not at all. It was rather crude except for the sculptures, all but one clinging to the stones.

Instantaneously, Emma found herself sitting in the lap of a Titan. It was one of seven living on the pyramid of stones — stones extracted from the excavation of the tunnel being built at the time. She was dazzled by the 140-year-old body, its muscles rippling, its face in quiet reflection. Built in 1879, the structure was dedicated to the builders of the Fréjus Rail Tunnel, an 8.5-mile tunnel in the European Alps, linking Italy to France. It took 13 years to build and the lives of many workers.

Emma rose to the top of the monument where the angel Genius hovered, pen in hand, near a tablet with the names of the tunnel's engineers: Sommeiller, Grattoni and Grandis. She then circled the fountain delighting in a special close-up viewing of the seven Titans, some standing, others in repose and one poor Titan draped over the harsh, uneven stones, obviously exhausted from participating in the Herculean task. His head hung over a rock and his left arm dangled from a very sore shoulder. Water circulated throughout the mountain of stone and this time of year, colorful flowers and tall grasses grew from the cracks, creating a crude Alpine mountain. Emma visited each of the Titans, hovering within inches of their weathered noses, asking them questions, like "Aren't you tired of sitting here for over a hundred years?" and "Do you guys get together and party when no one's looking?" She was hoping they would have the ability to respond through vibration. One of the many guest authors at Quinley Books was a scientist named Teddy Forester. Even though Dr. Forester was a better hypnotist than speaker – practically lulling the audience to sleep with his deep, metronome-esque voice, reading from the newly published *Quantum Qi* – his topic was fascinating. He said that everything is made up of energy. The same energy that composes a human body is also the energy that makes up a car, a phone, animals, even the trees. Energy is constantly flowing and changing form. It stood to reason that the Titan energy could telepathically speak to Emma. She listened intently after asking her questions but heard and felt nothing. "It was worth a try," she muttered as she left the monument and stopped in on her next destination.

Turin is known as the city of white and black magic. It's built on the 45th parallel where the Po and Dora Rivers meet. It is also where a supernatural triangle is formed. The white magic cities are Prague, Lyon, and Turin. London, San Francisco, and Turin are involved in black magic. Occultists believe this is where the magic triangles meet. It is also where it is said that the Philosopher's Stone is located, underground in one of the grottos.

After Emma found posters of Turin at a local travel agency, she went to the library and found all the books she could on the famous city. She loved reading about its rich history, but what Emma found most captivating was the belief that three alchemical caves reside under the city. Two had been found, but the third one was undiscovered. Legend has it that it is the home to the Philosopher's Stone, transparent, glass-like with red and purple hues. It can turn base metals like mercury into gold or silver. As if that wasn't enough to make the stone voraciously sought after, it also claimed to rejuvenate and give those in its possession immortality.

Emma saw enough renderings of what researchers believed the cave would look like. She conjured up the images and willed herself there, hoping it was a real place and not a fable. The outdoor monument was instantaneously replaced with darkness. The cave walls were damp, the ceiling low, and the floor consisted of compacted dirt and irregular shaped rocks, making it an imperfect, unattractive location, an unlikely setting for a stone that held immense power, but there it was, a brilliant rock. Fuchsia and lavender light radiated from the palm-sized miracle. Emma's spirit pulsed, merging with the energy of the stone. She bathed in its luminescent glow. Emma was so mesmerized by the alchemical object, that it took her a moment to notice the hundreds of other spirits, pinpoints of light, in the cave all in awe of the stone. And all aware that its physical powers were useless to them. Nonetheless, they enjoyed the brilliant energy it emitted.

"It's glorious, is it not?" a fellow spirit asked telepathically. "I come here often to delight in its wondrous glow." He looked like a teenager, but not from America or even from Italy. With his faded tartan kilt, blood-stained dirty white shirt, and leather boots, he looked like he had come straight from a Scottish battlefield.

"It is glorious," Emma replied. "Did you fight with Braveheart? What was his name? Mel Gibson? No! He portrayed him in the movie. Was it William Wallace?"

"Aye and it's Sir William Wallace. I fought beside him. A great man. Better that I died on the battlefield than he."

Emma nodded. She turned her attention to the other spirits, so many she couldn't count. Men, women, young children, even babies, all displaying their preferred human age and all basking in the mystical stone's energy. She communicated with many of them, learning about their lives as humans and their adventures as spirits. It was exhilarating and fun. She was surprised at how much she enjoyed social interactions more than she had in human form.

"You're new here, aren't you? Recently deceased?" The elderly woman had her white hair in long braids. She gazed gently at Emma. When she smiled, a crop of wrinkles graced her face.

"Yes, I died a little over a week ago. Ironically, I was on my way to Turin. I guess you can say that I reached my destination regardless of the accident. Compared to conventional air travel, spirit transport is so much faster. I'm Emma."

"Cynthia. Nice to meet you. I sense you're from California. San Francisco? That's where I lived."

"Yes! You can say that I still live there." Emma told Cynthia about her unusual circumstances. "I've heard about spirits like you, but never met one. You're so lucky, man. It sucks having to body snatch, but hey, you get to live again. How groovy is that?"

Cynthia had lived in Haight Ashbury, personifying the archetypal hippie lifestyle. She worked in a record store, had a tie dye business on the side – You Name it, We'll Dye It. She lived in an apartment at 635 Ashbury Street, one floor above Janis Joplin's apartment.

"The first party at Joplin's I went to, some dude handed me a glass of punch. I didn't know it had been laced with LSD until I saw mushrooms growing out of the floor. It was a real trip! It lasted about…" Cynthia stopped talking. Her new friend vanished. Unwillingly, Emma returned to her artificial body.

9

iss me Marilyn? Emma settled in, after being plucked from
Turin. She would definitely revisit the city and the grotto.
As a spiritual being, the experience of meeting others like
her was heightened, akin to turning up the volume past ten. She
vibrated with their energy. The Philosopher's Stone increased the
intensity. The word that came to mind was euphoria.

Paradoxically, Emma felt secure in the doll, safely ensconced in the
hard plastic cocoon. She innately knew she was safe. If the doll was
destroyed, Emma would be a free spirit. She could choose to
reincarnate or continue to explore the planet's many treasures, as well
as soar through the galaxy, visiting planets, stars, any place she desired.
She also knew that it was highly unlikely that Marilyn would meet an
untimely death, so time was running out. In less than a week, Emma
had to find a body to take over before she became permanently attached
to the doll. *I feel like a character in the movie, Invasion of the Body
Snatchers. Like an alien.* It felt wrong, but she didn't have a choice.

Oh choices. She'd made great ones like dating Sydney Zammit.
And bad ones, like dumping Sydney Zammit for Nick, the pathological
liar. Once they split up, she referred to him as Nick the Dick the Hick
the Prick. There were other regrets. She went over them one by one,
chiding herself for not following the path that felt right, the one her gut
told her to lean toward, not the one that could potentially crush her ego.
Like with Brendon.

Emma was so enamored with best-selling author Brendon Brooks,
she neglected to answer a question from the audience. It was her third
year as store manager for Quinley Books on the corner of Sutter and
Montgomery Streets, the largest independent bookseller in the city.
One of Emma's duties was to secure speakers for the store's monthly

book signings. Brooks' novel, *I Like it That Way*, held the number one slot on the New York Times' Bestseller List for five weeks. Naturally, he was being sought after for speaking engagements by bookstores, as well as talk shows, blogs, and radio programs. Around the same age, Emma felt a kinship with Brooks, not just because they were both in their early 30s, but the protagonist in his first book, *Saline Solution*, could have been modeled after her. Garland Grady lived in a big city, aspired to become a writer, married a law student, got dumped for a fellow law student, male, and moved in with her sister when she lost her job at a clothing boutique. Emma remembers getting goosebumps as she read the book, turning the pages with anticipation and had an odd feeling that she was being watched, as if the pages were being written as she read. By the middle of the story, the women's lives veered. Garland ended up designing a clothing line and becoming wildly popular while Emma eventually got her own apartment when she landed the job at Quinley's. Her dreams of writing were usurped by falling in love with Cal Waters. A classic narcissist, Cal was controlling and demanded that all her attention and focus be directed to him. As a good girlfriend and afraid of losing him, Emma was only too willing to comply.

"I'm so sorry. What did you ask?" Emma blushed as she addressed the woman. Everyone in the room was looking at her for the answer.

"I wanted to know if you have, *I Like it That Way*, in hardcover."

"I believe we do." Emma checked her watch, then turned to Brendon Brooks. "This might be a good time to take questions from our audience. I'll find out where those hardcovers are."

Brendon nodded and gave Emma a big smile. She melted right then and there. The man wasn't classically handsome, but he bore an uncanny resemblance to a young Humphrey Bogart. When she turned to go, she considered asking the author out to dinner after the book signing. She was between boyfriends and was desperate to find out more about Garland Grady. Did he fashion the fictional character from a real person? If not, where did he get the inspiration to write the story? She reached the inventory room and went to the shelf where the books were stacked.

An attractive woman in her early 20s was holding up her hand. Emma placed the books on the signing table, just to the left of the podium where Brooks nodded to the woman. She stood, pulling down her short, short dress which barely covered her backside. When Brooks flashed the same smile to her as he had done to Emma, her heart dropped. It plummeted when the woman spoke. "I felt such a kinship with your protagonist, Lola Berkshire. It was as if you were writing about me! Where did you get the inspiration to create her?"

Brooks eyed the woman like he was about to devour her. "That's a secret I'll only share with you. Deal?"

"Absolutely."

Emma looked down at her outfit: faded jeans, cowboy boots and a long-sleeved Quinley's T-shirt. It was appropriate attire for the liberal bookstore, but it was no match for the blood red, form-fitting dress worn by the very sexy young woman.

Emma totally lost her nerve. She exchanged the normal pleasantries with the author: thank you so much for coming. I hope you have a wonderful stay in our city. It was clear that his attention was going to be concentrated on someone other than Quinley's store manager.

Inside the plastic doll, Emma's soul relived that night, and she regretted her decision. If she had invited Brooks to dinner and he declined, so what? If he accepted, who knows where she would be right now. If the flap of a butterfly's wings can change the trajectory of events, Emma's invitation and his possible acceptance could have done the same. Too bad she couldn't go back in time and rewrite the script. She blamed it on not believing in herself. She wondered if that attitude would change once she took on Sandy's body.

"Hey lazybones. Sorry, inappropriate expression. Let's try it again. Hey sleepyhead, come on out of there and let's see what's happening with the crazy Ekhart clan."

Emma materialized; her mood somber. Gigi caught it immediately. "Why so glum?"

"Reminiscing and regretting."

"Don't do that. You can't take back what you've done. You can, however, make new and improved decisions. What were you thinking about?"

"Brendon Brooks' book signing." Emma sighed.

"Oh yeah. I remember that. You let that tart take him away from you. Once you have a new body, you won't make those same mistakes, right?"

"I will have a younger body, albeit one that's been abused by alcohol and drugs, but I bet I can whip it into shape. I can't wait to have tighter skin, no wrinkles, and joints that don't ache."

Gigi said, "Now you're talking. Let's blow this popsicle stand and head over to soap opera central."

"Before we descend upon the Ekharts, do you mind going somewhere first?"

"Honey, unlike you, all I got is time. Lead away."

Gigi didn't recognize the house at first. It was gray and white, the architecture was arts and crafts, not the typical Victorian, ubiquitous in San Francisco. A 'for sale' sign stood on the lawn. Despite the drought, the lawn was green and the flowers lining the walkway were vibrant, as were the star jasmine bushes that abutted the house.

Emma could tell that her sister didn't know where she was. "My home. I moved here when I separated from Vin."

The inside of the house was unrecognizable. All of Emma's belongings were gone. Her dining room table made from reclaimed wood, the watercolor painting of daisies that hung above her antique side table. All gone and replaced with ultra-modern furniture and décor.

Gigi scanned the living room and adjoining dining room. "Cute house, but I don't remember you having such antiseptic taste."

Emma shook her head. "You think I would have a glass and chrome coffee table? And a leather couch? Really? The paintings look like they're from Goodwill. My stuff is gone. This is all staged."

Instead of checking out the rest of the rooms, the sisters drifted over to the house next door. Emma wanted to see Petal again. The woman was a bright star in the neighborhood. She was young enough to be Emma's daughter, but the two got along like old friends. Reeling from the impending divorce, Emma's move was anything but joyful. She couldn't wait to leave the home that she and Vin had lived in for the past three years. It may have been four times larger, but the bad memories it held in the walls, the Olympic-sized pool, the California King-sized bed, and austere, functional furniture gave it a toxic glow. Especially their bed. It wasn't until she caught Vin cheating that she told him how much she hated living in a McMansion. The faux Tudor-style home reeked of nouveau rich. Vin had hired a decorator to fill his home with expensive, but nondescript furnishings, void of personality and life. His family had lived in a three-room house, slightly nicer than a shed, in rural Kentucky. The outhouse was accessible from the back door. Vincent Farthington was born Vinton Fugate and was the seventh child of Mulda and Vern Fugate. He was the first of their children to go to college where he studied finance. He changed his name when he was accepted into Mary Williams University. After graduation, he made it his life's goal to become a banker. That's where the money is, his daddy used to say. He also used to say that it doesn't matter how you make it to the finish line as long as you make it. Vin fast tracked into investment banking with the help of a mentor who happened to be his sugar momma. As soon as he was making over a million a year, his sugar momma became too sweet to swallow. She was unceremoniously dumped for a much younger and tighter version. By the time Emma met Mr. Fugate, he was newly single as was she. It wasn't until they were married for two and a half years that the sugar momma got her revenge. A meticulously thorough investigation into his career uncovered a trail of bribery, falsification of records, perjury, and a wide assortment of broken promises. Too bad Vinton Fugate's daddy didn't tell him that a woman scorned is one hell of an adversary.

Vin lost his job and his money. With his infinite gift of southern charm mixed with deceit, he managed to stay out of jail. It wasn't until he was caught with his lawyer's paralegal, Cindy Dole, that he lost his wife. After her husband's poor dealings made it onto the front page of the San Francisco Examiner, Emma knew her marriage was over. Finding him in bed with Cindy made the decision to divorce him immediate.

At Petal's house, Gigi looked at the small blue bottles sitting on her kitchen countertop. There were three pots on the stove and a large ceramic bowl of rose petals sitting next to a jar of organic sesame oil. They could hear Petal humming in the bathroom. Emma swirled above the workspace, trying to inhale the intoxicating scents. Her ethereal body was enveloped by the vapors.

"Don't you feel energized?" Emma asked her sister.

"Actually, I do. Petal's a breath of fresh air after hanging around Norma, Bob and their oh-so-lovely daughter."

Still humming, Petal walked into the kitchen. Suddenly, she stopped humming and looked up at the ceiling. Closing her eyes, Petal took a deep breath, held it for a few seconds, and then slowly let it out. She stood in silence for a full minute. When she opened her eyes, tears ran down her face. She went into the living room and picked up a photo of herself and Emma. It was taken during a summer solstice party in her backyard. Both women were wearing flower garlands. Their arms around each other. Big smiles. "I miss you, Emma."

"I miss you, too, dear Petal." Emma looked toward her sister. "Does she know we're here?"

"She can sense our presence. The woman works with essential oils and the essence of flowers. I can tell Petal is tuned in with her own energy, so it doesn't surprise me that she can feel ours. Conversely, the entire Ekhart clan is so involved with their own personal dramas, they wouldn't feel a horde of spirits if they walked into a reincarnation reunion."

"Is there such a thing?"

Gigi laughed. "No. The idea does put a smile on my non-existent face."

"Do you mind if we hang out here for a while? It's very calming."

"Not at all."

The sisters watched as Petal created her oil blends. They agreed she seemed to be in an altered state. She moved around her workspace with an intense clarity. Every scent was noted and analyzed for its properties. Whether she was checking on the barely heated oils or gently pouring the cooling oil blends into the blue bottles, Petal was a perfectly suited aromatherapist. By the time they left, it was twilight, and they were curious as to how Sandy was faring. They found her entering the Harmony Soup Kitchen. She appeared to be sober. Emma gave her a cosmic gold star.

When Sandy reached the front of the line, she was given a red plastic tray, silverware, and a napkin. It was her first time receiving a free meal, one she didn't have to beg for since being on the street. Even though she was told that Ellis was in police custody, she couldn't help but scan the crowd. She recognized a few of the patrons, like the old woman who wore a faded Forty-Niners baseball cap backwards. And the uncomfortably tall man with long braids, Willie Nelson's poor, giant twin. Sandy wondered what people thought of her. Did they assess her unwashed hair? Her weary worn expression? Did she look homeless to her fellow diners, or did she look like she was weeks-removed from living in a comfortable apartment with a refrigerator and stove, a bathroom with a door? She never had to wonder where her next meal was coming from. She looked down at her tray, a thin silver knife lay next to a fork, its tines slightly askew from overzealous diners. The napkin reminded her of the ones they had in the high school cafeteria. It was square and impossibly thin. Suddenly she felt very tired. What was she doing here? How did she end up in a soup kitchen line, her stomach empty, craving whatever they had to offer? She didn't have to think very hard.

A white-haired man with a handlebar moustache placed a sourdough roll on her tray. She thanked him and moved down the line. Standing behind an industrial sized pot was Dr. Will Remini. "Hi Sandy. I'm glad you made it for chili night." He lifted the ladle filled to the rim with the bean and tofu dish.

"Well, if it isn't Mother Teresa." She looked at the person to Will's right. "Who's your sidekick?"

"I'm Makelo. Willy's my uncle." He held out a small bowl of salad. "Would you like some salad?"

"Why not?"

"How are you feeling?" Will asked as Sandy began to move down the line to the dessert.

"Once the drugs kick in, I feel fine. Otherwise, the pain is pretty intense." She pointed to the chili. "I'll give you my critique later."

"Okay."

Will watched as Sandy held out her tray for a piece of chocolate cake. She wasn't a bad looking woman. With high cheekbones and light turquoise eyes, she could have looked every bit the woman of privilege she was born into, and it was eating at Will, the desire to know what had happened.

"Do you know her, Uncle Willy?"

"Yes, I do."

Once the line slowed down to a trickle, Will asked the white-haired man to take over his station for a few minutes and to keep an eye on his nephew, then he sat down next to Sandy. She was near a family of four whose children looked around Makelo's age.

"What's the verdict?" Will asked as Sandy swallowed the last spoonful of chili.

"I give it a thumbs up. Very tasty and despite my aversion to tofu,

I found it full of flavor."

Will put his hand over his heart. "I'm honored. Thank you."

Sandy stuck her bent fork into the chocolate cake and took a bite. She made a face. "Tastes like it's from Costco."

Will laughed and adjusted his glasses. "It is. You should be a food critic."

"As soon as I give notice at my current job, I'll look into it." She could see that Will was about to question her. "Just kidding. Currently unemployed."

"What did you do?"

Sandy lied. "Worked as a paralegal."

"Did you like it?"

"The work was okay, but I didn't like the people, so I left."

"Without having another job lined up?"

Sandy gave Will a dirty look. "It appears that way, doesn't it?"

"I'm sorry. That didn't come out right." Will took a business card out of his wallet and handed it to Sandy. "After what you've been through, you may want to check out The Rescue Mission. It isn't far from here. They have comfortable beds, meals, and even provide culinary training if you feel like trying something new."

Sandy inspected the card. "Do they have rules?"

"Well, sure. They have hours when they serve meals and last call for…"

Sandy handed him back the card. "Thanks, but no thanks." She got up to leave. "And unless an after-dinner port is being served, I have to jet."

Will refused to take the card. "Keep it. You may change your mind."

Sandy nodded and stuffed it into her pants pocket. She went over to the designated tray drop-off and, without another look, set down her tray and walked into the night. Will returned to his place behind the food table.

Makelo said, "That lady has pretty eyes."

"Yeah, she does. They'd be even prettier if she was happy."

Makelo looked up at his uncle with concern. "Do you think she ever will be?"

Will looked over at the door. "Yeah, I do."

"Then I do, too."

Will checked his watch. "The kitchen closes in five minutes. You want to help me bring the dishes to the kitchen for clean up? Afterwards, I'll take you to Bambino's Nice Cream."

"Sounds like a good plan to me." Without any prompting, Makelo went over to the tray station and picked up a tub full of dirty dishes. It was heavy, but he managed to walk it to the kitchen. The white-haired volunteer standing next to Will took a bite out of a sourdough roll, then he pointed it in the direction of the kitchen.

"That is one special kid. An old soul. That's what he is."

Will nodded. "Yeah, he's a keeper."

Gigi noticed that her sister was quiet. Unusually quiet. They were following Sandy out of the soup kitchen.

"What's up?" Gigi said.

"That was depressing. All those people who can't afford a meal. Families, teenagers, seniors. Did you see that kid with the horrible acne? His tennis shoes had holes on top. You can bet the soles had holes, too. And that old lady with no teeth? She could barely eat her food. She must be someone's mother or grandmother. What's happened to them? I counted over sixty people. Most of them probably homeless. This is one of thousands of kitchens across America. I bet they're feeding millions of people at poverty level. And that's just this country. Across the world people are starving, living in filth, and have no idea where their next meal is coming from. Their pain and hopelessness is overwhelming."

Gigi knew her sister was right. The pain was palpable in the large, utilitarian room where meals were doled out three times a day, every day of the year and there was never a shortage of diners. "Listen, there are always going to be people who can't take care of themselves. The human species is flawed in so many ways. Mental illness is just one of the maladies. At least there are those who look out for many of them, providing them with food and shelter."

Emma shook her head. "It's not enough. Everyone should chip in. Do their part."

"I see. Did you when you were alive? Were you volunteering at shelters or handing out food? Did you sacrifice your time trying to find these people jobs and homes and medical care?"

Emma stopped following Sandy and looked at her sister, a glowing image of her past incarnation. Sometimes, Emma felt as if she was staring back at herself, their resemblance was that close: the strong jawline and intense blue eyes. The slightly arched eyebrows and porcelain colored skin. "I had my charities and I contributed to them, but you're right. I never got my hands dirty. I wouldn't even make eye contact with a homeless person because I was afraid that they'd ask me for money, and I didn't want to give them a dime because I thought they'd spend it on booze or drugs. And they probably would have. I admit it. I'm a hypocrite."

"I wasn't trying to shame you, Emma."

"Yes you were."

"Yeah, I guess I was, but when you come back as Sandy, you'll be able to help these people. And if we can find out how to tap into Sandy's family's money, you'll have the potential to help a lot more people."

Emma looked dejected. "Great. I could help, what, thousands of people? Compared to the tens of millions suffering, it's nothing."

"It's something to those thousands. To even one of those people."

"Don't you see, this planet will always have pain, suffering, and premature death. I could never eliminate it. The human condition envelops it." She watched as Sandy entered the homeless encampment, walking past the makeshift shelters, tents, and flattened cardboard boxes that substituted for beds. She accidentally tripped on the edge of a reflective traffic cone, its base protruding into the dirt walkway. It was one of four, each stationed at a corner forming the foundation for a tarp that was placed over the top of the cones. The cone tipped over, causing the tarp to dip and the occupant under it to yell.

"Watch where you're going!" A gloved hand appeared from under the blue tarp, quickly righted the cone and just as quickly disappeared.

Sandy corrected herself before she fell onto a neon orange tent on the other side of the walkway. "Sorry." A couple of hundred more feet and she arrived at her pile of clothes and sleeping bag. They were stowed to the right of Kaitlin's tent. Sandy pulled her backpack off her shoulders and grabbed the half empty bottle of Smirnoff vodka. She hit the side of the tent a couple of times with the palm of her hand. "Come on out here and share a drink with me."

The tent moved and wiggled as the occupant crawled toward the entrance. A man in his twenties with a mop of blonde hair and big ears stuck his head out of the opening. "She ain't here anymore."

Surprised, Sandy put the bottle on the ground and stared at the sallow-faced man, his pale blue eyes watery, and the whites a light yellow. "What are you talking about? I saw her a couple of hours ago. That's her tent you're in and I suggest you get out before she comes back. She'll be pissed."

"She ain't coming back because she's dead." The young man pointed a bony finger toward the street. "She got hit by a car. The morgue mobile took her away, so get your shit away from my tent. I'm done talking." He zipped up the nylon door and crawled back to the other end of the tent.

Sandy sat down next to her meager belongings. Her head began to ache. She wasn't cut out for this life. She grew up in a house with over 8,000 square feet of living space. Her bedroom was the size of a studio apartment. It had a walk-in closet, an alcove for her dressing table, and a Bayview window with a view of the Golden Gate Bridge. She also had to endure Norma and Bob, parents that tipped the scales at evil and apathetic. The last place she wanted to live again was with them, despite the situation she found herself in. She sat there, on the dirt, for what seemed like five minutes. Sandy knew Kaitlin for only a few days, but she was her only friend, the only person who treated her with kindness at the encampment. Without her, she wouldn't have gone to the doctor. She wouldn't have gotten the medication she needed for the infection or the pain pills. Ellis wouldn't be in jail, and she wouldn't have met Dr. Remini.

Head down and eyes closed, she absently reached for the bottle of vodka. Sandy unscrewed the cap, tossed it next to the tent, and drank half the contents. She wiped the tears off her cheeks.

Emma looked down at her possible new 'vessel' and felt profoundly sad for Sandy. And herself. Did she want to take over the body of a young woman who used alcohol as her preferred numbing agent? According to the Akashic Records, the young woman's history didn't include alcoholism or even binge drinking at parties. She was pretty boring. Sandy and Sandra's big weekend fete consisted of a game of Hearts, pizza, a glass of wine, and catching up on their favorite television show, *Game of Thrones*. Her life up to this unfortunate point read more like an ascetic's than a high society debutante. Gigi interrupted her thoughts.

"I think you should try and take her tonight after she's passed out."

A sense of panic set in. Emma still wasn't sure if she wanted to become Sandy Ekhart. Taking over her body meant becoming part of the Ekhart dynasty. Along with the notoriety and money came dysfunction and tumult. "I don't know if I'm ready. I haven't learned everything about Sandy or her family. Wouldn't that be disastrous, taking on someone's body without knowing her entire history?"

"I can show you how to access her records and you'd be a master of Ms. Ekhart's life and past lives in a matter of seconds. Remember, the spiritual world doesn't work on linear time. It's all relative."

"I think we should wait a little longer. I'll scope her out, physically, too. I don't want to jump into her body without knowing it intimately, you know?" Emma felt a wave of decreased energy. It rippled through her spiritual body like someone plugged her into a socket, but instead of being energized, it pulled the energy from her.

Gigi saw her sister's light flicker, like a soft breeze on a candle flame. She came up to Emma, their bodies almost touching. "Are you okay?"

"Feeling a tad woozy. What happened?" Emma looked at her arms as they flickered. It reminded her of a light bulb before it died.

"You're getting more acclimated to the doll as your earth body. I'm going to say good-bye before you're pulled back for a while. And I want to say that I'm sorry for pushing you. This must be a very difficult decision. You'll be coming back to Earth in human form, and not the one you'd been living in for nearly sixty years. Forgive me."

Before Emma could respond, she was gone. Gigi sighed. She never imagined that she would be experiencing her sister in this situation. She regarded Sandy who, by now, had rolled out her sleeping bag and fell asleep. Her moaning was barely audible. Could Emma have found a better human to 'become?' Definitely, but Gigi had faith in her sister. She knew that she could bring out the woman's potential. Perhaps Emma would write the novel that she'd been contemplating for years, but with an entirely new plot.

10

Her heart was pounding to the rhythm of the hooves. Her breathing became shallow, and her eyes narrowed as she watched the horses race to the finish line.

Norma wasn't aware of anyone else in the room. She was transfixed on the 150-inch television screen. Rick had turned up the volume, despite Marlo's protest that the furniture seemed to be vibrating. He wanted to feel like he and his guests were at the Kentucky Derby. They did.

Bob took a sip of his mint julep. The frosted glass and fresh sprig of mint added to the refreshing taste of the Southern drink. He placed it next to the cheese and cracker tray. He wasn't as enamored with horse racing as his wife. His favorite aspect was the betting. It added to the allure of the sport. Norma would drag him to the Lassiter Racetrack in Santa Clara sometimes as often as once a month. She didn't need to get there early since they had a private box suite, but she insisted on leaving an hour before they needed to in case there was traffic. Once there, she made sure she said hello to the regulars; the ones sitting in the exclusive box seats; made sure they all saw her in her new racetrack attire. From her hat to her shoes, Norma could have stepped out of Vanity Fair's society page. Walking to the coveted reserved seating, she radiated wealth and influence.

Built in 1955, Lassiter was forty miles south of San Francisco. Before the Silicon Valley newly minted millionaires graced the stands, the track looked more like a refuge for low level gamblers, mostly men and a few women who would drive or bus it to the grandstands after work. They'd grab a slice of cheese pizza or a dollar frank at the concession stand, fulfill their vegetable requirement by squirting ketchup and relish between the dog and the bun, wash it down with

Miller draft beer, then spend the evening hours betting their money away on the horses. Due to demand from the moneyed patrons, the Lassiter Horse Clubhouse and exclusive skylight viewing rooms underwent major renovations. While they were at it, they gave the entire place a facelift, turning the racetrack into a premiere destination for locals and tourists alike.

Still, Norma favored Del Mar's track in Southern California. She'd fly down once a week if her social life wasn't so frenetic, absorbed in charity events, parties, and her coveted project. The historic racetrack embodied the pomp and circumstance that she loved and craved. After all, she grew up among the wealthy and influential in San Francisco. She felt most at home in the spotlight, where her celebrity was minor but still had heft, especially with old money. Her friendships with ex-mayor Willie Brown, Dianne Feinstein, and former Governor Jerry Brown were strong. Rumors that she had a fling with famous columnist Herb Caen were unfounded, but Norma never discouraged the gossip. It only added to her notoriety.

Rick Standish glanced over at his guest, thrilled that she was thoroughly enjoying the sensory experience he had painstakingly planned, despite his wife's reluctance to participate. She begrudgingly prepared for the evening, requesting that their chef design caviar and crackers in the shape of a horse head, prepare a platter filled with horseshoe-shaped crudité, and recreate the classic Louisiana mint juleps. Glass vases were filled with dozens of red and white roses and placed throughout the massive family room. An art deco coffee table held two of the Lalique vases, dormer columns on either side of the picture window displayed bouquets of the perfectly shaped roses as well. Rick's personal favorite was the mural-sized painting of the famous race where Secretariat won by a landslide. The excitement and energy of the historic event was captured in the oil painting. Norma made him promise that he would leave it to her in his will. He gladly complied. He knew Marlo could care less about the $30,000 painting and if it made the largest investor of Francisco Downs happy, he was happy.

After one mint julep, Rick opted for a glass of single malt scotch. Glen Fiddich was his favorite. Cooled by two horseshoe-shaped ice cubes, he savored the sweet and subtle oak flavors.

"Come on, Bucky Dent! Pass Holier Than Thou. You can do it!"

Norma was standing, shouting at the screen. Her competitive energy rivaled the race. Following her lead, more out of respect than desire, Rick jumped up, dislodging Marlo's hand from his leg.

"Run Miss Dahlia, run!" The scotch sloshed around in the highball glass, a few drops spilling onto the antique Persian rug.

Bob turned his attention to Marlo, a sight much more desirable than what was on the screen. She gave him a look as if to say, 'I'd rather be anywhere else.' He nodded in agreement, then lifted his drink and finished it, leaving the ice cubes, now reduced to small u's.

Coming around the bend for the finish line, the horses literally were running for their lives. Whipped with riding crops and being screamed at from the crowd and millions of TV viewers, they gave it everything they had. Nearly side by side, Bucky Dent and Red Rum were ahead of the others. As they crossed the finish line, Red Rum won by a head. Norma fell back on the couch, exhausted by the anticipation of the win. "He'll win next time."

Bob leaned in to console his wife, but she got up and went over to Rick who was replenishing his drink at the bar. "I love the new TV. Did you get that for the derby?"

He nodded. "Of course."

Marlo cut in. "What do you think of the caviar?"

Norma gave the horse head a cursory once over. She thought it was tacky. "Clever." She turned her attention again to Rick. "Good thing I only had a couple of thousand on Bucky Dent."

"I told you he wouldn't win. He's just not lean enough."

"He lost by a head. I didn't see Miss Dahlia in the final two."

Rick held up his drink. "Touché, Mrs. Ekhart."

"I think horse racing is more for people than the horses." Marlo surprised herself by blurting out a fair condemnation of the popular sport. She put her mint julep down, silently cursing the alcohol for loosening her lips. Bob would have concurred, but he stayed silent for two reasons: he may get lucky tonight so he didn't want to dampen his wife's mood, and incurring the wrath of Norma Ekhart wasn't on his list of priorities, so he kept his mouth shut. Still, he felt sorry for Marlo.

Rick gave Norma a look as if to say, 'Let's not go there, okay?' Out of respect to her friend and business partner, Norma kept her temper in check. Before she responded, her eyes scanned the top of Marlo's lush, long shiny hair to her gravity-defying breasts, down to her long, shapely legs. The woman was a work of art.

"Marlo dear, you realize that your husband is investing in the construction of one of the largest racetracks in the country, if not the world. Do you honestly think he would sink millions of dollars into a business that blatantly abused animals, an animal as magnificent as a racehorse?"

The penetration of those turquoise eyes was unsettling. Marlo stammered, "It's just that I've read that the horses are…"

Norma interrupted. "Where did you read this, dear?"

"On…online at the PETA website."

Norma almost grunted. "The PETA site? Really? You realize that organization wants to eliminate owning pets? They don't believe in eating animals either. Are you a vegan, dear?" She glanced over at the caviar horse head. "Last time I checked, caviar and cheese are on PETA's long list of no no's. Why don't you go in the kitchen and make a lettuce horse head or maybe a broccoli wreath, you know, like the flower wreath they grace the winner of the race with?"

Red faced, Marlo waited for her husband to offer his support. Instead, Rick cast his eyes down, avoiding his wife's pleading eyes. He took a long sip of his drink, then said, "Why don't we go out to the patio? The wind will pick up soon and drive us back in before long."

Hands balled into tight fists, Marlo walked past the kitchen into the guest bathroom. After locking the door, she took a deep breath as she pulled a small piece of paper out of her incredibly skintight jeans. Unfolding it, she sat on the toilet lid and silently read, *I am grateful for my beautiful home and generous husband. I am grateful for my wonderful parents and my amazing brother. I am so grateful for my looks and near perfect body. I am grateful for my friends and for living in such an amazing city.* Marlo stood and tucked the folded piece of paper in her back pocket. She looked in the mirror and re-fluffed her hair, then said aloud, "But I hate that fucking bitch."

Gigi lay back against the buoy. Actually, she pretended to, since her spiritual body would have disappeared into the red and white striped floatie. The waves pushed the nine-ton structure back and forth, then side to side. There was no method to the ocean's madness.

She sighed.

"Damn Emma, you sure do whine a lot. Were you like this before the big bang, 'cause I don't remember you complaining this much or ever calling you Debbie Downer, which I am prone to at this moment…Debbie."

"Don't you think I have a right to vent? After all, I just lost my body and I'm doomed to live in a kid's All American doll for eternity unless I find a flesh and blood body. I think even Miss Manners would grant me bitching rights, so get off my case woman."

"Sorry, you can't afford to be in self-pity mode. We need that soul of yours in peak form, void of negativity, doubt, and gloom. What you need, my dear, is a psychic cleansing." Gigi held up her arms and shot up into the night sky. Emma watched her sister's beam of light disappear only to return seconds later, brighter than ever. It looked like she was holding a glowing stick in her hand. It reminded Emma of a pixie stick, except it wasn't striped and she knew it wasn't filled with flavored sugar. Gigi held out her hand, the stick glowing even stronger. "Throughout your lifetimes you've accumulated what's called psychic garbage. All the crap that we tend to believe about ourselves. All the crap that others have inflicted upon us. It weighs us down, penetrating every fiber. A lot of it is embedded in our corporeal bodies, but when we die, our soul doesn't escape the internal trash. This little tool will help you expel some of it."

As it pulsated in her sister's hand flecks of green, blue, red, yellow, purple, and orange flew off the stick, like confetti bursting out of a party popper in slow motion. It was mesmerizing. Before Emma could ask a question, Gigi said, "When I engage the wand with your body, it will draw out thoughts, regrets, complaints, and some errant memories. Afterwards, I promise you'll feel lighter, more focused, and less negative. Are you ready?"

Emma nodded. "Why the colors?"

Gigi shrugged. "Why not?"

Gigi lovingly touched Emma with the wand. Flecks of color became animated, gently bouncing in, out and around her soul. She could feel things being pulled out of her. "I was three years old and went into the garage. When I got up on my tiptoes to grab a jar of nails on an old desk, it fell and broke. Pieces of glass were everywhere. I thought I'd be punished, so I hid in the desk's chair well for hours, too scared to move. When I found out Vin had an affair, I went to Macy's and bought $5,000 worth of clothes and jewelry on his credit card. I still feel it was unjustified. It was a petty and juvenile way to seek revenge. I should have shot him instead. Why didn't I stop and help that Collie who was running on Lombard Street? Its eyes were wild with fear and it looked so scared. I found out later it was hit by a car and killed. I wanted to have children, but the time never felt right. I should have had a child with Del. I hated getting old. I would look in the magnifying mirror twice a day, daring my body to make another wrinkle. I despise every single company that makes anti-aging products with the promise that they'll lessen wrinkles. They don't work. I didn't miss Dad after he died. It made me feel like I was cold and heartless, but I loved him dearly. When I was six, I decapitated an ant and still feel bad about it. I should have walked Toby more often. The poor dog barely got exercise, but I was so preoccupied in high school that I didn't care. I resented you for not being home enough, so the burden of helping mom was on me. Why did I get so emotional when I talked about the Coen brothers' movies? They infuriated me, but I didn't have to defend my position so vehemently."

Gigi listened to her sister's venting. She remembered when she was introduced to psychic cleansing. It was shortly after her death and, admittedly, she was enraged. Fatal car accidents are almost always bloody and messy. Twisted metal and broken, torn bodies. Killed instantly, her spirit rose slowly out of her body, giving her a chance to view the carnage. It took a psychic dumping to remove the vision of her crushed skull, arms smashed into her torso and enmeshed in the steering wheel. Her anger at being taken away from her devoted husband and gratifying career as an accountant was washed away, the multi-colored flecks absorbing the anger, the hate, the regrets, unwarranted vituperations, and even some benign memories. When her session ended, she literally drifted on a cumulus cloud for days, not concerned with where or who she was. It didn't matter. Gigi wasn't any more enlightened than before the cleansing. She was energetically more positive. Her perspective of life on earth was altered, as well. She wasn't sure she wanted to be human again. When she thought about returning to a planet where the beauty and good in humanity was rivaled by the horrors of the species' greed and lust for power, whatever negativity was left inside began to rise up. She wasn't sure if she would ever return. Unfortunately for Emma, she didn't have a celestial alternative. She was stuck in the doll until it was destroyed. Recalling how a friend of hers had a doll collection with some of them dating back to the 1800s, Gigi was determined to help her sister reenter the human population, even if that meant usurping the body of a homeless woman.

Gigi returned from her reverie only to find Emma continuing a steady stream of psychic dumping.

"…stole the candy bar from Safeway. I always wanted to tell Grandie that she never let me speak. The conversation was more like a speech from her. I felt horrible when I interrupted Spence and told him that he said, 'you know' too much. He was hurt, but he stopped using that phrase." Emma closed her psychic eyes and listened to the deep, dark waves splash against the buoy. When she opened them, she felt calm, serene. "If this is what unbridled euphoria feels like, I should have done this a long time ago."

Gigi extended her hand to Emma. "It's like thirty years of psychoanalysis in an instant. I knew you'd appreciate it. Too bad it's not available to humans. I have to return this." She held up the wand. "Be right back."

Before Emma could ask her where she was going, her sister shot into the sky, returning seconds later without the valuable tool. "Why don't we check out your new mom and dad. I'm sure they're up to no good."

"And I was feeling so unfettered. Now we have to endure the putrid air of dysfunctional San Francisco royalty?" Emma sighed. "Fine. Let's get it over with."

Lonnie finished the can of Pepsi and threw it in the back seat of his Toyota Camry. The late model sedan had been filled with a lot worse than a soda can even if a few drops fell between the cushion and back seat crack. Lonnie pulled the visor down and slid open the mirror. He grabbed the moustache comb from his jean pocket and swept it through the tuft of hair below his lower lip. He winked at his reflection and said, "Time to fly."

"Who is it?" Sandra Henstrom shouted and paused the rerun of *CSI Miami*. She stood on her toes and looked through the peephole.

She didn't expect to see a grown man resembling a surfer dude on the other side. She could tell he was trying to look through the small one-way hole.

"Lonnie King, private investigator. I'd like to ask you some questions about your friend, Sandy Ekhart."

Suspicious, Sandra said, "How do I know you're who you say you are?"

Lonnie fielded this question all the time, especially from women. "I was hired by Sandy's mother, Norma Ekhart. Hold on. Let me get her number and you can call her to confirm my legitimacy." He pulled one of his business cards from his shirt pocket, took out his cell and scrolled down to Norma's number. After he slid the card under the door, he said, "415...673...4499. Got that?"

Sandra picked up Lonnie's card. "I got to get my phone. Be right back." She padded away in her stocking feet, grabbed her cell, and returned. "Say the number again."

Lonnie repeated it. After four rings, it went to voicemail. "Hi Mrs. Ekhart, it's Sandra Henstrom, Sandy's friend. Did you hire a private investigator named Lonnie King to look for Sandy? If so, please give me a call." Sandra left her number and hung up. "Listen Mr. King, you can either wait until Mrs. Ekhart calls me back or you can ask me questions through the door."

"I'm going to go with option number two. Sandy lived with you, right?

"Yes. Up until a few weeks ago. She lived here for about six months."

"Can you be more specific? Exactly when did she move out and why?" Lonnie grabbed his small notepad and pen. He scribbled *six months*, then waited for her answer.

Sandra pulled one of the dining room chairs next to the front door and sat down. "I found out that she was lying about having a job and that was two Sundays ago, the...sixth. She moved out three days later. The woman did nothing around the apartment. The whole time she was living here, she claimed that she was a paralegal at a firm in the financial district. Turns out, she didn't have a job at all. She was home every day, lazing around. I gave her an ultimatum and when she failed that, I booted her. It's a shame because Sandy and I have known each other since high school. We did everything together. I had no idea that living with her would ruin our friendship. If you ask me, her mother is to blame for her being so messed up."

Lonnie scribbled away. "Yeah, well, we all have our opinions. Do you know where she went?"

"Not a clue. I haven't spoken to her since. You'd think she would have had a lot of money, a trust fund or something similar, but she hadn't paid rent the last two months she lived here, so either she went to her parent's or family members for a loan or – and I doubt she did this – is living on the street. Honestly, I think I was the only friend she had."

"That was my next question. You sure she didn't have anyone else she could go to?"

Sandra thought about it. She tried to recall conversations Sandy had on the phone or if she ever went out with anyone besides herself. "Sandy was a loner. I don't think she ever mentioned aunts or uncles, or even cousins. Wow, she was truly alone."

"Looks that way." Lonnie put away his notepad. "You've been helpful, Ms. Henstrom. If you hear from Sandy, please give me a call. Enjoy the rest of your evening."

"You, too." Sandra put the dining room chair back in its place at the head of the table. She slowly sat down on the couch and wrapped the faux fur throw around her shoulders and grabbed the remote. She hit the play button and just as quickly pressed pause. Sandy Ekhart. The name evoked both fond and infuriating memories. Sandra wanted to understand what her friend was going through, growing up with privilege, but little love and attention. She welcomed Sandy into her apartment. Allowing her to stay until she could find a place of her own was a little more than an inconvenience, but she didn't mind because she believed Sandy would be living with her for no more than a month or two. Sandra converted her office into a bedroom and shared her small bathroom, giving Sandy half the shelf space.

The first few weeks were ideal. It was like old times. They watched their favorite movies, played High School Musical more than once, went out dancing, and even hit the skating rink a few times. When one month went by and then three, Sandra began to wonder if her friend was ever going to look for another place to live. It was only when Sandra came home early from work, a migraine forcing her to leave, that she learned the truth. Sandy was spread out on the couch in her pajamas watching daytime television. Crying, she told Sandra that she had lost her job and was looking for another paralegal position. After insisting that Sandy tell her the truth, Sandra was told that there never was a job.

Incensed, Sandra was done with the friendship and wanted her apartment back. When Sandy finally moved out, she felt only relief and no regret whatsoever, but after the visit from Lonnie, Sandra's conscience was beginning to bother her. Regardless of the lies and lack of initiative, Sandy had been her best friend. While Sandra couldn't even fathom that Sandy could be living on the street, searching through trash cans for her next meal, she couldn't come up with another scenario for where she might be. Sandra made a mental note to call the private investigator in a couple of days to find out if he had located Sandy. Satisfied, she pressed 'play' and continued to watch the CSI Miami investigator collect evidence from a swing at the playground where the episode's latest victim was last seen.

11

Despite wearing two sweaters, jeans and thick, wool socks, Sandy shivered herself awake. The morning mist left a sheet of moisture on her sleeping bag, and even though it didn't penetrate the fabric, her clothes felt damp. Someone was making coffee, the smell pervading the chilled air. The familiar aroma gave the day a bit of brightness. Just a bit.

Sandy sat up too fast and felt the ache in her head grow, like a time lapse video of a rosebud turning into a flower in a matter of seconds, but the result wasn't pretty at all. She closed her eyes as the pain intensified. As much as she would have liked to go back to sleep, the headache was too much to take. She remembered the pain pills she received from the clinic and, despite the discomfort, opened her eyes and dug around in her backpack until she found the bottle. Eagerly, Sandy popped two Tylenol into her bone-dry mouth and swallowed them with what was left of a 13-ounce bottle of Crystal Geyser Spring water.

An hour later, the headache was barely noticeable, and the sun warmed her chilled bones. The person responsible for making the pot of coffee filled a used Styrofoam cup with a passable cup of dark brown liquid and handed it to Sandy. She drank it with a bagel found in a dumpster behind Starbucks. It was in a bag along with six other day-old bagels. Kaitlin taught Sandy how to find semi-fresh food for free, a skill that came in handy living on the street.

I need a plan of action. Yeah, a plan of action. Sandy repeated the phrase like a mantra. She ran her fingers through her unwashed hair. It stayed in place, the dirt and oil daring it to move. She had no idea what she was going to do, but without a home or a job or a family, she was convinced that a plan was necessary. She couldn't and wouldn't live in the encampment for long. Her survival instincts on the street were practically non-existent. Life in the Ekhart home didn't prepare her for life, period. She thought about living in the shelter that Dr. Remini mentioned. That would be a fair transition, a safe and warm place to live until she figured out what to do next. She couldn't wait to take a hot shower.

Sandy finished breakfast and with a new resolve, picked up her belongings and headed over to the free clinic. She lost the card Will had given her and couldn't remember the address of the shelter, and no one she asked seemed to know. Will had told her it wasn't far from the clinic, so she figured that would be a good place to start.

"I appreciate the help."

"Not at all, Mr. King. Please have a seat and I'll let Dr. Remini know you're here."

Lonnie searched the room for a spot where he didn't have to sit next to anyone else. Not everyone in the free clinic's waiting room looked sick or dirty, but he didn't want to take the chance of catching some deadly disease. Despite his laid-back appearance, he had excellent hygiene. At least he thought so.

Lonnie sat down next to the magazine rack. He was tempted to thumb through *Car & Driver* magazine on the third tier but thought better of it. Someone with a communicable illness may have touched it last. Instead, he pulled out his iPhone and checked his texts. There was one from Norma requesting his progress. He wrote back, *Getting close. Will let you know when I find her*. He was about to check his emails when the nurse called his name. Lonnie was led through the hallway, a narrow corridor painted light pink on one side and lemon yellow on the other. Warm, soothing colors. Ideal for a health center.

"Have a seat, Mr. King. The doctor will be here momentarily."

Lonnie sat down in a well-worn chair, the naugahyde cracking as he settled in. He assumed the doctor's office wouldn't be plush or even decent, so it was no surprise that the nicest objects in the office were Dr. Remini's framed diplomas from Stanford and UC Davis. They hung above the credenza to the right of the desk. Lonnie was tempted to look through a five-inch stack of manila folders. They sat less than an arm's length from him and they looked like the patients' files. He opted against it and was glad he did because a few seconds later Dr. Will Remini opened the door to his office. He walked toward Lonnie, arm extended.

"Dr. Remini. And you are?"

Lonnie stood. "I'm Lonnie King, private investigator."

Will sat down behind his desk. "What can I do for you, Mr. King?"

Lonnie pulled out a photo of Sandy Ekhart and placed it in front of the doctor. "I've been hired by Sandy Ekhart's mother to find her daughter. There's been a family emergency and she's desperate to find her."

Will had a feeling someone would be looking for Sandy. A woman of good breeding didn't normally end up homeless and visiting the free clinic. Will also knew his patients' rights and by law he wasn't allowed to comply, regardless of who was requesting information. "How long have you been a P.I.?"

"I know. I know. It's against the law to release information on your clients. I knew that coming in, but Sandy's parents are sick with worry. Her mother's been unable to function since she disappeared."

A faint smile appeared on Will's face. "Why didn't she call the police and file a missing person's report? That's more logical and a lot less expensive, wouldn't you say?"

Without flinching, Lonnie replied, "She has filed, but she wanted additional help. You know how the cops are. They drag their feet with missing persons, believing that eventually they'll return. Sandy and her mother are very close, so when her daughter disappeared, she understandably became concerned. I realize you're not at liberty to divulge any information, but she would certainly appreciate knowing if you've seen her and/or treated her." Lonnie had been leaning forward. He sat back and the naugahyde once again stretched and cracked under the man's weight.

With as much false sincerity as he could conjure up, Will said, "I really would like to help you, Mr. King. However, I am unable at this time to tell you if I have ever met or treated Ms. Ekhart. I am sorry. I truly am." Will stood and again extended his hand. Lonnie shook it.

"Thank you for your time, Dr. Remini."

Disappointed but undeterred, Lonnie returned to the waiting

room. While holding his breath, he went up to a group of men standing in the far corner. They all looked like they were dipped in mud and halfheartedly dusted off. All donned unkempt beards and greasy, matted hair. With a photo in hand, he spoke barely above a whisper so as not to attract the attention of the receptionist. "Excuse me. Have any of you seen this woman? She's about five foot six with light brown hair." He let the men pass around the photograph. In it, Sandy was sporting a pasted-on smile. It was obvious to anyone who saw it that she was told to look happy.

A big grin emanated from one of the men. His two front teeth were missing and the rest of his pearlies were far from white. When he spoke, a smattering of spit flew through the gap, avoiding Lonnie by inches. "She a pretty lady. She must be lost and you want to find her. How much is it worth to ya for an answer?"

Lonnie said, "You don't beat around the bush, do you?"

"Son, I don't even have a bush to beat. You want info or not?"

The man's friends watched the exchange with amusement.

"Have you seen her?"

"She looks familiar."

Lonnie was taking his wallet out of his back pocket when the receptionist window flew open. In a booming voice, the woman yelled, "Mr. King, I'm going to ask you to leave. Right now. Otherwise, I'm calling the police."

The waiting room suddenly became quiet. All eyes were on Lonnie. "Pardon me, ma'am, but I'm not doing anything wrong."

The receptionist left her station and strode over to Lonnie. She was nearly as tall and he was over six feet. "If you want to ask about the whereabouts of someone, don't do it here. Take it outside." She stood face to face with the P.I., daring him to oppose her. Instead, he tucked his wallet into his back pocket, tipped his imaginary hat, gave the toothless man a nod, and headed out the front door. The man followed.

"For twenty dollars, can you tell me where you saw this woman?"

With his hand outstretched and his other hand pulling up his pants, he replied, "I think so. She's pretty."

"You said that."

"Yeah, well I could say it again. You don't see many lookers in the camp."

Lonnie eyes lit up. "Homeless camp?"

"No, Camp Sunshine. Yeah, the camp on Center." He grabbed the twenty and pushed it down his shirt.

Out of habit, Lonnie put out his hand to shake, then retracted it. The thought of touching the man's hand gave him the willies. "Thanks a lot. You've been helpful."

Without answering, the man went back inside the clinic. Lonnie got in his car and pulled away from the curb.

When Sandy emerged from the drugstore, she was momentarily disoriented. She walked almost two blocks in the wrong direction before she realized her error. The mistake cost her a few minutes delay, but resulted in her missing Lonnie. She sat on a stoop and took a brush out of her backpack. Once she removed all the knots, she grabbed one of the ponytail bands she bought and tied it back. Before resuming her walk, she washed down her pain medication with a swig from the bottled water, then poured some of the water in her hands and splashed her face. She dried off with a washcloth Kaitlin had given her. A couple passed her by, trying not to stare as she adjusted her backpack. A few weeks ago, the sideways glances would have bothered her. Today was different. Sandy's resolve to get her life back in order resonated through her being. She was determined to get off the streets.

Sandy tapped on the glass. When the receptionist slid the small window open, she said, "You have an appointment?"

"No. I was hoping I could talk to Dr. Remini for a second." She knew the woman behind the glass could tell her where the homeless shelter was. She probably could have asked the cashier at the drugstore or the cop she passed on the street.

"He's kind of busy." For emphasis, the receptionist looked around the waiting room at the dozen or more patients.

Sandy sighed. "It'll just take a minute. Please."

"Hold on."

Shortly, the side door opened and Dr. Remini poked his head out. He smiled and waved Sandy in. She followed him into his office. Instead of sitting behind his desk, Will sat in the chair next to the one Lonnie King had been in moments earlier. He directed Sandy to the chair. Once seated, he said, "You're just the person I wanted to see."

Sandy felt her heart gently leap in her chest. It was the first time in weeks she felt happy. "I am?"

Will nodded. "First, tell me why you're here. I know your

appointment isn't for another week."

Sandy nervously pushed a few errant hairs behind her ear. "I forgot where the shelter was you told me about. I wanted to check it out."

"That's great. I'm glad to hear it." Will shifted in his seat and leaned closer to Sandy. "If I remember your first appointment, you expressed animosity toward your mother. Is that accurate?"

Sandy's face and heart dropped. "You want to talk about my relationship with Norma?"

"Not really, but I need to know."

"It's accurate. I hate her."

"I was visited by a private investigator hired by your mother to find you."

Sandy's eyes widened and her whole body tightened. Will reached out and touched her on her shoulder. "Don't worry. I didn't tell him a thing. I couldn't even if I wanted to. Doctor patient confidentiality. He did say that you were very close to your mother. That was the first red flag."

"What was the second?"

"He said there was a family emergency and your parents were desperate to find you. It may be true, but it sounded like a ruse to force my hand and dispense information."

Out of habit, Sandy wrapped her arms around her knees, head down, as if turning into a human ball would save her from the reality of the situation. She began to rock. When she was a little girl and her mother would verbally berate her over her appearance or her attitude or for just being Sandy, she would run to her room, sit in her closet, and squeeze her legs until she couldn't feel her arms. Sometimes, she would fall asleep, only to wake up in the middle of the night in a panic, completely disoriented.

Dr. Remini glanced up at the clock. He had already kept his patient waiting for five minutes, but he couldn't abandon Sandy, especially in the state she was in. In a gentle voice, he said, "I think your timing is perfect for entering the shelter. If you want, I'll have one of the nurses take you over there and she can help get you checked in. Tell them about the P.I. so they're aware and they can protect you. Does that sound okay?"

Sandy lifted her head. Her eyes were red from squeezing them tight, her skin flushed. "Yes."

Sandy gathered her gear and waited for the nurse, who told her that her shift would end in about five minutes. Her eyes darted to the left, then the right, wondering if someone in the room was watching her. The longer she waited, the more she questioned her mother's intentions for finding her. Deep down inside, Sandy was glad that her mother was looking for her. Maybe she and her father were worried about her. Maybe they did care after all.

After signing out, the nurse finally grabbed her coat and walked into the waiting room. She searched the crowded space for Sandy, scanning the faces. She wasn't there. Outside, she looked up and down the street. Not a sign of the young woman. The nurse shrugged and walked to her car, assuming Sandy decided to go to the shelter by herself.

Emma felt empty. Her energy level flat. Normally, she would be out of Marilyn as soon as Paige left for school. The house was quiet and she was undisturbed. Today, she wanted to stay put. She wasn't as enamored with the world.

There were times away from the doll, the air felt prickly, like tiny knives were poking her delicate spirit. Other ventures found the air hostile and thick. And this was only in San Francisco, the place where she grew up and vowed to never leave. Following and observing Sandy as she navigated her new environs, Emma was struck by the hundreds, if not thousands, of homeless. Despite government programs and compassionate people who tried to help them, these lost souls were broken. Some damaged beyond repair. And their ranks were growing. Yet people like Sandy's parents lived in mansions. Their net worth in the millions. Their spending off the charts on extravagant items. Jewelry, yachts, cars – all toys to amuse themselves. And as they walked down the street, their diamond bracelets' reflections would cast a privileged light on the tattered, dirty blankets of the destitute, the hopeless.

"Hey soul sista. Get your spirit ass out of there and let's fly. We're on a mission." Gigi was hovering above Marilyn. Paige had placed her doll on the bed in front of her pink, cloud-shaped pillows. On one side of her was a blue pony. On the other was a smurf, his goofy smile a sharp contrast to Marilyn's composed and ever-present stare.

"I'm going to pass today."

Gigi sensed something wasn't right. Emma's attitude was getting increasingly negative, and her energy was sagging. She knew it was imperative that her sister take over Sandy's body sooner than later. She tried again. "Why don't we visit Petal? I don't know about you, but I find her house invigorating. It must be the pervading scent of essential oils. What do you say?"

"Maybe tonight or tomorrow. The darkness is comforting and I'm tired."

Gigi tried another tactic. "I followed Sandy today to the clinic. That cute doctor told her that a private investigator is looking for her. Hired by her mother. I think Norma is up to something and it's not good. Your new body may be in trouble, and I need your help, Emma. Sandy needs our help, so please stop pouting and get out here."

Very slowly, Emma emerged from the doll. The vibrancy from only a week earlier was gone, replaced with a faint glow. It was difficult to make out her features. Her sister's appearance took Gigi by surprise. "Sweetie, we've got to revitalize your soul. You're starting to attach to the doll."

"I don't think that's it."

"It is."

Emma shook her head. "I don't want to be human again."

"Of course you do."

"No. Humans have made a mess of this world. I watched as a man on the street beat his dog for pulling too hard on its leash. That poor animal was howling, and no one did a thing to help it. I'm sick of humans' greed and apathy. Pollution is everywhere. Did you know that they've found mercury in the blood of penguins in the North Pole? The air is dirty, there are wars being fought on three continents. Homicide is up across the country and..."

"Hold it there, Esmerelda! I don't need a lesson on how messed up the human race is, okay? I worked in insurance and believe me, I saw deceit and corruption on both sides of the desk. It was a microcosm of the human condition: ego, greed and power. It sickened me. Why do you think I haven't come back yet in human form? The thought of going through infancy and childhood, living amongst the good people and the bad and the evil, is unappealing. But you, my dear, don't have the choices I have. If you don't get the hell out of Marilyn and into flesh and blood and bone, your existence could conceivably consist of darkness, nearly 24/7. You may have moments of exteriorization, but essentially, you'll cease to exist. Is that what you want?"

Emma stared at her sister. She knew Gigi was right. Her spirit swirled with visions of every ill that humans were capable of and before she realized it, the doom infiltrated every ray of light in her being. Her mood darkened and she watched Gigi's face contort into agony as Emma was sucked back into the doll. "Leave me alone."

Emma's soul was in shutdown mode and, at least for the time being, nothing her sister could do would elevate her.

Outside the Andersen home, Gigi decided her next stop was Pacific Heights. In an instant, she was close enough to Bob Ekhart to kiss him, though she would have preferred to slap him. His body exuded a passive aggressive energy that Gigi was only too familiar with. She watched as he balled his hands into fists, then released them, stretching his fingers wide only to repeat the movement. Norma had just told him that Sandy had been located. His elation turned to anger when he found out why his wife had hired a private eye to search for their daughter. Bob tempered his voice. He didn't want to set Norma off. Her hair-trigger temper unleashed left a lasting emotional scar, if only temporarily, but as Bob touched the scab on his forehead, he feared another physical assault. "You're telling me now that Sandy has a trust fund worth over twenty million dollars?"

Norma twirled her ruby drop earring between her fingers. Make-up deftly applied, hair styled, stunning in an emerald green chiffon shirt and a black skirt, she had wanted to leave the house before Bob awakened. He caught her as she was finishing breakfast. Betsy, the part-time maid, cleared the remnants of the soft-boiled egg and sourdough toast, rinsing off the plates and putting them in the dishwasher. She smirked as she heard Norma groan when Bob padded into the dining room, his thinning hair sticking out in all directions. With his round, dark brown eyes and thin lips, Betsy swore he resembled a baby orangutan. Of the two, she preferred Bob. At least he said 'please' and 'thank you.'

"It's not a big deal. Your mother loved Sandy, but she knew the girl wasn't terribly bright. Remember how long it took her to tie her own shoes? Mother was afraid that our daughter would blow through the trust, so she asked me to look after the money and make sure that it was given to Sandy only when I felt she was capable of handling such a large sum. Finding dear Sandra living in a homeless encampment justifies her concerns."

"Norma, I am your husband and..."

"You certainly are." Norma gave him an insincere smile.

"And I should have been told that my mother had a trust for Sandy. I can't believe she didn't let me know."

Norma grabbed her purse from the dining room chair. "Perhaps she didn't trust you to oversee such a hefty sum. After all, you did take half of our money earmarked for Francisco Downs and invest it in god-knows-what venture. I have to deliver forty million dollars to the bank by the end of next week. You yourself said that your investment won't be able to pay out by then. I simply want to use our homeless daughter's trust fund money. I'll pay it back when you get your investment payout." As she headed for the door, Bob beat her to it and blocked her exit. It was a bold move. His heart was pounding. Norma looked at her husband as if for the first time. "What are you doing? Get out of my way."

From the kitchen, Betsy tiptoed to the doorway between the kitchen and dining room. She wanted to witness Bob the Blob becoming Bob the Bold. It may be the only time, but when Norma saw her in the doorway, she motioned for her to leave. Dutifully, Betsy walked back to the kitchen sink and continued filling the dishwasher. Gigi was also transfixed on the couple. Despite learning about Sandy's love-deprived childhood and verbal beratings, she was still shocked at Norma's intentions.

Arms outstretched against the door, eyes wide, Bob looked more ape-like than before. "How are you going to get Sandy to sign her trust away? She's living on the street for god's sake. You don't think she'll want to have some of that money to live on? What are you going to do, threaten her?"

Norma's turquoise eyes turned a deeper blue, piercing her husband's stare. Instead of caving, Bob stood firm. His arms were getting tired, but he knew if he changed his stance, Norma would win. "Answer me."

Norma softened. She hadn't counted on Bob growing balls and obstructing her plan. She realized that she had better eliminate the interference before it worsened. "If she won't sign the papers, I'll find another way to obtain the money. Besides, this is a moot point. Lonnie confirmed that she'd been staying at the homeless camp, but she wasn't there when he stopped by. One of the bums said they saw her walking off with her backpack and sleeping bag. Can you imagine an Ekhart sleeping on the streets? She's surpassed even my low expectations of her." Norma straightened her skirt and re-adjusted her purse. "Now, do you mind getting out of my way so I can go to the bank?"

Bob put down his arms and stepped aside. He didn't believe Norma's answer, but his arms ached and exerting himself was exhausting. As soon as Norma got into her Mercedes-Benz, she slammed the door. "That little prick. If he even tries to get in my way again, I'll do to him what I'll do to our filthy, little tramp."

The car leaped forward and nearly skidded out of the driveway, leaving Gigi dumbstruck as the severity of Norma's words sunk in.

In the darkness, Emma saw the dog being beaten. It played over and over, like a Facebook post of a video that's on a loop until you hit pause. The more she watched, the harder it was to stop. The howling, the menacing look on the man's face as he whipped the poor animal with its own leash. The image switched off, replaced with an industrial pig farm under water, the result of a hurricane in North Carolina. Twenty to thirty pigs were on the roof of the nearly submerged building, clinging as best they could to the structure, while the drowned bodies of others floated nearby. No efforts were being made to save the animals, brought into this world only to be slaughtered, their flesh consumed. The more she watched, the heavier she felt, like she was being sucked into a vortex. Even if she wanted to stop her downward descent, she didn't know how. But she didn't want to – there were too many humans and non-humans suffering. Mother Earth was suffocating, her lungs choked by the myriad of pollutants infiltrating the delicate lining of her lungs. Emma watched in horror as Mother twisted and turned in agony, trying to fight off the billions of humans vying for her flesh. *I won't hurt you anymore. I promise.*

12

The protein bar was slightly melted, but Lonnie didn't mind. He sat in his car on Center Street, across from the homeless encampment. The camp could be entered a number of ways, however Lonnie was told that Sandy had left from the unofficial entrance, which was near the corner of Center and Goring, so he patiently waited, hoping she would return.

Fifteen minutes later, Lonnie spotted a woman walking up the street. She was carrying a sleeping bag and wearing a backpack. Her hair was pulled back and he could clearly see her face. He picked up the photo of Sandy on the passenger seat and studied it, then looked back up at the woman. "Bingo."

Lonnie grabbed the bank document from the manila envelope, sticking it inside his jacket. There was a big red X next to the signature line and another X next to a blank space for the date. He had no idea what the document contained, and he didn't care. He was paid to deliver the goods, regardless of what those goods entailed. One more swipe of the brush on the small smudge of hair below his lip and he was ready to sew up this assignment.

Sandy was about to cross the street when Lonnie approached her. He tried to look and sound as unassuming as possible, somewhat difficult considering his nearly six-foot-two-inch stature. "Excuse me, Ms. Ekhart? Sandra Ekhart?" Lonnie was taken aback when Sandy gave him a big, expectant smile. He was expecting a rebuff.

"Yes?"

"Um, can I talk to you for a minute?" Lonnie pointed to a bus stop bench. She nodded and followed him over, then sat down next to him, dropping her sleeping bag on the ground.

A gust of wind blew against them and Lonnie got a whiff of

Sandy's body odor. He did his best not to outwardly react to her musty, unwashed stench, but it was hard. He produced the piece of paper and a pen. "Your mother and father have been looking all over the city for you. If you could sign right here, I'll let them know that you're okay, staying over at the encampment, right?"

Sandy's mood changed drastically. She felt nauseous. How could she even think that her parents cared about her welfare when they rarely showed concern when she was a child? She grabbed the document and, without looking at it, shoved it back into Lonnie's hands, causing him to drop the pen. "Don't be like that, Sandy. Your mother said that this…"

"I don't give a shit what Norma said. Tell her to shove it up her uptight ass. We're done here."

Sandy grabbed her sleeping bag and ran across the street. A black Ford pick-up truck slammed on its brakes, skidding to the right, missing her by inches. Unfazed, Sandy continued to the encampment, disappearing behind the myriad of tents and cardboard structures.

Lonnie dialed Norma. He was glad when she didn't pick up. "It's Lonnie. Call me when you get this message." He knew it was pointless to go after her. He wondered if, when the sun went down, Sandy danced with the bottle. If so, getting her signature would be a lot easier. Lonnie stood up and stretched. A deli sign up the street caught his eye and he realized he was hungry. One more glance in Sandy's direction, then he headed to Mort's Deli.

Sandy stopped running when she came to the spot next to Kaitlin's usurped tent, a familiar location. She was too mad to cry. She dropped the sleeping bag on the ground and sat on it with her arms around her body. Her ribs ached and she was breathing heavily. *What an idiot I am*, she thought. *I should have known that Norma and Bob wanted something from me.* In her anger, she failed to look at the piece of paper, so she had no idea what they wanted her to sign or why her signature could be important at all. Sandy owned nothing. She had nothing. Yet, her mother hired a detective to find her.

As her breathing returned to normal, Sandy looked around, expecting to find the tall P.I. standing beside her, but the only person close by was an older man everyone called Gent. Higher than a Macy's Day balloon, the bow-legged, scrawny man stumbled over imaginary impediments, making his way to the entrance of Kaitlin's old tent. He knocked on the wind flap, then yelled, "You in there, Doogie Howser?"

"I ain't Doogie Hoosier. Go away, Gent. Git."

"You sure look like him and I got this bump on my leg and it's killing me. Come take a look at it." Gent pulled up his pant leg and revealed an oozing sore the size of an egg.

"Go away!" The tent shook as the young man scooted to the far end, doing his best to avoid contact with the old man and his troubles.

Gent shook his head and said to Sandy, "Don't doctors have an oblige to treat people? Talk to Doogie. Tell him to help me."

"He's not a doctor, Gent." She looked at his sore and cringed. "That looks really bad. Go to the free clinic and let them help you."

Gent's vacant eyes stared into Sandy's. She wondered if any of what she said registered. With a heavy sigh, she said, "I'll take you there, if you'd like."

"Okay."

She realized she needed to leave anyway. The detective would most certainly return and the next time she may not be able to get away without signing the paper. She also knew that if he didn't find her here, he may go to other encampments and the homeless shelter. Perhaps Dr. Remini would have different advice knowing what the P.I. wanted. Reluctantly, she picked up her sleeping bag and secured her backpack. "Follow me, Gent. It's not too far." Under her breath, she mumbled. "I should know. I was just there."

Across town, the Andersen house was anything but peaceful and serene. Rebecca did what any loving and caring grandmother would have done. Instead of getting a big hug and thank you, her good deed was met with horror and tears. A lot of tears. Paige was beside herself.

"How could you throw Marilyn away without even asking me? I loved her. I love her. Get her back!" Paige grabbed the 'new Marilyn,' an exact replica of her old doll apart from singed hair, soot-covered clothes, and the sickening smell of burned plastic, and threw her across the room. Anaya's gray beret flew off her head and landed a few feet from her body. "Paige!" Rebecca ran over and picked up the doll, then retrieved the beret and placed it on the doll's head. She pulled Anaya's arms down to her sides, then looked sideways at her granddaughter. This behavior was not what she expected. She decided to wait until Paige calmed down before she tried talking to her. In the meantime, she put Anaya back in her box, went out behind the house, then opened the back gate to the alley. That morning, she had placed the doll in the trash can. Rebecca's heart sank when she saw the can on its side, its contents strewn around the dirty concrete ground. Tentatively, she looked inside, hoping to see Marilyn's disheveled body. She saw remnants from last night's dinner: 3 corn cobs minus the corn, lettuce and garbanzo beans from the salad, and the empty chocolate wrapper. Rebecca made a face and stuck her hand into the can, moving trash aside, hoping Marilyn was underneath, even though she knew she had placed her on top of the refuse that morning. She stood the can up and began searching the immediate area. Some of their trash made it across the alleyway. A plastic bag was stuck on an azalea bush. As Rebecca retrieved it, she heard a rustling. She got down on her hands and knees and looked under the bush. A small dog, she guessed a Jack Russell Terrier, was going to town on Marilyn's leg, gnawing it like it was a juicy bone. Without thinking, Rebecca yelled at the dog, "Leave it!" and then she grabbed Marilyn by the hair and pulled. There was a slight tussle, but the dog gave up and trotted down the alleyway as if nothing had happened.

Rebecca examined Marilyn as she walked back into the house. She had more than a few puncture wounds on her left leg and her hair was askew. Her beret was missing, but her face was unscathed. She actually looked serene, as if it was just another busy day in the life of an American Girl doll.

"Marilyn is back, Paige. I'm sorry I threw her away."

Lying on the couch, face down, with her hands over her eyes, Paige stopped crying and sat up. Through teary eyes, she could just make out her doll in her grandma's hands. "What happened to her?" She wiped her eyes.

"She got a little dirty in the trash can. You wait right here and I'll clean her up."

Paige bounded off the couch and held out her hands. "Let me."

Reluctantly, Rebecca handed the survivor over to her rightful owner, then went into the bathroom to grab some cleaning tools. Paige looked Marilyn over very carefully. She took off her own ponytail band, finger-combed the doll's hair, braided it and secured it with the band. She ran her fingers over the bite marks.

"What happened to your leg, Marilyn? Did you get into a fight?" She looked at Rebecca who had returned with a wet, soapy washcloth and a towel.

"She got into an argument with a little terrier." Rebecca offered the washcloth to Paige who took it and began wiping down Marilyn's limbs and face.

From the moment Marilyn was placed, or rather thrown, into the trash can, Emma knew something wasn't right. The energy had shifted. The Andersen home was loving and warm and friendly. This new environment was not. It was lifeless and indifferent. Emma's first inclination was to leave Marilyn and find out what had caused the change. She decided to stay. What did it matter? She was going to remain indefinitely in the doll whether she was surrounded by love or apathy, and this new environment better suited her mood.

Sometime later, Emma felt the energy change drastically. It was charged with a mixture of aggression and excitement. Extremely curious, Emma left the doll. To her horror, she saw a small dog gleefully chewing Marilyn's leg. She screamed for the dog to leave, but telepathy wasn't the animal's strong suit, so it continued to gnaw. All her attempts to chase the Jack Russell away were futile, so Emma was thrilled when Rebecca discovered the ruckus under the bush and rescued Marilyn just in time.

Before returning to her 'body,' Emma decided to remain exteriorized. She watched as Paige lovingly tended to Marilyn, washing off the dirt and food particles from the trash, rearranging her dress, and setting the new doll's beret on top of Marilyn's newly styled hair.

As Paige hugged Marilyn close to her, she said, "You were so brave with that nasty dog. Mamma would be so proud of you." She looked up and Emma swore she was looking at her. "See Mamma? Marilyn is as good as new."

Emma sat next to Paige and put her arms around her. She had no idea if the little girl could feel the outpouring of love that she was emitting, but Emma felt the warmth and love from Paige. Quickly, she re-entered the doll before the yearning for human touch became overpowering.

Rebecca wiped the tears from her eyes. What was she thinking, replacing Marilyn? Her daughter had been gone less than a month. How could it not have occurred to her that the doll was Paige's connection to Janet? Her granddaughter had watched as Marilyn was tossed to her mother, then she was gone from her life. She leaned over and kissed Paige on the forehead. "Sweetie, I'm so sorry I got rid of Marilyn. I don't know what I was thinking. I do know that we have to tell your father about this, so he doesn't make the same mistake."

Paige nodded slightly as she continued to hold Marilyn tight.

"Can't you walk a little bit faster?" Despite holding a sleeping bag and lugging what felt like a 50-pound backpack, Sandy wanted to pick up the pace. Gent trailed her by a few steps, the tattered cuffs of his pants dragging on the pavement. He stopped short and cocked his head.

"I got me a big bump on my leg here. You saw it, right?" Gent was about to pick up his pant leg when Sandy stopped him.

"I saw it, Gent. I really don't want to see it again." She took a deep breath and waited for him to catch up. Once again, they set off, Sandy walking in step with her acquaintance. They had another quarter mile before they reached their destination. "What happened?"

Gent said, "To what?"

"Your leg. The sore."

"The bump? Well, it's not a nice story. You sure you want to hear it?"

Sandy nodded.

Gent scratched his head and small flakes of dandruff floated down from his greasy hair and clung to his dark brown jacket. He reached into his pants pocket and produced a small flask. The once shiny silver container was tarnished and dented. He unscrewed the top and took a gulp. "Want some?"

Conflicted, Sandy stared at Gent's outstretched hand. She didn't want Dr. Remini to see her drunk, but she could taste the alcohol on her lips, going down her throat, making her feel warm. Making her forget her shame. Dulling the ugly world around her. Sandy grabbed the flask, prepared to take a small gulp, but when the whiskey hit her lips, she found it difficult to part with the amber liquid.

"Slow down, Cinderella." Gent yanked the flask away from Sandy, careful not to spill any. "I ain't no millionaire and this stuff don't grow on trees."

"Sorry, but I am doing you a favor. That hideous growth on your leg could be malignant or it could be the beginning of gangrene. Getting you to the doctor could save your leg...or your life. Isn't that worth a couple of swigs from your precious little flask?"

Gent gave the cap an extra twist, then tucked the flask into his pocket. He motioned for Sandy to start walking. It was as if Sandy never said a thing. She figured he had been in survival mode for so long, his hearing was selective. She shrugged and trudged on. Her gait was a little unsteady, but she didn't care. The whiskey had taken the edge off an otherwise tense day.

The clinic was packed, standing room only. Originally, Sandy wanted to see Will. She would have liked to tell him about her encounter with Lonnie and get his advice on how to proceed, but it was clear he wouldn't have time. She left Gent and stood outside the clinic, deciding what to do next. Her inclination was to head over to the shelter and stay there until she could get back on her feet. She could then visit Sandra and hope that she would help her find a job. After all, they had been best friends.

Halfway to the shelter, Sandy walked by a liquor store. She licked her lips as she eyed the small bottles of vodka and scotch on display in front of the first aisle. At last count, $150 remained -- all that was left from her checking account, the one she closed after Sandra booted her out. She still felt a buzz from Gent's whiskey. She wanted to elongate it. She liked being comfortably numb. It didn't take her long to rationalize the purchase. She knew alcohol wasn't tolerated at the shelter. This could be her last hurrah. A celebration for the beginning of her new life.

Sandy raised the bottle to the sky. "Here's to eventual sobriety." She took a nice swig, felt the whiskey burn her throat as it made its way down to her stomach. Sitting with her back against the liquor store's side wall, she smiled as she watched the world get soft and slightly off-center. Life was calmer, situations were less dramatic. Even memories filled with Norma were easier to take.

She never made it to the shelter. After nearly finishing the bottle, Sandy fell asleep on the sidewalk, her body hugging the sleeping bag, her backpack doubling as a pillow. When she awoke, it was dark. She rubbed her neck in an attempt to alleviate the pain shooting down her left side while trying to remember where she was. She reached into her backpack for a bottle of water. It wasn't there.

The neon sign above the liquor store sputtered on and off, its light spilling onto the street and creating a demented rainbow in a mud puddle in the gutter. Sandy looked up at Phil's Liquors' sign and she remembered where she was and where she was supposed to go. "Son of a bitch!" She yelled as she tried to get up, only to lose her balance and fall against the wall.

Cold and disoriented, Sandy hugged her knees close to her body and rocked back and forth. It helped keep her warm, but her mouth was so dry she was spitting cotton, as her Grandbee used to say. She forced herself to get up and head into the liquor store. She grabbed a bottled water and gave the clerk two dollars. She must have looked frightful because the clerk wouldn't make eye contact. She didn't care. Her goal was to rehydrate then make it to the shelter before they closed their doors for the evening.

"How far is it to the Rescue Mission?" Sandy asked the clerk, an elderly Asian man.

"About half a mile, but it's a straight shot up this street and then take a right on Wakona."

"Thanks." Sandy drank half the bottle of water, then gathered her things and slowly made the trek to her new digs.

As she approached the entrance to the Rescue Mission, she was alarmed to see the private investigator walking out of the shelter. He looked to his right, then left. Sandy must have been in the shadows because instead of walking toward her, he crossed the street and got into his car.

Heart pounding, Sandy turned and walked far enough away so she was out of Lonnie's view. She watched him sit in his car, talking on his cell. She wondered if he was reporting to Norma. She also wondered how long he was going to stay parked across the street from the shelter. Again, she chided herself for not paying attention to the document he wanted her to sign.

Lonnie ended the call and took a sip of coffee. His instructions were clear: find Sandy and either get her to sign the document or get rid of her. In his long career as a P.I., he'd had directives that were similar, but never from a mother regarding her daughter. While Lonnie acknowledged that his client was a greedy, cold woman, he could barely criticize her. After all, he took the job and would be successful with or without a signature. He opened the glove box. His Smith & Wesson was in its holster, sitting on top of a map of San Francisco. Lonnie closed the glove box. "Where are you, Sandra Ekhart?" He glanced in the rear-view mirror, hoping he'd catch her walking up the street. Behind him, the sidewalk was empty. Across the street, hidden by a mature elm tree, Sandy stood stick still, her breathing shallow, praying the private investigator would leave. When it was clear he wasn't going anywhere, she decided to go to the one place she was positive he'd never find her.

Emma remembers the event like it was yesterday. She had just gotten off the phone with Vin. Upset, she went out back to vent. She tried to express her displeasure and frustration with a minimal amount of noise, but needed to expel the pent up anger. She figured this would be a good time to plant the apple tree. Digging a deep hole would be an effective release. She grunted as she plunged the shovel into the semi-hard dirt. From the other side of the fence, she heard someone say, "Are you okay?"

Normally, Emma would have lied and told the concerned neighbor that she was great, but there seemed a genuine concern in the woman's voice. "Actually, I'm furious and really upset and I'm sorry to have disturbed you."

"You didn't disturb me." The woman's head appeared above the fence. She was young, in her twenties, with soft, delicate features and clear blue eyes. "I'm Petal. Come on over and I'll make you a nice cup of catnip and chamomile tea."

Emma threw the shovel down, walked over to the fence, and couldn't help but smile back. "I'm Emma and I'm sorry that you had to meet me under these circumstances."

"Not a problem at all. Give me a couple of minutes to straighten up and then bring your anger and stress next door and I promise I'll make it go away."

"You got yourself a challenge."

Ten minutes later, Emma knocked on Petal's door. "Come in!" The first thing that struck Emma was the delicious scent in the air. It was a mixture of chocolate, roses, and lavender. She inhaled deeply. If that didn't immediately bring a sense of calm to her frayed nerves, she was delighted by an array of plants and flowers that were everywhere: wall shelves held African violets in colorful pots, on either side of the door were Ficus trees and a peace lily had its own chair next to the upright piano. She had an urge to touch the maidenhair ferns and the five-foot tall Arrow bamboo.

"I'm in the kitchen," Petal said. Her voice light and soothing.

The counters were covered with small, cobalt blue bottles. They were arranged in a heart formation. All 38 of them, waiting to receive the aromatherapeutic oil that was being prepared. A large bowl filled with small, irregular shaped shiny black rocks sat next to the bottles. Petal was dressed in purple sweats and a light pink tank top with purple letters that said, *Animals are My Friends and I Don't Eat My Friends*. She had her long auburn-colored hair tied back in a braid. A few freckles were sprinkled across her nose and forehead. She smiled as Emma walked into the kitchen and stopped stirring the contents in an eight-quart pot. She turned the stove burner off.

"The tea should be ready soon. It needs to steep a few more minutes. Please sit." Petal pointed to a retro yellow and black Formica table. Salt and pepper shakers in the form of Pepe Le Pew and his girlfriend Penelope Pussycat sat in the middle of the table next to a vase filled with lavender.

Emma picked up the shakers, admiring them. "I used to watch this cartoon as a kid. You weren't even born when Pepe was hopping from flower to flower, smelling them and then picking them for his girlfriend, Penelope."

Petal said, "They were my mom's and no, they don't air the cartoons anymore, especially since Pepe stalked poor Penelope. Back then, it was no big deal, but when you watch it in today's times, Pepe was quite the insensitive lout."

"A lot of the cartoons in my day were very sexist. So were the television programs." She put Pepe back in his spot. "Still, Pepe and Penelope are very cute as shakers."

From the cupboard, Petal grabbed a box of cookies. "Have you tried these? They're raw, vegan brownie bites." She arranged them on a plate, then brought them over to the table with the mugs of tea.

"I haven't, but they sound interesting."

Petal placed the cookies between them. "So tell me, why are you upset?"

Emma shook her head. "You really want to know?"

"Yeah, I do. My dad always said that I'd make a great therapist because I enjoy listening to people's dilemmas." She looked at the bottles sitting on her counter. "I chose another profession, but I'm still a great listener."

Emma took a sip of the tea. "Okay. Here goes. I had just gotten off the phone with Vin, my soon-to-be ex-husband. He's my third and most likely my last husband. The nimrod played around on me in addition to lying about his finances. I feel like an idiot because I ignored the signs. Huge red flags. He called and asked me for forgiveness. Can you believe it? I couldn't. I lost it, big time. When you heard me out back, I was still venting, using the shovel to release the angry vapors. What gets me is that I wasted precious time being with the dolt. He led me to believe that he was wealthy, and I didn't have to work anymore. I was finally going to take the time and write the novel that's been gestating inside my mind." She held her thumb and forefinger an inch away from each other. "I was this close to quitting my job when the bottom dropped out of Vin's financial floor. Now look at me. I'm almost sixty years old. Too old to pen a book. My upper lip went all vertical lines on me, my skin is saggy no matter how much I seem to exercise, and as much as I'd like to be with a man again, I don't know if I'll ever be attracted to someone my age. I see younger men and internally swoon, all the while knowing that they wouldn't give me a second look. I'm invisible to them and that crushes me. If I'm not attracted to the way I look, I doubt I'll ever be attracted to another wrinkled prune." Emma popped a brownie bite in her mouth and washed it down with the tea. "I envy your youth and beauty. You don't think about your skin falling off your bones or your face showing the effects of gravity. I sound bitter because I am. I wish I was one of those women who welcomed getting older. They flaunt their gray hair and smile unapologetically with crow's feet, laugh lines and cheek wrinkles galore. Me? The thought of aging and looking like an old lady terrifies me. I don't want to be an old lady."

When Emma looked up at Petal, she noticed tears in her eyes. "What's the matter? I'm the one who should be crying!"

Petal wiped her eyes. "When I look at you, I see this beautiful, vibrant woman. I don't notice your wrinkles or sagging skin. You have amazing posture and a great figure, despite what you think. You feel this way because of our society's obsession with youth. Can you name one fashion or even celebrity magazine where the womens' entire faces and bodies aren't airbrushed? Every little wrinkle, dimple, and mole are wiped off her from head to toe. Carrie Fisher was on the cover of a magazine, I think it was Elle, and they completely neutralized her face. No wrinkles, no age spots, but no identity. I wasn't sure who it was at first. I had to read the cover. Every human ages. Every being ages. It's not like you're doing it alone. Can you imagine what Cher, Raquel Welch, and Dolly Parton, just to name a few, would look like without plastic surgery?"

"Me!" Emma glanced at her arm against the table and noticed how the skin sagged against the surface. She re-adjusted it, hoping Petal didn't notice.

Petal laughed. "The public has made it nearly impossible for celebrities to look their age. If they do, the tabloids slam them for appearing haggard and worn. If they get nipped and tucked and stretched, the tabloids slam them for getting altered. Very few give the finger to the illusion of looking ageless and I applaud them." Petal got up and stirred the pot on the stove. "Advice about aging coming from a twenty-four-year-old may not be welcome, but I'm going to give it to you anyway. You've been on this planet for almost sixty years. Your life has had highs and lows, unique experiences that you alone have witnessed and moments with others that are invaluable. What you look like is a result of living. Wear it proudly. Wake up every morning, look in the mirror, smile and say, 'I feel wonderful and I'm grateful for everything I have.' Do it even if you don't want to because eventually you will believe it and you'll be happy with who you are. Proud even."

"Do you really think that years of conditioning, believing that a youthful appearance is preferred, if not rewarded, will change by looking in the mirror and giving myself a thumbs-up?"

"Yes I do." Petal moved the large pot from the stove to a hot plate beside the cobalt bottles. She then grabbed what looked like a small turkey baster and proceeded to fill the bottles with the cooled liquid. "The first few times you do it, you may be gritting your teeth and cursing my name. After a while, it will become second nature. You'll look forward to greeting your mirror image and starting the day with a smile and gratitude."

"Sounds kind of hippy dippy to me." Emma stood and walked over to the kitchen counter. "I don't know what you're making, but it smells divine."

"Promise me you'll try it for twenty-one days."

"I promise."

"Good!" Petal held up one of the bottles. "This is a tonic for grounding. Once the bottles are filled, I place a piece of Shungite in each one. Ever hear of it?"

"I work at a bookstore and…"

"Which one?"

"Quinley's on the corner of…"

"I know where it is. I love that bookstore. Sorry to interrupt. Continue."

"Not too long ago, a teenager asked me if we had any books on The Adventures of Shuggy. I had no idea what he was talking about. Turns out, it's a video game. When you mentioned Shungite, I thought of Shuggy. I'm guessing the two aren't related."

"Not quite." Petal picked up one of the rocks and held it up to the light. It was shiny like obsidian and as dense. The light reflected off it, not through it. "Shungite is one of the most powerful stones for restoring emotional balance. It's not a very sexy stone, like rose quartz or amethyst, but it has so many amazing properties."

Petal dropped a triangular piece of Shungite into one of the bottles, screwed on the spray cap and handed it to Emma. "Fresh off the assembly line. Shake it before you use it."

Dutifully, Emma gave it a good shake, sprayed it twelve inches above and in front of her, then walked into it. She inhaled deeply. "I love the scent."

Petal gave Emma a heartfelt hug. "Welcome to the neighborhood. Do me one more favor. Start writing that novel."

Emma rolled her eyes. "Petal, that ship has sailed, hit rough waters and sank."

"Bullshit. Laura Ingalls Wilder was sixty-five when she published her first book, *Little House in the Big Woods* – the first in the series of Little House on the Prairie books. Compared to her, you're a young'un, so get typing."

Emma saluted her. "Yes, Ma'am."

As Emma walked back to her home, her anger was gone. She held up her forearm and inhaled the lingering scent of the spray. She had to smile at the irony. Not more than an hour ago, she was ready to tear her hair out, her rage was so raw. Because of that anger, she met a woman who epitomized grace and serenity, and set Emma on a different path. A path that would unfortunately be cut short.

13

akelo stood patiently while his uncle spoke to the person on desk duty at the Rescue Mission, requesting that she double check to make sure Sandy Ekhart wasn't admitted. He remembered meeting the woman at the soup kitchen because his uncle seemed to show her more attention than the other diners that night. To Makelo, she came across as rude and ungrateful. It wasn't until they were driving home that Will explained the many ways people can end up homeless with nothing but the clothes they're wearing and the bundles they're holding. "I've seen homeless people with shopping carts. I bet there's a lot of stuff in there." His uncle nodded. "How many things from your room could you fit in a shopping cart?" Makelo imagined throwing clothes, toys, his favorite books, PlayStation, and shoes into the metal structure. He turned to Will. "Quite a bit, actually."

"Is your pillow in there and your blanket?" Makelo shook his head. Will continued, "How about your sheets and a lamp? Wait, you'd have nothing to plug it into, so when the sun goes down, so do the lights, unless you end up sleeping under a streetlamp."

Makelo looked down. "It must be so hard for them. And except for others on the street, they're all alone." He fell silent. Will let his nephew sit with his thoughts.

Anne, an angular-faced woman in her thirties with bright red hair and Clark Kent glasses, looked up from the computer monitor. "I'm sorry Dr. Remini, but there's no one here by that name. Rolf is checking the back room, just in case." Moments later, Rolf walked over to the desk.

"No Sandra Ekhart in the back. Any chance she went to the Potrero Hill Shelter?"

Will sighed. "I doubt it, but it's worth checking. I'll give them a call. Thanks for your help. Makelo and I will be in the kitchen."

Makelo added, "Uncle Will and I are going to make his famous vegan chili."

Rolf said, "We're very familiar with that dish. It's my favorite." He looked at Anne for confirmation.

"Sorry. Chili gives me tremendous gas."

"So, you haven't tried my chili?" said Will.

Anne shook her head.

"There's a secret to making chili so you don't toot. I soak and rinse the beans, cook them thoroughly and add ginger, cumin, and fennel. They help to neutralize the gas-producing starches. I think you need to have a bowl of my chili tonight. If it doesn't agree with you, I'd be surprised."

Anne threw up her hands. "Fine. I'll try it. After all, you're the doctor."

It took Sandy the better part of an hour walking from the shelter to Pacific Heights. She turned left on Broadway and headed toward 2705, one of the Gold Coast's most cherished mansions. Her feet ached and she was beginning to get a chill from the relentless wind pushing against her back. The San Francisco gusts could take a temperate, sunny day and turn it into a bone-chilling one.

Sandy remembered that Darby did her shopping every Thursday afternoon, returning to the house by 5:00 p.m. As a child, to escape her mother's demands and verbal barbs, she would hide on the side of the house, between a large cypress and the high brick wall separating them from the McGinty's estate. The tree was probably there before any of the houses replaced the lush landscape, leaving few trees, vestiges of a once flourishing hillside. The concave trunk, created organically, proved a perfect hiding place for a young girl who wanted to disappear into its belly. The rough skin and natural energy of the hundred-year-old tree was more comforting than her mother's touch.

Exhausted, Sandy placed her sleeping bag inside the trunk, eased into the opening, and leaned against her backpack. She closed her eyes and let her hands drop to her sides, but quickly raised her left hand as it brushed up against something foreign. Sandy's heart leapt, fearing that she touched a sleeping animal or worse, a brown recluse or black widow spider. She reluctantly looked down into the trunk and saw a shiny object sticking out of the bark. Curious, Sandy pulled on it, lightly at first, then more forcefully when it didn't budge. Released from the quarter-inch crack in the tree's trunk, Sandy's eyes filled with tears as she stared at a partially rusted lipstick case. It was thin with white lines running up the sides. She tried to pull the top off, but it was rusted shut. Then she tried twisting it, to no avail. "Watermelon punch," she said as a tear dropped onto her pants and was absorbed into the dirty, faded jeans. She held the case tight in her hand until it hurt, the base digging into her palm.

"Sandy?" Darby held two large tote bags filled with groceries. In her late fifties, the Ekhart's cook was short and thin. Her skin was nearly wrinkle-free, due to her aversion to the sun. Of Irish descent, Darby Houlihan knew that, with her fair skin, she was meant to stay in Ireland, where the dewy air and gray skies would keep it supple and smooth. Living in San Francisco for forty years, the woman from Killarney did her best to keep the rays away, owning no less than ten hats. With her pale green eyes and silver hair, Darby easily looked ten years younger.

Sandy opened her eyes. Staring in disbelief, Darby asked again. "Is that you, Sandy?"

"Yeah." She couldn't look at the woman who had cooked her meals since she was a child. It's the person she trekked all this way to see, yet coming face-to-face with the woman who watched her go from first grade to high school senior, the reality of Sandy's living situation hit her hard. She hadn't showered in over a week. Her clothes were dirty, her hair greasy, and she probably inherited the body odor of someone who spent more time inebriated than sober. She inhaled and could detect a slightly sour, pungent scent. Darby must find her revolting. She couldn't even stomach herself. Sandy quickly stood. Her feet still ached, and her body was fatigued. She grabbed her sleeping bag and started to leave. Darby dropped one of the totes and held out her arm, blocking the walkway. She motioned to the side door. "You can go to my room. It's Betsy's day off, so she's in Oakland visiting her sister. I doubt your mother or father have even been in the hallway to my quarters. They wouldn't know if I was operating a prostitution ring out of this place." Darby added, "But I'm not."

"Thank you. If I had somewhere else to go, I would have." She shook her head. "There's no one."

Darby picked up the tote bag full of groceries. "Don't you worry, dear. We'll get you all cleaned up and fed. Then you can tell me what happened."

"Norma is what happened," Sandy said as she followed the cook into the kitchen.

Darby unlocked the door to her bedroom. Sandy had always imagined a room with cheap, second-hand furniture and posters from discount stores, like Ross and TJ Maxx.

Sandy looked in wonderment at the place Darby occupied for close to sixteen years. It reminded her of the Taos signature look out of a Southwestern home furnishings catalog. The predominant colors were bright turquoise, sunflower yellow, and light peach. Sandy half-expected Darby to offer her a Margarita. The cook caught the expression on Sandy's face.

"What were you expecting, something along the lines of a quaint, Irish cottage? My parents left Ireland when I was three. I grew up in Michigan. You're more Irish than me."

"I'm not Irish at all," Sandy said.

"Exactly." Darby led her to the bathroom. Colorful metal fish hung from the ceiling with multi-colored wires. The walls were deep blue. Even the toilet seat was mauve with a seashell design. "My dream is to retire in Santa Fe, New Mexico. I can only put up with your parents for a few more years, then adios, bye bye, Ekharts. I can feel the sun on my pale skin right now, and if it begins to look like an iguana's, I don't care." Darby grabbed a bath towel and a washcloth from the cupboard. "Put your clothes outside the door. I'll bring you some clean ones while you're taking a shower. And really, don't worry about your parents finding you here. They wouldn't have a clue."

While Sandy was in the shower, Darby reheated a big bowl of pasta primavera from the night before. She sliced two pieces off a sourdough baguette, slathered them with margarine, crushed garlic, a sprinkle of celery salt and paprika, and then put the bread in the toaster oven. All the while, Darby was anticipating Sandy's explanation of her condition. Bob Ekhart's side of the family wasn't the friendliest to the cook, but they had always shown his daughter affection and generosity. Norma's kinfolk were tougher to explain. When they weren't fighting over an inheritance, they were flaunting their latest acquisitions. Petty, entitled and pompous best described the lot of them.

After Darby placed Sandy's dinner on a tray and set it down on the coffee table across from her television, she gingerly picked up Sandy's clothes and threw them into the washing machine, along with a pile of cleaning rags. When Sandy emerged from the bathroom, she looked the way Darby had remembered, which wasn't that long ago. She had pulled her hair back in a braid, revealing a fresh scrubbed face. Her eyes weren't as bright and vibrant as they had been, but with the film of dirt removed from her skin, she looked pretty. Darby's beige slacks and lime green pullover sweater fit her perfectly. The bra was a little tight, but Sandy didn't care. She loved the smell of her ensemble. Darby liked to use lavender sachets in the dryer. It delicately scented the clothes, the lingering smell settled on her skin.

"I feel so much better. I can't thank you enough, Darby."

"You're welcome, dear. You must be starving, so eat up. I'll be back after putting away the groceries."

"Do you mind if I watch TV?"

"Heavens, no." Darby picked up the remote and turned the television on. She placed it by the tray. "Knock yourself out."

Sandy flipped through the channels until she came to a rerun of *Modern Family*. She would have loved to shove as much food in her mouth as possible, the hunger pangs were so intense. Instead, her upbringing won out and she ate as if seated at the formal dining table upstairs. She also wanted to savor every bite. The pasta was cooked al dente with broccoli florets, mushrooms, zucchini, slivers of red pepper, and cauliflower bathed in a garlic olive oil tomato sauce. It was one of Darby's signature dishes and had always been one of Sandy's favorites.

"I see you've enjoyed the meal," Darby said as Sandy finished the last piece of garlic bread. She sat down next to her on the sofa.

"It was delicious."

Darby muted the television, then turned to her guest. "What happened, dear?"

Sandy eyed a bottle of port sitting on the end table under the window. "Do you mind if I have a glass of port?"

Darby looked her right in the eyes. "Yeah, I do. I found a near empty bottle of vodka in your backpack. I'm not scratching that itch.

What happened to you? When you were in high school and college, I don't remember you ever coming home drunk."

Sandy stared at the wall, not wanting to make eye contact. "I'm not sure. I moved in with Sandra and she said I could stay with her until I found my own place. Six months later, she kicked me out."

"Did you look for an apartment?"

"I was going to. First, I had to find a job."

Darby looked confused. "Your parents told me that you had a job when you moved out."

Small drops of rain hit the window, sporadic at first, then harder. It was warm inside, a comfortable seventy degrees, but when Sandy looked out the window, she shivered. The thought of being outside for another night sickened her. A crack of thunder made her jump.

"You didn't have a job, did you?"

Sandy shook her head. "I wanted to leave this place so badly that I told everyone I got a job as a paralegal. I figured once I escaped from Norma's prison, I could easily find a job. The problem was, there were so few openings, and I didn't have any experience."

"Sandy, your father has connections. Why didn't you ask him for help?"

"I wanted to do it on my own. I wanted to show them that I could make it." She put her head in her hands. "But I couldn't. Norma was right. I'm an incompetent, worthless idiot. I stopped looking for a job after a couple of months. Then I stopped paying Sandra rent. I don't blame her for telling me to leave."

Darby went over to Sandy and put her arm around her shoulders. "I bet your parents would let you come back, just until you get on your feet again."

"No!" Sandy pushed Darby's arm away and went over to the window. She watched the rain pelting the glass. "My mother hired a private investigator to find me. And he did."

"Maybe she was worried about you."

"Not a chance. She wants something from me. I have no idea what it could be, but he wanted me to sign something. It looked like a legal document. I refused. Later that day, I saw him in front of the homeless shelter, waiting for me. That's when I came here."

"Is there something you're not telling me?"

Sandy looked confused. "Like what?"

"I don't know. The document must have been some sort of release form. Do you have a savings account or a trust fund?"

Sandy laughed. "Darby, do you honestly think I'd be living on the streets of San Francisco if I had more than $150...I mean, $110 to my name?"

"No. If your mother is that intent on finding you, though, there must be money involved. I'll try to find out more, but your parents are pretty tight-lipped when I'm around. Actually, they don't talk that much to each other anymore. Heavens knows why they stay together."

Sandy was about to make a guess when the washing machine buzzed, signaling the end of the cycle. Darby put the clothes into the dryer, turned the knob to fifty minutes and pressed the button. When she returned to her room, Sandy had unmuted the TV and was watching Judge Judy. "I miss hot meals and a bed, clean clothes, and a shower, but television? Not really."

Darby agreed. "I watch more movies on the DVD player than TV shows."

Sandy hit the 'off' button in the middle of Judge Judy berating the defendant. "I know why my parents stay together. Divorce isn't an option for dear old dad. I overheard him telling Uncle Don that no one in the Ekhart family has divorced and he's certainly not going to break the tradition. How could he not be miserable with Norma? And Mommy Dearest loves Bob's money. His family has more prestige and nobility than hers. She's not giving that up. Let's face it. They belong together. Two little rotten peas in a defective pod." Sandy looked down at herself. "And this little pea didn't fall far from the pod."

Darby was about to assuage Sandy's badly bruised ego when she heard the front door from upstairs slam shut. "I have to fix dinner. Make yourself comfortable." She went over and lifted the bottle of port, tucked it under her arm and closed the door behind her. She could hear Norma stomping around. Even though her voice was louder and more shrill than usual, Darby couldn't make out what she was saying.

"What do you mean, you lost her?" Norma was apoplectic. She had to come up with the remaining twenty million dollars in less than two weeks. She knew once Sandy signed over her trust, releasing the funds could take as long as eight working days.

Lonnie wasn't used to failing. His success rate was near perfect. If he couldn't find Sandy again, he knew that Norma would trash his reputation within her circle of friends. And it was a large, very wealthy circle. "Don't worry. I'll find her."

"I am worried. You have to find her and fast." Automatically, her hand went up to her earring. She began twirling it, pressing the precious ruby hard. Too hard. She twisted it right off its gold stem. "Damn it!" Norma threw the broken earring across the floor. It skittered into the study, the Persian rug ending its run. "Call me as soon as you find her."

"Definitely. If I…when I do locate her and she refuses to sign the paper, what do you want me to do?"

Norma took off her shoes and began to ascend the stairs to her bedroom. She looked down at her manicured nails. "Get rid of her."

There was a pause on the other end of the line. Then, "That will be extra."

"I know." Norma opened the door to her walk-in closet and threw her shoes toward the shoe rack. "I need the signature, or I need to be childless. Get it done."

"Will do, Norma."

"Mrs. Ekhart, Lonnie."

"Yes, Mrs. Ekhart."

Norma practically ripped her dress off and threw it on the closet floor. "What am I going to do if he can't find her?" she muttered as she slipped on a pair of slacks and a light blue cashmere pullover sweater. "Goddamn Bob and his dubious investments. What was he thinking?"

"Are you talking about me, dear?" Bob opened the closet door and smiled.

Norma glared back at him. "What are you so perky about?"

"I should be asking you why you're in such a nasty mood, but then that's a rhetorical question, isn't it?"

"Fuck off, Bob. I have a lot on my mind."

"Keep your voice down. Do you want Darby to hear?"

"I don't give a damn who hears. You want me to open the windows and shout it out to the world how my idiot husband took twenty million dollars and squandered it?" Norma started for the window, but Bob grabbed her arm, pulling her away from the window. Stunned by Bob's assertiveness, the second time in a matter of days, Norma yanked herself free from her husband's grasp. "Someone's been eating his Wheaties…or you're having an affair. Which one is it Bob, Wheaties or a sweetie?"

Bob was about to answer, then thought better of it. No sense prolonging the conversation. Without another word, he turned and walked out of the room, leaving Norma to wonder what caused her husband's unexpected pluck. For almost thirty years, she controlled the marriage, from how they raised their daughter, to where they vacationed, who their friends were, to their investments. Until now. Norma instinctively went to grab her earring. Realizing it was broken, she methodically took it off, then took off the other one, placing them in an antique tray on her dresser. She walked out of the room as if hypnotized. It was the only way she could deal with the recent events without going full-on crazy.

Marlo stared intently at the computer screen. She removed her black horn-rimmed glasses and wiped away a tear as it ran down her cheek. The headline read, *Seven Horses in 10 days Dead at Del Mar Racetrack*. More than 90 percent of the breakdowns were caused by pre-existing injuries to the horses' legs. Despite veterinarian inspections, the injuries weren't detected. When she first began researching horse racing, she assumed that she would read about a few unscrupulous breeders and rigged races. She had no idea it was such a nefarious sport. More like a blood sport, she thought. Marlo knew that horse racing had been around for centuries. What she didn't realize was that it was a 300 billion dollar industry. With the financial stakes high, horses were bred for speed. Those who didn't make the cut were many times killed or sold to slaughterhouses. Many horses were raced too young, before their skeletal structure was mature, causing injuries, many permanent. Drugs, legal and illegal, were administered to the horses before a race, numbing an injury. A staggering twelve horses a week died on American racetracks, if not while racing, then away from public view, behind a hospital-like curtain, shot in the head. Their lifeless bodies hauled away, dumped in a junkyard or shipped to Canada or overseas where they'd be served on a plate alongside a baked potato and glazed carrots.

Marlo clicked on a link to an article about rampant drug use in the racing industry when she heard Rick coming up the stairs. She quickly took off her glasses and put them in the desk drawer behind a ream of copy paper. She removed the ponytail band from her hair and let the golden-brown locks fall past her shoulders. Rick walked in just as she was closing her laptop. She walked over to him.

"There's my gorgeous wife." Rick put his arms around Marlo's waist, hugging her close and kissing her.

Marlo pulled away first and gave her husband a light kiss on his nose. "How was your day?" she said as she rubbed his shoulders.

"Much better now. I spent half of it talking to the contractors for Francisco Downs. You would think they're building the Taj Mahal."

"About that. The racetrack. Can't you invest our money somewhere else?"

Rick put his hand up to his eyes and pushed hard against the brows as if staving off an oncoming headache. "Marlo, sweetie, don't start. The industry isn't as evil as you think it is. There are some bad apples, but for the most part the racehorse owners and jockeys love those animals. This is a profitable investment for *my* money."

"I wish I could believe you, but from what I've read, the abuse is widespread."

"Don't tell me, you've been on the animal rights sites? Those organizations want to eliminate all animal entertainment. The worst of the lot is PETA. Those fanatics don't even want us to have pets. Our racetrack will make sure that everyone is above board. Believe me."

"The New York Times did a huge exposé on the industry, not PETA or the Humane Society. It's a great article. You should read it. So many racehorses die on and off the track and suffer all sorts of problems like joint disease, pneumonia, and stomach ulcers." Marlo opened her laptop. "Please read the article." Without her glasses, the screen was blurry, but she managed to find the right keys.

Rick came around the desk and before Marlo could bring up the New York Times website, he closed the computer, nearly catching his wife's hands in the process. "Enough already. I don't want to hear any more about this 'horrible industry' that, by the way, is one of the oldest sports in history. You think it would have survived if it was replete with abuse? I've visited the horse farms and talked to the owners. They treat these animals better than most parents treat their children. The stalls are spotless and the horses are fed the highest quality grains available. Marlo, honey, you've seen these horses run. It's poetry in motion. You can see how much they love it. And they want to win. You think they're being forced to run that fast?"

Arms crossed, Marlo wasn't buying it. Under her breath, she said, "Jockeys use a shock device."

"What?"

"Some jockeys shock the horse with a device as they approach the finish line."

Rick threw his hands up. "They can't do that. It's illegal."

"So are all the drugs that are given to the horses, but they're still used."

Rick softened his stance. He knew Marlo was stubborn and the more he argued, the further she would dig her beautifully shaped, perfect heels into the ultra-plush carpet that he bought. "Tell you what. Why don't we take a drive out to Stone Meadows Farm this weekend? Shelly Stone's been raising thoroughbreds since before you were born. You can ask her all the questions you want. Bring the damn article. I don't care. To tell you the truth, I was going to take you out there anyway."

Marlo realized that this was one argument she wasn't going to win. Not now. Rick was set on investing in Francisco Downs, and she knew he wasn't about to see her side. She gave him a quick kiss and said, "That sounds fine, honey." She looked up at the clock on the wall. "It's almost time for dinner. Why don't you change and I'll go see if Alice needs any help?"

Rick laughed. "I pay Alice to do all the work. All you have to do is sit down and enjoy the meal. What's she making, by the way?"

"I believe we're having chateaubriand with scalloped potatoes and asparagus."

"Sounds delicious."

Marlo didn't respond.

14

When Will Remini was with his patients, they had his full attention. His concern for their health was genuine, but when they left his office, he didn't really think about them until their next appointment. If he did, his life would constantly revolve around illness, poverty, homelessness, and disease. Rarely had he ever taken such an intense interest as he had done with Sandy. He had to admit that part of it was his fascination with her chosen lifestyle. She was part of San Francisco's royalty. Now she was missing, and he was determined to find her.

It was nearly 10:00 a.m. After placing the dirty dishes in the sink, Will returned to his balcony to finish reading the paper before heading over to the homeless encampment where he assumed Sandy had lived. Opening the Business section, he grimaced. An article on the front page read, *Plans to Begin Construction on Target for San Francisco Racetrack*. The article stated that, despite a delay from an environmental group questioning the project's proximity to Sternwood Creek, they would be breaking ground within the next couple of months. Will jotted down the name of the group and continued reading.

As he pulled up to the homeless encampment, Will was surprised to see seven Harley Davidsons parked on the curb. Sensing trouble from a motorcycle gang, he quickly parked and ran across the street. Cellphone in hand, he was ready to call the police. Expecting violence, he was shocked to instead find a group of black-clad women handing out a variety of items to the camp's residents. As he approached, he saw the emblem of the viper wrapped around a large red V.

"I'm guessing you don't live here." Ronnie smiled as she noted Will's appearance: Clean, white button-down shirt tucked into intentionally faded blue jeans and loafers. She held out her hand and Will shook it. "I'm Veronica, but my friends and enemies call me Ronnie."

"Will Remini. Nice to meet you. So…you're a viper?"

"A vegan viper. Never heard of us? I'm crushed."

"Would it help alleviate the pain if I told you I'm also vegan?"

Ronnie's blue eyes lit up. It had been a while since she met a man she was attracted to, especially since her sphere of vegan suitors was fairly small. The vegan community in the Bay Area was larger than most. Still, she had trouble meeting men her age that shared her lifestyle and her passion for animal rights. "Elaborate, please."

"Let's see. I'm a doctor at the free clinic, the one on Wilson. I try to convince my patients to eat a plant-based diet, but you can imagine how difficult that can be when they tend to eat whatever they can afford or pick up off the street. I do make a mean vegan chili at the soup kitchen every Wednesday night."

"Ever been to the Big V?"

"What vegan hasn't? It's one of my favorite restaurants. Their carrot cake is amazing."

"Good answer. You're looking at the owner and chef." Ronnie pulled a sweater out of her bag and handed it to a reed thin, teenage girl. She thanked Ronnie and immediately put it on, covering her torn short-sleeved shirt.

Will was beyond impressed. The woman who stood before him was talented, compassionate, generous, and very attractive. "I always thought that if I didn't become a doctor, I would open a restaurant. My chili may pale in comparison to your skillfully prepared dishes, but I still think you should come by on Wednesday and give it a professional taste test."

"I'd prefer to try your chili in the comfort of my home. Are you game?" Ronnie was determined not to let Will get off easy. Her confidence was unwavering.

"Only if it's in the comfort of my home." Will took a business card out of his pocket and handed it to her. "Do you have a card?"

"When I'm not handing out goodies, I'm at the Big V. You can call me there. Glad we bumped into each other. By the way, why are you here?"

"I'm actually looking for a woman, a patient of mine, who I believe lives here or she used to." Will scanned the crowd, which was around forty. He'd never been to the encampment before and didn't realize how big it was. There were tents and lean-tos in every direction.

"Do you have a photo?" Ronnie said.

"I do." Will pulled a piece of paper out of his back pocket. He unfolded it and showed the picture to Ronnie. "I took it off the internet. Her name is Sandra Ekhart."

"Of *the* Ekharts?"

"Yup."

"Ouch. That's gotta hurt. One day she's closing her eyes in a gold-plated bed, the next day she's removing rocks from underneath her cardboard box so she can sleep." Ronnie looked out over the crowd. "Do you know what happened?"

Will raised his eyebrows. "Not really, but if I did, I couldn't tell you. Doctor patient privilege."

Ronnie hit her forehead with her hand. "Of course. How invasive of me. I just figured, both being vegans, we're in the same club."

"Nice try." Will lightly touched Ronnie's shoulder. "It was good meeting you and I'll definitely give you a call for chili night."

"At your place," Ronnie reminded him.

"At my place." As he walked through the crowd hoping to spot Sandy, he looked back at Ronnie. Being born and raised in San Francisco, men tend to grow up around a lot of strong, independent women. Feisty females were synonymous with San Francisco. His sister was like that, and he appreciated and respected it. Will wondered if Ronnie was really that self-aware and confident or she put on a great outer layer. He'd find out on chili night.

The energy from hugging Paige lasted longer than Emma expected. It faintly tingled and tiny points of heat pulsated upon her soul. She liked it. But didn't want to. The thought of re-inhabiting a human body left her feeling dizzy. Why would she put herself through the heartache and disappointments again? Life can be indescribably beautiful and full of love and joy and excitement. It was knowing that billions of beings were in pain all over the world and she was helpless to do anything about it. Coming back to earth would only bring the same feeling of guilt and helplessness.

"Houston, we have a problem."

Emma knew Gigi couldn't stay away long. Her sister wouldn't accept her refusal to find another body without a fight. Typical Gigi. It reminded her of the time the girls were in their early teens. Emma tried out for the talent show at school, playing guitar and singing a song she wrote about their dog, Parness. The family lavished praise on the budding singer/songwriter. At the audition, Emma sang her heart out. When it was over, she hadn't noticed a few of the judges giggling. Apparently, the dog's name in song sounded like penis, especially in the stanza, *You're a big one, Parness, a big one indeed*. She was accepted into the talent show, but felt humiliated and, when she got home, went to her room and cried. She made it clear, through her tears, that she wasn't going to participate. Undaunted, Gigi told her to knock it off. "Change our dog's name in the song, that's all. It's not a big deal. I heard that Paul McCartney had the same problem at his high school talent show. He changed the lyrics and look what became of him! Chin up, Esmerelda. There are going to be a lot worse problems in your life than this." She was right. Emma turned Parness into Clyde, tweaked the lyrics, and ended up winning top prize at the talent show.

Gigi persisted. "You still in there, Esmerelda Conklin Banks?"

"I'm here. What is it?"

"Huge news. Come on out and I'll tell you."

"Tell me now."

Gigi hovered an inch in front of Marilyn's glassy, vacant eyes. "Norma's planning on having her daughter killed." Upon her declaration, she assumed her sister would pop out of the doll like a jack in the box. Instead, she was met with silence. "Did you hear me?"

"Sure did."

"I'm not making this up just to get you out of your slump."

Emma snickered. "My slump? How about humanity's slump? Humanity's permanent slump is their inability to get out of the mindset of greed and power. Jealousy and revenge. If Sandy's killed, her death will be one of many at that moment, that day, that month, that..."

"Got it. You made your point. People are hopelessly messed up."

"Exactly."

"Fine. I'm leaving. For good. Have a nice life in total darkness for who knows how long." Before Gigi took flight, a small voice emanated from the doll.

"Is she really planning on having Sandy killed?"

Gigi didn't answer. She waited for her sister to exteriorize. After a while, she heard a heavy sigh, then silence. Crushed by Emma's apathy, Gigi left Paige's room, wondering if she would return. She shot into the sky, not knowing where she was headed. Not caring. She wanted to get as far away from earth and her sister as possible.

Light years away from the planet she used to call home, her ethereal body longing for support, Gigi settled into a cloud of lights, emitting a feeling akin to a long, enveloping hug. They were varying shades of blue and violet, and Gigi's white light absorbed as much of the 'hug' as she could. They recharged her. They offered her unconditional love. As she immersed herself in the cloud, she thought of Emma's hopelessness. She could understand her sister's reluctance to being human again. Gigi's human death was two years ago, yet she remained a spirit, not knowing if she wanted to return to earth and start over. The traumatic birthing process, infant to toddler, the frustration of not being able to communicate until you'd mastered the language, then the teen years when you didn't know what your hormones were going to make you say or do. Or not do. Young adulthood, then middle-age. Gigi never made it to becoming a senior. Not in the previous life. But her many incarnations throughout the years had afforded her the opportunity to die of old age. And she wasn't sure if the pleasure of inhabiting human form was worth the pain and trauma also experienced. No life could escape tragedy, drama, pain, sorrow.

Existence was so simple as a spirit. It was also peaceful and serene and loving and pure. It didn't involve any of the human foibles. Greed and the thirst for power didn't exist. There was no ego. Despite a fulfilling career and happy marriage, Gigi struggled with the problems facing humanity. Every day, she would sit down to breakfast and read the San Francisco Chronicle. The front page almost always screamed of death, environmental crises, terrorist threats, kidnappings, shootings, and corruption. Any good news was relegated to the Towns or Lifestyle Sections. The more she read about the ills of the world, the more she felt compelled to cancel her subscription to the paper, use the television only for movies, and forbid anyone from talking about the news. She knew it wasn't realistic, but maybe it was one of the ways she could live a life where she didn't feel guilty for being a 'have' amongst so many 'have-nots.'

Gigi had to do something very soon to convince Emma to take over Sandy Ekhart's body. She knew that Lonnie King would find her and, if he couldn't get her signature, she would be joining the spirit world sooner than she expected.

15

Sandy hadn't slept so soundly in weeks. She fell asleep on Darby's couch – even though her hostess insisted that she take her bed – and had a dreamless night. When Darby's alarm awoke her at 6:00 in the morning, Sandy wasn't tired. She did have a slight residual hangover from the day before, but nothing like she was used to at the homeless camp. She pushed the cotton blanket off her body and stood. The pajamas Darby had given her to wear were a little short in the legs and sleeves, but were clean and had that intoxicating lavender scent. She stretched her arms toward the ceiling, feeling some of the aches and pains she accumulated over the days of sleeping on the ground. The thought of leaving the warm, safe room made Sandy shiver. She wondered how long Darby would let her stay. On the chair next to her backpack, Sandy's clean clothes were folded.

"Good morning," Darby said as she walked past Sandy on her way to the bathroom, wearing pink and white polka dot pajamas and holding her work dress. "I'll only be a few minutes, then the bathroom is yours."

"Thanks."

"I hope you got some sleep last night."

Confused, Sandy said, "I slept great. Why?"

"You were talking in your sleep. Even shouted a few times. Most of it was gibberish, but you did say, 'Thank you, Will' more than once.

"Wow. I didn't think I dreamt at all last night. It's a good thing your room is miles away from my parents' bedroom."

"You can say that again." A few moments later, Darby emerged from the bathroom. She was wearing the same uniform that she'd donned when Sandy was growing up: a light gray knee-length dress, hair net when she was preparing the food, and ultra-practical black shoes with rubber soles. She tucked some errant hairs into the hair net. "So, who's Will?"

Eager to use the toilet, Sandy zipped past Darby and closed the bathroom door after her. "He's a doctor at the free clinic. He's been very helpful."

"Anything else about the good doctor you want to tell me?"

"Like what?"

"Is he a looker?"

"Darby!"

"Is he?"

"Yeah, he's pretty cute. Too cute to look twice at me, especially when he's seen me covered in dirty clothes, smelling like booze. I'm such a loser."

Sandy flushed the toilet. She went to the sink to wash her hands and found a new toothbrush and toothpaste next to a glass. She smiled as she picked up the soap and lathered up her hands, then washed her face. Darby knocked on the bathroom door. "Come on in."

"I have to fix breakfast for your parents. Give me about a half hour and I'll bring you something, too." Darby put her hands on Sandy's shoulders. "I've known you for a very long time. You haven't had an easy life dear, despite living in this gorgeous home. I know what it's like living with your mother and father. There were so many times I wanted to say something. Of course, I couldn't without being fired. This may sound trite or unrealistic considering what you've gone through, but I'm asking you to believe in yourself. Don't go back on the streets. You can stay with me while you look for a job. Use my laptop if you'd like."

Sandy turned to face the cook and hugged her hard. "Thank you so much."

With a lump in her throat, Darby said, "You're very welcome."

Dressed in a clean pair of jeans and a long-sleeved T-shirt, Sandy sat down to her second warm meal in two days. The pancakes were smothered in pure maple syrup and the orange juice was freshly squeezed. Sandy picked up the oversized mug of coffee and took a sip. "Kona coffee. Only the best for Norma and Bob." The pancakes were fluffy, just as Sandy remembered them. She had always admired Darby's cooking but realized how much she took it for granted after moving out and living with Sandra, whose cooking skills were on par with the school chef at Trinity High. At least her roommate had rudimentary kitchen skills. She knew how to boil spaghetti and pour store bought marinara sauce on it with a sprinkle of parmesan cheese. She also made a great mushroom omelet. Sandy's culinary calling? The closest she got to a pot or pan was interrupting Darby cleaning them to thank her for yet another splendid meal.

Sandy eyed the bottle of port and licked her lips. She could hear Darby in the kitchen. It sounded like she was rinsing off the dishes and putting them in the dishwasher. It wouldn't hurt to have a small taste, she thought, just enough to make the morning last a little longer before looking for a job. Sandy walked over to the end table where the bottle sat next to a vase in the shape of a four-leaf clover, holding a solitary white rose. She leaned over and inhaled the flower's soothing fragrance. A writing pad with a mechanical pencil also shared the space. She was about to pick up the bottle when she heard Norma's voice. She froze and felt her heart in her throat. Quietly, she went over to the door.

"Darby, I'm having guests over for dinner tonight. I'd like you to make leg of lamb, your rosemary roasted potatoes and glazed carrots. Surprise me with dessert."

"Yes, Mrs. Ekhart."

Norma turned to leave, then stopped. "Did you know that Sandy is missing?"

"You mean she's not living with her friend anymore?" Darby tried to sound as nonchalant as possible, despite feeling a little weak in the knees.

Norma shook her head. "I don't know if she'll try to contact you, but if she does, please let me know as soon as possible. Will you do that?"

"Of course."

"Good. Oh, I left my coffee cup on the dining room table. Could you please get it?"

"Yes, Mrs. Ekhart."

Without another word, Norma ascended the stairs to the dining room, grabbed her purse from the entryway table and walked out the front door.

Darby retrieved the Lenox Westchester cup. She examined the gold border with its elaborate etching, carefully turning it in her hands. Not long ago, she googled the Ekhart's dinnerware and discovered the sixty-piece set was worth close to $6,000. Sandy was homeless and Norma was drinking coffee out of a $100 cup.

Respecting her privacy, Darby knocked on the door before she walked into her room. She looked around her small living space, expecting to find her guest watching television or using her laptop. "Sandy, are you in the bathroom?" Not waiting for an answer, Darby walked over to the bathroom, its door ajar. She knocked. "Hello."

Her heart pounding, she went back into her room and that's when she noticed Sandy's backpack and sleeping bag were gone. Her eyes shot over to the end table. The bottle of Ficklin 10 Year Tawny Port was still there.

On the floor, under the coffee table, sat a small, partially rusty tube of lipstick. Darby knew it wasn't hers. She couldn't remember the last time she wore anything but lip balm with SPF 30. She opened the end table drawer and set it next to her playing cards. Then she prayed that Sandy would be okay.

With barely enough time to grab her things, Sandy practically ran down the street. The sound of her mother's voice shook her to her core. She was afraid that Norma would sense she was there, in the house, under her roof. She couldn't take the chance. Every time a car went by, she hunched down, burying her face in her jacket. A ball cap covered her head. Her new clothes, thanks to Darby, felt good on her skin, her clean skin. They kept her warm. She tucked the sleeping bag under her arm and stuck her hands in the jacket pockets. The fingers on her right hand touched what felt like thin pieces of paper. She pulled them out and discovered ten, twenty-dollar bills. Stuck between them was a bright pink post-it note. *Wish it was more, Love Darby*. Sandy smiled to herself. The woman was a life saver. If she survived this ordeal, she didn't know how or when, but she would repay Darby. There was one other place where Sandy felt safe. It would take her over an hour to get there, but she was convinced it was her only option.

Norma Ekhart made a left out of the driveway and headed to Annie Corolla's estate less than a mile away. Annie had called a special meeting of the Beckford Women's Group to discuss their latest fundraiser, a benefit dinner for the Special Olympics. She glanced over at her purse on the passenger seat and grabbed her phone. At that moment, she passed a young girl wearing a baseball cap, sporting a backpack and a sleeping bag tucked under her arm. Catching her image in the rearview mirror, Norma snickered, "I wish those bums would stay out of our neighborhood. They denigrate the ambiance."

Will was starting to worry that Sandy may be in danger. He knew someone could easily disappear, even in a city only 49.2 square miles, but he thought that he would have found Sandy or that she would have contacted him by now. He didn't know if she was safe or still being pursued by the private investigator. He went to the Portrero Hill Shelter on the corner of Rhode Island and 18th Street, hoping Sandy would be staying there. The converted three-story Victorian, with its orchid-colored trim against a purple façade provided food and shelter for forty people. Will was impressed with the atmosphere. The residents were given clean clothes, shoes, and toiletries. The kitchen staff prided itself on serving healthy meals, regardless of getting flak from some of their patrons. The director, Lisa Wimple, a petite Asian woman with her bleached blonde hair in a short pageboy, checked their roster, the waiting list, and even the meticulous notes taken by the front desk when visited by a potential resident. She told a disappointed Will that Sandy hadn't been by, but took his number and promised to call if she did. She added that he was the second person asking for Sandy in two days. Will was pretty sure he knew who the first one was.

By the time Sandy arrived at the Sutter Street Apartments, she was sweating. The sun decided to break through the fog and the wind was on vacation. As much as she appreciated not having to ward off a chill in the air, the weight of her backpack against her sweater made her perspire as did the sleeping bag she was now carrying in front. She wiped her brow and rested against the side of the building despite dirty looks from a young couple. She may have been clean and her clothes freshly pressed, but lugging a bulky sleeping bag was a dead giveaway that she was a transient.

Gigi had been following Sandy since she woke up that morning. She had been hoping that her sister would be joining her, but Emma's resolve to stay in the doll hadn't wavered, so Gigi continued to observe the poor little rich girl. She was thrilled to see her appearance improve as well as having been given $200, though Gigi was convinced that most of the money would be used for liquor.

Gathering her courage, Sandy pushed the button for apartment 324. After a while, a voice crackled over the intercom. "Yeah?"

"Greg?"

"That's me."

"It's Sandy. Sandy Ekhart." Silence on the other end. "Sandra's ex-roommate?"

"I know who you are."

The tone in Greg's voice made Sandy reconsider her visit. He sounded guarded, unfriendly. She continued, despite the hesitation, partly because she was desperate. "I was wondering if I could come up and talk."

Without another word, Greg pressed the buzzer long enough for his visitor to open the security door.

She knocked on apartment 324 and when the door opened, Sandy was greeted with a terse smile. His face dropped when he realized she was probably holding and wearing everything she owned. Sandy caught Greg's look and averted her eyes. When she first met Greg, she had just moved in with Sandra. She was thrilled to be living on her own and it showed. Instead of the shy, introverted young woman who had lived with her parents, Greg had been introduced to someone who had a sense of humor and a small hop in her step. They would sometimes chat outside his apartment. Both were fans of the 49ers and occasionally they would walk down the street to Big Al's Billiards and play pool. Despite Sandy's attraction to Greg, he was comfortable with their friendship and never intimated that he would be interested in taking it to the next level.

"How's it going?" Sandy tried to sound upbeat, but the judgmental look on Greg's face gave away his disdain.

"Doing okay. Hanging in there, you know?"

"Yeah."

"Sandra told me you moved out."

"She was driving me crazy. I had to get out that nut house. Any chance I could crash at your place for a day or two, only until I find my own place?" Sandy peered behind Greg and noticed a sectional. "I could sleep on the couch. You wouldn't even know I'm there. And I could cook for you, too."

Greg pulled the door closer to his body, shielding his living room from Sandy's view. "Sandra told me that she kicked you out." He waited for a response. When he didn't get one, he continued. "She also said you didn't have a job. Is that true?"

Sandy nodded.

Greg looked once more at the sleeping bag and backpack. "I'm sorry, but it just won't work. Have you tried the shelter on Portrero Hill? I hear it's nice."

Sandy shook her head and turned to go.

"Sandy?"

Expectantly, she turned back, "Yes?"

"I wish you the best of luck. I really do."

Without trying to sound too sarcastic, she said, "Thanks, Greg. I'm sure you do."

Gigi watched as Sandy walked, more determined than ever, to Rolley's Liquors. "That didn't take long" she said to herself.

"Is that the girl Emma was going to take over?" Lloyd Banks hovered close to his daughter while staring intently at Sandy.

"Is going to, not was, Dad."

"And how do you plan on changing Emma's mind? You know how stubborn she is, even without a body to stamp her feet and scream at the top of her lungs."

Gigi laughed. "Aren't you going back in time a little too far? It's been a while since Emma had temper tantrums."

Lloyd said, "Yeah, but it feels like they were yesterday. That kid knew how to get attention." He watched Sandy walk out of the liquor store, her hand holding a paper bag. She jaywalked across the street, deftly avoiding the oncoming traffic, and sat down under a large oak tree. As soon as she leaned against her sleeping bag, eyes defocused, the bottle was unscrewed, and she was taking a healthy swig of Johnnie Walker Black. As Gigi and Lloyd got closer, they noticed tears running down her face.

Lloyd said, "I wish we could help her."

"We can. Emma can. I totally understand why she'd rather not come back to earth. Helping one person out of the millions suffering seems pointless."

"Except that one person." Gigi nodded. Lloyd pointed to Big Al's Billiards at the far end of the block. "See that place? Your mother and I would hire a sitter and go there to unwind. She was one hell of a pool player."

Gigi turned to her father. "That's where you and mom went on date night? How romantic."

"Hey now, don't blame me. Your mother loved that place. She would order us a large plate of curly fries and smother them in mustard and ketchup. We'd wash them down with Anchor Steam on tap. We had a blast. She was something, your mom."

Gigi moved in closer to her father. "So were you, dad. So *are* you." She focused again on Sandy, who was close to finishing half of the bottle. "I think you should pay a visit to your youngest daughter. Maybe you'll have better luck with her than I. When she feels my presence, she hunkers down, even more determined than ever to remain in her plastic refuge."

Sandy's head snapped up. To onlookers, she appeared to be staring up at the gnarled tree limb above. To Gigi and Lloyd, they could have sworn she was looking directly at them. She pointed her finger, eyes red from crying, and shouted, "You have no right to judge me. No right at all. You try living with Norma. I dare you. I dare anyone to live with her and survives, except Bob. What a fucking wimp."

Startled, Gigi said, "There's no way she heard us, right?"

Lloyd shook his head. "Nope. I think she's just jabbering away. It's the alcohol talking."

Sandy continued. "Couldn't you have stuck up for me once, Dad? Just once? Maybe if you did, I wouldn't be sitting here like a fucking homeless person. 'Cause that's what I am. Shit." She took another swig.

"Couldn't you and Emma have picked a better specimen? You have millions, no billions of people to choose from." Lloyd said as he studied Sandy sympathetically as she wiped her runny nose with her jacket sleeve.

"I know right now she doesn't look like much, but Sandy has potential. I believe a lot of potential. If we succeed, she'll have the emotional support she needs from Emma and the financial support from her trust fund. Will you talk to her?"

"I'll do my best, Griselda. You're a good sister."

"Thanks, Pop."

Norma stood in the middle of the expansive field. Thirty acres, to be exact. There wasn't much to look at: scrub dotted the dusty terrain. Weeds and errant scraps of paper, empty cans and broken glass filled in the rest of the landscape. She closed her eyes and imagined standing in her custom luxury box, reserved for her and the other investors, a martini in one hand and a race sheet in the other. The sound of hooves pounding against the track increased in intensity as her visualization came into focus. The horses reminded her of well-oiled machines, moving gracefully and with purpose. Gulls squawked above, circling the area, disrupting Norma's concentration. She opened her eyes and glared at the seagulls, then she checked her watch. He was five minutes early. In the distance, Norma watched as he parked next to her Lexus.

Lonnie was taller than she remembered. And scruffier. He was waving a piece of paper in the air. Norma sensed trouble.

"Hey there, Mrs. Ekhart."

"Lonnie."

"I wish I had better news. I'm still looking for your daughter. She's very good at disappearing."

Norma said, "That's why I hired you. Private investigators are supposedly in the business of finding missing persons."

"I'll find her."

"Is that what you came here to tell me?"

Again, Lonnie presented the paper, handling it carefully, so as not to diminish its quality. "This is." He gave it to Norma. Believing it was a new document, she began to read it, then realized what it was. She handed it back. "This is what I gave you to have Sandy sign."

"Yup."

"Is this a joke?"

"Nope."

Norma shook her head in frustration. "Jesus Christ, Lonnie, what do you want?"

"I want more money, Mrs. Ekhart."

"We agreed on $1,000 for you to find Sandy and get her to sign the paper."

Lonnie nodded slowly. "That's correct, but if she doesn't sign and I, pardon the expression, off her, it's going to cost you a lot more than $1,000. More like $50,000."

Norma didn't flinch. "Fine. Is that all?"

"Pretty much." Lonnie was used to dealing with people who were eager to rid the earth of those they deemed undesirable, useless. He got it. It was part of the job, and he handled the task from start to finish with little or no emotion, but as he looked into Norma Ekhart's deep turquoise eyes, he saw determination and greed. There wasn't an ounce of regret or sadness in her decision to have her daughter murdered. Lonnie didn't know why she wanted Sandy's trust. It didn't matter. She was willing to sacrifice her daughter's life for money. After this job was done, he decided he was going to take a vacation. Maybe Cancun. Maybe Tahiti. Somewhere warm.

Norma opened her car door. "Call me when you have her signature."

"Yes, ma'am." Lonnie watched her drive away. What she lacked in empathy and compassion, she more than made up for in confidence and style. She exuded wealth and grace. And those eyes. Lonnie had never seen that color outside a fictional character in a comic book or a painting. Turquoise eyes, black heart.

Lonnie slipped the key into the ignition and his Toyota Camry hummed to life. A small voice told him to return to the homeless encampment. Even though he knew he had spooked her, he had a feeling that she would go back to a familiar place. At least that's where he hoped he would find the $50,000 woman.

16

Emma didn't mind being the only woman on the camping trip. Her husband Dale had assured her that Peter's and Matt's girlfriends would be going with them to the Yuba River for the four-day weekend. Meandering through the Sierras, the Yuba was a popular camping site for Bay Area residents. If you had a tent and an inner tube, you were set. At the last minute, Peter's girlfriend, Heidi, had to work and Jenny, Matt's girlfriend, came down with the flu. Emma knew both men and enjoyed their company. Still, it would have been nice to have female companionship for the trip.

They had planned on arriving at the south end of the river in the early evening, but traffic delayed their ETA by three hours. They arrived after dark, making the hike down to the river's edge a little more treacherous than expected. With two flashlights between them, the quartet stayed close together, navigating through sagebrush, scrub, and uneven trails. Peter slipped, scraping his arm and spraining his ankle. By the time they set up their tents and settled in for the night, it was nearly 1:00 in the morning.

Bleary-eyed and still smarting from the fall, Peter unzipped the tent's door flap and looked out of his home for the next four days. At twenty-four, he was the youngest of the campers. He wrapped the blanket around his thin frame, bony shoulders shivering in the morning air.

"What the fuck?"

The sunrise afforded him a glorious view of the river and the realization that they'd set up their tents less than fifty yards from what looked like a Hell's Angel's convention. Next to the black tents with the Harley Davidson logo emblazoned on the canvas and a campfire large enough to roast four San Franciscans, were beefy, imposing motorcycles lined up in a row in a campsite parking lot. Two years ago, Matt had camped at the Yuba, extolling the beauty and privacy of the campsite he'd discovered. Without the benefit of daylight, he'd mistakenly parked almost a mile from the original site. After Peter's fall, Matt assured him that it was worth the journey.

Peter's declaration awakened Matt, who was sharing the tent with his friend. "What's going on, Dude?"

"This is what's going on, douche." Peter opened the flap wider so Matt could get a perfect view of the Angel's camp. "Am I dreaming or is that a parking lot?"

Matt crawled to the edge of the tent door. "This is not where I camped last time."

"You think?" Peter picked up a small stone and threw it at Emma and Dale's army green tent. He heard some rustling, then their door flap being unzipped. Emma was the first to pop her head out. "Good morning."

"Is it?" Peter said as he pointed to the other campsite. Emma's eyes got big and, in a voice, too loud, she said,

"What the…"

Peter immediately put his finger to his lips. "Shhh! You don't want to wake them. I hear that they're very grouchy in the morning and raw flesh calms them. I suggest we pack up as quietly as possible and stake our claim somewhere else. Who's with me?"

By this time, Dale was aware of the circumstances. He, along with Emma and Matt, enthusiastically nodded in agreement. As they were gathering their things, Emma said, "I wonder why they didn't hear us come in last night. We weren't exactly quiet."

Dale rolled up his sleeping bag. "Maybe they were partying a little too hard before we arrived and passed out."

As the four began their journey up the hillside to their car, they glanced back at the Angel's camp, amazed that they were extricating themselves from the delicate and uncomfortable situation with nary a sound coming from the camp. Emma said, "I hope they're okay. I mean, it's unnaturally quiet."

Matt said, "Why don't you go down and check, Emma? Just knock on one of the big, black tents with the skull and crossbones on it and ask if they're okay?"

"Not funny, Matt."

Halfway to the top, the friends could hear the campsite residents waking up. A lot of coughing, hocking, and louder than normal voices drifted up the hillside. They had left not a moment too soon.

Back at the car, Matt reassured the group that, in daylight, he knew exactly where he was heading, however he did ask for complete silence so he could concentrate. Two false stops later, he confidently parked the car and declared that their camping adventure had officially begun.

The spot was idyllic. Surrounded by the forest on three sides and the expansive river on the fourth, their privacy was all but guaranteed.

It took some convincing, but the guys eventually talked Emma into eating mushrooms, the psychedelic kind. All three assured her that she would be fine. Dale promised to protect and safeguard her from harm. An hour later, she was gently floating down the river on an inner tube, wearing a bathing suit and a lopsided grin. She watched in fascination as the water appeared to change from fluid to solid, from blue to green, purple and fuchsia. Each water droplet on her arm was gold and blue. She swore she saw green luminous fish swimming just beneath the surface. "I thought you said I wouldn't hallucinate," she said to Dale as he caught the edge of her inner tube and brought her close to him. After a long, luxurious kiss, he said, "You must be confusing me with your other husband. He tried to kiss her again, but as he leaned forward, the inner tube tipped over and he went, headfirst, into the water. At first, Emma giggled, it then progressed into laughter and then ultimately she couldn't catch her breath she was laughing so hard.

That evening, around the campfire, they wrapped russet potatoes, zucchini, broccoli, and onions in foil, after drizzling it in olive oil and sprinkling the vegetables with salt, pepper, and garlic powder. After dinner, they sipped Bailey's and coffee, a long-standing tradition, according to Matt. With her head resting on Dale's shoulder, inhaling the scent of the smoldering sticks, pine cones, and logs from the campfire, and listening as the river lazily flowed past their campsite, Emma had rarely felt so peaceful. So very satisfied. She looked up at the black sky, emblazoned with billions of stars. They really were twinkling. From Sausalito, the lights of San Francisco were beautiful, but they couldn't compare to the real thing.

Long after she recalled the memory of thirty-four years ago, Emma began to feel the pangs of loneliness. The touch of another human being. A caress. A slow, tempered kiss. Even holding another person's hand was missed. She was torn between knowing that nothing could hurt her while encased in the doll and the uncertainty of living in the carnal world where she could experience the joys of life and its tragedies as well. She bemoaned the fact that her spirit didn't experience a smooth transition from incarnation to freedom. She wondered if Gigi would visit her again. It was hard to fathom Gigi giving up so soon, especially since Sandy's life was in danger. Sandy was a damaged young woman with low self-esteem and a lower self-image. Emma was positive she could transform her into a strong, confident person, but could she do it before the private investigator found her? Paige turned over in bed and Marilyn fell to the ground. The fall startled Emma. Is this the life she really wanted to live for years? She wasn't so sure anymore.

"Emma? Are you in there?" The voice was very familiar.

"Dad?"

"That's me."

"What are you doing here? Did Gigi send you?" Emma's query was awash in conflict and irritation. "I wish she'd butt out of my life."

Lloyd Banks surveyed the room where his youngest daughter lived. It reminded him of the girls' room when they were growing up. Awash in various shades of pink, a poster from the movie *Frozen*, and a hand-drawn mural depicting a pasture with grazing horses. What was it about little girls and horses, Lloyd thought. He lit just above the doll. "Do you remember your guitar teacher, Mr. Farney?"

"You didn't answer my question. Did Gigi ask you to come here?"

"She did. Now, tell me. Do you remember him?"

"Of course, I do. He used to play in a fairly popular band back when he was younger. I think they were called, The Farmer's Sons. He had dyed, red hair which looked strange next to his very wrinkled face. I thought he was old, but I'm guessing now he was around fifty. He was a great teacher. Patient, sweet disposition. Did you know that he smoked unfiltered cigarettes in that little sound-proof room the entire lesson? No wonder I developed such an intolerance to cigarette smoke."

"He couldn't get away with that nowadays. Do you remember when he invited us to see him play at that Shakey's Pizza Parlor in Burlingame?"

"Of course. I was so excited and proud. My guitar teacher was performing in front of an audience." Emma reflected on the memory. "My first disappointment was when we pulled up to the restaurant. It was in a lousy part of town and the 'S' in Shakey's hung at an angle, threatening to fall off. Gigi kept calling it Hakey's. The second shock was walking into the restaurant. Kids were running around, yelling. For lack of a better description, the patrons looked low class. They were talking while stuffing pizza into their mouths. No one was paying attention to Phil Farney, who was up on the makeshift stage playing his banjo and singing at the top of his lungs. I believe he was playing, *Oh Susanna*. My heart went out to him." Emma was quiet. "Why did you bring up Mr. Farney, Dad?"

"I'll never forget that evening, either. You begged your mom and I to take you to see Mr. Farney perform. I could have guessed that you would be disappointed, but I'll tell you something. Your teacher was so happy to see you. He was so glad you came. You could see it in his eyes, and he sang and played that banjo as if he was at the Concord Pavilion in front of thousands of adoring fans. He rose to the occasion. He gave it his best shot."

"You're actually comparing my situation to a washed-up performer playing at Shakey's? I thought your spirit was more evolved than that."

"Emma, the earth is filled with indescribable beauty, compassion, and love. It's also a world filled with unspeakable cruelty. Living in darkness you avoid that cruelty, but you also miss out on all the good stuff and, honey, there's a lot of good stuff. Mr. Farney may have looked out over the crowd while he was performing and saw the children running amok and their parents gorging on greasy slices of pepperoni pizza, completely ignoring him. When we walked in and listened to him singing and strumming his banjo and applauded, we made his night. I bet if you asked him, he would say that it was worth it."

"We won't ever know. He died about ten years ago. Lung cancer." Emma rose out of the doll. It was more difficult than ever. It felt like she was moving through molasses.

Her father's spirit was before her. He took the form of his younger self, around thirty-two. She had seen photos of her parents when they were in their thirties. She forgot how handsome her dad was with his thick, black hair and small, aquiline nose. She reached out to him and their 'hands' lightly touched. "So, you think I need to get back on stage at Hakey's and start singing my heart out?"

"More or less."

"I'll think about it."

"You better think fast. I watched you emerge from the doll, and it took you a lot longer than it should have. You don't have much time, Emma.

Emma nodded. "I still need a little more time. I love you, Dad."

As his daughter returned to Marilyn, Lloyd Banks said, "I love you, too, sweetheart."

Anticipating his upcoming date with Ronnie, Will was thankful that the workday was over. He got in the shower and turned the water on as hot as he could take it. Any stress or anxiety was washed away, the peppermint soap erasing every last remnant. Inhaling the scent had an immediate calming effect on his nervous system.

After towel drying his hair, he went to the closet and picked out a hunter green button down, long-sleeved shirt. Jeans were a given, as were his sneakers. Will picked up a small sample vial of Glenn Hatfield cologne for men. He pulled out the stopper and took a whiff. He almost put it on, then laughed out loud. "As if a woman like Ronnie would go for a guy wearing cologne." He tossed the vial in the trash. The ding of the oven timer brought him into the kitchen where he checked on the chili. After a small taste, he covered it and turned the heat down to low.

So involved was he at the clinic that Will couldn't remember the last date he went on. He thought it was a woman that his sister set him up with, but he wasn't sure. She was pleasant and very attractive. The problem was her sense of humor. She didn't have one. In Will's book of prospects, that was a necessity. He would easily choose a less attractive woman to one who didn't share his love of laughter. He checked himself in the mirror one more time, then went to set the table. As he placed the wine glass next to the dinner plate, the doorbell rang.

"You're right on time," Will said as he let Ronnie in. Out of her motorcycle gear, she wore a pale pink sweater and skinny cargo pants with brown ankle boots. Her hair was slicked back, and she wore minimal makeup. "May I say you look beautiful?"

"You may say it and as often as you like. Thank you." She handed Will a bottle of wine. "The wine expert at Rainbow Grocery assured me that it was vegan and very tasty."

Will read the label. "How did you know that zinfandel is my favorite?"

"I'll never tell." Ronnie placed her purse on the couch while checking out the apartment's living room. She loved Will's décor. She called it the unstaged planned look. She could see that every object and piece of furniture was not bought on a whim or out of necessity. They were all waiting for Will to discover them. Ronnie picked up a swirly white stone. It was about two inches wide, four inches tall and had a bumpy snow-white texture. She turned it around a few times, then said, "I give up. What is this?" She handed it to Will. He held it up between his thumb and index finger.

"Does it remind you of anything?"

Ronnie was going to say, 'a piece of petrified poop,' but she decided against it. Maybe when they'd gotten to know each other better. "Not at all."

"It's a seal balancing a ball on its nose."

Ronnie got a better look. "Oh…sorry, can't see it. Please tell me you didn't pay a fortune for this work of art."

Will shook his head and smiled. "I found it on the beach. As soon as I picked it up, I saw a seal." He pointed to the top of the stone. "This is the ball."

"Whatever you say, Picasso." Ronnie went into the kitchen. She lifted the lid on the pot. "Smells amazing and I'm not a huge chili fan."

"You will be after this dinner. I can almost guarantee it."

"Aren't you Mr. Confident?"

"Actually, it's Dr. Confident to you."

Ronnie bowed. "I stand corrected." She turned in the direction of the balcony. "Do you have a cat? There's something scratching outside."

"That must be Minky. Come on. I'll introduce you."

Ronnie followed Will outside. There, in the mini-log cabin, sat Minky scratching the side of his house, impatiently waiting for his nightly snack. The rat with the luxurious coat sniffed the air. His nose worked overtime as his whiskers fluttered wildly. He didn't recognize Ronnie's scent. Will opened a jar of nuts sitting on the patio table and poured a sizable amount into Minky's food bowl. His water bottle was half full.

"What a cute little fella. Was he a city rat before you domesticated him?"

Will nodded. "I don't know how tame he is, but he definitely prefers being fed to having to forage for his meals and risk getting injured or killed."

"Or poisoned. Along with pigs, rats are one of the most maligned animals. Their names are used only in a derogatory context, like 'that guy is such a rat,' or 'did you rat on me?' or my personal favorite, 'you're nothing but a filthy, stinking rat.' It's disgusting."

"I agree. The negative language justifies the continued subjugation and malevolence toward animals. What's the big deal about killing and eating a pig? Everyone knows they're dirty and sweaty and live in filth. Of course, we know none of that is true, but breaking people of the habit of maligning them is near impossible. On that note, how about we open the bottle of zin and sip it like the respectable rat and pig that we are."

"You really know how to make a woman feel special."

Will laughed. "I've heard I have that effect on women. They're either offended or..."

Ronnie interrupted, "Deaf?"

"That's one way to put it."

Will uncorked the wine and poured them each a healthy glass of Babbling Brook Zinfandel. He tasted it. "Very nice."

Ronnie agreed. "This should go very well with the chili, which I'm looking forward to judging." She sat back on the sofa and turned her attention to her host. He reminded her of a studious looking Ryan Gosling. It was the horn-rimmed glasses that gave him a conservative, yet sexy look. She imagined Will without his glasses and his hair tousled. A small smile crept across her face.

"What?" Will said.

Without a hint of embarrassment, she said, "I was trying to imagine you without your specs on and your hair mussed up. I think they call it the bedroom look."

Will blushed. "You certainly don't pull any punches, do you?"

"Not one bit. Honestly leaves very little room for misinterpretation and I hate it when I'm misinterpreted."

"I find it admirable. Here's to honesty." Will raised his glass and Ronnie lightly tapped hers against it. "How did you get involved with feeding the homeless?"

"As you know, the Big V isn't in the best part of the city. On my way to work, I would walk past people living on the sidewalk, begging for money or food. I was never the kind of person who saw them as worthless. I also did very little to help them. As the restaurant grew in popularity, I found myself more obligated than ever to do something for those who had nothing. After a catering event, the hostess insisted that I take the leftover food. She was leaving on a trip the following day and didn't want it to go to waste. On my way back from the party, I drove by the homeless camp where I met you. I set up catering tables in the middle of the camp and, along with my employees, we served this gourmet meal. They loved it. Some of them came up to me afterwards and hugged me. One woman thanked me with tears streaming down her face. She said her daughter was a caterer, too, but she hadn't seen her in years. It was a humbling experience. I decided then to recruit other vegan chefs and make the food drive a regular event. Lydia Highland from The Olive Branch and Cecily Cruz from The Sprouted Plate were the first two to come on board. Gretchen, Lydia, Tammy, and Wanda joined soon after. We came up with the name Vegan Vipers and, believe it or not, we were all into motorcycles as teenagers, but none of us owned one. Within three months, we all graduated from Henry Higgins Motorcycle Safety School, bought our bikes, and began distributing the leftover food from the restaurants. Lydia's suggestion to add clothing and toiletries to the mix was adopted about six months ago."

"You vipers are doing a great service to the city's homeless. Have you told other city's vegan restauranteurs about your operation? It could be a great way to further the vegan cause, as well."

"As a matter of fact, we're helping the owners of Veggie World in Portland and Veganmania in Los Angeles launch their programs. I was interviewed by a Los Angeles Times reporter. He asked me if our intention was to turn the homeless into vegans. I said, 'No, we're trying to keep them alive.' Even when vegans are trying to do good, idiot omnivores try to work in an angle."

"Sadly, we're still in the minority and will have to suffer the slings and arrows of unconscious meat-eaters. I'm surprised with everything you do that you had time for dinner with me."

"All work and no play makes Ronnie a dull girl. I'm loving this wine, by the way. I'm going to have to order some for the restaurant."

Will stood. "Are you ready for dinner?"

"Definitely. Bring on Dr. Confident's famous chili."

After finishing the salad, Will placed a bowl of chili topped with shredded vegan mozzarella cheese in front of Ronnie, then prepared a bowl for himself. Once he sat down, Ronnie mixed the cheese into the chili and took a bite. "Whoa. This is delicious. You are one talented cook. I may have to get your recipe and add this dish to the menu."

Will smiled broadly. "That means a lot coming from you. Thanks."

"You are most welcome. I've been meaning to ask you if you ever found the Ekhart woman. What was her name?"

"Sandy. And no, I have no idea where she is. I even checked the Portrero Hill shelter. She must think she's in danger and I'm beginning to believe it myself."

Ronnie ate another spoonful of chili and washed it down with the wine. "I don't want to be oppositional, but do you think she might be a tad paranoid? After all, she's living on the streets and survival mode can mess with your mind."

"Under normal circumstances I would agree, but Sandy said the man wanted her to sign a document. If the only reason her parents want to find her is so that she can sign a piece of paper, then I'm betting it has something to do with a transfer of money. Lots of money. I'm thinking that they'll do whatever it takes to get that signature."

"Doctor, gourmet cook, sleuth. What don't you do?"

Will put his hand up to his heart. "I hate to admit it, because my father was an amazing baker, but I'm lousy at it. Bread doesn't rise, cookies are like rocks and pies are mushy. We all have our Achilles heel. What's yours?"

Ronnie thought about it for a while. "I have so many. I'll narrow it down to two and fill you in on my more personal foibles when I know you better. I'm a really slow reader due to dyslexia and no matter how hard I try, I can't master the art of fencing. I have the height and the discipline. I was told I even had the body of a fencer, but every student in my class beat me. A 12-year-old girl whooped my ass. It was embarrassing and humbling."

"Bad fencer? This friendship is not going to work. I suggest we have dessert before I force you out of my apartment with a saber."

"If you made the dessert, I may just leave sooner than later."

"Touché." Will went to the freezer and brought out a pint of Carly's Caramel & Fudge frozen dessert. "Have you had this?"

"Are you kidding? It's my favorite non-dairy dessert. Carly's also makes an amazing coconut milk espresso ice cream."

"Had it and love it."

Will spooned out two big scoops of the dessert into bowls. They finished it in record time.

Ronnie said, "I hate to cut this shindig short, but I have to get up super early tomorrow. We're catering an afternoon wedding in Napa. Lunch for 200 guests." She leaned over and gave Will a quick kiss on his lips. "To say I had a great time is an understatement. Thank you so much for a wonderful evening."

Will leaned in and kissed her again. This time it was longer and more heartfelt. "I had a great time, too. Can I see you again?"

"Of course. If anything, I want to see that saber of yours."

They both laughed. "You are definitely a vegan viper," said Will.

"I most definitely am."

After doing the dishes, Will went outside and sat on the balcony. Most nights, he liked to read. Tonight, he was finding it hard to concentrate. He replayed the evening with Ronnie in his mind, from her assessment of his seal rock to the delicious kiss. He had never been with a woman so comfortable in her own skin. Her confidence was refreshing, not brash or arrogant. And he knew, from dining at the Big V, that she was an excellent chef. Her dishes reminded him of the film, *Like Water for Chocolate*, where the chef infuses her recipes with her current emotional state. The difference is that all Ronnie's meals made you feel fantastic. Will had meant to ask her if she attended a culinary academy. He also wanted to know where she grew up and if she had siblings. Will's thoughts were interrupted by the ringing of his cellphone.

"Hello?"

"I was getting ready for bed and had an urge to call you." Ronnie laid back on her pillow.

"You were most likely picking up on my vibes. I was thinking about you, too. I realized that I don't know your last name. It isn't

Viper, is it?"

"Very funny. It's Schatzki."

"Polish?"

"It ain't Italian, Dr. Remini. Actually, I'm Polish on my father's side and Russian, Polish, and French on my mother's. My brother and I are mutts. Are you a purebred?"

"Nope. Dad's Italian and my mother's family is from Croatia. When tempers flared between my parents, my sister and I left the house lest we got caught in the firestorm. Luckily, I didn't inherit my temperament from either of them."

"Good to know." Ronnie pulled the covers up to her chin and turned out the light. "Sleep well. I'll talk to you later."

"Good night." Will hung up and said to himself, "And so it begins."

"Marlo, I have to go to the investor's meeting. It's crucial." Rick was attempting to get dressed, but his wife was insistent upon him staying in bed, pulling his shirt off as soon as he put it on.

"Having sex with me is more enjoyable than sitting around a table with a group of money-hungry animal abusers, isn't it?"

"You forget, dear, that I'm one of those money-hungry investors. And we're not animal abusers, for God's sake."

Marlo slid out of bed, her naked body wrapping itself around her husband. She nibbled on his ear. "Come on back to bed, you sexy man. The she-devil can fill you in on the meeting."

Rick had tried to resist his young wife's pleas, but the temptation was too strong. He was a man, after all, and the desire of being entwined with an ex-model was overpowering. His shirt already on the floor, he let Marlo remove his pants and Rolex, then he slid back under the covers. At his age, if he were to have a fatal heart attack, he'd much prefer to remember his last moments on earth looking into his wife's eyes as she straddled him, than in a room full of investors.

Norma glanced at her watch. She feigned irritation. "He's late." The truth was, Norma needed more time to recoup the $20 million that Bob borrowed from the investment account. Granted, this meeting was merely a perfunctory one. Their lawyer, Jerry Zeller, would be updating them on the status of the environmental impact statement.

"Did you try his cell?" asked Donald Parledo, one of the partners. He was sitting to Norma's right, an investment banker with a rotund body and a comb-over so bad, it looked like he took a mini-weedwhacker to his ten remaining hairs, then pulled them over his liver-spotted head. He pushed his tortoise-shell glasses further up on the bridge of his bulbous nose as he checked his emails.

Norma nodded. "It went straight to voicemail. If he doesn't get here in the next ten minutes, I move to reschedule the meeting."

Craig Schaffer agreed. "You'd think Rick would be on time, considering we're holding the meeting in his office."

Just then, Rick's secretary opened the door to the conference room. "I received a call from Mr. Standish. He apologizes for his absence, but he's been interminably delayed and needs to reschedule."

"Did he give a reason for the delay?" Craig asked.

"He did not. Sorry gentlemen and Ms. Ekhart."

Norma stood. "Well, that was a waste of my time." She turned to Jerry Zeller. "Will you reschedule and text us the new date?"

"Of course."

Before anyone could engage her in conversation, Norma hurried out of the conference room. In the elevator, she called Lonnie. After two rings, it went to voicemail. "If you haven't found my daughter in twenty-four hours, I'm taking you off the case." Next, she called her husband.

"Any news on the $20 million you stole from our investment account?"

Bob rolled his eyes. "No, Norma. I told you that when…"

"I didn't think so." She hung up the phone, wondering why she stayed married to such an irresponsible man.

Gigi stood so close to Norma that if she could smell, she was convinced she'd be able to inhale the wealth that the woman emanated. In life, Gigi had never personally experienced another human so self-absorbed and self-serving. She could feel Norma's energy, that insatiable need for personal gratification. Before she left to visit her sister for another round of begging, she was compelled to stay with Norma a little bit longer, hoping that she'd pick up more ammunition for her quest.

After realizing that Norma was making the rounds in Union

Square, San Francisco's upscale shopping district, Gigi left and went straight to the home of Paige Andersen, the proud owner of one All-American doll named Marilyn who was perhaps the only doll in the world with a soul.

17

Emma sat in Petal's living room, surrounded by candles, varying in size and color. Smoke from vanilla incense erratically climbed into the air. Quartz crystals were strategically placed, the light from the candles catching in their facets. In the corner sat a three-foot tall amethyst geode. Its brilliance and beauty was mesmerizing. Emma was immediately drawn to it. She could feel its energy emanating from the dozens of six-sided violet-colored prisms.

Petal carried a tray with two steaming mugs of tea and a pitcher of coconut milk over to the coffee table and set it down. She placed one of the mugs on a coaster in front of Emma. "Dragonwell green tea helps with my concentration. It keeps me on track."

Emma took a sip. "I like it. It has a sweet chestnutty taste. Very nice." She put the mug down. "Tell me again why you think I should meditate."

Petal pulled her hair back and twisted it into a bun, then secured it with a ponytail band. "Your divorce has created so much tension and malcontent. Your mind is working overtime, trying to deal with the event as well as with everyday issues, like work and friends and family and life. You read the paper, right? Look what's going on in the world. Everything, no matter how remote you think it is, affects you on every level: emotional, physical, and spiritual. When you read about someone murdered or the Syrian refugee crisis, your heart hurts, right?"

"Yeah. I never thought about it, really. The other night, I was watching the news and they were reporting live from a refugee camp. I started crying. Ten minutes later, they're recapping the Forty-Niner game and I got wrapped up in the highlights, cheering and applauding their victory. Refugees, what refugees?"

Petal pointed to her heart. "They're right here." She took a sip of tea. "Meditating clears the mind and gives it a chance to recalibrate. When you meditate, you're in the present. The past and future don't exist. All that matters is now and that soothes the soul. Are you ready?"

"How long will it take?" Emma asked as she sipped the tea.

Petal sighed. "That's not important."

"It kind of is. NCIS is on in twenty-five minutes."

"Watching a television program takes precedence over your peace of mind? This is exactly why you need to meditate."

Emma gave Petal a look of concern. Petal relented. "Why don't we meditate for ten minutes?"

"Sounds perfect. What do I do?"

Petal took a sip of tea, sat back on the couch, and crossed her legs. "Get comfortable. You can either cross your legs or sit with your feet touching the floor. Hands can be in your lap or on your thighs, palms facing up. Now close your eyes and begin to inhale deeply through your nose and exhale through your nose. Concentrate on your breathing. If your mind wanders, bring it back. If images appear, send them love and put them in a rowboat and let them float away. Don't worry about the time. I'll let you know when ten minutes is up."

Emma crossed her legs and placed her hands in her lap. She closed her eyes and began to inhale deeply, the scent of the incense helped calm her. After two inhalations, Vin's angry face appeared in her mind's eye. The thought of sending him love felt uncomfortable, so she sent the vision away without a boat, Vin's head bobbing in the water without her blessing. More errant thoughts invaded her mind and she was able to ship them off. Emma was surprised at how active her mind was. She felt like she was playing tennis against a ball machine. As soon as she knocked a ball away, another came flying at her. Finally, her animated brain slowed down. She felt calm and peaceful when Petal said, "Take a deep breath and count down from five with every breath thereafter. When you've reached one, open your eyes."

Thirty seconds later, Emma opened her eyes. She smiled. "I feel great. Like I took a nap for about an hour." She stretched her arms above her head. "Wouldn't it be great if meditation could get rid of wrinkles?"

Petal took a long sip of her tea, which by now was room temperature. She looked into Emma's sleepy eyes. "You look wonderful, and you really have very few wrinkles."

"Please. Turn up the lights and you'll see scads of wrinkles and saggy skin. And it's getting so thin. I bumped into my refrigerator the other day and I got a bruise on my thigh the size of a grapefruit. It looks like someone smacked me with a mace. My eyes water in the morning when I wake up and my nose runs indiscriminately. I panic if I don't have a tissue on me at all times. I swear, if I could come back at any age, I would be twenty-three again."

"First of all, that's not going to happen. Second, learn to love who you are, wrinkles and bruises and runny nose and all. You were twenty-three and twenty-four and thirty-four and, you get the picture. Relish who you are and where you are. Everyone ages."

"That's easy for you to say. You're young and your skin is toned with nary a wrinkle in sight. Wait until you're my age. I'll ask you then how you feel."

"I can't wait to be fifty and sixty. Even seventy. I'm going to rock it."

Emma marveled at this young woman with so much more maturity and breadth than herself. "I believe you, kid. I really do." She glanced up at the clock. It was five minutes until the hour. "NCIS is calling. Thanks so much for the lesson."

"Anytime you want to come over and meditate together, I'm here."

They hugged, then Emma walked across the yard to her home. She turned on the television and poured herself a glass of iced tea. The program erupted on the screen with a high-speed chase, followed by the pursued car crashing and exploding. Flames jumped high into the air. Normally, the violence wouldn't have phased her. Tonight, it was disturbing and clashed with her serenity. For the first time, Emma turned off her favorite show, opting instead to take a hot shower and finish off the night reading in bed. She was looking forward to finding a good book in the kindle library. Someone had recommended a book by first-time author, Audrey Slocum. They said it was a love story. It sounded perfect.

In the darkness, inside her hard plastic tomb, Emma let the memory of that evening saturate her soul. She missed Petal immensely and hoped that someday she would see the beautiful woman again in the flesh or otherwise.

18

Marlo thought she'd feel like a yuppie at a Grateful Dead concert, so she dressed in jeans, albeit $250 designer jeans, a white tank top and light pink sweater. Used to wearing heels, she ditched them for her running shoes. When she walked into the Citizens for Environmental Protection meeting, she expected to be hit with the smell of patchouli oil and a surplus of tie dye. Instead, the woman at the sign-in table was dressed eerily similar to Marlo. The attractive thirty-something blonde with friendly coffee brown eyes, was wearing a pullover sweater that Marlo had seen in the Saks Fifth Avenue store window. The price tag? A mere $375.

"Hi. Is this your first-time here?" The woman gave Marlo a warm smile.

"It is."

"Welcome. I'm Suzy." She grabbed a pamphlet off the table and handed it to Marlo. "This will give you a little background on our organization. If you'd like to get on our mailing list, sign here." Suzy pointed to a clipboard.

"Thanks so much." Marlo folded the pamphlet in half and put it in her purse. As much as she would have liked to receive emails from the group, she didn't want to take the chance that Rick would see them. She had a few minutes before the meeting began, so she took a seat close to the rear of the auxiliary room in St. John's Baptist Church. Trying not to stare, Marlo took in the scene. There must have been at least fifty people. Most looked to be in their late twenties, early thirties. From their attire, they appeared to be middle to upper middle class. There were some teenagers and several older men and women. Out of the group, Marlo spotted a couple, the only two people wearing what she thought would have been the norm: tie dye sweatshirts, baggy jeans, and Birkenstock sandals. At least that's what the man was wearing. He appeared to be in his late fifties, his long gray hair tied back in a sloppy ponytail. His wife or girlfriend was wearing matching sandals, but she rocked a maxi dress, its tie dye colors of yellow, green, black, and orange complimented her long, wavy salt and pepper hair. She had on enough turquoise and silver jewelry to open a pop-up jewelry store right there in the meeting room. The man caught Marlo staring at them. He flashed her the peace sign and smiled, his straight, white teeth destroying her stereotype of the 'dirty hippie.' Instinctively, she returned the sign and smiled.

With some time to spare, Marlo retrieved the brochure from her purse and began reading it. Not more than thirty seconds later, a woman stood next to her. "Is this seat taken?"

Marlo shook her head.

The woman sat down and took out her cellphone. At the risk of being rude, Marlo said, "I hope you don't mind me asking, but what perfume are you wearing? It smells amazing."

"Thank you. It's my own blend of essential oils. I customize each scent for the person wearing it. I'm Petal, as in the flower not the bicycle part."

"What a pretty name. I'm Marlo. So, it's your business?"

"Uh huh. If you'd like me to create a personal perfume for you, I'd be happy to." She fished a business card out of her purse and handed it to Marlo, who eagerly accepted it. "I also make aromatherapy sprays using essential oils. What do you do? Wait, don't tell me. You're a model."

Marlo laughed. "I used to be. Now, I'm a very bored housewife. When I met my husband, I was living in Manhattan, working hard on moving up the modeling ladder which is, as you can imagine, a very crowded ladder. Rick literally swept me off my feet. I moved to San Francisco to be with him."

"Would you want to get back into modeling?"

"Not really, but even if I wanted to, Rick wouldn't let me. He wants his wife to be there when he gets home." Marlo saw the look of disdain on Petal's face. "I know. It sounds so old fashioned, but I fell in love with the man and the lifestyle, so here I am, living in San Francisco with nothing to do."

The woman's lifestyle was so different from her own, yet there was something about Marlo's energy that Petal was drawn to, otherwise she never would have said, "I don't know if you're interested or even if your husband would approve, but if you would like me to show you how to work with essential oils, I'd be happy to. For some reason, I think you'd be a natural. No pressure. I felt compelled to put it out there."

Marlo looked dumbstruck. "Are you clairvoyant? I was just thinking how much fun it would be to be in your line of work." She looked around, as if she expected to see Rick lurking amongst the environmentalists. "I don't care what Rick says. I'm going to do it." She quickly added, "Of course, I'll do my best to make sure he doesn't find out. I'm not that emancipated!"

At that moment, a middle-aged man with a short beard and healthy head of black hair walked up on the stage and stood behind the podium. He tapped the microphone to ensure it was on. "If everyone could please take their seats, we'd like to begin the meeting." He waited a few moments while those standing settled in, then he began. "I'd like to welcome you all to the Citizens for Environmental Protection's emergency meeting. I appreciate you all showing up at such short notice, but we've got one helluva battle on our hands. We're dedicating tonight to discuss how to fight Francisco Downs, the racetrack slated to begin construction near Sternwood Creek despite our efforts to delay it. According to the Environmental Impact Report, the Kayteen Investment Group's project has a number of violations, one of which is building the horse stables too close to the creek. Runoff is imminent and will pollute the water. Another glaring violation is the impact a racetrack will have on the neighborhood. There will definitely be an increase in traffic and noise. Due to gambling, a jump in criminal activity is highly probable." A woman in the third row raised their hand. The speaker pointed to her. "Yes, Denise?"

Denise Orden, a petite, well-dressed woman in her thirties, stood. "John, it's my understanding that the project can't continue without a clean EIR, so why an emergency meeting?"

"We received an anonymous call from someone close to the project. They said that the group is planning to bribe the judge in charge of the ruling. Even though we can't verify the caller or the information, we felt we should come up with a contingency plan if the project is approved. The caller went on to say that funding is going through within the next few weeks."

Denise shook her head in disgust. "I'm not surprised. These assholes will do whatever it takes to push their projects through. Do we have any legal leverage at all?"

Before John could answer, a few more hands shot up from the crowd.

Petal turned to Marlo and whispered, "The last thing we need is another venue where animals are exploited. The racing industry is absolutely the worst for horses."

"Tell me about it. That's why I'm here. It's more about the horses than the environmental aspect, even though that's really harsh, too."

Petal smiled. "I don't think it was an accident that we sat next to each other."

"I think you're right."

When Marlo married Rick Standish, his friends became her friends, for better or for worse, and for the most part, it was the worst. Rick's friends were society people, couples from the country club, charity functions, and business events. Marlo felt closer to her housekeeper than any of the social climbers, least of all Norma and Bob Ekhart. In private, she referred to Bob as Bob the Blob and Norma, the Wicked Witch of the West Coast. Marlo knew that not all old money treated the nouveau rich with disdain and, if they did, they hid it well. Norma didn't even try – her condescending attitude toward Marlo was blatant and her jealousy was obvious. It's true, she was smarter and richer than Marlo and, when she was younger, Norma would have given Marlo serious competition. Now, Marlo could turn heads quicker than Norma could flash her checkbook and she knew it. It was the only thing she could lord over her husband's business partner and that was fine with her. For now.

John continued. "I think it's vital that we let the public know what's going on. We need their help to put pressure on the courts and the city of San Francisco and expose the graft. Let's put a permanent halt to Francisco Downs. I'm asking for volunteers to make calls. We're also requesting donations to help fund an ad campaign. Any social media professionals out there?"

The audience chuckled as more than ten hands shot up. Looking for a techie in San Francisco was like looking for ice in the North Pole.

Marlo and Petal offered to make calls, and both made donations, Marlo's extraordinarily more substantial. When the meeting was over,

Petal invited her new friend out for coffee.

"I'd love to, but I have to get back home. I'm getting up early and need to get things done before I go to bed. I'll take a raincheck, though, and I really do want to learn more about your business."

"I hope you call because I think…no, I know that you're going to be an excellent aromatherapist." As Petal walked to her car, her thoughts immediately went to Emma. She found it perplexing. It also saddened her. She looked up at the stars, faded from the lights of the city. "I hope you're in a better place, Emma. I miss you."

"If you only knew," Gigi said as she looked down on Petal. Suddenly, Gigi got an idea. She didn't think about its feasibility, only its outcome. It felt like it might work. In a split second, she was gone.

Marlo's drive home to Pacific Heights was less than twenty minutes. It gave her a chance to reflect on the evening. She was looking forward to learning all she could from Petal and for the first time since giving up her career, Marlo felt a sense of purpose. She couldn't justify her modeling career as important as helping a social movement, animals, or the environment. It was simply a means to an end. It paid well and, she could now admit, it served its purpose of landing her a wealthy, albeit older, husband. Her life was effortless, her duties minimal. She thought that being pampered and cared for was what she wanted. Turns out, Marlo couldn't wait to get her manicured nails dirty. She couldn't wait to expose the horse racing industry for what it was: greed, greed and more greed. She knew there were people who enjoyed watching the horses run, blind to the lives most of the thoroughbreds led when they weren't performing for the owners and bettors. It was anything but glamorous. Any twinge of guilt she felt for upending her husband's business investment was allayed by the fact that Rick Standish would parlay the money into another venture. He had the money and the means to do so. She also knew if he found out she was involved in Francisco Downs's demise, he would be furious. Her conscience didn't care.

"Hurry up, Marlo. I don't want to be late." Rick left the door to their four-car garage open and started up the Canary yellow 488 Ferrari. At Rick's insistence, his wife wore a riding outfit he had picked up the night before. Technically, his secretary bought it with the company credit card. She looked like she walked out of the pages of *Dressage Today*. Every inch the model, Marlo adjusted the seat to accommodate her long legs. "You look beautiful, honey."

Marlo smiled. Her thoughts were not focused on the imminent tour of Stone Meadows Horse Farm. Instead, she was thinking about the script she had been given by John at the CEP meeting the night before. She knew she had to carefully choose where she'd be calling lest someone recognize her voice. Of course, she wouldn't be using her real name and she was debating whether she should use her cellphone. The organization's offices weren't far from the house and their phones were available for use.

"I've only been to the stables a few times, but every time has been a treat. Shelly's horses are spectacular. Did I tell you that their bloodline is from Danny Boy? You know who he is, right?"

"No, but I'm guessing he won a lot of races." Marlo tried to sound interested. Rick didn't buy it. He shifted into second gear.

"Yeah, he won a lot of races: The Kentucky Derby twice and the Triple Crown back in 1990. Please try to show more enthusiasm when you're at the farm. Please. Shelly's a good friend of mine."

Not one to shy away from expressing her opinion, Marlo took a few moments to construct her response. She didn't doubt Rick's love for her and, although he would have preferred a more compliant wife, she also knew that he enjoyed her spunk. She was well aware of his tolerance level and, unless he witnessed the abuse of the racehorses that she purported, he wasn't going put up with her resistance to the racing industry and his investment much longer. She sighed internally and decided to play the game. It wouldn't have been the first time. Marlo shifted in her seat so she could face her husband. At fifty-seven, he had a full head of silver hair. Money has a way of making even the homeliest man look attractive. With a net worth of $45 million, Marlo ignored Rick's double chin and focused on his gray green eyes and high cheekbones. She thought he looked very sexy, especially behind the wheel of a Ferrari.

"I'm actually looking forward to meeting Shelly. She sounds like a fascinating woman. How long did you say it would take to get there?"

"Depending on traffic, between one to two hours."

Marlo turned on the radio and tuned it to Sirius XM. Lady Gaga's

Bad Romance filled the car. "I didn't know you were a Lady Gaga fan."

"I thought I should expand my music selection. You like Lady Gaga?"

"I do. Welcome to 21st century music, Mr. Standish."

"Thank you so much, Mrs. Standish. It's great to be here."

Rick intentionally drove slowly up the private drive so Marlo could take in the lush landscape of Stone Meadows Farm. The requisite white picket fence lined both sides of the road where azalea bushes were in full bloom, showing off their white, hot pink, orange, and lavender flowers. Thoroughbreds grazed in the expansive meadow, their glossy coats glistening in the sun. It was too picturesque. Too perfect. She could acknowledge that the horses were enjoying their lives at the moment. The racing scene was a completely different picture. This was but a small aspect of their lives.

"Pretty amazing, huh?" Rick looked over at his wife, hoping she was impressed.

"It's beautiful. I feel like I'm in Kentucky. That's where they have all the horse farms, right?"

Rick nodded. He pointed up the road. "There's Shelly." A woman in her late fifties was walking a horse back to the stables. Her chestnut brown hair matched the horse's mane. That wasn't the only feature they shared. Shelly Stone, with her large brown eyes, long face and thin lips had distinctly equine features. Even her body was long and lean.

Shelly waved as the car approached. "I'll be right back. Have to put Slender Josie in her stall."

Rick parked next to a dark green Mercedes in front of a ranch-style house.

"Nice place," Marlo said as she got out of the car and stretched. "Does Shelly live alone?"

"For now. She tends to go through men at breakneck speed."

"Like a racehorse, huh?"

Rick laughed. "Exactly."

Shelly walked up to Rick and gave him a big hug and kiss. "It's about time you came down to visit me. It's been way too long." She turned her attention to Marlo. "Well, aren't you gorgeous? Rick told me about you, but honey, you are downright stunning." Before Marlo could reply, Shelly bear hugged her, too.

Once released, Marlo thanked Shelly for the compliment. "It's a pleasure meeting you. Rick waxes poetic about you and your farm."

"He better. Without Rick, I wouldn't be where I am today." Shelly started walking to the house. "Why don't we have a bite to eat before I show you around?"

The dining room table had been set. Pictures of racing horses graced the dinner plates. The water glasses carried the horse motif as well. Shelly served her guests salad and homemade cannelloni.

"That was delicious. You're a great cook, Shelly."

"Why thank you. Besides raising champion horses, cooking is my second love." She wiped her mouth with a horseshoe patterned napkin then stood. "We can have dessert on the veranda after I show you my babies, the most magnificent creatures you'll ever meet."

Marlo and Rick followed Shelly out to the stables. As they walked along the brick path, Marlo hadn't yet decided if she was going to ask Shelly, a clearly devoted horse lover, questions about the nefarious practices of the horse racing industry. She knew that her husband was growing tired of her opposition. She didn't want to feel his ire on the drive home. She also didn't want him to suspect that she had anything to do with the inevitable public backlash once the phone calls and marketing campaign began.

'Stone Meadows' was emblazoned on the front of the main stable in large, fire engine red letters, a declaration to all who passed under it that they were entering the farm's inner sanctum. Two smaller buildings that each housed three stalls were connected to the main one, all were white with black roofs, and shutters graced the front and side windows. It was impressive and the interior was even more so. Immaculate was the word that came to mind as Marlo walked through the stable. The hay covering the stall floors was fresh and golden yellow. The walls were so white and clean, she suspected they were scrubbed daily. Salt licks were in each stall as were water troughs and feed trays.

The first stall was home to Catch A Star, his name on a placard that hung from a gold Fleur-de-lis hook. He turned around when they approached and nuzzled up to Shelly. She stroked his black mane. "How's my big, beautiful boy? Looks like you've just been groomed." She turned to her guests. "This is one of the studs. He's been with me for over ten years now. His daughter, Calliope, won the Belmont

Stakes in 2015. His son Coltrane won the Prix de L'Arc de Triomphe in Paris two years ago. He's sired other winners, but I have a feeling we're going to get another big winner out of him before he's spent. Maybe the Triple Crown. Wouldn't that be fantastic?"

"Without a doubt," Rick said. "May I pet him?"

"Of course. Don't be shy." She motioned for the couple to come closer. Together, they stroked the elegant horse's head and back. He graciously allowed them to touch his gleaming coat, his $3.1 million coat to be exact. Marlo was completely in awe. She felt like she was in the presence of royalty. It was then she understood the lure and enticement of horse racing.

"He is beautiful, I mean handsome," Marlo said as she rubbed Catch A Star's velvety soft nose.

"Let's not spend all our time with this boy. I want to show you the others and we've renovated the training barn. It's twice the size."

As the trio was leaving the side barn, Marlo heard some commotion at the far end of the stable. She turned around and saw two men restraining one of the horses. It was putting up a fight, snorting and moving its head up and down as it was being forced into a small metal enclosure inside the stall. One of the men was yelling at the other. Marlo couldn't make out what he was saying. Shelly quickly ushered them out of the stable.

"What was that all about?" Marlo asked.

"I believe Greg and Carlos were administering medication to Redbone. Obviously, she's not fond of getting it."

Marlo was about to respond when Rick cut her off. "My wife thinks that the racing industry is replete with animal abuse."

Shelly laughed. It sounded like a whinny. "Ah yes. You must have been reading that crap propaganda from PETA and Animal Liberation. If it were up to those fanatics, we wouldn't be allowed to ride horses and race them. Racehorses are athletes and, just like human athletes, they get injuries. Do you know how many NFL football players get on the field with injuries? Almost all of them! They're able to play, thanks to painkillers. I read an article the other day that said almost every player is shot full of Toradol, an NSAID. It's no different with racehorses. These babies give their all on the track and the track can be unforgiving. We can't wait for them to recover from a leg injury when they have another race to compete in. We prefer administering

Salix because it prevents the common problem of bleeding in the lungs."

"Good for you for using Salix," Rick said. "I knew you cared about your horses." He looked at Marlo as if to say, 'I told you so.'

Marlo wanted to puke. She had told Rick that she read the in-depth article about rampant abuse in the racing industry in the New York Times. Apparently, he chose to ignore that small fact. At that moment, she looked at Rick in a whole new light, one that was shrouded in greed.

Shelly continued. "Of course I love my babies. They're everything to me. When one of them becomes lame or injured, I hate saying goodbye."

"Wait. What? You sell them? Why don't you keep them on the farm and take care of them?" Marlo was stunned.

"Honey," Shelly said in a voice used to placate a crying child, "Do you know what the annual upkeep is on a racehorse?" She eyed the emerald and diamond necklace Marlo was wearing. "Not as much as that bauble around your neck, but pretty damn close. I can't afford to feed and tend to a horse that's going to hang out in the pasture."

"But didn't they make you a lot of money when they were racing?"

Before Shelly could answer, Rick said, "I know this is not easy for you to understand, sweetheart, but Shelly runs a business. If she retained every horse she'd ever bred, she couldn't sustain a viable living. Believe me, those horses are sold to good people." He looked at Shelly. "Right?"

Shelly's brief hesitation was noted by Marlo. And Rick. "Of course, now let's move on, shall we? I've saved the best for last." She winked at Rick, then led them to a pasture at the far end of the property. It was the only one that abutted a lake. A lone horse grazed. Her brownish-red coat contrasted beautifully with her jet black mane and tail. Her legs were black a little past her elbows and knees. When she saw the trio approaching, she gracefully walked over to them, stopping in front of Marlo and nudging her shoulder. Surprised, Marlo gently stroked the mare's mane.

"How fitting," Shelly said with a tinge of jealousy. "I raised this little girl. Her name is Belle du Lac. Beauty of the lake. As a foal, she loved to run to the lake and play there."

"She certainly is a beauty. And so sweet. How old is she?" Marlo continued to pet the mare.

"Two years old. One more year and she'll be racing. I think she's going to be spectacular on the track. Mark my words."

A tremor went through Marlo's body. She couldn't imagine, didn't want to imagine, the treatment Belle du Lac might endure as a money-making machine. Shelly was no different from the breeders she read about. Her 'babies' were a commodity. They were a lot more glamorous than computers or furniture or even cars, but they were her merchandise just the same.

Rick said, "Do you like her?"

"Of course. She seems very sweet and gentle."

"She's yours," Rick said and gave Belle du Lac a pat on her hind quarter.

"Oh my! Thank you!" Marlo wrapped her arms around her husband and gave him a kiss. Shelly looked on, arms crossed, bemused.

"Now that you own a future racehorse, perhaps you'll change your views when Belle du Lac starts making you money," Rick said.

"Time will tell, won't it?" Marlo replied. Her mind had been made up long before their visit to Stone Meadows. She had more than an inkling Rick had bought her a racehorse. She had one year to plan for her horse's exclusion in the racing industry. It was a challenge she accepted with pleasure.

Back at the house, Marlo barely listened as Rick and Shelly talked about racing. She ate her slice of peach pie and nodded from time to time as if she was actually paying attention to their ramblings. She couldn't wait to call her new friend and tell her about Belle du Lac, the horse whose hoofs would never touch the racing turf.

19

Despite her fear of being cornered by the private detective, Sandy returned to the homeless camp. She knew some of the residents by sight only, not taking the time to learn their names. She wasn't planning on staying there long enough to create any lasting friendships but standing at the entrance to her 'home away from home,' she wished she had gotten to know some of her fellow homeless better. She could use a confidante, a friendly face. Instead, few residents made eye contact. The ones who did were high or inebriated, their gaze unfocused. Sandy walked cautiously down the main pathway, her eyes darting back and forth, looking for any sign of the P.I. She jumped when one of the tents shook. Seconds later, a young woman emerged from behind the tent. She practically hissed, "Don't even think about taking my space. Not for sale."

Sandy shook her head. "Not even thinking about it." Heart pounding, she continued through the city of tents and cardboard boxes, offensive smells and trash strewn walkways. As Sandy reached the perimeter of the homeless camp, she thought she recognized a woman sitting in a lawn chair next to a huge cardboard box. It was the size of a car. She walked over to the woman.

"That's some box you got there. Looks like a car could fit in it."

"Lucky guess." She pointed to the far side of the box. The Amazon logo was proudly displayed, its black 'smile' seemed out of place in the encampment. "Some dude ordered a car, then had the box driven here and gave it to me. Problem is, I don't have enough stuff to furnish it, except my blankets and this chair, plus some other stuff." The forty-something woman with short, chopped sienna brown hair, cloudy brown eyes, and wrinkled jowls eyed Sandy. "Weren't you friends with Kaitlin?"

"Yeah. I can't believe she was killed. She was nice."

"Are you kidding me? She was a nut job. One minute she was sharing her booze with me and the next she was throwing the bottle at my head. Loony bin. That's what she was. She's in a better place where her mind isn't so tangled and swimming in booze. Speaking of which, would you like some?" The woman held up her mug. Disney characters danced around its rim, Mickey chasing Pluto who was chasing Minnie who was running after Goofy. A chip in the mug gouged out half of Goofy's head. "Name's Olive, what's yours?"

"Sandy." She dropped her sleeping bag next to Olive's chair and sat on it. Then she took a cup out of her backpack and gave it to Olive, who promptly filled it with Smirnoff Vodka. She handed it back.

"Nothing gets you there like straight V. Am I right or what?" Olive coughed. It sounded like a death rattle, wet and raspy.

Instinctively, Sandy leaned away. Her life was bad enough without catching a disease. "Cheers." The liquor stung the back of her throat, but she continued to drink it, the elixir burning up Sandy's reality. She knew she had to be aware of her surroundings, lest the private eye find her, but she also wanted to dull her mind to the point where she no longer felt the intense loneliness and discomfort that was her life. Olive, Kaitlin, and any other resident would never fill the void. She desperately wanted to see Darby again, but hearing her mother's voice sent tremors down her spine. Going back to the mansion was no longer an option.

Olive took a large swallow from her mug and began coughing. It was more violent than the first. When it subsided, she had tears streaming down her face and her nose was running. She grabbed a soiled napkin from her pocket and blew her nose. She wiped the tears away with her jacket sleeve, then chuckled when she saw the concerned look on Sandy's face. "Don't worry, dear, it's not contagious. Too many years smoking non-filtered cigarettes. I gotta get to the clinic for more extra-strength cough medicine. That reminds me. One of the doctors from there was looking for you. He was showing your picture to everyone here, asking if we've seen you. I'd recognized you when you were hanging out with Kaitlin, but that was a couple of days ago."

Sandy's mood lightened. "Was it Dr. Remini?"

"I don't know the guy's name. It could have been. I just remember him saying that he worked at the free clinic. I told him I had to get over there soon. He was here when those vegan vipers came by. Too bad you missed it. One of them gave me this loaf of bread with nuts and raisins in it. Damn, it was good. I still have some. You want a slice?"

"Sure. Thanks. I have some food, too." Sandy rooted around in her backpack and held up an apple. She put it on the ground. "I know I have some protein bars. Ah, here they are."

"Looks like we got a real feast. I'll drink to that!"

Never a big drinker, Sandy found that alcohol made living on the fringe of society tolerable, just shy of fun. She drank half the contents. "I'd still be living with my parents if I had known that a steady dose of alcohol would have made life easier."

Olive cocked her head to the right and closed one eye, giving her guest a thorough look-over. "Aren't you kinda old to be living with mommy and daddy?"

"I'm only twenty-three," she said defensively as she took another swig, finishing the vodka. "Besides, my parent's house is big enough to get lost in. I could have successfully avoided them for days."

"Pardon me, Miss Rich Girl, but what the hell are you doing here?"

Sandy realized she had said too much. The last thing she wanted was to be associated with her family's money. She backpedaled. "When I say big, I mean, like 2,000 square feet. I should have said that it would have been easy to avoid them if I got up after they left the house for work and went to my room before they got home." She pointed to her clothes. "Do I look rich to you?"

"No, but you said…"

"I know what I said. It was the liquor talking. Speaking of which…" Sandy pulled out a bottle of Old Jameson. "Ta da. I love mixing vodka and whiskey, don't you?"

"One of my favorite things. Fill 'er up, Miss Rich Girl."

"Please don't call me that. I'm not rich."

"Fine. No need to get snippy. Play your cards and bottles right and you may just be able to spend the night in the palatial cardboard estate of one Olive Rostemeyer."

"Does it have central heating?"

Olive held up the bottle of vodka. "You're looking at it."

A few miles away, Will knocked on his sister's door. He heard Makelo shout, "I'll get it!" and shortly after, the door swung open. "Uncle Will!"

"Nephew Makelo. What's happening, buddy?"

"Dinner."

"Is that why I'm holding a bottle of wine and a box of cupcakes?"

Makelo held out his hands and Will gave him the box. He ran into the kitchen. "Uncle Will brought cupcakes from The Big V."

Danya was watching The Great Goon Babies, her favorite show. When she heard the word cupcakes, she paused the DVD and ran to the kitchen. "Let's see! let's see!" Her small hands pried the top open. Her eyes widened as she took in the variety of all twelve cupcakes.

"I didn't know The Big V made cupcakes," Gloria said as she gave her brother a hug.

Monica wiped her hands in her apron and wrapped her arms around her brother-in-law. "I'm more interested in the wine," she said as she took the bottle. "Iron Dog Cellars. Love the label. Why does it have a V for vegan? Aren't all wines vegan?"

"Not at all," said Will. "Some of the fining agents used to clarify wine are fish bladders, egg whites, and gelatin."

"Ew, gross." Makelo held his nose.

Will agreed. "I know. Iron Dog Cellars makes one of the best pinots around and they're not only vegan, but they are biodynamic as well."

Makelo said, "What does that mean?"

"It's very cool. Basically, the concept behind biodynamics is that everything in the universe is interconnected and gives off a resonance, a vibration. It includes the moon, planets, and stars. The winemakers balance this resonance between their vineyards, the people who make the wine, the earth's vibe, the planets, and the stars."

"I want to do that," said Makelo, "but do I have to make wine?"

"It refers to agriculture, but anything you want to do, you can apply the biodynamic concept. Take for instance the paper that you're writing on a homeless person. Look at that human being in relationship to their surroundings. Look up to the heavens to find out where they came from. And I don't mean their deceased relatives. Who were they before? Does that have a bearing on who they are now?"

Gloria had been setting the table while listening to the

conversation. "Aren't you getting a tad too esoteric, Dr. Remini? Makelo's eight."

Before Will could answer, Makelo said, "I've been reading a book on reincarnation, and I believe in it. I think it would blow my teacher away if I used it in my paper."

Gloria said, "I stand corrected. Once again, my son, you have dispelled the myth that eight-year-olds aren't sophisticated enough to understand anything past Pokémon Go."

"I find that insulting, Mom."

Monica said, "Me, too. Our kid is brilliant." She motioned for everyone to take their seats at the dining room table. "Where did you find a book on reincarnation, kiddo?"

Makelo took his seat and Sisi immediately jumped into his lap. She curled up into a little black and white ball, resembling a fuzzy domino more than a cat. "A couple of weeks ago, our class went on a field trip to the bookstore. At the end of the tour, the lady told us we could each have one book from the sale rack. All the books were for kids. I didn't see anything I liked. Then I saw *Reincarnation for Dummies* on another sale rack and asked Mrs. Kornfeld if I could have that one. She said yes. It's not really for dummies. Mrs. Kornfeld said that the title is deceptive. She said that reincarnation is explained so people can understand it easier."

Will stabbed a couple of roasted Fingerling potatoes with his fork and placed them on his plate next to the grilled eggplant and zucchini. He then drizzled tahini sauce over the vegetables. "So tell me, Makelo, why do you believe in reincarnation?"

"When I lived in Turkey, I used to dream all the time that I was flying over the orphanage. I would circle around it, visit the stray cats, and then fly to other parts of the town. Sometimes, I would shoot straight up into the black sky. One time, I flew over to another part of the village and saw a man running down the street. He stopped, grabbed his chest, and fell to the ground. The next day, one of the ladies at the orphanage was crying. She said her father died of a heart attack last night. They found him in the middle of the street. After reading in the book how our spirit wakes up and flies all over the place when we go to sleep, I don't think I was dreaming."

Gloria was surprised. "Honey, you were three years old when we adopted you. How can you remember so much about your dreams, especially witnessing the man's death?"

Makelo shrugged. "I guess I have a really good memory. Mom, do you believe in reincarnation?"

Gloria said, "Honestly, I don't know. I vacillate between wanting to believe that the purpose of life is spiritual growth and there have been a lot of believable stories of people under hypnosis who remember their past lives, but then I see so much violence and hurtful things that people to do each other, to the earth and to animals. I find it hard to believe the human spirit has grown at all. People are worse than they've ever been."

Danya had been playing with her Sparkle Pony while poking at her dinner. She stopped, her eyes moist with tears. "Am I worse, too?"

Monica gave Gloria the look, one that questioned yet again why her wife didn't screen her comments. It wasn't uncommon for Gloria to speak unfiltered in front of the children, yet she seemed to realize, after the fact, that she should have been more careful with her opinion.

Gloria went over to Danya and gave her a big hug. "Not at all, sweetheart. You're fantastic."

Danya held up her Sparkle Pony. "Is she fantastic, too?"

"Absolutely. As a matter of fact, everyone here is very good." Gloria went into the kitchen. Feeling hot, she pulled her hair back and put it in a ponytail.

In a hushed voice, Will said to Makelo, "Why don't we talk about this after dinner?"

Makelo nodded. "I also want to go to the soup kitchen with you. I still have to interview a homeless person. Do you think Old Joe will talk to me?"

"Sure he will. That man loves to talk, whether you want to listen or not. He's a chatterbox."

Danya said, "Uncle Willy, can I have a cupcake? I finished my dinner."

Monica said, "You did? Then why is there so much food on your plate? I think Sparkle Pony ate more than you. I want to see half the food on your plate eaten, Miss Danya, then you can have a cupcake." She turned to Will. "Makelo told me that you were looking for Sandy Ekhart the other day. Is she okay?"

"I don't know. She told me that she would leave the homeless camp and stay at the shelter, but when I inquired, they said she never arrived.

I checked the Portrero Hill shelter, too. Not a sign of her."

From the time Will walked into his sister's house, Gigi was there, tailing the young doctor like a vapor trail. His interest in Sandy's welfare drew her to him, hoping that her knowledge of the homeless woman's predicament and her whereabouts would, like osmosis, seep into Will's mind. So far, no luck. Whenever she was within close proximity to a human, she used all her concentration to radiate a presence. The closest anyone had come to feeling her company was Petal. Even then, she was unable to convey a message. Still, Gigi persisted, convinced that there were people; not many of them; with an acute sensitivity to the spiritual world. Self-proclaimed psychics and clairvoyants abounded, but few actually possessed the ability to tell the future or communicate with the spirit world. She had yet to meet one.

As a tiny pinprick of light, Gigi listened to the family's conversation next to the chandelier above the dining room table. She knew immediately that Makelo's spirit had experienced hundreds of incarnations. The eight-year-old's eyes gleamed with knowledge and wisdom.

"Uncle Will, I think we should look for her again. If she's in trouble, then we could help her, right?"

Gloria cut in. "If she's in trouble, she could also be in danger and I don't want you anywhere near her, my little boy." Monica nodded in agreement.

"But I want to help her," said Makelo, his voice filled with emotion. Sensing his anxiety, Sisi sat up. She looked into Makelo's large, brown eyes as she climbed up his chest and licked his cheek. No one paid much attention, since it was a regular routine with the two Turkish immigrants.

Will put his arm around his nephew. "Tell you what. Come with me to the soup kitchen tomorrow night. After we serve dinner, you can interview Old Joe. If Sandy's not there, we'll take a quick ride to the Portrero Hill Shelter. If we find her, great, but if not, I'll take you home so your moms don't worry." He shot his sister a look. "How does that sound?"

"Fine with me. Mon?"

Satisfied that Danya had finished half the food on her plate, Monica placed the cupcakes on a large platter and set it in the middle of the table. She looked directly at Will. "Only if you're super careful."

"I will guard him with my life." He turned his attention to the decorated mini cakes. "Let's see if I can remember the flavors. The ones with the orange and white striped frosting are dreamsicle-flavored."

"What's that?" Danya said as she slid her finger across the side of the cupcake.

"Vanilla and orange. You want to try it?" Will asked his niece.

Danya pointed to a chocolate cupcake with pink frosting and chocolate jimmies. "Sparkle Pony wants to know what flavor that one is."

"Of course she does, because it matches her mane. I do believe that it's chocolate bubble gum."

Danya's face lit up. "That one. I want that one!"

The adults ate their cupcakes with coffee while the children each had a glass of almond milk with theirs.

"These are amazing." Gloria popped the last bite of her caramel macchiato cupcake in her mouth.

"You've been to the Big V. Everything Ronnie makes is amazing." Will smiled. It was a sly little smile.

"What are you not telling us, brother o' mine?"

"Have you heard of the Vegan Vipers?"

Monica said, "Are they a compassionate group of snakes that eat tofu mice?"

"Very funny. They're a group of Harley riding, vegan chefs that bring food and other living necessities to the homeless. Ronnie started the group a few years ago. They're quite a vision. I think there are seven of them. They wear vegan leathers with a stylized illustration of a viper on their jackets. I met them when I went to the homeless encampment looking for Sandy. Ronnie and I started talking and, before I knew it, she was asking me out. I swear! The woman's got chutzpah. I made her my signature chili the other night."

"Did she meet Minky?" Makelo asked. He went to grab another cupcake, but Monica stopped him.

"You've had two, dear. That's enough. We'll save one for your lunch tomorrow, okay?" Makelo nodded, reluctantly.

Will said, "She did indeed meet the famous Minky. They got along famously."

"I'm guessing you two did, as well." Gloria was elated. Between the clinic and the soup kitchen, her brother barely had time to visit the family. He made time and that's what made him such a special person.

"As a matter of fact, we did. We'll definitely be seeing each other again."

"Hallelujah and pass the kale. I couldn't be happier for you. She's a fantastic cook, a vegan, charitable, and I'm guessing attractive, especially in her viper outfit straddling a Harley. What more could you ask for?" Gloria went over and gave her brother a big kiss.

Makelo looked confused. "What's the big deal? It's just a girl."

Gloria said, "You'll understand when you're older. For now, be happy for your uncle." She turned to Will. "I have to put the kids to bed. Stay. I'll be down in a little while."

"I want Uncle Willy to put me to bed," Danya cried.

"I would be happy to, my little niece, under one condition." Will went over and put her little face in his hands. "Let's leave off the fairy dust, okay?" He gave her nose a little tap, then turned to his sister. "One of my patients was coming off Ecstasy and swore I had been anointed king of the fairies. He wouldn't stop bowing before me. I thought I had removed all the glitter. Apparently, I hadn't."

Gloria let out a hearty laugh. "Imagine that, my brother a fairy!"

Gigi also laughed, yet no one heard.

"Paige, honey, it's time for bed. Go brush your teeth, please." Alec walked into his daughter's room. She was sitting cross-legged on her bed, listening to her grandmother read a book. Marilyn sat straight-legged next to her, her torn dress and the discoloration from the concrete dust remained. "What are you reading?"

Rebecca looked up from the book and held it up for him to see. "The Giving Tree. My mother used to read it to me. It was one of my favorites."

Rebecca looked at Paige. "I read this story, this same book, to your mother. Shall I finish? We're almost done."

Paige nodded. "Marilyn wants to hear the end, too, don't you Marilyn?"

All eyes were on the doll. Emma couldn't see them, but she could feel the energy in the room directed to her. It was loving and it was heartbreaking. It also slightly energized her weakening spirit. Marilyn reminded the family that, if it weren't for her, Janet Andersen may still be alive. Emma wondered if she would still be alive if the American Girl doll hadn't fallen out of Paige's backpack. What if. The world was full of what ifs. Most of them didn't end in death. Since her father's visit, Emma wasn't sure what to do. Her energy was dropping. Soon, she wouldn't have a choice. She didn't want to suffer the loss and heartache and searing emotional pain that came with being human. If she did take over Sandy's body, she would have her work cut out for her. The woman had racked up so many psychic scars that even with a 'new and improved' spirit, Emma didn't know how much of Sandy's personality had seeped into her bones and muscle, sinew, and skin. Would Sandy gain a new perspective and attitude on life only to doubt herself? Without a playbook, it was a crapshoot. Emma wasn't sure she wanted to take that chance.

While Emma was ruminating, Rebecca finished reading the book. She took a tissue out of her pocket and wiped her eyes. "The end gets to me every time."

Paige said, "Because the tree is only a stump, but still loves the man and she's happy because he's happy?"

"That pretty much sums it up. It's called unconditional love and if every human on this planet practiced it, this place would be pure paradise."

"Would mommy still be alive if everyone had unconditional love?"

"Definitely." Rebecca put the book on the dresser. "Go brush your teeth. It's past your bedtime."

Paige jumped off the bed and ran to the bathroom. "Do you have unconditional love, Grammy?"

Rebecca thought about the men who placed the bomb in the airport terminal. The men who took her daughter's life. Snatched away a mother, wife, human. She shook her head, wanting to dislodge the image. "I'm working on it, sweetheart."

In another room, Alec was crying. The Giving Tree reminded him of Janet. His confidante. Her generosity was boundless. She loved Paige with every ounce of her being and would have done anything to protect her. He always thought of Janet as practicing unconditional love. Would she feel that way if it was Paige who died instead of her? Could she have forgiven those who took away her child?

In a moment of nostalgia, Emma decided to leave the doll for a while and observe the family. She missed watching Paige get ready for bed. She wanted to see Rebeca make a pot of tea, then sit in the living room and read the thrillers she so loved. And Alec, as he washed the dishes while he sang along to the tunes on his iPhone.

When she attempted to exteriorize, she was hit with a wave of sluggishness. Her spirit, once able to leap out of Marilyn, was having a difficult time. It felt like she was stuck in tar, thick and viscous, unrelenting. By the time she got halfway out, she was overcome with exhaustion. As she slipped back into her home, she was again surrounded by darkness. The reality of never leaving this tomb sent Emma into shock. She prayed that Gigi hadn't given up on her, but even if she did come to Emma's aid, could she help her?

Norma was getting nervous. She hadn't heard from Lonnie since they met at the future site of the racetrack. She wanted to keep her contact with him minimal, but she also wanted to know if Lonnie had been having any success at finding her daughter. He said he would call her as soon as there was a development. His silence meant he was failing, which would result in Norma unable to meet her financial deadline. She briefly considered asking her parents for a loan, but her pride wouldn't allow it. Bob also refused to turn to his family.

Sitting at the dining room table, finishing her morning cup of coffee, Norma's attempt at reading the San Francisco Chronicle was weak. She merely went through the motions, skimming an article on the new art installation at the de Young Museum. As she turned the page, she caught the subheading in an article: *Environmentalists go to the phones to inform residents about racetrack dangers*. The more Norma read about the Citizens for Environmental Protection's plan to disrupt the construction of Francisco Downs through the EIS, the more she could feel her heart rate increasing. The future racetrack had been intentionally kept under the radar. Rick had used his influence with the newspaper to keep it out of the Chronicle's pages. Another investor had ties with The Franciscan Group, a media conglomerate that owned over half the radio stations, magazines, and local television stations in the Bay Area.

"How the hell did this get into the paper?" she shouted. Walking into the dining room from the study, Bob said, "What's the matter, Norma?" His tone implied he could care less what upset her.

Norma threw the newspaper across the expansive table. Pages scattered. "Those tree-huggers are trying to stop construction of the track over a trickle of a creek. They've even begun calling the surrounding neighborhoods, attempting to evoke antipathy toward the racetrack, saying that it's going to be an eyesore in their community and an environmental nightmare for the creek's water quality. Environmentalists aren't trying to save anything worth saving. They're more like Nazis and their target is progress. I wish they'd all choke on the twigs and branches they want so desperately to save."

Secretly, Bob was thrilled. He wasn't a horseracing fan. Nor was he that excited about investing their money in a venture that was dependent upon the health of the economy. The recession in 2008 saw at least two casinos and a racetrack file for bankruptcy.

"Sternwood Creek empties into the San Francisco Bay. It's not an insignificant body of water."

Norma glared at her husband. "Since when are you an environmental Nazi sympathizer?"

Nervously, Bob tightened the belt on his bathrobe. He pulled it a little too tight and gasped. He didn't like disagreeing with Norma, but he was getting tired of having to defend his opinion every time it contradicted hers. "All I'm saying is…"

"All I'm saying, all I'm saying. You don't know what you're saying. I'd like to hear you tell me that the $20 million is back in our account. I'd love to hear that. Can you tell me that, Bob? Can you?"

The familiar sound of the Kentucky Derby Trumpet Call interrupted their conversation. Norma turned her back on Bob and reached into her purse. She answered the call before the trumpet sounded again. "This is Norma."

"I think I found Sandy."

"Finally, some good news."

When she made the decision to go, she was running late. Marlo kept waffling about whether she should follow through with volunteering for Citizens for Environmental Protection. She had agreed to make the calls at Petal's house and then her hostess was going to give her a rudimentary introduction to aromatherapy. Marlo's desire to spend the day at Petal's was as strong as her anxiety over the decision to go.

If she made all the lights, she'd still be a couple of minutes late, so she forwent her daily routine and for the first time since she met Rick, she ran out of the house without make-up. Marlo balled up her long, caramel brown locks into a bun and secured it with chopsticks. Black and white checkered tennis shoes, jeans and a pink cotton long-sleeved Ralph Lauren polo shirt completed the ensemble. As she re-adjusted the seat in the Mercedes to give her ample leg room, Marlo pulled down the visor and looked in the mirror. "Ugh. I hope Petal recognizes me. I don't even recognize me."

From Marlo's neighborhood to Petal's was like visiting Disneyland, then going to Fairyland in Oakland, sweet but it paled in comparison. It reminded Marlo of her neighborhood growing up. The cottages were built in the 50s. One was distinguished from the other in color, landscaping, and roof composition. Petal's home stood out from the others. It was French vanilla with sage green shutters. A brick chimney sat on the dark grey shingled roof. Instead of a lawn, an herb garden graced the right side of the brick walkway, and the left side was awash in color and fragrance with gardenia and rose bushes, lantana, and a miniature lemon tree. Marlo used the brass frog knocker on the maroon-colored door.

"I'm sorry I'm late," Marlo said as Petal greeted her.

"Don't worry about it." Petal observed her new friend and fellow volunteer. "I didn't think it was possible, but you look better without make-up. Radiant, even."

Marlo blushed. "How sweet of you to say. My husband would strongly disagree. The more dolled up the better." She inhaled deeply. "There's that wonderful scent again, but it's mixed with other fragrances." She closed her eyes and inhaled again. "I already feel more relaxed." Marlo took in the eclectic décor. "I love your home, Petal. It's so warm and inviting."

"Thank you. Would you like a cup of tea?"

Marlo nodded. She walked over to a clay sculpture of a cougar stretching, its front paws hanging off the shelf. "This is exquisite."

Petal joined her and stroked the cat's back. "My brother is a sculptor, among other things. This was one of his first pieces. I love how it flows. The cougar looks so relaxed and at peace."

When the kettle began to whistle, Petal turned off the heat and poured the boiling water into two mugs. "Are you ready to make calls? I personally have never done this before. I'm a little nervous. What if people get mad at me and hang up?"

"When I first went on modeling auditions, I was subjected to some really insensitive jerks. We women were a dime a dozen, like Barbie dolls coming off the assembly line, and they treated us like we were idiots. It was humiliating and for the first couple of months, I was offended until I stopped taking it personally. That's what you must do. If someone's rude, thank them for their time and hang up. Show's over. Move on. Make your next call. Don't stop to think about it. Keep the vision of a clean, toxic-free creek in your head. Focus on why we're doing this."

"You could be a motivational speaker. I appreciate the advice. We'll see if I can keep those words of wisdom in mind when someone yells at me."

Marlo took a sip of tea. "Mm, this is delicious."

"Thanks. It's my special blend of green and white tea leaves, dried loquats, and lavender buds."

"Never in a million years would I have put those ingredients together."

"I love to experiment with different combinations, mix it up. I do it with my oils, too."

"I have a feeling I'm going to be learning a lot from you."

Petal gazed intently at Marlo. "If you were to create your own tea blend, what would you use?"

"I never thought about it before. Let's see, I would start with white tea leaves. Then I'd add dried black cherries and cinnamon, two of my favorite flavors. Can I include chocolate and vanilla?"

Petal laughed. "I love your creativity! Yes, all those ingredients would make a satisfying and healthy tea. You are going to be so easy to teach."

Marlo blushed. "Thanks, Petal. All this feels very natural to me.

Like I'm returning to a place where I never wanted to leave."

After the women spent a couple of hours on the phones, they decided to sit out on the back porch and reward their selfless behavior with homemade fudge and espressos. Marlo observed Petal as she took a long sip from her coffee. Petal caught the look out of the corner of her eye. She was at once self-conscious. "Do I have some fudge on my face?" She lightly swatted her cheek.

"No. I was just admiring your haircut. It's a great look for you. It complements your features." Marlo removed the chopsticks from her hair. The golden brown strands fell past her shoulders, down to the middle of her back. She grabbed a handful of her shiny locks and pulled them away from her face. "Do you think I would look good with short hair?"

"Definitely. And it's so easy to take care of." She gave her head a quick shake.

Marlo took another look at her long locks and thought about how labor intensive the upkeep was. She glanced back at Petal. "Let's do it."

"Huh? You want to go to a salon now?"

"No silly. I want you to cut it."

"I make great fudge and my teas and oils are exceptional, but I don't cut hair!"

"I do." Forest was standing just inside the patio door. He was average height with short, curly black hair and a goatee. He was wearing shorts, a muscle shirt, and flip flops.

Petal stood. "Isn't it a little cool for beach wear?"

"I just came from the gym. Besides, it's in the mid-60s. In San Francisco, that's like seventy-five degrees everywhere else." Forest turned his attention to Marlo. He held out his hand. "I'm Forest. Petal's brother. Are you sure you want to cut your hair? It's beautiful."

Marlo shook his hand. "Marlo Standish." She pushed her hair behind her ears. "I can't remember ever having short hair. My mother wouldn't let me cut it past my shoulders. When I started dating, guys begged me to keep it long. And even though he's never said not to shorten it, I know my husband loves it."

Forest said, "It sounds like you need to do what you want, not what others tell you to do. I used to date a hair stylist and she taught me how to dry cut. It's more difficult working with dry hair, but it's so much easier to see how the style is taking shape. She compared it to sculpting, which I do for a living, and it makes perfect sense." Forest walked up behind Marlo and put his hands on either side of her head. "May I?"

"Sure."

Forest picked up Marlo's hair and felt its weight and texture. "Did you want it to look like Petal's? You both have straight, fine hair."

"Do you have professional scissors? I remember my hairdresser telling me that she paid over $900 for hers."

Forest said, "I'll tell you what. I won't cut it as short as Petal's with my cheap, but sharp, scissors, so if you don't like it, you can go to your hairdresser and let her finish my work with her uber expensive shears. Deal?"

Marlo took a deep breath and let it out slowly. "If I don't do it now, I'm going to lose my nerve, and I dream of washing short hair and leaving my hairdryer under the sink, along with the flat iron. Let's do it."

Petal said, "Normally, I wouldn't let a neophyte cut my hair, but Forest is an artist and I think you're in good hands. Of course, if he messes up, I had nothing to do with this!"

Forest rubbed his hands together. "I'll be right back."

Petal set up a makeshift salon in her dining room. She spread a sheet on the floor under the chair. She also secured a towel around her friend's neck. Marlo turned down the option of facing a mirror. Petal put a drop of Cloud Eleven on the palm of Marlo's hand and instructed her to rub her palms together to create heat, then put them up to her nose and slowly inhale. "It will give you a sense of serenity. I have a feeling you'll need that."

Scissors poised to begin, Forest said, "Ready?"

Marlo closed her eyes. "Just do it."

Forest separated Marlo's hair into four sections, then snipped the back section. "Are you also an aromatherapist, Marlo?"

"No, but I'm hoping your sister will teach me how to become one. I find it fascinating and the aromas intoxicating."

"What are you doing now?"

Marlo ignored the question. Instead, she put her palms up to her nose. "Can I have another drop of that oil? It's working, but I'd like to feel just a tad more fluffy."

Petal laughed. She brought the bottle over and added another drop on Marlo's palm. "This is one of my biggest sellers."

"I can certainly see why. It's wonderful. My head feels lighter already."

Petal looked down at the sheet. "I think that's because you just lost about ten pounds of hair. Are you sure you don't want me to bring over a mirror? I can lean it up against the side table."

"Nope. I want to be completely surprised. By the way, Forest, I love your cougar sculpture. It really captures the cat's grace."

Forest cut another large section of hair. "Thanks. I've always been intrigued by cougars. They're my favorite big cat."

Petal sat at the other end of the table, finishing her espresso, watching her brother perform a work of art on a complete stranger. Both siblings inherited a strong sense of self-confidence from their parents, but Petal wondered if she had the fearlessness her brother possessed. If she did, she had yet to test it.

Thirty minutes later, Forest held Marlo's hand as she walked with eyes closed into the bathroom. When she opened them, she saw a woman with chin length hair and soft bangs staring back at her. She ran her hands through her hair then shook her head and laughed. "I absolutely love it!" She gave Forest a hug and kissed him on the cheek. "You are an artist. An incredible artist."

Forest took a bow.

"By the way, why did you come over?" his sister asked.

Forest gave his sister a sly smile. "I had a feeling I was needed."

"So, it wasn't to pick up the box of fudge I told you I had waiting for you?"

"Yeah. That, too." Forest looked around. "Where did Marlo go?"

Marlo reappeared in the bathroom doorway. "I went to get my purse. What do I owe you?" She pulled out her checkbook, poised to write.

Forest looked at Petal. "Is she kidding?" He stared in disbelief at Marlo. "Are you kidding?"

Suddenly, Marlo felt very small. "I just thought you deserved something for all your effort. I didn't mean to offend you."

"I'm not offended, just surprised that you would think that I'd charge you for doing something I offered to do, or that you would feel obligated to pay me."

"How about this. When your sister teaches me how to make my

own aromatherapy potions, you'll receive my first gift pack." Marlo tucked her checkbook back in her purse.

"Works for me."

Marlo glanced at herself in the mirror and giggled. "I can't believe how happy I am with my new 'do.' I feel so liberated and suddenly empowered, like the reverse of Samson. You know, of Samson and Delilah fame. I know I'm going to get shit for this when I get home, but it's worth it."

Once Marlo left, Forest turned to his sister. "How did you meet Marlo?"

"I sat next to her at the environmental group's meeting. She's also opposed to the racetrack at the other end of the city. We were making phone calls to people in the vicinity of the future track, asking them to fight its construction. Isn't she great?"

Forest grabbed a piece of fudge from the plate. Before he took a bite, he said, "This is raw, right?"

"Absolutely."

Forest popped the dark chocolate square in his mouth. He closed his eyes. "Unbelievable. You really should market this."

"I have my hands full creating and marketing my oils. Maybe when I have more time." Petal began cleaning up the kitchen. "So, what did you think of Marlo?"

"I think it's amazing that the wife of one of the investors is fighting against the project. I bet hubby doesn't know."

Petal nearly dropped the bowl she was washing. She turned off the water and stared at her brother. "What are you talking about?"

Forest took a bite out of his second piece of fudge. He brought the espresso cups in from the patio table and placed them next to the sink where Petal was standing, still in shock. "A few years ago, an investment group was planning on purchasing, then demolishing the Vicktor Theater on Broderick. They were bidding against a group bent on preserving the building, which was one of the few left standing after the 1904 quake. They were going to renovate it and bring it back as a music hall. The investment group won the bid. In less than a year, the theater was torn down and replaced with elite condos. Ironically, the residents have a private theater in the building. Rick Standish was the spokesperson for the group. When she told me her name, it sounded familiar, but she didn't look like a socialite at all. No make-up, jeans, and tennis shoes? It wasn't until about halfway through cutting her hair that she began to look familiar. Then I remembered hearing Standish speak at the ribbon cutting ceremony, Marlo by his side. The old fart must be thirty years her senior. No wonder she offered to pay me. The woman's loaded."

"The woman has chutzpah, that's for sure. When we spoke, she actually seemed more concerned about the mistreatment of the horses than the creek's welfare. Whatever the reason, Ricky's not going to be happy when he finds out."

"If he finds out." Forest filled up a glass with water and took a sip. "I have a prediction to make. Within the next couple of years, if not sooner, Marlo is going to leave Mr. Moneybags. That woman has a conscience and it's going to be getting too loud for her to ignore. Remember that movie, *Sleeping With the Enemy?*"

Petal's eyes narrowed. "Yeah, I do, and it's a completely different scenario."

"I know. The title's the only thing they have in common."

Petal laughed. "You want to stay for dinner?"

"Would love to, but I need to finish a project. I have to deliver an owl sculpture to my client tomorrow. She wants it on display at her housewarming party. You want to see it?"

Petal nodded and walked over to her brother while he found photos of the sculpture in its various stages of development. Forest thumbed through the photos of the white, gold and charcoal-colored bird while his sister oohed and aahed.

Across town, someone else was admiring Forest's handiwork. The Standish's maid, Christina, a thirty-year-old refugee from Afghanistan, walked around Marlo in awe.

"I love it! You look even more beautiful than before." Her English was nearly flawless as she had spent a good deal of her twenties in Manhattan before moving to San Francisco to be closer to her brother. She took her hair in her hand. It was in a long, thick braid. "You think your friend would cut my hair, too?"

Marlo said, "I'll tell you what. Set up an appointment with my hair stylist and I'll pay. It will be my gift to you."

Christina's large, almond-shaped eyes, widened. "That is so kind of you. Thank you so much, Mrs. Standish."

"I'm happy to do it."

Impulsively, Christina gave Marlo a heartfelt hug. Rick walked through the front door and caught the embrace. "What did I miss? Wait, Marlo, what happened to your hair?"

Christina said, "Isn't it lovely?"

Rick's face darkened. "No, it isn't. What the hell have you done?"

Marlo's first instinct was to run upstairs to the bedroom to avoid a confrontation. She hated fighting, especially because she was atrocious at defending herself. She would get tongue-tied and her brain would go into shutdown mode. But she stayed. She didn't want to be that Marlo anymore. Spending time with Petal and Forest made her feel smart and funny and capable of making her own decisions. Their confidence empowered her.

Rick held out his overcoat and briefcase and Christina dutifully took it and delivered it to its rightful place in the study. Alone with Marlo, Rick continued his assault. "Why didn't you tell me that you were going to chop off all your hair so you could look like a little boy?"

Marlo looked down at her long legs and tiny waist, her ample breasts that defied gravity. "My hair shouldn't define my femininity. Plus, I've never seen a little boy with a body like this. Have you?"

"You know what I mean."

"No Rick, I don't. It's my hair that I lopped off. I've been wanting to do it for years and I finally had the courage to do it." She put her arms around her husband's neck. "Feel it."

Tentatively, Rick ran his hand through her hair. "It's soft." He slid his hand up the nape of her neck to the top of her head. "Very soft." He then stepped away and looked at Marlo. A small smile crept across his face. "You don't look like a little boy and when you have make-up on, you'll be as stunning as ever."

Marlo hugged her husband. She decided this wouldn't be the best time to tell him that she was going to start wearing less make-up. One shock at a time.

20

Makelo felt tiny beads of sweat on his hairline. He helped his uncle carry the hard plastic bowls out to the dining area. As soon as he placed them next to the huge pot of chili, steam seeping out of the loose-fitting lid, he wiped his brow. Other volunteers were cleaning off the long tables and chairs, wiping the crumbs and stains from the last meal.

"When can I interview Old Joe, Uncle Will? Before or after dinner?" Makelo checked his back pocket, lightly touching the mini recorder his mother let him borrow.

Will set the spoons next to the bowls. "First, you need to ask him if you can interview him, then I would wait until after he eats. Old Joe loves to talk, so I don't think you'll have a problem there."

"That sounds like a plan."

A few minutes later, the doors opened, and a line began to form at the front of the food station. It snaked its way around the dining room and out the door. Will shook his head. The line grew longer every year. San Francisco rents were unrealistically high and the young techies pouring into the city with high-paying jobs were driving the rents higher, pushing out lower income residents and rendering more than a few of them homeless. Will was determined to create decent, affordable housing through San Francisco's Department of Housing and Urban Development. He was nearly finished with his proposal. In the meantime, he offered his services to these marginalized San Franciscans whenever he could.

Twenty minutes into serving, Makelo spotted Old Joe. "There he is!" His enthusiasm was contagious, and Will couldn't help but get excited for his nephew. There weren't many eight-year-olds that were eager to interview a homeless man. A crusty, old homeless man.

When Old Joe shuffled up and took a bowl of chili from Makelo, the little boy said, "Hey, Old Joe. How are you tonight?"

"Same as last night. Achy, cold, and hungry." He scratched his crotch and Will winced. He would have preferred Makelo didn't see that, but his nephew looked unfazed. "You want to give me a little more of that chili?" He held out the bowl long enough for Will to top it off. "Thanks." Before he moved on, Makelo said,

"After dinner, can I interview you for a school assignment?"

Old Joe scratched his head. More than a few white flecks fell from his head as he considered the question. He looked at Makelo whose face was filled with hope and anticipation. "Sure. Why not. You're not going to pepper me with personal questions, are you?"

Makelo shook his head. "Oh, no. And if I do, you don't have to answer. Okay?"

"Deal." He pointed to a table at the far end of the dining hall. "Meet me over there in about twenty minutes. Be there or be square or oblong or obtuse."

Once Old Joe shuffled down the line, Makelo turned to Will and said, "What does that mean, be there or be square or oblong or antuse?"

"It's just a saying. Actually, it's be there or be square. Old Joe added his own spin to it. He's basically telling you to come over, and it's obtuse, not antuse. So, do you have your questions written down?" Will ladled a generous helping of chili into a bowl. Makelo pointed to his head.

"They're all up here. I memorized them. Will you let me know when it's twenty minutes from now?"

"Sure."

There were five people in the dinner line when Will told Makelo that it was time for the interview. Dutifully, Makelo practically skipped over to where Old Joe was putting the last bite of cornbread into his mouth.

Old Joe patted the seat next to him. "Well, aren't you Johnny on the spot?"

"You have a lot of funny sayings. What does that mean?"

"It means you're on time. A good trait to have." He rubbed his hands together. "Let's get this party started. That means you can ask me your first question."

Makelo said, "I knew what that meant." He put the recorder on the table, checked to make sure the volume was turned up and hit 'record.' The red light went on. "Is Old Joe your real name?"

The man laughed. It was a throaty, phlegmy laugh. His teeth were deep yellow and small pieces of food were stuck between them. He wiped his mouth with the napkin. "I was born Joseph Ryder Phelps, Junior. All my life, I had been called junior. I hated it. When I turned fifty, I insisted that I be called Old Joe."

"Where were you born?"

"Schenectady, New York."

"When?"

"I thought you said you weren't going to ask personal questions?"

"If you like being called Old Joe, why don't you want to tell me when you were born?"

Joe smiled. "I like you, kid. You're smart. I was born in 1945. That makes me how old?"

Makelo counted off the decades on his fingers. "Seventy-one. Next question. What do you like the most and the least about your life?"

Without missing a beat, he said, "The freedom to do what I want, when I want and not have to pay Uncle Sam a dime. The downside is not having the money to stay warm and clean and sated. That means having a belly full of food, something I'm sure you don't have to worry about."

Makelo went on to ask Joe a few more questions, but after a while the old man was getting restless and promptly ended the interview. Makelo shut off the tape recorder and put it back in his pocket and took out his mom Gloria's cellphone. "Thanks for talking to me, Old Joe. Do you mind if I take your picture?"

"Snap away." As he stood, Makelo heard the old man's legs creak under his army green pants. They were worn, but clean. Old Joe moved his head from side to side – more creaking and pops jumped from his overused muscles and bones. "When you've written the paper, can you bring me a copy? I'd like to read it."

"Sure. See you later. Stay warm."

"I'll try. You, too."

Makelo ran into the kitchen where Will was washing dishes. He grabbed a pile of dirty plates and brought them over to the sink. Lucy, one of the volunteers, a pretty blonde with a hot pink nose ring and a tattoo garden covering both arms, went up to Makelo. "I saw you talking to OJ. What's up?"

"I interviewed him for a class assignment."

Lucy tousled the little boy's hair. "Good for you, kiddo. That's the kind of interview all the kids in your class should be doing."

"So how did it go?" Will said.

"Good. Old Joe's had a really interesting life. Did you know he used to be married?"

"No, I didn't."

"Well, he was. He also used to be an insurance salesman." Makelo slipped the dishes into the soapy water. "He wants me to bring him a copy of the paper."

"That's terrific. You're going to have to make a copy for me, too, so I can share it with the rest of the volunteers here. Did you enjoy the interview process?"

"Yes, but I also forgot to ask him some questions. Next time, I'm going to write them down." Makelo got up on the stool in front of the sink, kitchen towel over his shoulder. "I'll dry if you wash."

Will rinsed off a plate and handed it to Makelo. "You're on."

21

One more step and Emma swore she was going to scream in agony. It was their third date and she was determined not to wimp out. She had wanted to impress Jeremy, Mr. Outdoors, with her athletic skills. The man was in amazing shape. His body was a work of art. He biked and hiked and kayaked and skied. She was surprised he had time for anything else. When he asked Emma if she liked to hike, she told him that she loved it and regularly took to the mountain trails above Mill Valley, the Marin County town that looked every bit as wealthy as its residents. With that in mind, Jeremy took Emma to the Cutcliff Pass, an infamous swath of dirt and rocks that led from the base of Mt. Lindenhort to the summit.

Emma had the look of a professional hiker, from her Eddie Bauer mountain climbing boots to her navy blue cargo shorts. Her toes, however, felt like they were going to explode. Each digit had its own special brand of pain. In contrast, Jeremy looked like he was walking on air. His effortless gait and perpetual smile made Emma want to stab him with her hiking stick. She couldn't even detect a drop of sweat on his perfectly tanned face. She changed her look of agony into one of complete elation when Jeremy glanced her way.

"Isn't this the best trail?" Jeremy said.

"Oh, for sure," Emma said through gritted teeth. Nonchalantly, she asked, "Are we close to the summit?"

"If we keep up this pace, we'll be there in less than five minutes." He turned back around and forged ahead. She took the opportunity to silently scream and wipe her face with her shirt sleeve.

If we keep up this pace, you're going to have to drag me up to the top, Emma thought. Instead, she said, "Sounds like a plan."

Five minutes later, Emma did her best imitation of a happy hiker while her feet felt like they had been put through a grinder, as they reached the top of the mountain. The view caught her off-guard. The sun was making its western descent, silently disappearing into the horizon. Its final shards of light shone over the Pacific Ocean and the clouds were a deep pink and orange.

"Look!" Jeremy said as he pointed to a pod of dolphins close to the breaking waves. There must have been at least seven of them, following the surf, jumping out of the water.

Pain temporarily forgotten, Emma experienced the moment as if she'd never seen a sunset before. As if she was seeing the ocean for the first time and those magnificent, glistening mammals were performing for her alone. They stood together, silent, refusing to disrupt the natural sounds of the mountain and the ocean below. Unfortunately, this was their last date. She found out that he wasn't a doctor as he professed, but worked behind the counter at Better Copy Service. The Mercedes SUV he drove was his father's. He had loaned it to Jeremy while his beater truck was in the shop.

I want to see the sunset again and the ocean, seagulls, the sky. Dammit, I want to see again, Emma moaned from inside her self-imposed tomb. Can't I take back what I said? She would have screamed, but her energy level was too depleted. Leaving Marilyn was almost impossible and, when she was able to push herself out, her time was severely limited. Five minutes, maybe ten, then her soul was pulled back into its vestibule. In her last conversation with her sister, she was adamant. Human brutality and insensitivity were overpowering her desire to revisit a corporeal form. But her tune changed when she became lethargic and heavy. She knew that in a few days, she wouldn't be able to move. The solitude and peace she craved became a living crypt. Her only hope was that Gigi would return and, somehow, infuse her with enough energy to take over Sandy's body. She didn't even know if it was possible. In her desperation, she was hoping that the spirit world held that kind of power.

Lonnie laid back on his jet black, leather sectional. The townhouse personified masculine interior design. Lonnie had seen a spread of Sylvester Stallone's penthouse in an ex-girlfriend's *House Beautiful*

magazine. It was from the late 70s after the success of Rocky. Lonnie thought it was the coolest place and vowed to re-create it when he had the money. It took a couple of years, but eventually he succeeded, from the black and white photographs of various sporting events to the monochrome color scheme and amber-colored lamp shades on top of large, chunky chain link stands.

Lonnie took a huge hit from his multi-colored bong and filled his lungs with Vanilla Crunch, his favorite strain of marijuana. The plan was to get so high that he would forget he told Norma he had located her daughter. Normally, his instincts were spot-on. For the first couple of days, finding and tracking Sandy Ekhart was easy. When she ditched him at the free clinic, his radar seemed to go on the fritz. All his regular informants were clueless as to her whereabouts. He stopped blaming himself when he was convinced that Norma's energy was interfering with his own. And since it was her fault, Lonnie didn't feel guilty lying to his client. He told her that he found Sandy at the south end of the city, living in an artist's commune. His plan was to infiltrate the group, disguised as a starving artist, and get her to sign the release document. If she refused, he'd kill her. Simple. At least it sounded like an excellent plan when Norma approved it. As an ex-mercenary, murdering someone for money didn't bother Lonnie at all. What he found disturbing was the ease with which a mother could approve the execution of her daughter over money. Granted, it was a lot of money, but still it was her daughter, not her wimpy husband. Lonnie took another mega-hit. He could have sworn he felt the thick smoke permeating his brain, spiraling down his spinal cord, and wrapping itself around each toe. Soon, the vapor swirled around the images of Norma and Sandy, the homeless camp, and the free clinic. The sweet-smelling smoke then wiped it away leaving nary a trace.

Lonnie picked up the remote and turned on the TV. "I'll find the bitch tomorrow," he said aloud. "Right now, it's South Park time!" He grabbed the family size bag of Skittles and began popping them in his mouth with machine gun precision. He flashed on Norma and started laughing. "She'd split a gut if she could see me now."

The omnipresent Gigi sat on the chair facing Lonnie. She glared at him. "She'd split more than that, you insensitive dolt. I'm thrilled that you can't locate our heroine, but you better hope Norma doesn't find out how incompetent you are."

Fifteen minutes into *South Park*, Lonnie fell asleep. A small pile of Skittles pooled on the floor below the bag. Gigi was long gone. As much as she had wanted to explore the cosmos and disappear into the stars, she felt an obligation to check up on Sandy. It wasn't too late for Emma to change her mind and agree to take over the young woman's body. Gigi knew that she would have to make another attempt at convincing her sister to abandon Marilyn. Perhaps she would visit the Andersen house after stopping in on Sandy. The last time she saw Ms. Ekhart, the young woman was sucking down a bottle of vodka like she was in a chugging contest with a woman who lived in an industrial-sized cardboard box. She had watched Sandy lose herself in a drunken stupor and wondered what she would do if she found herself homeless. It was a ridiculous question because Gigi never would have had to choose to live on the street. She always had someone to run to, whatever the emergency. She had found it hard to believe that, with a large extended family, Sandy ended up homeless, until she read the woman's Akashic records. She witnessed the degradation and humiliation Sandy endured at the hands of her mother. She was stricken by Bob's indifference to his daughter's pain. Sandy's self-worth had been extricated from her psyche at a young age, never having the chance to develop a healthy ego, a vibrant self-worth. Gigi knew that Sandy felt she didn't deserve to be treated well by family or friends. Friend. Sandra seemed to have been the only one. Co-existing with the homeless crowd wasn't going to win her any lifelong friends, either.

As Gigi scanned the homeless encampment, she felt like she was being struck with a psychic mallet. The amount of misery and pain and hopelessness in the camp represented a microcosm of the world. On every continent, in every country, city, town, swath of land where humans inhabited, despair existed. It's what kept Gigi away from re-entering human form. She realized now that it was what should be bringing her back. She knew that she could choose her path before her birth. Since Emma's death, Gigi had been beating the drum for her sister's return to earth, yet she wasn't following her own advice. She felt like a hypocrite. Olive's raspy voice drew her out of her rumination.

"I said, Missy Prissy, that you could share my home if you share your booze and you ain't doing it." Olive waved an empty bottle of vodka in the air like a victory flag, then she drop-kicked it into a stretch of land known as quicksand alley. The camp inhabitants used the thin stretch of dirt between the edge of the camp and the fence separating it from another property as their dumpsite. The bottle hit another empty liquor bottle and both shattered, the sound barely causing attention.

The wind had picked up, determined to penetrate the three layers of clothing Sandy was wearing. She took her sleeping bag that she had been sitting on and wrapped it around her body. Olive snickered. When Sandy looked at her drinking buddy, she saw two Olives staring back at her. Sandy pointed her finger at both of them. "You just finished my bottle. Isn't that sharing?"

Olive said, "You were sharing it, but it's gone, isn't it, and you said you don't have any more." In a sweeping, exaggerated gesture with her hand, she continued. "Therefore, you're not sharing. See how that works?"

"Olive, if I had more, I'd share with you. Please let me sleep in your shelter. I'll get more vodka in the morning." Sandy sat down on the ground to stop from swaying, but she continued to shake.

Sandy's weakness fed Olive's ego. Rarely did she hold power over anybody or anything. She practically swaggered over to where Sandy was sitting and looked down at her. "Vodka in the morning doesn't help us now. Either you go find some hooch for us or go back to living with mama and papa in that huge palace on the hill."

"They don't live on a hill."

"I don't give a flying patookie where they live." She glared at Sandy as the young woman cowered.

Gigi thought, *this girl is not cut out for drinking or living on her own. We have got to get her that trust fund.* Before she witnessed Sandy's attempt to stand, only to fall and break down in tears, she flew to the Andersen home, hoping her sister would change her mind.

It sounded like someone was calling her name, speaking through thick gauze. Was it Paige? The voice was deeper than a child's. *Emma! Can you hear me? It's Gigi.* Gigi! She knew she'd come back. A faint spark ignited Emma's spirit. Enough that she could answer.

"I'm here. I'm so sorry. I should have listened to you."

"It's okay. Come on out and I'll catch you up on the life and despair of Sandy Ekhart. It's a doozy."

Emma willed herself to leave the doll, but her spirit wasn't strong enough to push through the thick, hard plastic. She tried again. Nothing happened. The effort sapped her energy.

"I...can't...get...out."

Gigi looked at the doll lying beside Paige, the child oblivious to the spiritual dialogue taking place. She clutched Marilyn, holding onto her as if her life depended on it, not realizing that a spiritual being's life depended on the doll's demise.

"I'm so sorry for not coming sooner, Emma, and I don't know how to help."

"You...didn't...read...the...manual?"

"Very funny. Hold onto that sense of humor. You may need it more than you realize." Gigi felt so helpless. She was clueless as to how she could help her sister, and time was running out for Sandy. Lonnie was going to revisit the homeless camp tomorrow night and there was a very good chance that Sandy would still be there. She'd be cold and hungry and hungover, but she had nowhere else to go. If she signed the document, she'd be signing away her trust fund worth millions of dollars. If she refused to sign, she would die. "We don't have much time for you or Sandy. If anyone can help us, it would be the Source. It's where souls are created. Maybe the answer is there. I hope it's there." Gigi held the image of Emma as she remembered her, a vibrant woman in her fifties with shoulder-length brown hair, sea green eyes and a slightly crooked, but thoroughly adorable, smile. "I'll be back. Stay hopeful!"

With her sister gone, Emma tried desperately to think of a way out of her prison. She envisioned Paige shaking her out of the doll, even though she knew that wasn't the way the spirit body worked. She saw Marilyn on top of an immense bonfire. Her plastic body melting onto the charred firewood. Emma would be released, but she would also be officially without a body, and she would remain a spirit like Gigi or she would be re-birthed into another human. Again, an unrealistic scenario. No one had any intention of casting Marilyn onto a pile of burning wood. And then, as if a spiritual lightbulb went off, Emma figured out a way to be released, but she needed Gigi to make it happen. She prayed her sister would return before it was too late.

22

Before Bob Ekhart could knock on the massive, ornately carved oak door, Norma said, "Ring the doorbell, dear. You'll hurt your knuckles."

Bob gave his wife a dirty look. "How could I ever survive without you?"

"That's a question I ask myself on a near constant basis." She stared at the doorbell and pulled her white fox stole tighter around her shoulders, suppressing a shiver. "Press it."

Dutifully, Bob pressed extra hard. The door was answered before he could withdraw his finger. The butler greeted the Ekharts at the door. "Nice to see you again, Mr. and Mrs. Ekhart. Mr. and Mrs. Standish are in the living room. May I take your coat and wrap?"

As they walked into the foyer, Bob and Norma handed their jackets over to the butler. Bob said, "Thanks, Rudy. How are you this evening?"

"Fine, sir, and you?"

"Just dandy."

Norma rolled her eyes. She took her cell out of her purse and checked it, then smoothed her floral tunic and adjusted the deep turquoise satin cigarette pants. The color accentuated her eyes. As much as Bob resented his wife's demeaning personality, he never got tired of looking into her eyes. He was confident that somewhere behind those turquoise orbs was a decent, caring woman. Bob wondered if he would ever have the chance to experience *that* Norma. He had been married to her for twenty-five years. The odds were against him.

Rick and Marlo were standing by the fireplace, brandy snifters in their hands. When Norma saw Marlo's new hairdo, her mouth involuntarily dropped. She was thrilled. Marlo strode over to Rick's friends, her oversized lemon-yellow knit sweater hid her figure, but her long legs were accentuated by skinny jeans and deep red pumps. She gave Bob a heartfelt hug, then air-kissed Norma. By this time, she had closed her mouth, but was still in shock. Marlo was a beautiful woman, but her hair was her crowning glory. It personified her femininity. Now it was gone. And Norma couldn't be happier.

Norma said, "I barely recognized you without those long, gorgeous tresses. Whatever possessed you to lop them off?"

Marlo's self-confidence was solid. Very little tipped her off-balance, especially Norma, whose remarks and back-handed compliments she was intimately familiar with and grew to expect. She combed her hand through her hair, then shook her head, her hair barely moving. "I should have done it a long time ago. It's super easy to take care of and I'm tempted to give away my hair dryer and flat iron. Don't you like it, Norma?" She waited for the dig.

"It's very sweet. Reminds me of Mary Martin when she played Peter Pan."

"I'll have to look her up on the internet. She's way before my time. Wait, I think my mother mentioned something about seeing a woman playing Peter Pan. Or was that my grandmother?"

Richard went up to his wife and gave her a kiss on the cheek. "I think she looks ravishing. Marlo, you could put a rusty bucket on your head and it wouldn't diminish your beauty at all."

Without thinking, Bob said, "I totally agree." As soon as he said it, he could feel those turquoise eyes boring holes into the back of his head.

Marlo said, "Thank you Bob." She walked over to the wet bar. "Can I get you two a brandy?"

"Please," said Bob.

Norma simply nodded. "You promised to give us an update on the site's EIS. Please tell me it's been approved, and those environmental pests can crawl back into their holes."

Rick finished his brandy and refilled his snifter. "If it were only that simple. Citizens for Environmental Protection have launched an offensive, calling the residents in neighborhoods close to the property, casting doom and gloom over the project. They're claiming that runoff from the stables will destroy the creek."

Norma said, "That's ridiculous. With gutters and a retaining wall, the runoff will circumvent the creek."

"That was the original plan and the one written into the EIS, but the CEP is questioning its effectiveness. We do live in earthquake country. A jolt of 5.5 or greater could feasibly compromise the safeguards, resulting in an environmental nightmare."

Norma was getting worked up. "No shit, Sherlock. A quake could wreak havoc on a lot of structures, not just the racetrack's. Seismic activity has a way of undoing many a good, solid building."

Marlo sat back against the wing backed chair, sipping her brandy. She loved the way it warmed her throat. Norma's displeasure added to her enjoyment. She noticed how Norma played with her earrings when she became agitated or nervous. Marlo watched her furiously twist the black pearl earring.

Norma continued. "Have you heard from Mayor Winston? Why isn't he fast-tracking the project through to approval? We gave him what he asked for. Does he want a horse named after him?"

A nearly inaudible snap was heard. Norma looked at the black pearl between her fingers, disgusted. "Cheap earrings. You told me you bought these at Nordstrom's. Where did you really go, Bob, across the street to Forever 21? Are they even real gold?"

Bob had been daydreaming, his mind drifting as far as it could go. He was fantasizing about Marlo, the two of them having delicious sex, Bob running his hands through her short, sexy hair. He heard his name and a mention of real gold. "What is it, Norma?"

She walked over to her husband and dropped the pearl in his hand. "Nordstrom's or Forever 21, Bob? Are they real?"

Bob put the pearl in his pocket. "Of course, they're real. You want me to show you the credit card statement? The way you twist your earrings, it's no wonder you have any at all."

Rick said, "Can we get back to the conversation? The bottom line is that the bank is getting nervous. It's taking too long for the approval and they're becoming increasingly uncomfortable with financing the project."

"Tell them it hit a snag, but we're back on track."

Rick looked at her like she was a child. "We're not dealing with a small investment. You know that, Norma. Bank executives, even if they're on our side, are always looking at the bottom line. They don't want to be on the losing end."

"Don't talk to me like I'm a neophyte. I know exactly how big business operates. This isn't my first venture."

"No, it's your third or fourth. I do this for a living."

Bob and Marlo looked at each other at the same time and mentally shrugged. Marlo held up her brandy. Bob did the same and they toasted from across the room. Norma peripherally caught the gesture. "Speaking of neophytes. Are we boring you?"

Before Bob could answer, Marlo said, "As a matter of fact, you are. For the past couple of months, this seems to be all we, you two talk about. We invited you over for dinner. Can't you and Rick discuss the abuse track, I mean racetrack during business hours?"

All startled eyes were on Marlo. She surprised herself, as well. It must be the haircut, she thought. She flashed on looking at her new 'do in the mirror at Petal's house, Forest behind her, apparently pleased with his latest creation. Dark, wavy hair framing his angular face. His black eyebrows slightly arched. A self-satisfied smile showing white, straight teeth. She glanced over at Rick and suddenly his face looked doughy. His lips thin, the bags under his eyes accentuated by dark circles.

"Marlo's right. Let's enjoy the evening," said Rick. He turned to Norma. "Okay?"

Norma rolled her eyes. "Whatever."

As Bob passed Marlo on the way to the dining room, he whispered, "Bravo."

She wanted to high five him, but then remembered that the older, wealthy crowd didn't subscribe to that form of congratulatory gesture. They simply gave a nod or a barely perceptible smile. I bet Forest high fives, Marlo thought, then she caught up to her husband and gave him a kiss on his slightly wrinkled jowl.

The dinner conversation was tame. Nothing said was controversial, stimulating, or racy. It was boring, but palatable. After Norma checked her cell for the second time, Bob said, "Are you expecting a call?"

"I am."

"May I ask from whom?" The timbre in Bob's voice barely concealed his irritation.

"Lonnie."

Rick said, "The private detective? What are you using him for?"

Norma wasn't sure she wanted to bring Sandy up in front of

Marlo. Rick knew very well the trouble they had had with their daughter. He may have even recounted especially memorable incidents to his wife. Still, it was a weakness in the Ekhart family that made Norma uncomfortable. She relented. "I would like to find my daughter." Despite her embarrassment, she exuded a stoicism that very few could effectively pull off.

Rick spooned the mushroom risotto onto his plate. "You still haven't found out what happened to her after she left her friend's apartment? Wasn't that almost a month ago?"

Norma shook her head. "Two weeks. Lonnie was certain that he had seen her and was following some leads. He said he'd call if he had good news."

Marlo was visibly stunned. "I had no idea she wasn't living with Sandra anymore. What happened between them?"

Norma gave Marlo a look of irritation. "Does it matter?"

Marlo replied, "Of course it does. If you knew what transpired in their last days together, it could make a huge difference in locating her."

Norma looked amused. "Transpired? I'm surprised you know what that means."

Bob stopped mid-bite and Rick was about to admonish his business partner, when Marlo said, "I'm full of surprises, Norma." She put her hand up to her gold hoop earring and twirled it. "Wait until you see what we have for dessert."

Once the dishes were cleared, a slice of chocolate cake was placed in front of the diners. Norma looked at the cake. Aside from the frosting, decorated with small, candied violets, it didn't look special at all. "Oh, this is such a surprise. Chocolate cake."

"Taste it," said Marlo.

Norma took a bite and chewed. "Butterscotch, mint, and cardamom. Fascinating flavor and the texture is smooth." She raised her eyebrows. "I stand corrected. I am surprised."

"Thank you." It was rare when Marlo won a round with Norma. The woman flung so many back-handed compliments, curt responses, and criticisms at her, she never felt she was fast enough with witty responses. "I bought it at the new vegan bakery on Union Street, Sweets With a V."

"Surprise number two. I thought vegan cakes would taste like sawdust mixed with paste." Norma took another healthy bite. "Delicious."

Bob looked at Marlo and winked.

Rick said, "Since when do you go to vegan bakeries?"

Marlo was about to say that her new friend introduced her to the divine bakery but stopped herself. She didn't want to divulge Petal's identity lest it led to the environmental organization. Instead, she said, "I was shopping on Union and hadn't seen it before. Curiosity got the better of me."

"I'm glad it did," said Bob. "I have to agree with Norma, though. I always thought that a cake made without eggs and milk would taste terrible. What's it called again?"

"Sweets With a V. It's run by one of the Vegan Vipers. You've heard of them, right?"

Marlo was met with blank stares. "Enlighten us, dear," Rick said.

They're a group of, I believe, seven or eight vegan chefs in San Francisco, who ride up on their Harleys to the different homeless camps in the city and give away the leftover food from their restaurants. The Examiner ran an article on them not too long ago."

Norma shook her head. "Giving bums free food only encourages them to beg and not take responsibility for their welfare. Typical vegans. It's not enough that they try to push their philosophy down our throats. Now they're trying to convert the homeless. Can't they just live and let live?"

Marlo chuckled. "I think that's the point of veganism."

Head cocked, Rick looked at his wife. "What's gotten into you?"

"I'm sorry. Have I somehow crossed a Pacific Height's line? Keep the status quo? Disregard different lifestyles other than our own?"

Norma finished the last bite of chocolate cake. She pointed her fork at Marlo. "Aren't you feisty?"

"Every once in a while, I enjoy coloring outside the lines. Will you excuse me for a moment?"

Once Marlo was out of earshot, Norma leaned forward and said to Rick, "Uh-oh. Another one of your child brides is getting a mind of her own. It won't be long before we'll be attending yet another wedding extravaganza, ala Rick Standish and bride number four or is it five?"

Bob was certain his wife was pushing buttons she shouldn't push, but Rick was unfazed. "Marlo stretches the envelope every now and then. It will pass."

Norma persisted. "If it doesn't?"

Rick sat back and picked up his brandy snifter. "It may not be long before you'll have another Mrs. Standish to needle and annoy." He finished off the last of his brandy, picked up the bottle and poured himself a healthy serving.

Petal answered her phone on one ring. "Hello?"

"Hi Petal, it's Marlo."

Petal was laying on a chaise lounge on her back porch, her body swathed in a blanket. The cool night air touched her face and hand, the only exposed parts of her body. She was enjoying a mug of hot chocolate when her cell rang. "Hey there. How does your husband like your new 'do?"

"After he threatened to banish me from the Standish kingdom, he said he liked it." As soon as she said it, she regretted it.

"I'm glad he likes it. So, what are you doing?"

"Taking a break from our dinner guests. They're so boring and narrow-minded. Unfortunately, I should get back. I was wondering if you had time this week to give me my first lesson in aromatherapy."

"Can I get back to you? I'm outside, rolled up in a blanket like a taquito. My calendar is in the house. Text me your available days and I'll let you know what works for me."

"Sounds like a plan. Thanks, Petal, or should I say Ms. Taquito?"

"That works. Try to enjoy your company. Adios."

"Adios."

When Marlo returned, Bob and Norma were getting ready to leave.

As Rick walked them to the foyer, he said, "As soon as I get an update on the EIS, I'll let you know."

"I appreciate it. Let's hope the news is good." Norma waited as Rudy handed Bob his jacket. He then placed the fox stole around Norma's shoulders. She gave Marlo a sly look. "Aren't you going to say something deleterious about my fur? I assume you're against wearing them."

Before her exploration into the inhumane treatment of racehorses, Marlo didn't think twice about owning a mink coat or an ermine stole. Her web search on horse racing landed her on websites that covered many animal rights topics. Fur was one of them. She had no idea how fur animals were raised. Honestly, she never thought about it. When she began reading what transpired at fur farms, she felt hollowed out. Then the guilt overpowered her. Pictures showed animals living in filthy cages so small, they could barely turn around. The animals were forced to live in extreme weather conditions without the aid of warmth in the winter. Hot days left them panting on the wire floors. When it was time for their fur to be stripped from their bodies, they were either anally electrocuted or stuffed into 'hot boxes,' where they were gassed. The unfortunate ones who didn't succumb to the gas, woke to find themselves being skinned alive. Marlo's fur inventory was donated to a local animal rights group where they were used in demonstrations and protests.

Marlo internally groaned. Instead of following through with her impulse to clock Norma between the eyes, she smiled as sweetly as she could muster and said, "When I look at your fur, all I see is misery and death."

Norma's retort was swift, "They're varmints, you know. Pests. Honestly, I look so much better in their fur then they did."

Before Marlo could answer, Bob swiftly escorted his wife out the door.

"What's gotten into you?" Rick said, his voice tinged with annoyance. "Pissing off my friend and business associate isn't the smartest thing to do."

"I was going to say that she started it, but that makes me sound like a child. You know she's jealous of me, Rick. I'm young and attractive and it drives her nuts because she's older and not necessarily wiser. Tell her to back off and then I won't have anything to respond to, okay?"

Before Rick could answer, Marlo climbed the stairs. "I'll be in the study."

"Be careful what you say, young lady. I have my limits, too."

She turned and glared at her husband. "Talk to me like I'm your daughter again and you won't have to worry about me saying anything offensive to any of your friends." She continued up the stairs, shaking with anger and the fear that her marriage could so easily crumble from the weight of her new sense of confidence.

Rick watched his third wife ascend the stairs. He sighed and said under his breath, "I sure am going to miss that body."

Ever since Gigi left Emma, she was scouring the heavens to find a way to help her sister. The Source offered no advice. Her parents didn't know what to tell her, as well as the many of the other spirits she contacted. They had never dealt with Emma's condition before. When they died, their spirits were free to leave earth, returning if they chose to. The few souls that became trapped by inanimate objects didn't identify themselves to the others. Many of them remained stuck, unaware of how to solve their dilemma.

Defeated and feeling infinitely helpless, Gigi returned to Paige's bedroom, dreading what she had to tell her sister. Marilyn was sitting on Paige's bed. The blank expression on the doll's face belied the misery within.

"Emma. Can you hear me? It's Gigi."

Emma heard her sister and was ecstatic that she had returned. By now, she felt like she was wrapped in blankets, encased in a closet, the finality of her new body was nearly complete. It took every bit of the energy she had left to communicate. "Push…me…out." Emma's voice was small and weak, nearly inaudible.

"What?"

"Push…me…out…of…Mar."

"Push you out of the doll? Of course! Why didn't I think of that?" Gigi's light was bright and vibrant. As suddenly as she became excited, she became still. "If I push you out of the doll, Marilyn will become my body and I'll have to find another human to take over. You'll be free."

Emma wanted to respond but couldn't. Perhaps it was best. She didn't want to lie to Gigi and tell her that she forgot that minor detail. She knew exactly what she was asking of her sister. It may not have been fair to ask Gigi to return to earth in human form. How many times had she told her that she wasn't sure if she wanted to come back? She regaled Emma with vivid descriptions of her journeys to other planets and galaxies. She wasn't burdened by corporeal problems, battling the ego for control, dealing with selfish, insensitive humans. Emma was also sure that Gigi didn't want her to be stuck inside a doll for an unterminated amount of time. Even if Marilyn was eventually relegated to the trash and ended up in a landfill, it could take hundreds of years, if ever, to decompose or be destroyed.

Emma was right. Gigi didn't think twice. Her decision was a no-brainer. "I've never done this before, so I don't know how difficult or easy it's going to be to oust you, but I'm going to try until I get it right. You're getting out of there no matter what, you hear me?" Gigi didn't wait for an answer. She knew Emma couldn't respond. She was hoping that her low vibration would make for an effortless takeover. "When I say three, I want you to give up any strength you have left. No thoughts. Basically, turn into a limp strand of linguine." Gigi silently said goodbye to her spiritual life. She was going to miss it. A part of her was a little bit excited about living in San Francisco again. She didn't know if she would retain her memory; If she would be able to recall her life, her thoughts, her sister. "Here we go. One...two...three."

Gig aimed for Marilyn's right ear. With all her might, she entered the doll and knocked into Emma. She expected to be engulfed in darkness. Instead, she found herself right back where she started, hovering just above Paige's bed. "Shit!"

Emma willed herself to relax, to become completely submissive. After Gigi said 'three,' she must have anticipated the jolt, because she felt a hard push, then nothing.

As if she knew what had transpired, Gigi said, "Let's try this again and don't tense up. Imagine seeing the Golden Gate Bridge and walking through Clearlake Park where the black swans live. Picture Ocean Beach. Feel complete elation, not anticipation." Without giving her warning, Gigi dove back into Marilyn, this time she went in through the stomach and pushed upward, believing that, even though it was an inanimate object, the top of the head was still an entry and exit point.

Another dull thunk. Gigi looked around Paige's room in disgust. And fear. What if this was an exercise in futility? "I'm not giving up, Emma. My energy level is optimal. I can and will do this until we're successful. You with me? I know you are."

After five more failed attempts, Gigi needed to try another tactic. Up to this point, she had been directing her energy at pushing a willing spirit out of its vessel. She had no idea why her sister was resisting, despite directing Emma's attention elsewhere. Gigi went over to Marilyn. She started at the head and worked her way down, rotating around the doll, looking for weak spots, places where the plastic was thinner or damaged.

In the middle of the right heel, the plastic was cracked. It was about an eighth of an inch long, just a sliver of an opening. Gigi prayed that this was Emma's Achilles' heel. "Emma, when you were able to exteriorize, did you leave the doll at the same spot every time? If so, concentrate on that spot. I have a feeling it's in Marilyn's heel. When you feel my presence, go to that spot, okay?"

Imagining that she was a gold-tipped arrow, Gigi propelled herself through the top of Marilyn's head, focusing all her energy on visualizing Emma's spirit leaving the doll through the damaged heel.

"I'm out! I can't believe I'm out!" Emma's exclamations sounded faint and strained, but they were music to her sister's ears. She wanted to psychically hug every piece of furniture in Paige's room.

"It sucks in here. I don't know how you could stand it." Leaving the same way as Emma, Gigi exteriorized. The two siblings' spiritual lights comingled, delighted in their success. "Believe it or not, what we just did was the easy part. If it was that difficult pushing you out of a piece of plastic, I can't imagine what I'm going to encounter with Sandy."

Emma was rapidly regaining her strength. She could feel the energy filling up her astral body from the inside out. She began to shine brighter, stronger. She stared into her sister's eyes. "I'm sorry I was so difficult before. I truly didn't want to be human again. All the negative memories, the painful memories, overwhelmed me. The thought of living amongst the living was so unappealing. I discovered that living in a tomb was even more unappealing. That's too light a word. It was downright horrifying." She felt a sudden wave of sadness. "I'm so sorry that I forced you to take my place."

Gigi shook her head. "You didn't force me. It's true that I wasn't thinking of becoming earthbound any time soon, but I have a feeling this happened for a reason. Maybe trading places was our destiny after all." She stared at Marilyn. "I'm on the clock now. Let's go check out my new body."

Lonnie stared at himself in the mirror. A dark brown wig covered his sandy blonde hair. The acrylic strands trailed down past his shoulders. He sported a four-day-old beard and moustache and even bought brown contact lenses in case he was spotted up close. His clothes were consistent with those of a vagrant. He pointed to his image "I don't even think my mom would recognize me. Mr. King, you've outdone yourself."

He checked his back pocket for the document and patted his chest, making contact with the .45. The silencer was attached. He grabbed the car keys from the table, put on his torn and tattered jacket, the inside pocket holding a pint of whiskey, took one more quick look in the mirror, smiled and said, "Showtime."

It was almost eight o'clock in the evening when Lonnie parked his car on Chestnut Street. After leaving his cellphone and wallet in the glove box, he locked his car and began to walk to the homeless camp. Unless she had the urge to leave again, he was sure that Sandy had settled back into her original spot. That's where she was the night before, getting wasted with some of the other residents. Lonnie was hoping that she would already be inebriated so it wouldn't be too difficult to get her alone, especially with the promise of some shots of Johnnie Walker Black. He would then trick her into signing away her trust fund. He would rather not use force, but if he had to, he would.

A few blocks away, Will and Ronnie were finishing up dinner at Delton's Bar & Grille, a hole-in-the-wall establishment that Ronnie had suggested. From the outside, it had the look of a condemned building. Inside wasn't much better: mismatched tables and chairs, walls filled with Starving Artist-style paintings, and the concrete floor stained from the many drinks and food stuffs spilled on it. But Ronnie was convinced they made the best vegan pasta carbonara in the city, including North Beach, famous for its Italian restaurants.

"I feel like a tick ready to pop." Ronnie wiped her mouth with her napkin and gently patted her stomach.

"Me, too. My mind told me I was full and to stop eating, but my taste buds begged me to keep going. How did you find this place? It looks like a dive from the outside." Will downed the last sip of Chianti.

"My friend Claire stumbled on it a few years ago. I think she had just run the *Bay to Breakers* and was starving. Delton was the name of her first boyfriend, so she decided to give it a try despite its shoddy appearance. She had no idea most of the items on the menu were vegan. After having a stellar meal, she told all her friends about it, hoping the increased business would give them enough money to fix up the place. Business quadrupled, but it turns out, they liked it just the way it was."

The waiter came over and placed the check on the table. He put the bag with two extra orders of pasta next to it.

"This place is definitely a keeper." Will took out his wallet and placed three twenty-dollar bills on top of the check. "Are you ready to go?"

Ronnie stood. "Thank you for dinner. I owe you one."

"My pleasure. Thank you for agreeing to go with me to find Sandy." Will grabbed the to-go bag and followed Ronnie out the door.

The night air was warmer than usual, so the couple decided to walk instead of drive to the homeless camp. Ronnie looked up at the night sky, the lights of the city obscuring the view of the stars. "It's nights like this that stop me from leaving the city. I love San Francisco, but sometimes I want to feel the sun on my face without that sharp, biting wind. I wish I could take a picture of the still, warm air. Friends from So Cal wouldn't believe it."

"Come on now. The crazy strong wind and cold nights makes our city the unique place it is. Nights like this are the icing on the foggy cake. Would you really want to have warm nights all the time?" Ronnie nodded enthusiastically. "Traitor! I'll have to report you, you know." Will nonchalantly took Ronnie's hand. It felt like a bold move since it was only their second date. Ronnie wondered what took him so long.

She stopped. "Before you turn me in to the authorities…" She stood on her toes and gave him a kiss.

Will said, "Keep that up and you may just get a reprieve." He kissed her again.

"Do we have to go check on Sandy? I'm sure she's fine and I can think of something a lot more fun to do than peeking inside tents and cardboard boxes looking for a homeless heiress."

"I have a strong sense that Sandy's in trouble. If we find her and convince her to let us take her to the shelter, I'll feel a whole lot better." He hugged Ronnie and kissed the top of her head. "Can we have fun afterwards?"

"You bet, Dr. Remini."

Lonnie had no trouble fitting in. His ensemble resembled a number of other men and women's fashion style scuttling about in the makeshift neighborhood. If he wasn't a familiar face, it didn't matter because he looked like one of them. It took his eyes a while to adjust to the monochrome landscape. Tents, clothing, even light brown cardboard boxes took on a dull veneer. Being homeless was everything it wasn't cracked up to be. In a rare moment, Lonnie felt grateful for his apartment, his car, his job; control over his actions. The thought of alcoholism or mental illness running his life sent a chill through his body. At that moment he convinced himself that if he had to kill Sandy, he was doing her a favor.

Navigating his way through the city's largest homeless encampment, he finally spotted Sandy sitting by herself, swaying from side to side. It was obvious that she was in an altered state. Perfect. His concern, though, was to get her alone. The warm evening air had brought most of the residents outside their enclosures, making them more social, lightening their moods.

"Got any food under that jacket?" A young woman with a shaved head stared up at Lonnie. She was holding a small dog. It looked like a Chihuahua, but it was hard to tell because it was wearing a hoodie, a pink one with rhinestones around the rim of the hood. It looked at Lonnie, its large, round wet eyes imploring him to feed them both. Lonnie fished an energy bar out of his inside pocket. He took a piece of lint off the wrapper and handed it to the woman. She stared at the offering. "Is it organic?"

"What are you, a homeless foodie?"

"Just asking. Don't get your panties in a bunch, asshole." Before Lonnie could fire back, she walked away. He heard her say, "What the hell is a foodie?" as she unwrapped what was most likely her only meal for the evening.

Lonnie sat on the ground, cross-legged and patiently waited to make his move. He had one eye on Sandy while he observed the other people filtering through his line of vision. Some walked by without a word, shuffling, limping. A child skipped slightly ahead of her mother. Another spoke in a soft voice, barely audible, to an invisible friend. From his intonation, the friend was being admonished. Lonnie said to no one in particular, "Every being on this planet is connected. We all come from one seed. Where did I read that?" He reached for his cellphone, then remembered he intentionally left it in the car. To an observer, Lonnie fit right in with the group, just another resident of 'camp of the forgotten, the refuse.'

Five minutes later, Sandy stood up. She took a couple of steps and stumbled. Lonnie jumped to his feet and helped her up. He kept his hand on her shoulder. "You need help going somewhere?"

Sandy tried to focus. She put her hand over her right eye to stop from seeing double. The man standing next to her didn't look familiar, but he had a friendly face. Ever since the night she was raped, she had a strong distrust of men. At the moment, she had to pee badly and it would be a lot easier walking to the bathroom with help. "Bathrooms. Gotta pee."

"No problem."

Lonnie could see one other person, an old man hunched over, waiting to use the portable toilets. He slowed his pace, hoping the man would be gone so they would be the only ones waiting. When they arrived, the man was going into the outhouse. Two more people vacated the gray and black toilets. Sandy didn't notice, so Lonnie said, "Looks like we have a bit of a wait."

"They better hurry. I really have to go bad."

"Don't worry, I won't let anyone go ahead of you." Lonnie took the document out of his pocket, along with a pen. "While we're waiting, I wonder if you would sign my petition. I'm trying to get the city to install more toilets here. It's obvious we need more, right? I only need a few more signatures."

Lonnie handed Sandy the pen and held the paper in his hands. He pointed to the signature line. "Sign right there."

Sandy looked at the pen in her hand and then at the piece of paper before her. Her eyes couldn't focus on the text, but even in her drunken state, it didn't look like a petition to her. "Where are the other signatures?"

Without skipping a beat, Lonnie said, "I thought it would be more effective if there was a letter for each person. More of an impact, you know?"

Sandy looked up at the toilets, hoping one of them would soon be vacant. "Damn, I wish they'd hurry." When she looked up at Lonnie, she was staring directly into his eyes. He looked desperate and that scared her. Her heart started pounding and she was suddenly very thirsty. "Do you have any water? I'm bone dry."

"Not on me. Sign this and I'll get you a bottle from the liquor store across the street."

Unbeknownst to Lonnie, one of the outhouses was occupied. The door opened and a child ran out and joined his father. Sandy began to walk in earnest to the vacated toilet. With a very short window of opportunity, Lonnie grabbed her arm and said, "I'd like to show you something really quick. It won't take long."

Struggling to free herself, Sandy said, "I have to go to the bathroom."

Lonnie ignored her pleas and pulled her toward an isolated area of the encampment. A burned-out streetlight helped conceal the dark corner where an accumulation of trash gave him the privacy he needed. "I was trying to do this the easy way, but even shitfaced, you're a pretty smart bitch."

Terrified, Sandy could only let out a whimper.

"Sandy! Is that you?" Will shouted as he and Ronnie ran toward her.

Disoriented, Sandy tried to look behind her, but Lonnie jerked her back, causing her to cry out in pain.

As Will and Ronnie got closer, Lonnie realized he had no time to get a signature. He also knew that his client had paid him to do a job. He picked up his pace, running as he pulled Sandy along, looking for an exit. He spotted an opening in a chain link fence about fifty yards away. "All you had to do was sign the damn paper." He threw Sandy to the ground, took out his gun, aimed at the woman's forehead, and pulled the trigger. Sandy screamed. Without checking his handiwork, Lonnie bolted toward the fence and slipped through as Will and Ronnie spotted Sandy lying on the ground. The light was dim, but Ronnie gasped when she saw Sandy's forehead covered in blood. She took out her cell and dialed 911.

"Sandy, can you hear me?" Will was on his knees. He took out a handkerchief and gently wiped Sandy's forehead. The smell of alcohol was pungent. He saw what looked like a deep gash just above the arch of her right eyebrow. He applied pressure to the wound.

Sandy opened her eyes. She smiled. "Is that you, Dr. Remini?" Her words were slightly jumbled.

"Yes."

"I think I peed my pants." Sandy tried to get up, but Will stopped her. He could see a puddle of dark liquid under her head. He took off his jacket and placed it under her head.

"An ambulance will be here soon. I don't know the extent of your injuries, so please don't move."

Ronnie knelt beside Will. She took Sandy's hand in hers. "You'll be fine."

"Who are you?" Before Ronnie could answer, Sandy said, "I don't feel so good." Despite Will's directive to remain still, Sandy turned on her side and threw up. She began to cough, and it was then that she put her hand on the back of her head and felt the blood mixed in with her hair. When she looked at her hand, she fainted.

"Now, Gigi! Do it now!" Emma felt electric. She knew that the timing was perfect. Sandy's body had suffered a major traumatic event and her spirit was at its most vulnerable. At first the sisters were devastated, certain that Lonnie killed Sandy, but her head had landed on a rock, causing Sandy's head to turn. The bullet grazed her temple instead of penetrating her skull. Lonnie sprinted away without realizing his miscalculation.

"It's not right." Gigi looked down at the drama being played out. Sirens could be heard in the distance. Her spiritual light flickered, as if a gentle breeze was moving her in an erratic dance.

Emma looked at her in disbelief. "What's not right? I don't understand. You may not have another chance to do this." She looked back down at Sandy, lying there helpless and vulnerable.

Gigi said, "I'll tell you later. Right now, we need to be somewhere else. Fast."

Emma had no choice but to follow Gigi. In an instant, they arrived at their destination. Emma looked around. The place looked very familiar: gold-plated banister, enormous dining room, and a marbled entrance hall. "What are we doing at Norma and Bob's?"

"I can do the most good as her." Gigi pointed to Norma as she seemingly glided down the stairs, belying gravity. The smile on her face was almost comical.

Emma looked doubtful. "If that woman doesn't have a tough spirit, I don't know who does. You had a helluva time taking over the doll and I was willing to leave." She studied her sister, her energy was sputtering, like a flame being blown out. "Are you okay?"

"Very shortly, I'll be back in a body. The thought terrifies me, but then I remember what it felt like to be in love or to taste a crisp Fuji apple for the first time or body surf in the ocean. And I really miss breakfast. I can't wait to have sourdough toast with peanut butter and sliced strawberries. And a hot, steaming cup of coffee.

"Humans are such flawed creatures. We have the intelligence and curiosity to discover black holes and the talent to express ourselves through dance, music, and art. And we have the ability to inflict the most heinous acts of cruelty on everything we get our hands on; fellow humans, animals, the planet. It's astounding to me that one person can carve the Pieta out of stone, and another can sadistically torture and murder without remorse.

"I'll be joining my fellow humans and not without reservation. Before you even became Esmerelda Conklin Banks, your destiny was planned out. You'll be part of the spirit world and I'll be returning to earth."

Emma let Gigi's words sink in, then replied, "I read an article in a magazine not too long ago. It was about finding ways to celebrate life every day. There were seven that stuck with me: get up early to watch the sunrise, put down electronic devices and gaze up at the clouds or stars, play amazing music and, if it feels right, dance to it, write about the time you were in awe of someone or something, visit a local or state national park, take a walk around your neighborhood and look at things as if for the first time. Do you think you can remember that?"

"Definitely."

Emma and Gigi followed Norma into the study and watched while she poured herself a healthy serving of Glenlivet Founder's Reserve, dropped an ice cube in the glass, and sat down on the couch, facing the fireplace. The warmth of the fire added to her good mood. She held up her drink and toasted. "To Lonnie. I knew you'd get it done one way or another." Norma swallowed the amber-colored single malt scotch, then made another toast, her turquoise eyes darkening to a deep sea blue. "Here's to not having to deal with offspring ever again."

Emma said, "Damn, she's evil. I sure hope her dastardly personality hasn't permeated her cells. Before you perform the switch, I want to know why you chose Norma."

Gigi studied Norma. "Because I can affect the most change becoming Mrs. Norma Ekhart. Through her, I can help Sandy. I can verbally dive bomb the racetrack's demise with information from the environmental group. And I can use the Ekhart fortune to effect positive changes for San Francisco's homeless."

"But you'll be coming back as a woman in her mid-fifties."

"Doesn't bother me a bit," said Gigi. "You're the one with the aging hang-up. You won't have to worry about that anymore. You'll be starting from scratch."

"If I decide to come back at all." Emma looked around the room. "*If* you can take over Norma's body, you'll be a multi-millionaire. I hope money won't affect your plans for altruism."

"I was getting to that. While I was trying to push you out of the doll, it occurred to me that, even in your weakened state, your spirit is a lot more evolved than Mrs. Cutthroat here. My theory, which will be tested very soon, is that new and/or deeply flawed spirits are easier to upend."

"I'm going to miss you all over again," Emma said, her telepathic voice cracking with emotion. "Please be careful in your new body. I'm sure over the years, Norma's made some enemies."

"I'll miss you, too, Esmerelda. You'll always be my best friend, no matter what."

Totally oblivious to the Banks sisters, Norma finished her drink. "I deserve another." She rose and not more than three steps later, the heel of her shoe came down on something hard in the rug. Her foot twisted, the glass of scotch flew out of her hand and shattered against the fireplace. Her head hit the corner of the coffee table, and she fell back against the unforgiving hardwood floor. In that instant, Gigi and Emma witnessed Norma's spirit fly out of her body. It hovered a few feet from Norma's crumpled form, looking down then looking directly at the sisters. Before Norma's spirit realized that the fall wasn't fatal, Gigi slid in. The spirit looked confused. It attempted to return but was unsuccessful. She then turned her attention to Emma, who was watching the interaction from a corner of the room. Emma knew she was safe. Spirits don't have the ability to harm each other, but still, it was Norma's. If anyone's spirit defied the rules, it was hers. Without warning, the newly dislodged soul flew straight up through the ceiling. Relieved, Emma turned her attention to Norma. She looked harmless lying on the floor, a lump quickly growing on her forehead. Emma went over to the spot where Norma lost her balance. Barely visible in the carpet was half of the ruby earring that Norma broke off days earlier. *Maybe there are no coincidences and things do happen for a reason*, Emma thought.

Norma's eyes fluttered open and for the first time in two years, Gigi was looking at the world through an optical lens. It felt like she was encased in a body suit filled with batting. She lay on the ground for a while in an attempt to adjust to being human again. The three-dimensional world looked like two. The luminescent glow that Gigi was used to was gone. She slowly lifted her right arm and watched in awe as she turned it, flexed her fingers, made a fist, and glided it back and forth. It was sore from the fall, but its movement captivated her.

Like water seeping into cement, filling the thousands of crevices and cracks, Gigi could feel herself integrating with Norma's psyche. Thoughts were co-mingling. Sensibilities merged. Norma was becoming an amalgam, yet Gigi's spirit persevered. When Norma tried to get up too fast, her head began to pound. She touched her forehead and cringed. The lump had grown to the size of a golf ball. She attempted to stand, this time moving slower, more deliberately. It still felt foreign, the movement of her body. She made it to the couch, relieved that she was on a softer, more forgiving surface. Norma gingerly touched her forehead again. "Son of a bitch." She laid her head against the back of the couch and closed her eyes. She felt disoriented, but strangely calm. She glanced up at the ceiling and smiled. Her turquoise eyes looked softer, warmer, welcoming. Emma could see Gigi shining through.

"I'll be back, Gigi. I can't wait to see the full transformation from the beast to the beauty. You're a brave, enlightened soul and I aspire to be like you. I love you."

And then Emma was gone. In that instant, Norma's heart fluttered. She looked toward the doorway, but no one was there. A faint image popped into her head: A woman around her age. As much as she tried to concentrate, she couldn't make out her face. Her mind was too foggy, and she could feel the beginnings of a headache, so she shrugged it off as another sign of getting older.

Norma pushed herself off the sofa and walked to the bathroom. She felt a little lighter, like a few layers of clothing were shed. She caught her breath when she looked at herself in the mirror. Her normally flawless skin sported a large, bloody bump. "That is one ugly sucker." It was starting to turn a dark gray and blue. Norma studied her face, as if for the first time. She turned to the right and to the left, observing her high cheekbones and perfectly arched eyebrows. She traced the outline of her small, straight aristocratic nose with her finger. "I'm really quite beautiful. And those eyes. Astounding." As soon as she said it, she chided herself for being so vain.

She had just placed a hot washcloth against her forehead when the telephone rang. She glanced at the caller ID readout: SF Police Department.

"This is Norma Ekhart."

"Mrs. Ekhart. My name is Detective Kyle Rhone and I'm with the San Francisco Police Department. I understand that your daughter is Sandra Ekhart. Is that correct?"

Norma began to shake. "Yes, it is. Is she okay?"

"She's a very lucky young woman. She was accosted by someone at the homeless encampment downtown and has been transported to San Francisco General Hospital with wounds to the head. I was told that they're not life-threatening."

Norma put the washcloth on the table. "Do you know what room she's in?"

"Room 1312. Please be forewarned that she asked us, actually pleaded with us, not to call you or your husband, but under law we are required to contact next of kin when a crime has been committed."

"I understand and I'm very grateful for the call. Thank you, detective."

This was it. Norma's moment of reckoning. She hadn't seen Sandy since she moved out six months ago. And now, she couldn't wait to see her and start repairing and building their relationship. She wondered if Sandy would let her.

"Darby!" Norma called to her cook from the dining room. Shortly, Darby appeared in the doorway. When she saw Norma's forehead, she gasped.

"Mrs. Ekhart, what happened?"

Norma shrugged it off. "I fell and hit my head on the coffee table. Don't worry, I'm okay. I do have some great news. I found Sandy."

Darby was stunned. First, Norma wasn't concerned about an injury to her precious face and then she appeared to be excited that Sandy was found. Darby prayed she was alive. "Is she okay?"

"Yes, thank goodness. I can't remember what her favorite meal is, can you?"

Of course I can, Darby thought. *It's your husband's favorite, too, for*

Christ's sake. "She loves my vegetable pot pies with extra carrots and peas."

"That's right." Norma didn't have a clue. "Please tell me you have some in the freezer."

Darby stood a little straighter and smiled. "I always have at least three in the freezer, and all have extra carrots and peas."

Norma was delighted. Almost giddy. "Wonderful! Please heat up one, no two. I'm hoping to bring my daughter back home."

"Shouldn't I defrost three? One for Mr. Ekhart?"

Norma almost laughed out loud. She forgot about Bob. Her husband of over twenty-six years. "Is he home?"

"I believe he told you at breakfast that he was going to be visiting his friend in Palo Alto. I can't remember his name."

"It doesn't matter. Why don't you defrost three pot pies? If Bob doesn't come home for dinner, you can join me and Sandy. I'm sure she'd love to see you again."

"Pardon me for saying this, ma'am, but what's going on?" Darby wondered if a jolt to the head could change someone's personality. In all the years she worked for the Ekharts, Norma was never this nice to her. She was barely civil.

Norma realized she'd better get used to those around her scratching their heads at her new persona. "I realized that I didn't like who I was. I want to change that."

"Good for you, Mrs. Ekhart."

Norma speed dialed her husband. It rang three times before Bob picked up. "Hello Norma."

"They found Sandy." Her voice was filled with joy.

"That's wonderful! Wait, why do you sound so happy? I thought you could care less what happened to our daughter."

Norma hesitated. How could she explain her sudden change in attitude and demeanor on the phone? "We can talk at the hospital. Sandy is at SF General, room 1312. I'm heading over there shortly."

"What happened? Why is she at the hospital?"

"The officer gave me very little information. He said that she was attacked and sustained injuries to her head, but that they weren't life threatening."

She heard Bob sigh. "I'm leaving Palo Alto now, so I should be at the hospital in about forty-five minutes." Without waiting for a reply,

Bob hung up. He rejoined Danny Slingham in the study.

Danny, a short, tubby man in his late fifties with a full head of white hair said, "Was that the wicked witch of Pacific Heights?"

Bob scratched his head with a bemused look on his face. "Kind of. It was Norma, but not the Norma I know and loathe. The good news is that Sandy is safe. She's at SF General. The bewildering news is that her mother is happy they found her. It wasn't more than a few days ago that she wanted to have nothing to do with her only child. Now, she's acting like they've discovered the cure for cancer."

"I'm relieved that Sandy's okay. Maybe someone was with her when she called you and she had to put on a show, pretend that she loves her daughter."

"I hadn't thought of that. It's a more feasible explanation than Norma growing a heart."

"Do you want me to go with you?"

"No, but thanks. I appreciate the offer. I'll call you from the hospital."

When Norma left the house for the hospital, Darby ran down to her room and turned on her computer. As soon as it booted up, she typed, *can a blow to the head change someone's personality?*

She scanned the results, then clicked on an article from the American Psychiatric Society and read in disbelief how, in rare instances, a concussion can affect a person's temperament and, indeed, their personality. One case study involved a woman who was cripplingly shy. She rarely left her home and, when she did, it was to go to the grocery store. After suffering a mild concussion from tripping on the frayed end of the bathroom rug, her personality took a dramatic turn for the better. She got to know her neighbors, reconnected with old friends, and even took up guitar lessons.

Miracles do exist, she thought. In Norma's case, she only wished it had happened sooner.

23

Norma couldn't remember the last time she was so nervous. She was rarely insecure. But her bravado had vanished when she fell. Gigi had plenty of insecurities and they were seeping into Norma's nooks and crannies, like melting margarine on an English muffin. She washed her face and did her best to cover up the bump on her forehead, but the best she could do was hide the bruise with foundation. The bulge over her left eye remained alarmingly large. She didn't have a Band-Aid big enough to cover the lump. She pulled her hair back into a ponytail and deliberately dressed casually, understated, in jeans and a light yellow sweater. She ditched the heels for a pair of black espadrilles. She studied herself in the mirror and decided she looked anything but intimidating.

Before Norma reached Sandy's room, she leaned against the wall and took some deep breaths. A nurse walking by stopped and put her hand on Norma's shoulder. "Are you okay?"

Norma nodded. "I'm fine. Thank you."

When she peered into room 1312, she was surprised to find a small group of people around her daughter's bed. Sandy was always a loner, save her friend, ex-friend, Sandra. Tentatively, she walked in. The conversation stopped and everyone turned in her direction.

Sandy was sitting up in bed, a large bandage covering a good portion of her forehead and right temple. Black and blue, ochre, and red surrounded her right eye. She was pale and her face drawn. When she saw Norma, her eyes widened, and her heart started pounding. The needle on the heart monitor leapt. "What are you doing here?"

Norma's heart felt like it was going to explode. Even when Sandy was born, her maternal instinct failed to kick in. Now, the love for her daughter broke through the once impenetrable dam and rushed in all at once. Her first impulse was to embrace Sandy and feel her in her arms, but she knew better. She expected resentment, no less than hatred for a mother who offered her daughter verbal barbs and nasty remarks, never compliments. Almost never adulation. She deserved whatever Sandy threw at her. "I wanted to see you. I'm so glad you're safe." She stepped closer.

Will and Ronnie were standing next to the bed. They started to move out of the way to make room for Norma. Sandy grabbed Will's arm. "I'm just fine and dandy. You can leave now."

Don't leave, Norma told herself. *This is your chance to make it right.* "I would appreciate a few moments alone with my daughter," she said to the people in the room.

Sandy said, "I don't want anyone else to leave, just you, Norma. Go."

Will gave Norma a tentative smile, then he said to Sandy, "I know this is hard for you, but give your mother a chance."

"A chance for what? To try and kill me again?" Sandy sat up straighter. "Are you going to deny that you hired that thug to shoot me?"

So much had transpired since the fall that Norma completely forgot her contract with Lonnie and the transfer of trustee ownership. For the last week, that was all she could think about besides breaking ground for Francisco Downs. Temporarily rattled, Norma made a mental note to contact Lonnie. She needed to end their relationship and make sure that their dealings never surfaced in public. She composed herself and tried again. "Sandy, I don't want to hurt you. I just want to talk to you. Please."

Sandy was about to object, but something stopped her. It was her mother's tone of voice. It was calm and, dare she say, loving? Confused and curious as to what Norma would say, she relented. "Fine."

As soon as Will and Ronnie closed the door, she approached the bed. Sandy immediately sensed a different energy surrounding her mother. She wasn't sucking the life out of the room. Her vulnerability was tangible. And the bump on her head highly visible. "What happened to your head?"

Norma automatically put her hand up to her forehead. "I fell against the table in the den."

Sandy pointed to her own forehead injury. "We look more like mother and daughter than ever before." She offered a weak smile.

With tears in her eyes, she lightly touched Sandy's arm. "I don't know how to make up for all the pain I've caused you, but I'm going to try. When I think of how I've treated you, I'm mortified and ashamed. I'm asking you for another chance."

Sandy wasn't sure if she was hearing correctly. Norma Ekhart, the mother whose rearing practices rivaled those of Joan Crawford's, was apologizing? She wondered out loud if the nurse gave her morphine for her pain instead of Tylenol.

Norma chuckled. "You're not hallucinating. You could say that I had an epiphany, a spiritual awakening. Honestly, I think it was the fall. It knocked some sense into me. And empathy. And a lot of attributes that apparently, I was missing."

"Do you know how crazy that sounds?"

"About as crazy as an Ekhart living on the street."

There was a knock on the door. Bob Ekhart walked in. He went around to the other side of the bed and kissed Sandy on her head. She grimaced. "Thank God you're okay. I was so worried about you."

"Were you?"

"Of course, I was." He gave Norma a dirty look, ignoring the glaring bump on her forehead. "What did you say to her?"

"Only good things," Norma replied.

"I find that hard to believe."

Sandy said, "It's true. It appears that Norma has had a metamorphosis, unless..." She took a deep breath. "What did you want me to sign?"

"Yeah, Norma. What *did* you want Sandy to sign, or should I say, sign away?"

Norma realized that if she was going to be a better person, she had to come clean with one exception. For the time being, she didn't have the mental strength to tell her daughter that she hired a man to kill her. That tidbit of exposition would have to wait. "I wanted you to sign over your trust to me."

It took Sandy a moment to understand what her mother had said. Aside from receiving a less than respectable allowance, Sandy never had a decent amount of cash. "What trust?"

Norma's head began to hurt, the bump throbbing. "Grandbee left you a trust and made me the trustee. I...I never told you about it."

"Or me," Bob practically spat out.

"How much?"

"Twenty million." Norma watched her daughter's eyes widen, then tears began to form and spill down her cheeks.

"I was sleeping on the ground. Living out of a backpack. Hungry. Scared." She wiped the tears off her face and looked at Norma, eyes narrowed. "How could you hide that from me? You're a monster." She turned to Bob. "And you. You never did a thing to protect me from her. I want you both to leave. Get out of my room. Get the hell out of my life."

Without another word, Norma and Bob walked by Will and Ronnie and the other visitors, averting their gaze.

"I'm going to have to ask you all to leave. Visiting hours are over." The nurse closed the door behind her. "Are you in pain?" she asked Sandy.

"I'm in a lot of pain," she said as she wiped the tears from her eyes. "If I could have something to knock me out so I can sleep for days, I'd appreciate it."

The nurse smiled. "How about a good night's sleep instead of a sleep-a-thon?"

Sandy wiped her nose. "If that's all you got, I'll take it."

The nurse took Sandy's vitals, then checked her bandages. Only hours earlier, her head wounds had been cleaned and the dressing applied. After she gave Sandy a mild sedative, she turned off the light and left the room. Sandy lay in the warm, clean bed. Physically, she was comfortable. Emotionally, she couldn't wrap her mind around her mother's confession. She was a millionaire. She also felt like an orphan. All her life, she wanted her mother's approval. She wanted to see love in her eyes, pride in her voice when she spoke about her only child. Tonight, Norma apologized. The indomitable cold, calculating woman who made Sandy's life miserable, who had Sandy praying on her knees every night before bed that she would wake up and her mother would love her, asked for her forgiveness.

The effects of the sleeping pill were beginning to blur the lines between elation and horror. As her eyes fluttered and her heart rate slowed, Sandy welcomed sleep. She almost wished that when she awoke, she would discover that her parent's visit was just a dream.

⁂

"I don't know about you, but I would love to know what transpired between Sandy and her parents." Ronnie locked the passenger door as Will pulled the car away from the curb.

"I wish I was the proverbial fly on the wall. From what little I know about their history and the way they left the room, I'm going to say the reunion wasn't a pleasant one." Will wanted to tell Ronnie about the encounter he had had with the private investigator, then thought better of it. Sandy had been his patient and he took patient confidentiality seriously.

"Aren't you perceptive?" Ronnie said sarcastically and adjusted her seat belt. "I've seen pictures of Norma Ekhart in the paper, usually on the society page. She always looked attractive, but in person, she's even more beautiful and reeks of wealth. I wonder how she got that knot on her forehead. I don't think we'll see her picture in the paper for a while."

Will slowed down as he approached a traffic light. "At the clinic, we call that injury a misstep. When patients come in with a lump that size, they were most likely high and/or drunk and missed the step."

"Do you mind stopping by my restaurant? I need to pick something up."

"Not at all." Will looked over at Ronnie. She smiled, exposing very white, straight teeth. Her front tooth was chipped. It added to her quirky personality. Will thought it was sexy.

"What?" She said, cocking her head slightly.

Will returned her smile. "I'm so glad I met you."

"Aw. I'm glad I met you, too, Doc. We're like two little peas in a vegan pod."

Will laughed. "That's one way of putting it."

Ronnie pulled down the visor and opened the mirror on the other side. She took out lip gloss and painted her lips deep burgundy. "I've been thinking about the homeless center you want to create. Since you're going to offer alternative healing modalities, have you thought about providing hypnotherapy, too? I've heard that it's very effective on people with addictive personalities. One of my chefs went through a program at Affirmative Change Hypnosis for alcoholism and he can't say enough good things about it. He also attends AA meetings."

"I hadn't thought about hypnotherapy, but that's an excellent idea. I don't know why it wasn't on my radar. I'll add that to the list of other services: acupuncture, Reiki, chiropractic, craniosacral, massage, homeopathic, naturopathic, and osteopathic."

"Wow. This center of yours sounds wonderful. I may consider being homeless just so I can utilize the services."

"You are a genius!" Will pulled off the road. He turned off the car and gave Ronnie a big kiss. "All this time, I wanted the city to fund my project. I still may need government assistance, but the center's practitioners can see regular folk, too. Instead of charging the current rates for appointments, we can lower them for the general public, and they'll essentially be paying for the residents' therapies."

"How's this for another idea: have a gym for the residents. Increasing their body image goes a long way. Of course, I personally wouldn't want to share that facility with the recently homeless. And I'm not saying that for hygienic reasons. I'd personally be afraid that one of them might come unglued and attack me with a barbell."

"Another gem from my good friend, Veronica Schatzki. The gym should be for residents only. I don't want to be fielding personal injury lawsuits." Will glanced at the clock on the dashboard. "It's getting late. Let's get you over to the restaurant. Did you leave something there?"

"I did."

Will said, "Are you going to tell me what it is?"

"You'll see."

Ten minutes later, Will watched as Ronnie locked the front door to The Big V. She was waving a postcard-size piece of paper.

Once inside the car, she handed the paper to Will. *Billy Grippo 415-378-1212.* He turned the paper over. It was blank. "I don't get it."

Ronnie gave Will a look of bemusement. "That name doesn't sound familiar at all?"

"Should it?"

"Uh, yeah. He's the founder of Dreamer.com, one of the largest entrepreneurial sites on the internet. The man's worth millions. Hundreds of millions. And he's vegan."

"Okay. What does this have to do with me? Or is it you? Does he want to fund another vegan restaurant?"

"The last time he was at the restaurant, I told him about you and your plans to build a complex for the homeless and how you wanted to serve only plant-based food. He was really impressed and told me to have you call him. He's interested in possibly funding it."

Will's hand started shaking, making the paper flutter. "This is incredible. You're incredible."

"I try." Ronnie cupped Will's face in her hands. "Great things happen to great people. You're an inspiration to all who know you. I'm convinced that you're going to build that center and others will use it as a blueprint for their cities."

"It may be premature, but I say we go back to my place and celebrate."

"Mind reader. You can add that to your list of talents."

Norma knew what she had to do to win Sandy's support and, ultimately, her love. First, Lonnie needed to be taken care of. As soon as she got home, she descended the stairs to the first-floor kitchen. She found Darby checking the pot pies in the oven. "Darby, would you mind if I used your room to make a quick phone call? I don't want Bob to hear."

"Not at all. The door is open." Darby watched in amazement as her employer disappeared into the one room Norma Ekhart had most likely never been in, save when they purchased the mansion over twenty-five years ago. As much as she would have loved to hear the call, Darby reluctantly walked to the other end of the kitchen and continued to prepare dinner.

Lonnie answered on one ring. "Hey Norma."

"Lonnie."

"The job is finished and in the designated time period. When can I expect payment?"

"Why don't we meet where we did the other day, at the racetrack site? Please bring the document and I'll bring your remuneration for services rendered."

"Sounds like a plan. When? Tonight?"

"I'd rather not meet in the dark. Shall we say 10:00 tomorrow morning?"

"See you then."

Lonnie thought he had killed Sandy. She could hear the

anticipation of getting a big payload. It was a job to him. That's all. Norma closed her eyes, grateful that he missed his intended target. She saw her daughter in her mind's eye, lying in the hospital bed, looking at her with venomous eyes, probably wishing she was dead. Norma had work to do. She didn't have to mend fences, she had to tear them down, and build new ones.

"Thank you, Darby. I owe you one." Norma walked over to the pot pies cooling off on the counter. She inhaled the savory aroma of the browned crust hiding chunks of vegetables in a lemon herb sauce. "I forgot how delicious your vegetable pot pies were. I can't wait to have one."

Tentatively hopeful, Darby asked, "Will Sandy be joining us?"

"Sadly, no. The hospital wanted to keep her overnight for observation. I do wish to bring her home tomorrow. Fingers crossed."

"It will be wonderful to see her again."

Norma nodded. "I would appreciate you setting the table for dinner and please set a place for yourself."

"Are you sure Mr. Ekhart won't mind?"

"I forgot about Bob. What the hell. Set a place for him and I don't care what he thinks. I'm more interested in talking to you."

"I'm flattered, Mrs. Ekhart. Thank you."

Norma smiled sincerely. "You're very welcome."

Returning upstairs, Norma found Bob sitting in the den, a glass of scotch in his hand. His head was back, eyes closed. His mouth was partially open, as if he were sleeping, but as she approached, he opened his eyes and glared at his wife. "I hope you're happy. You've turned our daughter against both of us with your hostility and greed." He knew he was poking the tiger, so he braced himself for the all too familiar tirade.

Norma calmly sat across from her husband. Her turquoise eyes misted over. Her posture was soft, not austere and unyielding. "I'm not going to defend myself. I have nothing to defend. I am deeply sorry for the pain that I have caused Sandy. I've been a poor excuse for a mother and a wife. I don't deny it." She lightly touched the bump above her eye. Despite Norma's expensive concealer, the purple bruise was bleeding through. It looked like she was involved in a brawl and some thug head-butted her. "Maybe getting hit on the head knocked some decency into me." Norma wiped her eyes.

Bob wasn't sure if he was in an alternative universe, where up was down, wrong was right and the evil were angelic. He stared at Norma for a long time, not knowing if she was trying to bait him. It was the first time since he'd met her that she had ever apologized. Except for the time they were playing tennis at the country club over twenty years ago. Despite Bob declaring that the ball was out of bounds, Norma thought she'd aced the serve. She insisted to the point of coming up to the net and pointing to where she claimed the ball landed. Normally submissive, Bob stood his ground. Ever defiant, Norma picked up her racket and hit the ball, aiming for her husband's head. It hit his groin instead and Bob dropped to the ground like a sack of potatoes. As he lay on the court, holding his crotch and moaning, Norma apologized. "I'm so sorry. I was aiming for your head." Recalling that day, Bob swore he could feel a throbbing in his groin.

"I'm finding your conciliatory stance hard to believe."

"I'm sure you do, but it's the truth. And my first step towards redemption is pulling out of Francisco Downs. I don't want to invest in an industry that is replete with abuse and greed. I'll admit it. Marlo was right."

Bob abruptly stood up and pointed his finger at Norma. "Liar! I know how much you love horse racing. I see the look in your eyes watching those animals running around the track. You once told me that it was better than sex. What's your angle, Norma?"

Exhausted from the day's events, Norma wasn't in the mood to deal with her husband. Part of her felt bad for him. He had endured living with a harpy for decades. He suffered privately and in public from Norma's hostility. On the other hand, no one was forcing him to stay married. It was his allegiance to the Ekhart family that he upheld the tradition of a divorce-free family tree.

Norma understood Bob's skepticism and she would have most likely reacted the same way. Without telling him the truth, she wasn't sure how else to explain her abrupt transformation. "I have no angle, Bob. You have every right to doubt my sincerity, so let's leave it at that. What is it they say, actions speak louder than words? In the coming days, I'll prove it." She stood up and held onto the chair's arm for support. "Right now, I'm hungry and would like to eat. Darby set the table for three. She'll be joining us for dinner. I have no idea who she is other than the woman who has cooked our meals and served us for as long as I can remember. It's time I found out."

Norma turned to go, expecting Bob to follow. Instead, mouth agape, he seemed frozen, unable to move. His mind couldn't comprehend what his wife just said.

"Are you joining us?"

"Uh…uh."

"Make up your mind. Nothing's worse than a cold pot pie."

24

If Bob hadn't offered to sleep in the guest room, Norma would have volunteered. She would have preferred never to see her husband again and she assumed he felt the same about her. Despite a restless night, the result of an overactive mind and the ongoing acclimation of Gigi's soul in human form, Norma awoke at 6:30. When her feet touched the soft carpet, she was momentarily disoriented. Her toes wiggled into the high pile, and it felt luxurious, yet the sensation was foreign. She stood, uneasily at first, her head aching and her mouth dry. Once she was steady, she walked to the bathroom, filled a glass with water and drank it. Through her tired, red-rimmed eyes, she took a long look at herself in the mirror, feeling her body as she studied its contours, her hands lingering on the smooth skin on her arms, belly and back. Her laugh lines were barely visible. As yet, no marionette lines. She ran her fingers through her ash blonde hair, then turned her attention to her part. The gray hairs were just starting to sprout. She smiled at her reflection. "With the exception of the knot on my head, I look damn good for an old broad."

After she showered and dressed, Norma went to the kitchen to fix breakfast. It was early and she didn't want to inconvenience Darby. Twenty-four hours earlier, that would never have crossed her mind.

The strong, sharp aroma of coffee brewing, filling up the kitchen with its scent, was intoxicating. The first bite of sourdough toast with almond butter and a smattering of raspberry preserves tasted divine. Norma savored the morning meal as if it was her first. Actually, her second. Last night, she received strange looks from Bob and Darby as she bit into her vegetable pot pie and wouldn't stop raving about it. The flavors were remarkable, the crust melted in her mouth. She made Darby promise that she would teach her how to make it. With the shock of Norma's transformation starting to wear off, Darby asked her employer if she would entertain the idea of getting a dog. Everyone who knew Norma was well aware of her distaste for pets. She claimed that she could smell their friend's dog, a Yorkshire terrier named Peek A Boo, when they went to their home, a 7,000 square foot manor on Nob Hill in San Francisco. The two-year-old, three-pound canine wasn't capable of emitting enough dog scent in a closet, let alone a mansion. Bob figured that Norma didn't like dogs, but wouldn't admit it, so she used the excuse that they smell bad. The new Norma smiled at Darby and said she thought it was a capital idea. Having a pet might be just the thing to make Sandy feel more at home. "And let's adopt a shelter dog. I hear there are so many in need of homes." Bob dropped his fork mid-bite, sending crust, peas, and carrots skittering across the table.

On her way to Francisco Down's future site, Norma mentally went over her conversation with Lonnie. She was hoping, no praying, that this encounter would be the last she ever had with the private investigator. She understood the cell phone records would preserve her relationship with the would-be killer for eons and Lonnie's own testimony, if charges were filed against her for conspiracy to commit murder, would put her away for life.

Norma decided to park her car a few blocks away as a precautionary measure. She didn't want her car in the same parking lot as her co-conspirator's. Make-up free, wearing a light blue sweatshirt and jeans, she looked like a middle-aged woman out on a stroll. She doubted that her friends would recognize her. Norma never left the house or entertained without being fully presentable. That meant, photo-worthy.

As she approached the site, she watched as Lonnie pulled into the lot and parked in the farthest corner. She stepped up her pace, wanting to get this over with as soon as possible.

"Good morning, Norma."

"Lonnie."

"All's well that ends well, wouldn't you say?"

"That I would, Mr. King. The document, please."

Lonnie handed over the release form for Sandy's trust fund.

"Thank you. Are you sure you weren't seen last night?"

Lonnie stood a little taller, his chest size increased. "Absolutely. It was dark and the only people who may have seen me with her were homeless druggies and alcoholics." He failed to tell Norma about being pursued. "I was watching TV this morning for any news on a homeless woman's murder, but nothing yet. I guess they haven't found her body."

"Would you mind showing a modicum of respect for my daughter, please?"

Lonnie slapped his head, exaggerating the move. "Gee, I'm sorry. She wouldn't be dead if it weren't for you, or did you forget that small piece of information?"

Norma ignored the question. She removed an envelope from her back pocket and opened it up. "This is your fee, plus the bonus you requested. Please take it out of the envelope."

Lonnie grabbed the money. As he counted it, the smile on his face grew larger. "It's all there. Pleasure working with you. Let's do it again, soon I hope."

Norma anticipated his answer. "Aren't you going to tell me that I overpaid you, Mr. King?"

Rarely, if ever, did Lonnie blush. He turned his crimson red face away from Norma. "I could have sworn that this was the bonus I requested."

"No, it's not. I added an extra $30,000. If you're wrong and someone did see you, there's a chance you could be called in for questioning. I think it would be wise to leave the Bay Area and put out your shingle in a city where they don't know you. With your penchant for wearing shorts and tropical shirts, I'd say Florida would be an ideal relocation site."

Lonnie stroked his soul patch. "Do you know something I don't know?"

"Absolutely not, but why take the chance? You murdered a young woman last night. Once she's identified, it's possible through people you spoke to about her, they may connect the dots. Do you really want to take that chance?"

Almost positive that he wasn't seen the night he shot Sandy, Lonnie thought about the conversations he had with Sandy's ex-roommate and her doctor at the clinic. Even the patient in the waiting room. Sandy wasn't his first hit, but he also didn't want her to be his last. He could feel the wad of cash in his pocket. It would be a shame not to be able to spend it. "I have an aunt in Miami. My mother said she works as a realtor. Maybe I should give her a call. Check out some homes."

"That sounds like a smart idea. I think we'll both breathe a little easier, don't you?"

Lonnie nodded.

"Goodbye, Mr. King." She quickly walked back to her car. Norma wanted to get as far away as she could from Mr. Lonnie King. She also had to go to the bathroom. She may have come off cool and under control, but underneath the façade, her nerves were on overload.

Norma knew there would always be a chance that her association with Lonnie could be exposed. That was why her next conversation would be the most important. If she failed, Gigi's new life as a human being could easily be spent behind bars.

Marlo was ready to knock on the door, but Petal had been watching for her through the living room window. She opened the door and Marlo nearly fell forward; her energy was that heightened.

"What was so important that you drove across town during lunch hour to tell me in person? I'm guessing this is going to be good."

"It's monumental!" Marlo gave Petal a big hug. It felt comforting to connect with another empathetic person. She took off her sunglasses. "Bob Ekhart called Rick this morning and told him that he thinks aliens abducted his wife and replaced her with a kinder, gentler being." Marlo went on to relate Norma's behavior to Petal, who stood wide-eyed, disbelieving. "And here's the real clincher. She's pulling out of the racetrack project. She said that I was right about the industry and wants no part of it. Norma said I was right! Without her backing, I don't think the remaining investors can fund the project." Marlo clapped her hands. "Of course, Rick was upset."

"That's fantastic." Petal feigned confusion. "Why would Bob Ekhart be telling your husband this?"

In her enthusiasm to relate the great news, Marlo completely forgot that she never told Petal about Rick's partnership in Francisco Downs. "I was so afraid that you would judge me or, worse, think I was a spy for the investors. It's not typical for the spouse of a pro-horse racer to volunteer to sabotage the investment. Please don't be mad at me."

Without admitting that she already knew, Petal gave her a warm smile and gently touched her arm. "I would have done the same thing. The important point is that you did what you felt was right. I'm proud of you."

"Thanks. I almost forgot. Bob also told Rick that they found their daughter, Sandy. She was shot last night, but the bullet grazed her head so she's okay. Right now, she's at the hospital. Rick and I were going to visit her this afternoon. The police told Bob that she had been living in a homeless camp. I think he said it was the big one off Crenella. Can you imagine an Ekhart sleeping on the street?"

"Only if it was paved with gold." Petal sat down and patted the seat next to her. Marlo obliged. "What do you think the reason is for Norma's drastic change?"

"Great question. The woman was barely civil to me. She would make a nasty remark whenever she could. And the most perplexing part is that she loved horse racing. She grew up going to the track with her family. She once told me that she could care less about the treatment of the horses because, deep down, they loved to run and win. She was such a bitch. So self-serving. Honestly, I didn't think she had an empathetic bone in her blue-blooded body. Bob said that Norma attributes the transformation to falling and hitting her head on the coffee table in their den. That's not possible, is it? A completely different personality?"

"Did you Google it?"

"Of course. I Google everything. Someone's personality can change after a traumatic brain injury. According to Bob, Norma has a large lump on her forehead. She lost consciousness, so she very well could have had an injury to her brain. I also googled, 'can aliens take over a human body?' and found an article on ten ways to tell if you've been abducted by aliens. Number six said that people who have been abducted suddenly have a calling to want to help the environment and others less fortunate than themselves."

With a smile, Petal said, "That must be what happened. Norma was abducted. The mothership saw the Ekhart's massive home from space and decided to check out the occupants. Seriously, whatever changed Norma's mind concerning the racetrack, I don't care. She just made our fight to stop the damn project a lot easier." Petal got up from the couch. "I'm going to make a pot of tea. You want?"

"Yes, please." Marlo followed her into the kitchen and watched Petal deftly combine three different kinds of dried tea leaves, herbs, and dried berries. She placed them into the ceramic teapot's stainless-steel sieve, then filled the tea kettle with water and turned on the stove burner.

Petal handed Marlo a chocolate ball covered in crushed almonds. "A friend of mine makes raw chocolate truffles. This one has bits of coconut and almonds in the center."

Marlo took a bite. "I don't think I've ever had raw chocolate before. It makes Hershey's and even Ghirardelli taste anemic." She took another bite. "My taste buds are standing at attention!" She popped the remaining bite into her mouth and licked her fingers. "Petal, in a few weeks, you have introduced me to new ideas and foods and remedies than I've ever been introduced to in my lifetime."

"Stick around gal. I've only just begun. And don't forget about your rockin' haircut, compliments of Forest, who, by the way, thinks you're very cute. Just saying."

"He knows I'm married."

"Still thinks you're the cat's pajamas."

Marlo looked confused.

"Google it."

Before Norma drove back to the hospital, she made sure that her daughter hadn't yet checked out. With trepidation, she made her way down the hall to Sandy's room.

Thankful that the other bed was unoccupied and no one else was visiting her daughter, Norma lightly knocked on the partially open door. Sandy looked away from the television. When she saw her mother, she thought she was going to lose it. She felt her anger swell from deep in her belly. She hissed, "I told you to leave me alone."

Cautiously, Norma approached Sandy. "I know, but I have to tell you something and when I'm finished, if you still want me out of your life, then I'll respect your wishes. Give me a few moments. Please."

Reluctantly, Sandy muted the sound on the game show she was watching, then motioned her mother over. "My whole life was spent trying to get you to really see me and now I can't get you to leave me alone. Talk about irony."

Norma laughed nervously. "True." She grabbed a chair by the door and brought it to the bedside. Before she could sit down, Sandy said, "No make-up? I don't think I have ever seen you leave the house without a minimum of foundation, mascara, eyeliner, and blush. My God, you don't even have lipstick on. And that bump on your head is looking worse than mine." Sandy touched her bandaged wound for emphasis.

"I told you I've changed, but you're never going to believe how. Actually, I hope you believe me. It's going to take an incredible leap of faith and after years of abuse and disdain that I've perpetrated upon you, I know I'm asking a lot." Norma closed her eyes and took in a deep breath. She held it for a few seconds, let it out. One more time and she was ready. She opened her eyes and with resolve she began. "Almost three weeks ago, there was a terrible accident at SFO. A bomb was detonated in the United Airlines terminal and five people died. One of them was a woman named Emma Banks. When Emma was killed, her spirit left her body. In its ascent, it collided with a doll and became trapped."

Understandably, her daughter was looking at her like she had completely flipped her lid. Sandy looked around the room. "Am I being filmed for a documentary on the homeless? Or are you testing my sanity because this is beyond bizarre. You know that, right?"

Norma reached for her daughter's arm, but Sandy pulled away. "Continue, Norma. I think."

"Trapped in the doll, Emma was forced to either stay in her new body or find another human body, meaning she would have to push out their spirit. Emma's sister, Gigi, who had died a few years ago, helped Emma find another body to inhabit." Norma looked into Sandy's skeptical eyes. "Emma chose you."

Sandy felt like she had been doused with ice water. A chill went up her spine. Before she could respond, Norma continued. "Emma wanted to find out more about you, so the two soul sisters followed you. They also eavesdropped on your father and me. The purpose was to get as much background and current information about you so the transition would be smooth. The problem was that Emma decided she didn't want to be human again. Our race, with all its flaws and barbs, disgusted her. She made the decision to stay in the doll. The downside was that her soul was becoming attached to Marilyn – that's the doll's name – and if she stayed, it would become permanent. She could no longer leave the doll whenever she wanted. Her energy level also lessened. It was like living in a coffin. Only her sense of hearing functioned. As you can imagine, the reality of that hell set in, and she asked Gigi for help. Here's where it gets very interesting. The sisters realized that the only way Emma could be set free was for Gigi to take her place. As a newly inhabited spirit, she would have the initial freedom to move in and out of Marilyn. Eventually she, too, would succumb to the doll's body." Norma retrieved a bottle of water from her purse and took a sip. "How are you doing with all this?"

"You have my attention. Whether I believe it or not is another thing. On the other hand, in my entire life, I have never known you to show the slightest interest in the supernatural or anything remotely spiritual."

"That's true. I always thought people who believed in reincarnation were afraid of the finality of death, so believing in an eternal spirit gave them comfort. I also thought they were idiots, but I digress." Norma pulled her hair back and secured it with a ponytail band. "So, the sisters had a dilemma, especially since Gigi hadn't wanted to return as a human. She had died in a car crash and wasn't in a hurry to come back to earth. Emma's situation changed that. Without hesitation, she pushed Emma's spirit out of the doll and took her spot. Now Emma was a free spirit and Gigi's time was critical. The sisters saw you get shot."

Sandy's eyes widened. She looked at her mother in disbelief. "Are you telling me that this Gigi spirit is in me?"

Norma's turquoise eyes filled with tears. She smiled lovingly at her daughter and said, "No, dear, her spirit is in me." She took her daughter's hand in hers and Sandy felt affection, acceptance, adoration, and love spreading throughout her body. She couldn't deny that her mother, a woman who always seemed cold to the touch, was the embodiment of warmth and sincerity. Still, Sandy had her doubts. She pulled her hand away.

"So, you hired that man to find me and force me sign over my trust to you?"

Norma took out a handkerchief and wiped her eyes. "I did."

"And if I didn't, you knew he was going to shoot me?"

Norma nodded. "It was before…" She touched the bump on her forehead. It was still very sore. "I really was a vile person. I apologize for who she – I was, but it's not me anymore."

Sandy lay back on her pillow and closed her eyes. Her head was pounding, and she didn't have the energy to fight. Her mother's story was so out there, so fantastical, that she was gravitating toward believing it. The Norma she knew would never invent such a crazy scenario as an excuse. The Norma she knew wouldn't have admitted to being a party to attempted murder. The Norma she knew wouldn't be sitting beside her in the hospital.

Norma continued. "My timing may not have been optimal, but you needed to know the truth. I also want you to come back home. Let's start over. Let me be the mother that you should have had."

Sandy opened her tired, bloodshot eyes. "Who are you?"

"What do you mean?"

Sandy sat up too fast. She could feel the blood pulsing behind her eyes. She put her hands over her eyes and could feel the sweat on her forehead and cheeks. A shot of vodka would help her cope right now.

"Are you okay? Do you want me to call the nurse?" Norma stood and fixed Sandy's pillow.

"I'm fine." She pulled the covers up to her chest. "I am asking who you are. Are you Gigi wearing Norma's body? Are you my mother with a new conscience? Forgive me, but this is the first time I've met a transspiritual."

Norma laughed. "I like that. Transspiritual is a great word, but it's not accurate. There's only one body and one soul. Remember as a child how you liked to mix the pink and blue Play-Dohs together? At first, you could clearly see pink and blue. Eventually, as you continued to knead the clay, it became purple. That's how I feel. My spirit is Gigi, but my Norma body has cellular memory. I remember almost everything, and some memories are more acute. I can feel myself being gently kneaded, body and soul melding into one. You can be assured that the old Norma will never rear her nasty head again."

"How can you reassure me? Do you really know what's going to happen?"

"Good question. It's going to take another leap of faith for you to trust me. Before I traded places with my sister, I tapped into the universal energy source. Everything and anything you want to know is there. Humans have access to it as well, but it's a lot easier to absorb the information when you're not encumbered by a mind, an ego, and constant external stimuli. I learned about spirit swapping, the initial experience, and the permanent results. My deliberate takeover of this body gave me the upper hand, so to speak, so I'll always have control."

Sandy looked intently into her mother's eyes. "You're asking me to trust you, move back to the home that's filled with lousy memories, and live with you and dad when I just found out I have $20 million dollars waiting for me as soon as I leave the hospital?"

"I'm not. I'm leaving your father and moving out. The house feels as foreign to me as much as it feels unpleasant to you."

"Is this a ploy?"

"No. I'm not going to spend my new life married to a weak-willed coward. The only reason your father won't divorce me is that he's loathe to break the Ekhart family tradition. Not one person in that gnarled family tree has been divorced. They believe marriage personifies conviction and strength. Instead, it's a perfect example of blind allegiance to a government-sanctioned institution. We're humans, not machines. We don't always choose the right partner. Why should we be stuck with them because we signed a document that said we would?"

"You really are the new and improved Norma. My mother would never digress like that." She pulled the covers closer to her body. "Is it colder in here? It feels colder to me."

Norma got up from the chair and felt Sandy's forehead. It was clammy. "Why don't we call the nurse? You're sweating."

Without making eye contact, Sandy said, "I think I need more pain medication. My head's throbbing."

"Is it okay if we come in?" Will and Ronnie stood at the entrance to the room. As it was his day off, Will was dressed in jeans and a pullover sweater. Ronnie wore her Vegan Vipers ensemble, getting more than a few looks from the hospital staff and visitors. She loved the attention. If it made people think, she was grateful. In the elevator, a woman tapped Ronnie on the back and asked what the Vegan Vipers were and where she could get the leather jacket. The question was asked so often, that Ronnie had crafted a short and succinct answer. "We're a group of female vegan restauranteurs who provide food and other necessities to the homeless. The jacket is made of pineapple leather." She would give them her card. One side had The Big V restaurant's information. The other side was dedicated to the vipers with a contact name for the jacket maker.

Norma turned to the door and beckoned them in. "Of course. Welcome. I'm Norma, Sandy's mother."

"Will Remini. Nice to meet you."

"Veronica Schatzki."

Norma said, "I love your outfit, but I thought vegans didn't wear leather."

Ronnie smiled. "We don't. This is made from pineapple skins."

Norma reached out to touch the jacket. "May I?"

Ronnie nodded and held out her arm. Norma felt the sleeve. "Remarkable. It looks and feels just like leather."

Will said, "And no animals were harmed in the process."

Sandy looked from her mother to Will, to Ronnie. She couldn't get over the normal conversation she was witnessing. She was still feeling chilled, so she pushed the button for the nurse.

Norma had forgotten about Sandy's request. She was intrigued by the couple in front of her. "Don't tell me you're a vegan, too?"

Will replied, "I am. I was also Sandy's doctor at the clinic on Fillmore."

"He and Ronnie are the ones who saved me last night."

Norma hugged Will, then Ronnie. "Thank you so much. You're heroes, you know that?"

Will said, "We're just thankful that the guy was a lousy shot." He glanced over at Sandy. She knew exactly what he was thinking. She knew she couldn't tell anybody about her mother's confession.

The nurse came up to Sandy's bedside. "Did you need something?"

"Pain meds, please. My head really hurts." Sandy's pallor was obvious. Her skin looked waxy and her eyes were red. Her hands shook slightly.

The nurse felt her forehead, then took her pulse. "Are you thirsty?"

"Yes."

The nurse poured Sandy a glass of water and placed it on the bedstand. "I'll be right back." She left abruptly, prompting Will to follow her.

Norma watched them leave. "What was that all about?"

Sandy burst into tears. "I think I know." She grabbed a tissue from the nightstand and blew her nose. "I'm not proud of what I'm about to say, but since you came clean with me, I think you should know that…living on the street was a lot easier when I was drunk. So, it was rare when I wasn't drinking. It became my new normal." She began crying again. "I thought I was a mess before Sandra kicked me out of her apartment. I've gone so far beyond a mess." She blew her nose again and looked toward the window. "Please don't think badly of me."

Ronnie's discomfort was usurped by her interest in Norma's reaction. Will hadn't told her much about the mother/daughter relationship, but after Sandy's outburst the night before and her parents' hasty departure from the hospital room, Ronnie was sure their relationship needed improvement.

Norma went up to Sandy's bed, leaned over and kissed her head. "The only person I think badly of is me." She took her daughter's face in her hands. "I said it before and I will say it again: I was a lousy mother. You deserved so much better, and I promise that I will make it up to you. You do not have to do this on your own."

Despite the IV in her arm, Sandy hugged her mother hard. As a child, she remembered how hugging Norma was akin to embracing a statue. She would stand stick still as if bracing for an unfortunate event. After a while, Sandy stopped hugging, even touching her, much to Norma's relief.

Neither woman wanted to let go. They were making up for all the years where intimacy was non-existent. A new bond was being created. A new, indelible link being forged. It was only when Will and the nurse returned with the doctor that they disengaged.

Dr. Sedie was a large man. He stood a little over six-foot-three. He ran his hand through his full head of dark, wavy hair, then took off his wire-rimmed glasses as he finished reading Sandy's chart. "Hello, Sandra, I'm Dr. Sedie. I saw you last night when you were admitted to the hospital. The nurse said you were complaining of pain." He pointed to the IV drip. "You're receiving 10 cc's of Percocet. That should be enough. I'd like to examine your wounds and make sure there's no infection."

Norma offered her hand to Dr. Sedie and he shook it. "I'm Sandy's mother, Norma Ekhart."

"A pleasure to meet you. You have quite a nasty wound on your forehead, as well."

Norma smiled. "Mine was the result of being clumsy, nothing as dramatic as Sandy's experience. Do you want us to leave while you examine my daughter?"

"I think that would be a good idea. We have a waiting room right down the hall. I can have the nurse let you know when I'm done."

As soon as they left, Dr. Sedie said, "Sandra, I realize you've been through a traumatic experience, but I need to ask you if you had been drinking alcoholic beverages to excess."

Sandy clasped her hands together to stop her from shaking. "Only over the past couple of weeks. Before that, I barely drank."

Dr. Sedie gently removed the bandage from Sandy's forehead. He placed it on the side table. As he moved closer to inspect the abrasion, he said, "Can you describe how you feel right now?"

"I have the chills and a monster headache." She held up her hands. "I can't control the shaking."

"Are you nauseous?"

Sandy shook her head. "But I'm also not hungry."

Dr. Sedie placed a fresh bandage on the wound, then instructed Sandy to sit forward so he could attend to the gash on the back of her head. "I'm going to make an educated guess as to the extent of your affliction based on your withdrawal symptoms. I don't think you're going to experience much worse than you are right now. Two to four weeks of binge drinking isn't good for your body, obviously, but it also won't take long for you to normalize, as long as you don't drink. I want to prescribe a benzodiazepine. It will help control the shaking and any anxiety you might feel. Have you ever taken Valium, Librium, or Ativan before?" Upon inspection, the wound looked clean. No signs of infection.

"I took Valium a few years ago when I had trouble sleeping."

"Any side effects?"

Sandy shook her head. "Nope. I quickly fell asleep and woke up feeling fine."

"Valium it is."

"When can I leave the hospital, Dr. Sedie?"

"That depends, Sandra..."

"Sandy, please."

"Sorry, Sandy." Dr. Sedie wrote something on her medical chart.

"Do you have a place to stay, and will there be someone who can be with you, to care for you?"

"Yes. I'll be staying with my parents."

"I'd like to monitor your progress one more day. If all looks good, you can go home tomorrow. How does that sound?"

"Fantastic."

"I'll ask the nurse to tell your guests they can return." Dr. Sedie placed the clipboard at the foot of the bed frame. A few minutes later, the gang came back. Will was the first to speak.

"So, what's the prognosis?"

"The good news is I'm going to live. The bad news is that the doctor wants me to stay one more day, so I'll be released tomorrow."

Ronnie said, "Your mom was telling us that when you were a little girl, you liked to cook. Does it still interest you?"

"It does. I find it very relaxing, especially baking."

"Tell you what. Once you get settled and are feeling up to it, why don't you come over to my restaurant and I'll give you a tour of the kitchen. If you're interested, I'll give you baking lessons."

Will looked at Ronnie with renewed admiration.

Sandy said, "You know I'm not vegan, right?"

"I know." Ronnie put her arm around Will's shoulders. "Hang around us long enough and you may just become one."

25

Marlo waited until she was sure Rick was gone. She watched the bright yellow Ferrari disappear down the street, then went into her closet and took down her biggest suitcase. The Ralph Lauren slacks and jeans went in first, followed by a dozen pullover cashmere sweaters in a variety of colors. Socks, bras, underwear – mostly lace thongs – quickly filled up her temporary closet. The more clothes she folded and placed in the Gucci bag, the lighter she felt. She had been contemplating leaving Rick, but his response to an article in the Examiner clinched it. When Marlo read the headline, she gasped. Rick looked up from the business section, his reading glasses low on his nose. "You okay?"

"No. Many Clouds, the 2015 Grand National winner, collapsed and died after winning the race at Cheltenham. She was ten years old."

Rick clucked his tongue. "What a shame." He went back to reading the paper.

"That's it? That's all you have to say?" Marlo was furious.

"Not this again. Honey, I'm sorry that I don't get all choked up over a racehorse dying. You said she was ten years old? She died doing what she loved. How many people can say that?"

Marlo could almost hear the last piece of her heart that cared for Rick break off. She could see Rick bracing for a fight, but she no longer had it in her. Instead, she turned the page so she wouldn't have to read the details and silently vowed that she would do everything in her power to fight for either the dissolution of the racing industry or for stricter, enforced regulations.

It was during a benefit gala for the Palomino Club's Scholarship Fund when Marlo met Rick Standish. Marlo's modeling career was growing, but she needed extra income, so she worked part-time for a caterer. When Rick was presented with a tray of appetizers, he accepted a stuffed mushroom and before popping it into his mouth, complimented Marlo on her exquisite presentation, all the while staring at her cleavage. Unruffled, she thanked the average looking, middle-aged man with a slight paunch, sans wedding ring. Throughout the evening, despite being with a date, Marlo would catch Rick staring at her. She would politely smile, and he would surreptitiously nod his head. When she had a chance, she asked her boss if he recognized the gentleman who exuded confidence. "Of course. That's Rick Standish, one of the most successful investment brokers in the city." Marlo heard 'most successful' and 'investment broker,' and the average looking man just got a whole lot better looking. In a field as competitive as modeling, she liked the idea of having life insurance – Rick could be her insurance for a better life.

Toward the end of the evening, as the guests were leaving, Marlo made sure she was in close proximity to Rick and his date. As anticipated, Rick said something to the woman. She nodded and walked to the exit.

"Could you direct me to the restroom, miss…?"

"Marlo and I believe the men's room is down that hall to the right."

"Thank you, Marlo. One more thing. Would it be possible to obtain your phone number? I find you simply irresistible."

As if on cue, she pulled a business card out of her pants pocket and demurely handed it to him. "Are you sure your date won't mind?"

"What date?" he said as he walked to the men's room.

Marlo saw her future that night. She saw gourmet meals instead of frozen dinners, a navy-blue Mercedes-Benz instead of her thirteen-year-old white Toyota Camry. And, without an ounce of disgust, she imagined her young, lithe body intertwined with a pale, doughy one. In a king-sized, four poster bed.

As she folded her violet satin teddy, she thought about the night she met her soon-to-be ex-husband. She didn't regret her decision to sublimate her energies into becoming Mrs. Marlo Standish. She knew exactly what she was getting herself into. She took one last look at her closet, a room larger than the studio apartment she was living in when she met Rick.

Marlo wasn't concerned about the divorce settlement. Whatever alimony Rick was willing to give her, she would accept. Money and opulence had become secondary. Her freedom to live as she pleased was more important. She couldn't wait to become Petal's apprentice, learning about aromatherapy, essential oils, and exploring her spiritual side. God knows she'd mastered her materialistic side.

When all three suitcases were placed in the trunk, Marlo backed her Mercedes out of the garage and headed over to her new apartment. She had a few more trips to make, then she'd wait for Rick to come home so she could deliver her news. In the years they'd been married, the man barely raised his voice to her. He was as kind and gentle as an alpha dog could be. Rick made sure that Marlo knew her place. It was on his arm in public, by his side listening attentively to his evening musings, and in his bed, compliant, creative, and grateful. Tonight, she wasn't sure how he would react to her leaving, but she had a feeling that he was as unhappy with her as she was with him. Despite a possible bruised ego, she was too impatient to wait for him to make the first move. Tomorrow, Marlo Standish was ending her reign in her Pacific Heights mansion as a trophy wife and starting anew in a one-bedroom apartment overlooking the Presidio. She couldn't wait to get started.

When Makelo was nervous, his left leg shook. At the moment, it nearly hit the underside of his desk. Caroline Busby was in front of the class, reading her oral presentation. He was up next. She had chosen to interview her Persian cat named Plum Cake. He had to admit that it was clever and funny. Who knew that Plum Cake's favorite television show was Hawaii 5-0 and that she dreamt of one day traveling to the Middle East where her breed is from? He laughed along with his fellow classmates, all the while wondering if his interview with Old Joe was too depressing or, worse, boring.

After the applause died down, Makelo slowly walked up to the front of the classroom. To the easel on his right, he placed a large photo of Old Joe. Some of the kids laughed. Others made disparaging remarks about the man's appearance. With his unkempt greasy hair, heavily lined, weathered face, and crooked smile, his visage was in sharp contrast to Plum Cake's caramel-colored eyes and elegant snow-white coat.

"This is Old Joe. I met him at the soup kitchen where my Uncle

Will and I volunteer. A lot of people who don't live in homes like you and me come to the soup kitchen to eat. It may be the only time they eat all day."

"That's because they're all drunks!" one kid shouted. Once again, laughter erupted in the classroom. The teacher, Mrs. Kornfeld, quickly stood up and addressed the class.

"Homelessness is not a laughing matter. And the homeless certainly should not be generalized. Show Makelo and his subject matter respect. If I hear another outburst, you'll be sent to the principal's office." She nodded to Makelo to continue.

"Old Joe's real name is Joseph Ryder Phelps, Junior, and he was born in 1945 in Schenectady, New York. He's seventy-one years old. You look at his photo and laugh and make fun of the way he looks. He's been homeless for almost ten years. His skin is hard and wrinkled. He can't see out of one eye because he was hit with a bottle during a fight over a sleeping bag. He's in a lot of pain because so many of his teeth are rotten, but he can't afford to go to a dentist. He also told me that he doesn't beg. He wasn't brought up to ask for handouts. If it weren't for the soup kitchen or the people that donate food and blankets, he probably would be dead.

"What keeps him alive? Having the freedom to do what he wants, where he wants and no one telling him what to do. He loves to go to the park and sit up against a tree or watch the birds fly above him. He says that they're truly free. As a kid, he just wanted to have a life like his parents. His dad was an insurance salesman, so he became one. He married a girl he went to high school with, and they had a daughter. Her name was Jackie. She died when she was sixteen. Joe said since her death, he was never the same. I'm sure you're all wondering how Joe became homeless. I was curious, too, but he wouldn't tell me. I think it may have had something to do with Jackie's death. He did tell me this: whether you believe in reincarnation or not, live like this is your only life. Be responsible for what you say and what you do because when it's over, you're the only one looking back. You're the only one who put one foot in front of the other and made it this far.

"When I thanked Old Joe for the interview, I could see in his eyes that I made him feel important and that makes standing up here worth it. My Uncle Will said there's a saying: Walk a mile in someone else's shoes. Until you do, don't judge people. Whatever happened to Joe, it must have been pretty horrible for him to end up living on the street without family, without friends. I still don't know a lot about him, but I do know that he would never make fun of any of you. Whether you're too short or too tall, have a teeny nose or a large one, he would show you respect."

Makelo replaced the photo of Old Joe with a photo of people being served dinner at the soup kitchen. In the center of the line was a family of four, one of the children was around the same age as the students. Her hair looked clean and brushed. Her clothes were ill-fitting and showed signs of aging, yet they were clean as well.

Behind the family, an elderly woman stared off into space. She hid most of her unkempt hair under a backwards baseball cap, while her choice in fashion redefined the art of layering. She was at least thirty pounds lighter than she looked, donning several T-shirts, sweaters, and a jacket.

Makelo was waiting for more snide remarks or snickers. There were none. Either his classmates didn't want to be sent to the principal's office or they were moved by Old Joe's story. Maybe it was a combination of both. "I'd like to end with a quote from Illinois Congresswoman Jan Schakowsky. 'There is a lot that happens around the world we cannot control. We cannot stop earthquakes, we cannot prevent droughts, and we cannot prevent all conflict, but when we know where the hungry, the homeless and the sick exist, then we can help.' Makelo looked at his classmates. He could feel tears forming and he did his best to keep it together. His moms told him that there's nothing wrong with crying and he believed them, however, he didn't want to break down in front of his class. He took a deep breath. "I volunteer at the soup kitchen once a week. They always need help and if anyone is interested, let me know and I'll give you the information."

After the class applauded, Makelo took his photographs and returned to his seat. Mrs. Kornfeld thanked her student for his presentation, then called Greg Phillips to the front of the room. Glad the presentation was over, Makelo half listened to Greg talk about his brother, a Marine in Afghanistan. He was still thinking about Old Joe and wondering if there was any way to convince him to move into the shelter. He was afraid something bad would happen to him if he continued to live on the street. For a brief moment, he even entertained the idea of asking his mothers if Joe could move in with them. It was a very brief moment. There must be other ways to house every homeless person. Makelo was determined to solve the problem.

Emma hovered above the Grand Canyon. The energy from the magnificent natural wonder energized her. She felt electrified. As a family, they had vacationed there when she was ten. Gigi said it looked like God took a serrated knife and, after lopping off the tops of the mountains, began carving them up.

She marveled how the sunset turned the banded sedimentary rocks bright orange, yellow and sienna. The vertical cumulonimbus clouds above her were dense, heavy with rainwater. She knew that if she stayed, she would be in the middle of a thunderstorm. She couldn't think of any other place she'd rather be. Moments later, the sun disappeared, and the rain started to fall, light at first, sprinkling the mountains. Then the downpour began. She watched as the rain pelted the canyon, turning a dramatic landscape into wet shadows. Lightning split apart the clouds above her and struck a plateau. The sound of thunder roared through her. She felt delighted being part of nature. Miles away, two more lightning bolts shattered the sky. The thunder was deafening, exhilarating. She dove into the Colorado River and witnessed the rain churning its waters. A large school of Speckled Dace raced by, as if trying to avoid the roiling waters. Emma laughed as their energy filled her. She was a flicker of light, a part of Mother Nature's organic performance. She was the rain and the lightning. It was a feeling the human body was incapable of experiencing: pure light and energy.

As the storm subsided, Emma had an urge to return to San Francisco, beckoned by her indelible tie to Gigi. She came in through the Ekhart's roof and lit on the table, an arm's length from Bob, who was visibly shaken. It looked like he was on the verge of tears, his lower lip trembling, his face a lighter shade of pale. He pointed his finger at Norma, who was sitting across from him. "We've been married over twenty-five years. It's not a perfect marriage, but it works."

Norma took a sip of tea. She was calm and poised. "I disagree. It is a perfect marriage. Perfectly dysfunctional. We have failed at mutual respect, we have failed at parenting, we no longer have a sex life and when we did it was only so-so. I've bullied you our entire marriage and you took it. What's worse is that you weren't there for Sandy and for that, I find it hard to forgive you."

Emma was so impressed with Norma's transformation, she zigzagged around the room, barely able to contain her enthusiasm.

Bob was nearly apoplectic. "You're the one who pushed me away from our daughter. The way you taunted her and criticized her. Telling her she wasn't good enough to be an Ekhart. I don't know how you can forgive yourself!"

Despite his agitated state, Norma got up and sat next to Bob. She looked into his eyes and said with genuine sincerity, "I am no longer the Norma you knew, and I don't want to be any part of who she was. I need to forgive myself for being an insensitive, ego-driven, vile person and I vow that I will never be that person again. I'm not blaming you for who I was, Bob. I blame you for who you were and, hopefully, will choose from this day forward not to be. I asked for Sandy's forgiveness and she gave it to me. Will you do the same?" Before Bob could answer, Norma added, "Sandy needs our unconditional love right now."

Bob closed his eyes. He couldn't believe he was having this conversation. Sandy forgave her mother for hiring a hitman to kill her? Was Norma telling him the truth? Despite her disfigured forehead, Norma looked radiant. He always thought she was gorgeous, but tonight she absolutely exuded an otherworldly grace and beauty. He finished his scotch. It helped coat the evening in a light film, creating a buffer between his raw emotions and the wife he thought he knew so well. "If I apologize to Sandy, will you stay with me? Now that you're the new and improved Norma, our marriage will be better, you'll see."

Is he dense or what? Emma thought to herself. It reminded her of the time she told Vin she wanted a divorce. The marriage was so off kilter even Dr. Phil couldn't save it.

Norma was tempted to pour herself a stiff drink, then thought better of it. She needed a clear head. Instead, she took a deep breath and slowly let it out. "You could find a cure for cancer and I still wouldn't want to stay in our marriage."

"That was mean."

"No Bob, I'm trying to express how I feel and what I want to do with my life moving forward. Staying with you is not an option. I don't want to live according to what others deem correct and proper. You may protest now, but I know that you are going to be much happier without me. And just think, you'll be the lone trailblazer in the Ekhart dynasty. I guarantee that once our divorce is final, other family members will be scrambling to undo their toxic marriages."

"I would be changing the family's paradigm."

"Definitely. With all due respect, they'd never expect such a ballsy move from you."

"Gee thanks," he said, his voice slightly sarcastic. Bob refilled his glass with brandy and took a healthy gulp. "I never thought I'd say this, but if you want a divorce, I won't contest it. I suppose you'll want the house."

"No, I don't. This place is much too big for me. I want to scale back dramatically, so it's all yours."

Another shock. Bob couldn't believe that Norma's extreme personality change could be the result of a fall. "Are you seeing someone else?"

Norma laughed. "No, I'm not seeing anyone else." I am someone else, she said to herself. She yawned. "I'm going to bed. I'm exhausted." She thought about giving Bob a kiss on the cheek but decided against it. She didn't want to give him any reason to think she would reconsider.

"I'm going to stay here and get completely sotted. Sleep well."

"Thank you. Don't forget to turn out the lights. Last month's electricity bill was high."

Bob was convinced. That fall completely turned Norma into another person.

Emma laughed. Gigi's devotion to the environment was rabid. It was so like her not to want to waste electricity.

The worst seemed to be over, Norma thought as lay in bed. Soon the reparations would begin, building a solid, loving relationship with Sandy. Once that was accomplished, she was determined to look up Grant Cantella, Gigi's husband. Their marriage was the polar opposite of Bob and Norma's. Grant used to say that she was the pepper to his salt. That became his nickname for her and got a kick out of calling her Pepper when they were in public. "What did you think of the movie, Pepper?" "I loved it. Did you, Salty?" For thirty years, their marriage was ideal. It was an anomaly in a culture where one out of four marriages fail and of the ones that survive, only sixty percent are content and flourish. The last time Gigi visited Grant, he was at work. She could feel his heartache as he sat behind his oak desk, plotting out formulas for the company's latest tooling machine. She stared into his light brown eyes, trying desperately to infuse his soul with happiness and contentment. Innately, she knew it wasn't possible, yet she tried.

Introducing herself to her husband would be easy. Convincing him that she inhabited his wife's spirit would be a challenge, hopefully not an insurmountable one. In the meantime, she vowed to watch every movie that involved soul swapping. She would take notes and practice her explanation before executing it. The first two on her list: *Prelude to a Kiss* and *Chances Are*. She'd make Sandy watch them with her. Maybe it would help strengthen their bond. Before she fell asleep, Norma's last image was of Lonnie King. She saw his smug face with that ridiculous soul patch. He treated as if it were prime real estate. She prayed he would take her advice and move 3,000 miles away to the land of sun and humidity, leaving the foggy, windy city behind for good.

26

Will was finishing up with paperwork from his last patient when there was a knock on his open door. He looked up to find Sandy Ekhart, the new and improved Sandy Ekhart, leaning against the entrance. She looked like a different woman. A beautiful woman whose resemblance to her mother was obvious. Her eyes were clear and they actually sparkled. She wore a baseball cap to hide the bandage covering the wound on the back of her head. It partially obscured the flesh-colored bandage on her forehead. Will guessed that the expensive-looking blouse and designer jeans were from her mother. She wore gold and white striped flats.

She flashed a big smile. "Hey there, vegan doc."

Will walked over to Sandy and gave her a big hug. "You clean up good. How do you feel?"

"Memories of my drinking still haunt me, but I'll survive. My head hurts, but I'll survive that, too. I wanted to thank you for helping me, for really caring about me. You saved my life." Sandy took a linen handkerchief out of her purse and carefully wiped her eyes, so as not to ruin her makeup.

Will took a short bow. "My pleasure. So tell me, where are you living?"

"I'm staying with my mother." She saw the surprised look on his face. "I won't go into an explanation now and even if I told you about my mother's unbelievable transformation, I don't think you'd believe me. Let's just say it's as if she was the victim of a body snatcher with a heart of gold. She and my dad are getting a divorce and she'll be moving out of the house as soon as she finds a place in – get this – Bernal Heights. She said it reminds her of her college days. She was part of a study group and one of the members lived there. It was the one place where she felt comfortable and at ease."

"Society's It Girl is giving up a Pacific Heights mansion for a modest home in the Land of Lesbians? I think she was a victim of a body snatcher."

Sandy would have loved to tell Will her mother's incredible story. She doubted he would believe her and being a doctor, albeit an open-minded one, she imagined that his beliefs were rooted more in science than spirituality. "I know. It's hard to believe, but she said she's no longer interested in her lifestyle. Of course, I never felt like I belonged in that tier of society. And to that end...," She pulled out a check and handed it to Will. "I want to do all I can to help the homeless."

Will stared at the piece of paper for a long time. "This is a check for ten million dollars."

"I know. It's for your homeless community."

"How did you find out about it?"

"Ronnie told me."

Still staring at the check, he asked tentatively, "Is there a catch?"

"There's always a catch, isn't there?"

"There is."

"Let me work there. Being homeless was brutal. It was demeaning. It also taught me humility. I want to keep others from ending up homeless and give those on the street a place to live and, hopefully, prosper."

"You realize that you're making my dream come true. I am almost speechless. You will always have a place at the community, especially since it will be named after you."

Sandy shook her head violently. "No! That's not why I'm doing this."

Will put his hand on her shoulder. "I know that, but I want to give the center your name because its inception won't be possible without this generous contribution. Let me do that for you in addition to hiring you as...what do you want to do?"

"I studied to be a paralegal, so I have skills in legal work. Perhaps I could assist with the vetting process, interviewing the residents and placing them in the appropriate programs, etcetera."

"That's a possibility. Why not join the planning committee? That way you can start on the ground floor and learn about all the positions we're going to need. By the time the community is finished, you'll know what suits you best. What will make you the happiest, the most fulfilled. Burnout is a huge factor when dealing with the homeless." Will realized what he had just said and paused. "That was thoughtless of me. I'm so sorry."

"Oh please. You don't think I know what a pain in the ass I was? I was belligerent and cocky. The homeless camp was full of people like me, in addition to those that were mentally unstable and alcoholics and drug addicts. It reminded me of the Ekhart family reunions, only we smelled and dressed a lot nicer."

Will laughed. He glanced up at the clock. "I hate to cut this short, but I have a patient in five minutes." He looked at the check again. "Sandy, you must know how grateful I am. Thank you again from the very bottom and top of my heart. As soon as I've worked out the details for the first planning meeting, I will be in touch."

The two hugged. "Here's my cell number. I can't wait to get started." Sandy handed Will a piece of paper then left. Until he was called into the examination room, he stared at the check sitting on his desk, still finding it hard to fathom that the center for the homeless would soon enough become a reality.

Dinner night at his sister's. Will practically ran to their house, knocking furiously on the door. He could hear scrambling on the other side and assumed that Makelo and Danya were vying for the job of turning the knob and letting their only uncle in. He was right. When the door opened, both had their hands on the doorknob.

Makelo said, "Danya, let go. I got here first."

"You let go."

Will interrupted the tussle. "Both of you close the door, then let go."

Obediently, they did as they were told. Will gave them each a kiss, then walked into the kitchen where Gloria was draining the spaghetti and Monica was putting dressing on the salad. As soon as she saw Will, she dropped the strainer in the sink, causing the spaghetti to slosh around. A few noodles escaped down the drain. Without drying her hands, she gave her brother a ferocious hug. "Tell me the huge news! I've been in a state of high alert ever since you called. It's good news, right?"

"Of course. I wouldn't make you wait for bad news. I told you it was good, didn't I?"

She shook her head. "You most certainly did not, Dr. Remini, physician who can be a bit sadistic at times."

Monica pushed, "Tell us already."

Without saying a word, Will produced the check and slapped it onto the kitchen table.

"What's that?" said Gloria. She pushed her hair out of her eyes and bent down to read the slip of paper. She screamed. "No fucking way! Ten million dollars made out to my favorite brother. Have I told you lately how much you resemble Ryan Gosling?"

Makelo and Danya ran into the room. Makelo said, "Are you okay, Mom?"

"I'm not sure. I think I need to sit down."

Monica said, "I can guess what this is for, but who is giving you ten mil?"

"Sandy Ekhart. And she wants to work there. At the community center. And get this: She and her mother have reconciled. And I think Norma is going to be your neighbor. She's getting a divorce and moving out of the Pacific Height's mansion. She wants to live in Bernal Heights." He saw the confused look on his sister and sister-in-law. "Pretty crazy."

"Crazy? Absolutely back asswards. Didn't you tell us that Norma fell and hit her head? Could that kind of injury change someone's personality so dramatically?"

Will shook his head. "I highly doubt it, but after getting this check, I wouldn't rule anything out. Sandy despised her mother. I got the impression that she would rather die on the streets than ask her mother for help. Now they're pals and living together so they can reconnect, make up for lost time and, from what I've heard about her childhood, they have a lot of making up to do."

Makelo said, "Did you get money for your homeless project?"

"I did."

"Can I work there, too? You don't have to pay me." Makelo knew his uncle's answer, but he thought it was only right to ask and not just tell him that he would do anything to help, and he meant anything. He couldn't explain the passion he felt toward helping those in need. It began before he could even articulate it, first saving Sisi the cat from imminent starvation, then befriending the least popular children that lived with him at the orphanage. He carried on the tradition when he began kindergarten. Just yesterday, he stuck up for a fellow student who was being bullied.

Will squatted so he was at eye level with his nephew. "When I realized that I was going to be able to fulfill my dream, the first thing on my to-do list was to hire you, with pay. You know why? I know that your sensibility is exactly what we need to make this community successful. I'm going to depend on you for ideas and suggestions. Are you up for that?"

Makelo burst into tears and hugged Will so hard his neck hurt.

Will laughed. "I'll take that as a yes."

Danya jumped on Will's back. "I want to help too and so does Sparkle Pony. What's a community?"

Before Will could answer, Monica lifted Danya off Will's back. "I'm sure Uncle Will can find something for you and Sparkle Pony to do at the community, which is a place where people who don't have anywhere to go will live. It's going to take a while to build it, so why don't we have dinner and talk about all the ways you can help, okay?"

"Okay." Danya looked at her brother. He was wiping his eyes and smiling. "Why are your eyes sad but your mouth is happy?"

Makelo said, "Sometimes when people are super happy, they cry. And right now, I'm super, super happy. Does that make sense?"

"Nope. I'm hungry." Danya skipped into the dining room and sat down.

Everyone else grabbed dishes filled with food and set it on the table. Dinner at Gloria and Monica's was always a pleasure, but tonight was special and everyone there could feel the buzz. The only thing better than being with his family would be if Ronnie was there. She was invited, but had to decline due to work. She promised to come over to Will's once she closed The Big V for the night. As if he could read Will's mind, Makelo said, "Does Ronnie know about the check?"

"Oh yeah. She's the one who told Sandy about my idea. It's synchronistic that the only reason I was at the homeless encampment and met Ronnie, was because I was looking for Sandy."

Gloria doled out the salad to Danya. "It sounds to me like the circle is complete."

Sisi jumped up on Makelo's lap. As he stroked her head, he said to his uncle, "Let's make more circles."

⚜

"We almost started without you," Petal said as she gave her guest a hug and welcomed her into her home.

Marlo took off her jacket and laid it on the arm of the sofa. "Sorry I'm late. I'm not used to my new neighborhood and I took a wrong turn. What do you mean 'we?' I thought you and I were going to have dinner alone."

Forest appeared around the corner, holding a glass of red wine. "I'm the admitted party crasher. I dropped off some supplies for Petal and she asked me to stay for dinner. If you wanted to discuss sensitive issues, I can leave."

"Please stay," Marlo said. "I just wasn't expecting anyone else to be here. Absolutely no problem at all." She inhaled deeply. "What smells so good? Please tell me it's our dinner and not another tincture."

Petal said, "Mushroom raviolis with a pumpkin sauce. And they're waiting for us to devour them."

After Petal poured the wine, she placed the bowl of raviolis on the table with the sauce on the side. "How does it feel being a single woman?"

Marlo held up her wine glass. "I love it! Here's to singledom." Petal and her brother joined in the toast. "I was going to wait until after dinner to tell you this, but I can't hold it in any longer. Remember when I told you about the American Wild Horse Preservation organization? They're going to be protesting the slaughter of wild horses at the Bureau of Land Management office in D.C. The night before the protest, they'll be hosting a fundraising event in Georgetown. It's next Saturday and I got two roundtrip tickets for you and me."

Petal said, "That sounds amazing, Marlo. I would love to go, but I have plans on Saturday and I can't cancel. It's with a potential distributor for my tinctures."

Forest raised his hand. "I'll go."

Marlo arched her eyebrow. "Will you now?"

"I will be the perfect gentleman, plus you'll need protection from all those animal rights zealots who will be clamoring over each other to get to you. We can't have that, can we?"

Petal rolled her eyes. "Oh boy."

Marlo gently put her hand on Forest's. "If you want to go, you are

262

more than welcome. I even booked two rooms at the Georgetown Inn, a turn of the century bed and breakfast. Since I thought Petal would be going with me, both rooms are very feminine. Canopy beds, ornate chandeliers, lots of lace and pink. I hope you don't mind."

"Not at all. It will give me a chance to explore my feminine side...in a spiritual way, of course. Plus, there's a gallery in Georgetown that carries my sculptures and I've never been there. It will be cool to stop in and check it out."

"Now I'm jealous," Petal said. "You two are going to have fun." She gave her brother a serious look. "Not too much fun, right Forest?"

Marlo cut in. "Leave him alone. He'll behave, won't you?" She smiled demurely.

"You bet." He took a bite of the ravioli. "How do you like your new place?"

Marlo became animated. "I love it! It's a one bedroom, one bath apartment with a spectacular view of the Presidio. The interior isn't much to look at, but it's all mine. It's quiet and cozy, not like the behemoth of a house I was living in. Way too big for two people, actually five if you count the butler, maid, and chef. After the settlement, I'll find a house, but for now, it's perfect."

Forest said, "I may be stepping over the line with this question, so if you don't want to answer, say so. Did you marry Rick for his money or were you in love with him?"

Marlo picked up her knife and pointed it at Forest. He recoiled in mock horror. "You got a lot of nerve, mister." She put the knife down and smiled. "The truth is that I really liked Rick when I met him and grew to love him after we dated. He was charming and just handsome enough. It was his wealth that tipped the scales. I admit it. I wouldn't have gone out with him if he didn't come with an oversized wallet. I wanted the big house and nice cars, five-star vacations, and having an unlimited amount of money to spend on clothes and shoes. Rick crossed over from tolerable to unacceptable in his attitude toward racehorses. I can't stand animal cruelty."

Forest looked at Petal. "Should I tell her?"

Petal knew exactly what her brother was talking about. "Be my guest."

"Is that sweater you're wearing cashmere?"

Clueless, Marlo rubbed the sleeve. "It is and it's so soft. Do you want to feel it?"

Forest shook his head. "The reason I asked is because the industry is not kind to the goats. Cashmere is made from the undercoat of cashmere goats. There are millions of them in China and Mongolia. When they shear the goats in midwinter, the animals can die of cold stress. Many of them are also killed and sold for meat."

Marlo hung her head. "Shit. I love...loved my cashmere sweaters and I have them in so many colors. I had no idea the animals were abused. In the near future, you may see homeless people wearing gorgeous sweaters in fuchsia, mint green, plum, pumpkin and lemon yellow."

Petal said, "Sorry, kid. Cashmere is the tip of the iceberg of cruelty in clothing. Wool, leather, even silk involves tremendous suffering, pain and death."

"I thought silkworms made silk. How cruel can that be?"

Forest said, "They boil the silkworms alive."

"Why?"

"After the silkworm has spun its cocoon, it transforms into a moth. Once the transformation is complete, it will begin to excrete a fluid that dissolves a hole in the silk so it can emerge. The silk farmers don't want their silk damaged by this fluid, so once the cocoon is completely formed, they toss all the sacks into boiling water to kill the silkworms."

"There goes another large portion of my wardrobe." Marlo sighed. "Believe it or not, I haven't worn leather for a while. I do know where it comes from and I'm not naïve enough to believe that it's humanely taken. Hanging out with you two is very educational and, at times, quite depressing."

Forest said, "Depressing in a good way, right?"

"Very funny. Actually, I'm glad I know about how the materials for my clothes were made. I don't like being ignorant. It isn't bliss."

After they ate, Petal got up from the table. "Did you know tonight is a full moon? It's when the moon emits the most energy. One of my tinctures isn't complete until I leave the bottles outside for the night. If you both help me put out the bottles, I'll make my rosemary and cardamom tea. We can drink it outside on the patio."

Marlo took Petal's hands in hers. "I really believe it was fate that brought us together. You've introduced me to a whole new lifestyle, and I will be forever grateful."

"I feel honored to know you, too, Marlo. I have a feeling you're going to surpass me in the aromatherapy realm. You may have the body and face for modeling, but you most definitely have the sensibility and intuitiveness needed for working with essential oils." Petal gave Marlo a hug and together they walked into the kitchen.

Darby sat across from Sandy at the dining room table. They were finishing up a breakfast that Sandy insisted on making. She also insisted that Darby wear her pedestrian clothes, not the uniform that she'd worn every working day of her life. She couldn't help but smile, moved by Sandy's transformation from timid and self-effacing to confident and self-assured.

"The pancakes were delicious. Where did you learn to make them?"

She laughed. "The back of the pancake mix box. The sliced strawberries and blueberries were my personal touch." Sandy pulled up her legs and sat crossed legged. She was still too thin from being homeless. Since being released from the hospital, her appetite had increased, and she had put on a few much-needed pounds. Her cheeks filled out and her eyes exuded a serenity that she had never before displayed.

"I know it was harsh on the streets, especially for someone like you, living in the lap of luxury for so long. How did you cope?"

"The truth? I didn't cope well at all. That's why I drank. I was able to look at my surroundings from a protected place. A numb place. When I was high, the wind wasn't as cold and the ground wasn't as hard. The people I lived with were tolerable and I didn't feel the sting as much when strangers would turn their heads as soon as they saw me. When the high disappeared, it was like someone slowly ripped off a Band-Aid. You know how that feels, but instead of waiting for the pain to subside, I would start drinking again."

"You know I would have let you stay with me as long as you needed to, right?"

"I know, Darby. I freaked out when I heard my mother's voice. I thought she would find me in your room and put us both through hell."

The women brought their plates and coffee mugs into the kitchen, placing them in the sink. Sandy said, "After Norma and I move out, are you going to continue to cook for my dad?"

Darby squeezed dishwashing liquid onto a sponge. "Your mom didn't tell you?"

"Tell me what?"

"She's persuaded me to take an early retirement. Of course, it didn't take much convincing after handing me an extremely generous check. My good friend, Darlene, recently moved to Ukiah and I'm seriously considering moving up there and opening a café. I had my heart set on retiring in Santa Fe, but Darlene is trying to convince me otherwise."

"I'm so happy for you, Darby! I know a woman who has a restaurant in the city. It's called The Big V. The V stands for vegan, in case you were wondering."

"Another word did cross my mind."

"I think that was her intent. Anyway, I'd be happy to introduce you to her. I bet she could give you some great tips on starting your own restaurant."

"I'd like that. Thank you." Darby shook her head. "In a million years, I wouldn't have been able to predict that I'd be having this conversation with you. And in ten million years, I wouldn't have been able to predict that your mother could have changed into her polar opposite. If stranger things have happened, I'm not aware."

"I couldn't agree more."

The kitchen door swung open. Bob stood there in his pajamas and bathrobe. His hair was uncombed, and he sported a three-day stubble.

"Good morning, Mr. Ekhart. Can I get you something to eat?"

"I guess."

"Good morning, Dad."

Bob didn't make eye contact with his daughter. He looked down, failing to notice that the fly in his pajama bottoms was open. "You still here?"

"I'm still here." Sandy stood motionless. She had no urge to comfort her father. After all she had been through, he had yet to console her or offer his sympathies for his shortcomings as a father.

"I thought you and your mother would have found a new nest as soon as possible so you wouldn't have to live with me any longer than you had to."

Sandy looked at her father and felt nothing but sympathy. She got her stature and looks from the Nesbitt's, but her personality was one hundred percent Ekhart. Her grandfather was what her grandma called a lily liver. When she asked her what it meant, she said that grandpa was spineless. It wasn't until Sandy was older that she learned 'spineless' meant meek and cowardly, not that he lacked a spinal cord. She knew exactly how Bob felt because she had been in the same state of mind countless times. But not anymore. Complete self-confidence hadn't reached full throttle, but it was inching closer. It didn't hurt that she inherited twenty million dollars.

It was doubtful that Bob would ever change and that's why Sandy pitied him. It would have been easy to bark back, releasing pent up disappointment and rage. It would have also been infantile and Sandy preferred growth over revenge. She approached him. "I made some pancakes. Would you like some?"

"If that's all we got." He sat down at the dining room table. "Coffee would be nice, too."

"Coming right up." Sandy grabbed a mug and filled it with coffee while Darby re-heated the remaining pancakes.

Sandy sat down next to her father. "I know you're upset with mom, and I can understand why, but believe me when I tell you that growing up I never saw you two express any affection for each other. Even in photos, you both look unhappy. That doesn't say loving marriage to me." She put her hand on his arm. "You'll be just fine."

Bob took a sip of coffee and held the mug against his lips. He slowly put the mug down. "Where is your mother?"

"She said she was going for a run."

Bob's eyes widened. "As in jogging?"

Sandy nodded.

"I didn't know your mother even had running shoes! Since I've known her, she hasn't gone running." Bob stood and began pacing. His hands waved erratically. "I don't know what to think anymore. Everything's topsy turvy. These past few days have been surreal. I don't know how much more I can take!"

Bob made a beeline for the stairs, then suddenly stopped. He sat down on the third step and looked longingly at his daughter. Finally, he said, "I'm not adjusting well to the changes, but you do deserve an apology. I was a crappy father and I'm sorry for what you went through.

I should have been there for you."

"Thanks, Dad. That means a lot to me." She wiped the tears from her cheeks and hugged her father. For the first time, his arms felt like those of a father's: strong and protective.

The front door opened, and Norma walked in. She was dressed in jogging pants and a T-shirt, her jacket tied around her waist. She pulled out the ponytail band, then ran her fingers through her hair trying to detangle it. The lump on her forehead was still visible, but about half its original size. Will had given her calendula salve and told her to apply it two to four times a day. "It smells good in here. Do I detect pancakes?"

Sandy said, "You do and I made them, believe it or not."

"Good for you. I didn't think you liked to cook. Wait, you did go through a baking phase, if I remember correctly."

"I did, but that was a long time ago. Now, I'm finding that I enjoy it. It's therapeutic."

Norma nodded to Bob. He nodded back, then she sat down next to Sandy and gave her a hug. Bob watched in disbelief. Even Sandy was still taken aback by Norma's warmth. "We should take a cooking class together. Wouldn't that be fun?"

"Why not? This might sound totally off the wall to you, but since I've known Dr. Remini and Ronnie – she's the woman who owns The Big V, the vegan restaurant – I'd really like to learn how to cook vegan food. Let's really get crazy and go plant-based and get super healthy. Are you game?"

"I am."

Bob stood. "Reconciling with your daughter, moving to Bernal Heights, jogging, going vegan. I think my head is going to explode from your extreme transformation."

"Please don't explode in the house. In case we sell it, it would be near impossible to get all the brain matter off the walls."

"Now that's the Norma I know. I'm going to take a shower."

Darby cleaned off the table. She said, "Would you like some breakfast, Mrs. Ekhart?"

"No thanks, Darby. I stopped off at a Starbucks on my way home." She turned to Sandy. "I have an appointment with a realtor in about an hour. We're going to look at a couple of homes for sale in the Berns. Want to come?"

Sandy said in a low voice. "Are you ever going to tell Dad who you really are?"

Norma let out a throaty laugh. "Oh yeah, that would go over really well. He'd probably have me committed. Only one other person will know what happened. Everyone else will be left scratching their heads."

Intrigued, Sandy asked, "Who's the other person?"

"Grant Cantella, my…Gigi's husband."

"Does he live in San Francisco?"

"Last time I checked."

"So, when are you going to talk to him?"

Norma said, "I'd like to spend more time with you before I pursue anything with Grant."

"That's very sweet of you, but aren't you afraid he'll meet someone else?"

She shrugged. "That's the chance I'm willing to take. Right now, our relationship is more important. I'm no longer involved in the racetrack, and I've resigned from the boards of most of my non-profits. I'd rather volunteer at an animal shelter or soup kitchen than organize benefit dinners and galas. It's not me. I shudder at the thought of attending events and having to schmooze with San Francisco's socialites. You're looking at me funny."

"I'm still not used to the new Norma. You loved the prestige of being the director of planning at the American Heart Association and the Cancer Society of San Francisco. I always thought you cared more about the adulation from the donors than you did from me."

"Truth? I did. I couldn't get enough praise from the other committee members and guests at the benefits. I felt accepted. Motherhood only made me feel burdened. God, I was a heartless bitch, wasn't I?"

Sandy reluctantly nodded. "I'm still processing my new mother and purging the old one from my memory." Sandy made sure they were alone, then said, "I know you have Gigi's spirit, but then how are you aware of Norma's past and her loves and hates and, well, everything?"

"There's a question worth asking the universe. I have no idea. I can tell you that when I took over, it felt like I was two people at the same time. It was confusing and overwhelming. Norma's body has cell memory, and my soul has Gigi's life experiences. The process felt like an internal zipper. Both entities were joined in the middle. My comfort level is getting better every day."

Sandy said, "That sounds freaky. Will you lose your memory of ever being Gigi?"

"I don't think so. She's taken over. The only remnants left of Norma are the memories." Norma held up her hand and gazed at it as she turned it from side to side. "I recognize this as my body and it feels comfortable, like putting on a glove. I was going to say a skin glove, but that sounds too *Silence of the Lambs*." Norma stood. "I'm going to get ready. See you in a bit."

Sandy watched her mother walk away. She had the same stride as the old Norma. Her hair swayed gently, lightly touching her slender shoulders just like it did when she walked out of Sandy's room after punishing her for doing something insignificant. The little girl knew her mother relished asserting her power. Walking away now was the new Norma. The compassionate, kind, and gracious Norma. Sandy never imagined that this would be the new direction her life would take. No more narrow, winding road where one side is an impenetrable mountainside and the other side a sheer cliff. She had choices and she had support, at least from her mother.

On the other hand, dear old dad was still treading water. The new Norma was a shock to his system. It was hard to tell which way he was headed: a nervous breakdown or the realization that he just got a *get out of jail free* card. Whatever direction his life took, Sandy vowed to be there for him. Being single was going to be an adjustment, especially for a man who was constantly being told what to do and how to do it. If therapy was what he needed, Sandy was willing to hold his hand through it all. *That's* what daughters do for their fathers.

27

Will surveyed the building, mentally checking off the number of rooms needed for his homeless community, otherwise known by its new name: the Ekhart Living Light Center. Sunlight poured in through the floor-to-ceiling windows in the main room, a 3,000 square foot space. Will imagined the room alive with the downtrodden and once hopeless being introduced to their new lives. He turned to Ronnie who was beaming at her boyfriend. "It's perfect. Absolutely perfect. You must be my guardian angel."

"Don't I have to be dead for that?"

"Let me rephrase that. You're my guardian viper."

"Much better. You know, it was sheer luck that I came across this property. I had been thinking about opening another restaurant, so I hired a realtor. This is the first place he took me. Can you imagine a 30,000 square foot restaurant?"

"You would have had to call it The Humongous V." Will pointed to a room in the front right corner of the two-story building. "That will be my office. I want to feel the hum of activity, not tucked away in a quiet space. This is going to be so great. I can't wait to begin working on the remodel. The contractor said he can start as soon as the sale is final." Will grabbed Ronnie by the waist and held her close. "This wasn't possible without you. Thank you for everything."

"There's a helluva lot more to come, buddy boy. I have more than a Humongous V up my sleeve."

Will pulled the cuff of Ronnie's long-sleeved shirt back and was looking into it when he heard the front door open. Makelo broke free from Gloria and ran over to the couple. "Wow, this place is ginormous. How are you going to fill it up?"

"That's the easy part, kiddo. Where's Monica?"

"She had to work."

Makelo ran over to Gloria. "Can we explore?"

"Of course. Shall we start upstairs?"

Makelo gave her an enthusiastic nod and took off running. He made it to the base of the north staircase and was about to take the stairs two at a time when Gloria asked him to wait for her. He obliged, though not without giving her a disapproving look. Makelo's intuition kicked into high gear. His energy level was so high, he felt he could fly upstairs. He knew this building had good bones. He knew his Uncle Will's enterprise was going to be a huge success. He felt it in his heart.

After parking in the Stockton Sutter Garage, Norma and Sandy walked up the crowded street. It was close to noon, and many were on their way to lunch. Sandy pointed to a restaurant on the opposite side of the street. "Grandbee took me to the Garden of Delights all the time. She knew it was my favorite restaurant. I loved their signature garden pasta."

Norma didn't hear a word. She was laser focused on a little girl with her father walking towards them. She was holding a doll. An American Girl doll. Sandy followed her mother's gaze and stopped in the middle of the sidewalk. "I know that girl." Norma said, "So do I."

Tentatively, Sandy walked up to Paige. "Do you remember me?" she asked. "I met you at the park and your grandmother kindly gave me her pink jacket."

Paige's eyes lit up. "You're the lady who lives in the park!"

Sandy laughed. "I am and I used to live in the park, but not anymore. And I would love to give your grandma her jacket back. You both were so kind to me. It meant a lot."

It wasn't until Norma kneeled in front of Paige that Sandy noticed tears streaming down her mother's face. "Thank you for helping my daughter. You're a very special little girl." Norma lightly touched the doll on the nose. "And Mari...your doll is very special, too."

Alec felt like he had stepped into a play, mid-act. Everyone but him knew their lines. Thoroughly and utterly confused, he said, "I would be most grateful if someone could tell me what's going on." He looked at Norma. "You were going to say Marilyn, weren't you? How did you know Paige's doll's name?"

Thinking fast, Norma said, "Marigold. I was going to say Marigold. That was the name of my childhood doll who, coincidentally, looks exactly like Marilyn here. She even had a gray beret." She paused. "I'm Norma, Sandy's mother."

It was Sandy's turn to explain. "I was at the park when your daughter came up to me and introduced herself. It was cold that day and she generously offered me her jacket, but her grandma stepped in and gave me hers. I still have it and would love to return it."

Alec smiled. "I do remember Rebecca telling me about meeting someone in the park. I'm sure my mother-in-law would like you to keep the jacket. As she would say, wear it in good health."

"Please tell her thank you for me." She leaned down and looked Paige in the eyes, her expressive, beautiful, loving eyes. "I'll never forget your kindness. Thank you."

Shyly, Paige said, "You're welcome."

As they walked away, Sandy said to her mother, "I didn't expect you to get so emotional."

Norma took out her cell and texted Will, *running late, will be there soon!* She turned to Sandy, "Let's go to The Garden of Delights for coffee. I need to recalibrate and tell you how I know Paige and Alec."

After they sat down in a booth and each ordered a cappuccino, Norma took a deep breath. She pulled her shoulders up to her ears and exhaled as they gently came back down. It took two more times to soften her muscles and slow her breath. Her turquoise eyes gleamed, the purity of her spirit shining through. "When Emma was killed at the airport, I told you that her spirit became trapped in a doll. You just met the doll."

The realization gave Sandy goosebumps. She shuddered, then reached out for her mother's hand. "How jarring that must have been for you."

"It was, but it also felt like closure." Norma looked toward the ceiling. "I wonder if Emma is watching. I hope she's happy with her decision to trade places with me."

Emma smiled and her spirit shone a brilliant golden white. "*I'm very happy, Gigi, I mean Norma. No, I mean Gigi.*" She felt a twinge of envy watching as mother and daughter bonded, their fingers entwined. It reminded Emma of the last time she hugged her sister. It was the day before Gigi's accident. The energy that had flowed through them in life was strong, satisfying. She missed that. Sandy took a sip of her cappuccino. Emma watched her wipe the foam from her upper lip, and she suddenly longed for a cup of Joe: cappuccino, espresso, mocha. She missed it all. Living on earth wasn't that bad, was it? She could have made it a lot better for herself if she had only listened to her intuition. She'd never be able to change all the violence that existed on the planet, but she could do something to alleviate the pain and suffering.

Emma suddenly heard her new favorite Beatles song blasting from the heavens, piercing through her spiritual coil. All you need is love, indeed.

When they finally arrived at the future site of the homeless center, Sandy said, "I'm so impressed! I can only imagine what it will look like when it's up and running."

Norma said, "I agree. So, do you have a name for this place?"

"The Ekhart Living Light Center," Will said and watched Sandy and Norma's faces light up.

Sandy spoke first. "I'm honored, but this is your baby."

"And my baby wouldn't have been born without your financial support. I think it's a perfect name."

"Speaking of financial support, I'm going to match my daughter's donation. If you really want to create the ultimate living space where the homeless can not only live comfortably, but provide food and medical services, you'll need more financial aid," said Norma.

Will was stunned. The generosity of the Ekharts was beyond his expectations. "Thank you, Norma. I feel truly blessed."

"You're very welcome. I have complete faith in you. Now, let's christen The Ekhart Living Light Center." She pulled a bottle of Saint Gregor's non-alcoholic Champagne out of a Chanel tote bag. "Believe it or not, I have champagne flutes in here, too, and vegan truffles."

Sandy laughed. "I believe it. Unfortunately, I don't think I should partake."

Her mother held up the bottle. "It's alcohol free."

The sentiment wasn't lost on anyone. Will glanced over at Ronnie and she nodded ever so slightly. Apart from the Chanel tote, there wasn't a trace left of Norma Ekhart, society's ice queen. Defrosted, the woman before them was a warm, gentle soul. What they didn't know was that she had only just begun to share the gift of her new life with her adopted community.

Before she left for Turin, hoping to reconnect with Cynthia from Haight Ashbury in the grotto, Emma Banks hovered over the group of friends. She was thrilled with the way things had turned out. She looked at Will and Ronnie and she shone even brighter. She hoped they would marry and, even more, she hoped they would have a child. If they did, she couldn't wait to be a part of their family. She wouldn't even mind if she came back as a boy.

— THE END —

Other books by
Carol Treacy

www.ingramcontent.com/pod-product-compliance
Lightning Source LLC
Chambersburg PA
CBHW070322260626
47160CB00003B/927